RESET, RESET

NATALIE TRIUMPHS

HOUSE OF INDIGO

Published by **House of Indigo**

www.houseofindigocollective.com

Ebook ISBN: 978-1-966187-11-0

Paperback ISBN: 978-1-966187-12-7

Natalie Triumphs has had numerous Number 1 Amazon Best Sellers, including an International Best Seller. Among the areas where her books have achieved #1 sales are:

#1 Best Seller in YA Politics & Government
#1 Best Seller in YA Adventures and Adventurers
#1 Best Seller in Human Rights Law
#1 Best Seller in Animal Law
#1 Best Seller in Environmental and Natural Resources Law
#1 Best Seller in Civil Law
#1 Best Seller in Public Law
#1 Best Seller in YA Schools and Education
#1 Best Seller in YA Fiction Alternative History
#1 Best Seller in YA Environmental Science and Ecosystems eBooks
#1 Best Seller in YA Media Studies eBooks
#1 New Release in YA Sociology eBooks
#1 New Release in Ecology
#1 New Release in Public Administration Law
#1 New Release in YA Fiction about Parents
#1 New Release in YA Diseases, Illnesses and Injuries Fiction eBooks

We are rapidly entering the age of no privacy, where everyone is open to surveillance at all times, where there are no secrets from government. -US Supreme Court Justice William O. Douglas

We know by now that if we make technology the predestined force of our lives, man will walk to the measure of its demands. We know how easy it is to computerize man and make him a servile thing in a vast industrial complex. -US Supreme Court Justice William O. Douglas

We'll know our disinformation program is complete when everything the American public believes is a lie. -Former CIA Director William Casey

If you tell a lie big enough and keep repeating it, people will eventually come to believe it. -Joseph Goebbels

Wrong is wrong, no matter who does it or who says it. -Malcolm X

Man is about to be an automaton; he is identifiable only in the computer. -U.S. Supreme Court Justice William O. Douglas

There are no illegal humans. -Eight-term U.S. Congressman and Presidential Candidate Dennis J. Kucinich (Los Angeles, CA, 2007)

CHAPTER 1

"Karmic extermination of depraved, immoral, disrespectful degenerates, fascist anarcho-communists, liars and disinformationists," the narrator summarized the justification for leaving the masses behind to be killed in Planet Earth's nuclear holocaust.

Images of angry crowds setting fire to buildings and cars, tents blocking city sidewalks, and people fighting with police, along with scenes of people and children marching, carrying signs with slogans, reading "Bankers are evil", "Take Down the Government," and "Defund Wall Street," flashed before us in the video we were watching on our holographic monitors above our desks.

In the midst of the depravity, an image in the background simultaneously sent a warm sensation and icy ripple through me. It was a child with a hoop twirling around his waist. He was smiling and laughing. In a world of chaos, he was happy.

I cautiously glanced around the room. The faces of my classmates carried the expressionless look of "We've seen this documentary before. We already know this stuff."

As the video concluded with mushroom clouds and firestorms sweeping across the cities, villages and homes, our holographic screens vanished. Students sat, rhymically applauding, no emotion visible on anyone's faces.

Professor Sargat stood. "This is what we escaped when we came to the underworld. While the parasites stayed above to be disintegrated by thermonuclear bombs that left nothing alive, those of us who were proper, moral and intelligent, those of us who were natural-born leaders, scientists, engineers, and intellectuals worked collectively to create a better society, free of violence, crime, homelessness and hunger. Dismissed."

We all rose and exited single file, not a student out of step. Outside, everyone knew where they next needed to go.

As Chanelle and I walked to the school lunchroom, we turned towards each other. "Best friends for life," we said in unison, clapping our hands together.

"We are so lucky to be down here," I said, trying to sound appropriately and unemotionally enthusiastic while simultaneously trying to ignore the inexplicable emptiness encapsulating my stomach. "All our needs are supplied. Everyone is healthy and safe. It couldn't be better." Yet, the kid with the hoop continued to haunt my thoughts. I tried to erase the image from my mind, but couldn't.

"It's nice."

"Of course, we've lived here all our lives. Do you ever wonder what it would be like if we weren't here?"

"No. We'd be dead. And those who didn't make it down here were stupid. They deserved to die," she said matter-of-factly.

But does anyone really deserve to die? What does intellect have to do with the right to live? I wasn't supposed to care about those left behind. Still, it seemed wrong to speak ill of the dead. Those who remained above were incinerated long ago as the world above became a radioactive wasteland. We were told they'd gone mad, ended themselves and rightly so. We were the sane ones, the ones who deserved to live.

I had to stop questioning, feeling.

"Happy Birthday." I pulled a small package from my pocket and handed it to Chanelle.

She opened it. It was a locket. She looked inside at a picture of the two of us. "That was a good picture. I remember when it was taken." She put it on.

"Your sixteen-year transition is today. Are you worried?"

"Why would I be worried? It will just facilitate my getting a little older and becoming the more perfect me. According to our history books, before the transitions, people used to get sick. Who would want that?"

"But you always look different afterwards. I wonder why the boys age more slowly, while most girls look so different after theirs. Are the quick-activating growth transitions really better than the slow ones?"

"Quick-acting growth hormones make us more attractive and wiser right away," she said. "I will become taller, more developed and more beautiful today. Boys have different biology. It's all good."

"But—" I paused, sliding my left hand and wrist deep into my pocket, hoping my wrist monitor wouldn't pick up my voice. "Will it change you and us? Will you stop clapping my hands? We once played tag and hide and seek—before—never mind." That was many transitions ago, and I wasn't supposed to miss what came before. I was taught to be proud of the alterations, but with each change Chanelle had undergone, I felt a sense of loss.

"Those were baby games."

I knew it was our duty to conform and focus on improving our abilities and knowledge, not trying to revert to babyhood. But a pang in the pit of my stomach missed the old days and didn't want her to transition again. I pushed into hazardous territory. "What if you skipped this one? Maybe wait until the next one. Do you really want to change?"

"Of course. I'll be better. I'm sure they know what they are doing. My dad says everyone goes through the sixteen-year transition and it's no big deal. You'll have yours in almost five months when you turn sixteen. Why are you questioning it? Did your mom put you up to testing me?"

Why am I so concerned when she isn't bothered or worried at all? "Do you remember your last transition? What did it feel like?"

"I don't remember. That's the beauty of it. We're not supposed to notice our own changes."

"I didn't notice any of my changes following my transitions."

"You're not supposed to."

"I guess not. But what if we didn't have any transitions and just grew up normally? Would it be so bad?"

"Why would you want to do that? We might look ugly, like those people in that video. Tell your mom, I passed the test."

"They weren't all—" I needed to stop. My mom had told me my questions would get me into trouble. Still, an uncanny fear kept nagging at me. She was my one true friend. Unthinkingly, I started to give her a hug.

"What's this for?" she asked, pulling back.

"I think it's something we used to do when we were younger."

"Nobody hugs anymore."

"Of course." Even my parents never hugged me—only each other, and then only in private. I seemed to have a sensory memory of my mom doing it when I was little. Those hugs could have just been my imagination, or maybe just a wish. "We'll still be best friends forever, right?"

"Sure. We've always been friends."

"Best friends. But do you ever just want to let go of your feelings and have a fun time, just for the enjoyment of it?"

"Is this part of the test? You're sounding weird, heretical?"

I almost frowned at her comment, but caught myself.

I didn't dare check whether my reaction could have been picked up by the cameras that were just about everywhere, in the streets, the hallways, the classrooms, the playgrounds, the vehicles and all the houses. There was also the one I wore under my sleeve. Their presence was for our protection and safety, or so we were told. But looking at the cameras would also be suspicious to anyone observing.

I had been told there were no microphones attached to public area cameras, as our leaders wanted the contents of their conversations to be confidential. I suspected that the Directors personal cameras—if they had them—didn't have microphones, either. Inside the homes, classrooms and playgrounds, the microphones were always on, though. I understood most kids and teens carried active microphones at all times. The AI monitor in my bracelet might already be analyzing my conversation with Chanelle.

"Right. You answered perfectly, but you weren't supposed to know you were being tested."

I had always felt there was something wrong with me. The other girls were so well-adjusted, content, and unquestioning. Chanelle was my closest friend, but even she would judge me if I got too radical.

"Maybe my mom will let me watch." I continued. Mom was conducting Chanelle's transition. She was the Western Region's top bio-physicist, well-renowned for her skills.

"There you are." It was Chanelle's brother, Kalandro. He sneered at me. "How is your monster of a mother?"

"You calling my mother names, again?" I couldn't stand Kalandro. He was consistently mean to me and very disrespectful to his sister. I remembered, or thought I remembered, a time long ago when Kalandro and I were friends and liked each other. One day, he just started hating me. Since then, he had had nothing nice to say to me, just insults, often calling me ugly and stupid.

"If you were human, you'd call her a monster too," he said, snidely but coolly, as if he were talking about the weather.

"How dare you!" I shouted, forgetting my mother had told me never to shout. I also forgot that she had told me not to slug anyone as I punched him in the stomach.

"For an android, you're pretty weak. Did your mother program you to be an emotional wreck?"

"If anyone is an android, it's you. How dare you call me that!"

I felt a pang of guilt over my words. Most of the help and much of society outside of those in positions of power were androids. They washed our clothes, prepared our food and drove us to field trips. I wasn't supposed to put them down. I hoped this didn't get back to my parents.

He shook his head. "You aren't supposed to get violent. Must be a defect in your programming."

"Natalia, what's with you?" Chanelle asked, calmly. "Why are you always so emotional?" Even my best friend sensed that something was wrong with me.

"I'm sure they'll take care of the flaw in your programming at your next transition," Kalandro said. "Or maybe they decided they needed to have some monster robots to match your mom's personality."

This time, I held my temper as I bit the inside of my upper lip, but I was sure I turned red. Kalandro walked away. I could taste and smell the blood in my mouth, but had to ignore that.

"Are you blushing? How is that possible?" Chanelle asked.

"It's the lighting." I remembered my mom leaving me an envelope marked confidential the other day. This morning, she asked me if I had opened it. I still hadn't and couldn't recall what I had done with it. Normally, I had a great memory. Maybe I didn't want to read it. I suspected it was about my blushing problem. *Why can't I be calm and unemotional like everyone else my age?*

"It was more than lighting," Chanelle said. "How did you do that?"

"I had to work at it," I lied. "It's a skill, like my dancing."

My mother would be upset if she knew I had been caught blushing again, and even more upset to know I had slugged someone. She had always insisted I hide any emotions. She warned there could be serious consequences if the wrong person noticed. I wondered what those consequences would be. The regional leaders, of which my dad was the top one, didn't approve of emotions—though I had seen him show anger when he didn't know I was looking.

My curiosity was another problem I needed to get under control. I kept wondering about the lost society, which had been blown out of existence.

In history class, I had learned that there used to be democracy in the USA, but it was a failure as people often elected unpredictable leaders and couldn't be trusted to vote in their own interests. Things were better for us now: no violence, no public nudity, no homelessness. We had no want of anything, and everyone was civil—that is, everyone but Kalandro.

I worked to get myself under control and calmly asked. "Why is your brother always so mean to me?"

"Why do you care?"

"I don't. We're supposed to get along, down here."

"Maybe future leaders are supposed to be that way, practice for when they take charge. He calls me names, too. It's no big deal."

"The other boys in Future Leaders don't call me names, and neither do the current leaders." *I have to keep calm, be normal. Why do I care what some stupid boy thinks of me?* "Right. No big deal."

***

We lived in Plathorya, the Capital of the Western Region. My mom's Bio-Enhancement Lab was located in the Government Central Operations Center.

Within the Center, not far from Mom's lab, were the Administrative Offices for the whole Western Region, which included the continental United States and Canada. We were told that the USA had perished, along with the rest of the world, but we'd won the war as we had bigger, more powerful weapons, including deep-earth bunker busters—though we had been the nonviolent ones. The insane ones, who died above, were responsible for the war.

The Operations Center also contained the power and environmental controls for the entire region. The electrical, oxygen replenishment and waterway system for all the sectors were linked to the Operation Center of Government Central and Plathorya—though local sectors could temporarily disable certain of their own functions for maintenance, and my dad would set up secured remote access to the main computers when he traveled to other sectors.

The Directorate made all the day-to-day decisions, as well as the rules and laws for the Western Region, although there was no crime. In school, we were taught that that was one of the benefits of our society. Those who didn't make it below were a lawless bunch who would kill their own mothers if they had the chance. Our survival was a lesson that our system was the most effective, the most humane.

The lab was open, and my mom was sobbing. She had generally avoided showing emotion, but today something was especially wrong. I hoped the cameras in the lab were off.

"What's upsetting you?"

"I was just thinking of my friend from long ago. I guess that's why I—"

"Who?"

"Shh," she said, hearing approaching footsteps in the lab's hallway monitor. "Be really quiet. It's best if you leave quickly."

"Mom, what is it?"

She shook her head and dried her cheeks.

"Go!" She instructed me firmly.

The door opened. "Oh, Natalia. It's good to see you." It was Chanelle's dad holding Chanelle's hand. Mom turned off her hallway monitor.

"Daddy, is this the lab you told me about?" Chanelle asked. "Natalia, it is very nice of you to come. Daddy, she can stay to watch my transition, can't she?"

"I don't see why not. After all, one day, she'll be following in her mother's footsteps."

"Good afternoon, Jason," my mom said. Jason Denton was the Deputy Chairman of the Western Region. He was second in command behind my dad, the Regional Chairman. My mother took orders from the Board, but they deferred to her on technical issues.

"Eterra," he greeted her. "Your work would be so much easier on you if you used AI to handle the transitions."

"Maybe I am AI."

He looked at her for a second and laughed. Laughing was something I had occasionally seen the Directors do, but very few others.

"With your efficiency, I wouldn't be surprised."

Chanelle peered around. "Look at all the heads."

There were a number of children's heads on shelves, some with varying lengths of blonde, black, brown and red hair. It looked almost like a mannequin shop, but seemed more real. I had often wondered about the purpose. I suppose it was related to my mom's refit work.

She was also in charge of procedures to restore injured people and kids with artificial parts, like arms and legs. But I had always wondered why there were heads in the lab.

"What is the surprise, Daddy?" Chanelle asked, not curiously, but like she was asking a question to a teacher.

"You're going to sit down in that chair and we're going to cover your eyes."

She sat down in a soft swivel chair that looked like something out of pictures of old barber shops. He put a bandana around her eyes. Then he pulled straps around her body to hold her firmly in place.

"What are the straps for?" she asked, casually. If she was bothered, it didn't show. I would have been freaking out.

"There's nothing to be scared of. You'll see. You'll love the surprise."

He motioned for my mother to come over. She attached electrodes to my friend's head. The electrodes were on a cord attached to Mom's primary computer.

"Don't you have a more sophisticated way of doing it yet?"

"This is less messy and less tamperable. It's a closed system, more secure."

"Secure from whom?"

"It's what was decided when we started the system," Mom replied calmly. "Until the rule is reversed, I have to follow protocol."

The computer indicated that it had completed its task.

My mom nodded. "Natalia, you've seen the start. You have things to do."

"Let her watch. Maybe one day, she'll take over for you," Denton said.

From the stiff look of her body, I could tell my mom wasn't happy about his comment, but Denton didn't seem to notice. Mom was different today. I thought about Mom's tears before Denton and Chanelle arrived. Something was really bothering her.

Jason walked to a glass case containing an ax. I had always wondered what it was for. My mom said it was a relic and she never used it.

"That's kind of messy. There are better ways," my mom said, quite calmly, almost monotone.

"Don't deny me my little pleasures."

He took it out of the case and strode back to his daughter. Was he going to cut the ropes? He held it high and swung it at Chanelle's neck.

As he did so, my mother covered my eyes and turned me away, rushing me to the door.

I couldn't see, but heard what sounded like a heavy ball hitting the floor.

CHAPTER 2

As I started to scream, my mom's hand covered my mouth. She pushed me out the door and closed it fast.

In the corridor, I controlled my reaction. I knew I was never allowed to scream, but I only made it a few feet when everything went dark, and I felt the floor slam hard against my body.

What has happened to me? Why did I collapse? I sat up, worried that the cameras might have caught my clumsiness or fainting. *Did I faint?*

I'd never fainted before. I had read that people experienced that in the Old World Order, but I had never heard of anyone down here ever fainting. *I must have tripped. That had to be the answer.*

With all the monitors, I could be in big trouble if my starting to scream was detected, but part of me didn't care. I had lost my best friend—my only real friend. I wasn't allowed to cry or react to anything. That had been drilled into me. It occurred to me, if they saw my reaction, maybe I would meet the same fate as Chanelle.

Had she shown emotion? Is that why she lost her head? She was always more controlled than me. Would I be executed for my sixteenth birthday transition in five months?

I went back to the door to listen. I heard Chanelle's father say, "Where did Natalia go?"

"Too much of a good thing is not good for any girl."

"It was good, wasn't it?" He sounded gleeful.

How could a father be gleeful about killing his own daughter? Poor Chanelle. At least, she didn't see it coming.

When I saw the ax, why didn't I rescue her? Did I put obedience above my best friend's life? What kind of person am I? I wanted to find a safe place to cry. I could barely hold myself together.

"We'd better throw the pieces into the incinerator." That was my mom's voice.

My heart was breaking, but I couldn't run. I slowly walked towards home.

The artificial occasional breeze brushed against my face, but I only felt numb. It was always the same temperature in the underworld, about seventy-five degrees—except in the recreation areas designed for competition skiing and snowboarding, where the temperature was set to just below thirty-two degrees. The air had an almost crisp scent that was uniform throughout most areas.

The sky was always blue. At night, it was royal blue and the stars were bright, but I didn't know if the nights and days were real or simply scheduled by the Directorate's orders. The snow in the ski locations and water in the rivers and lakes were always plentiful, but rain never fell from the artificial sky. The water parks, grass and flowers had what I assumed were the same smells as above. Sparkling rainbows appeared in the sky every evening before sunset, but rain never preceded them. And yet, I wondered whether the sky above looked the same as the one we saw down here.

I would gladly give up this perfectly engineered world, with all its luxuries, to have my best friend back.

My mind flashed to an example of "demented literature" we'd been taught to condemn. It was Emily Dickinson's poem, "The Loneliness One Dare Not Sound." Loneliness was a sign of a defect. It was viewed as evidence that poems and prose written by weak or mentally ill humans were inferior to those created by artificial intelligence. Yet, it was as if she had written about me and made me feel less alone.

I often found myself enjoying people-written literature we were supposed to hate. I kept my defective preference secret, hoping nobody would hold it against me. All literature and information were computerized. AI designated which literature was demented and to be hated and what was quality literature. Most of the pre-Reset literature I'd read had red warning marks about false concepts. I would always take the time to add my own negative comments on any refuted literature that I liked, so I wasn't stopped from reading more.

I walked by a park where Chanelle and I used to play when we were younger. After each transition, it took a while for her to warm up to me, though something was always lost. In time, we would hang out and share our hopes and dreams with each other again.

As long as I could remember, she had been good at hiding her emotions. No. That's not true. There was a time when we were small and she was happy and laughing. I guess that was before she learned to control herself. But looking back, for more than a decade, she hadn't blushed, hadn't cried and had been very muted in her responses. She had been well trained to fit in. I wished I had been that good. A tear started to fall down my cheek. I quickly patted my face, less conspicuous than a tear.

I knew there were video monitors in the park, and I always tried to avoid them. But I couldn't escape the monitor I carried with me at all times. I pulled my sleeve over it.

I pretended to drop something near a picnic table. I bent down and sat under it, hoping the monitors couldn't see the tears that flooded down my cheeks. My covered wrist was behind my back, and I hoped I wasn't making any sound as I cried. I wondered why the directors and some of the boys could show emotion, but all the girls I knew hid their feelings as if it was a natural skill.

As I sat there, Kalandro strode into the park. His fists were clenched, and he looked angry. Didn't his father tell him that was forbidden? I wondered if he knew his sister was gone. If anyone saw him angry, he could get kicked off the Youth Leadership Council. But maybe the boys in the leadership council had more privileges.

Kal grabbed a basketball and started making baskets as if making the shot was his only concern, but the glare in his eyes and the clench of his jaw told me he was anything but calm and okay.

He walked to my table. I feared he'd see me. He didn't look under. Instead, he smashed his fist down on the table, cracking the wood.

"A monster," he had called my mom. But it wasn't my mother who was the monster. It was his father who killed his sister and did so with joy. I was sure Kalandro would blame my mom. He hadn't seen what I saw.

He let out a groan. I wondered if the monitors picked that up.

Despite the coldness with which Kalandro regularly talked to his sister, he must have cared for her, too. I wanted to get up to speak with him, but I didn't dare say anything that might expose my feelings. As he collected his ball and turned to leave, I could have almost sworn I saw tears starting to fall down his cheeks.

At home, a large palatial estate in the area reserved for the families of the top Elites in the New Order, I closed the drapes, turned off the lights and tried to sleep. It was still daylight. We had very long days.

As I lay there, I couldn't think of anything but Chanelle.

A couple of hours later, I heard my mom enter. She came to my room and turned on the light, along with a loud digital music player. "Are you alright, honey?"

"Is this what you do for a living?"

"It's not that simple."

"Chanelle was my best friend. Was."

"Honey."

"I don't want to hear anymore!"

I got up and rushed out of my room and out of the house. Outside, I had to walk slowly so it didn't look like I was running from anything.

My dad had arrived home and was getting out of his car. His position as Chairman meant I had to do my best to follow the protocols at home and behave properly around him. My mom had made that perfectly clear.

"Hello, dear."

"Hello. I'm going out for a walk," I said matter-of-factly.

"I will see you later. I have something else to take care of at the office." He got back into his car. He was a good father. He never mistreated me. I always got the impression he saw me as one of his prized possessions.

My dad backed up his car and took off down the road. All vehicles were self-driving, but some could be manually operated. The cars and trams were recharged with electricity from the fusion generators in the power center that controlled the energy to the whole region.

I remembered overhearing a conversation my dad had had about how, at one point, a sector of the region questioned the management and suddenly found their power, oxygen and water cut. Later, when I asked about it, I was told that it had been a myth and everyone throughout the region was happy.

I walked back to the park and nearly collapsed in shock. "Chanelle?"

It was her, in the flesh.

CHAPTER 3

She looked a little older, bustier, and her hair had been clipped shorter. Gone were her recreational clothes. In her blazer, skirt and high heels, she was dressed as if she planned to go to an office. She no longer looked like a teenager. Despite her blasé outfit, there was something more sultry, sexier about her appearance.

"Chanelle?" I asked, again, in disbelief.

"Who else? You are my friend, right?"

"Yes. But I saw you—well, I don't understand."

"Of course, you've seen me. We're friends."

"Best friends for life." I picked up my hands to clap hers, but she just stared at me.

"Aren't we a bit old for childish games?"

It was Chanelle, but it wasn't.

"Would you like to play basketball or something?" Part of me was hoping that I had just imagined what happened in the lab. Maybe my emotions had made me delusional.

"I need to go home to prepare for work tomorrow."

"Work? No school?"

"They gave me my diploma today."

I shook my head. That's when I saw Kalandro start to walk back into the park.

"Hello, Kalandro," Chanelle said in a monotone.

He turned and walked away without saying anything.

I went home. Mom was there. Music was playing loudly. My dad was still out. As I arrived, she took off my bracelet and put it in the bedroom. She turned up the music, louder than before and pulled me into the bathroom. Both the shower and sink faucets were turned on full blast.

"I saw Chanelle, but she was killed."

"She is one of many Chanelles."

"How? Kalandro called us androids earlier."

"Honey."

"Did you replace my friend with a robot?"

She hesitated as if not wanting to say what came next. "She was replaced years ago."

"The transitions. They weren't about using medicines to make us mature fast. They were about being exterminated and replaced? Is that correct?"

"The memories and knowledge are uploaded onto the replacement and the earlier version is destroyed. That way, the youth age more appropriately."

"Then I—I'm not real?"

"You are special. Always remember that."

"A special robot?"

"Natalia."

"Can they hear us?"

"You have a removable monitor and the sound on it is defective. Your voice doesn't come through, but don't let anyone know you know that. Nobody can be trusted and we must always watch what we say."

"I see. If they hear us, they'll alter or debug me, I guess. I've been through how many transitions? I don't remember them."

"Nobody remembers the transitions. Otherwise, they would feel less human." Though we were alone in the bathroom, she looked around as if maybe there might be a secret monitor close by.

"But we aren't, are we? We're nothing more than fakes, machines."

"Natalia. I told you you're special. Different, but you can't say anything."

"I don't want to be special. I want to be human!"

"You have to lower your voice and not react. You have to fit in, hide your feelings," my mom whispered.

I knew that whatever she wanted to tell me, this was not the place to talk. Maybe nowhere was. There were ears everywhere. She was clearly guarded. "Do I have a monitoring microphone in me like the household robots? Is the bracelet just a game?"

She looked at my bare wrist and shook her head.

I pictured my mom setting a new head on my best friend, Chanelle. Not just a new head. She had a new body as well. *Was Kalandro right? How could my mom do that?* "She looks like eighteen now. But it's not really her. She doesn't care about me the way she did before."

"She has the memories. She just won't be a little girl anymore. She has a heart and all the same organs as a regular girl. She even has a red blood-like substance in her veins. She's a top-tier android, a regular girl."

"Top-tier, but her organs are synthetic, not real, right? How is that regular?" I thought back to a conversation I had overheard recently. "I heard Dad and Jason saying that long ago, girls had stopped being girls. There was something about using too many pronouns. Women had lost their sports and all their rights. I've never seen that. We have sports."

"That was before the Reset, when they were working on what they called 'population control.' It was felt that women were having too many babies. That doesn't happen anymore. The population is under control."

"And pronouns led to too many babies?"

"It was a game to trick girls into sterilization. If a girl didn't know she was a girl and switched to a boy, no baby problem."

"I can't have babies, can I?"

"Dear, why would you want to? Babies are messy. They poop."

"Poop? Like that dog we used to have before I could walk? But there are no more real dogs, are there? I haven't seen a real dog since I was a little girl. Who cares if they poop?"

"But aren't pets that don't poop nicer?"

"They aren't real. Back to my friend. Was Chanelle ever real?"

"Not for a very long time."

"She was once real? So, kids are born real and then changed?"

My mom didn't answer. Maybe she felt she had said too much.

"Are there any real dogs left?"

"I suppose there are some in the wild."

"What wild? I haven't seen any wild. I mean, we have forests, lakes and rivers, but I haven't seen any wild animals anywhere—not like the carnivorous animals I read they had before the Reset—the ones that ate people. But why replace kids? We don't eat people."

"Parents still want kids, well-behaved kids. Too many misbehaving kids wouldn't sit well with—" she pointed up with her hand, though it stayed low down between us as she looked around again. I assumed up meant leaders.

"But there are women having babies. I've seen women with new babies. And why do we go to school? Why don't they just program us with information and make us adults to begin with?"

"People want to raise kids—even if they aren't real. They want the parenting experience."

"Mom, why do I have emotions when almost none of the other android kids do?"

"They hold them in better. You need to control them. It is very important that you do."

"Do you think you are a monster?"

"I don't know. I hope not. Your dad will be home soon, and you need to act as if all is well."

"Mom, have you killed any kids?"

"No."

"Then, who does?"

My mom shook her head as if she didn't want to say anymore. "How about a pre-dinner snack?"

"No, thank you." I wanted to know more. "Mom, was it really that terrible before the Reset?"

"That's what they tell people."

"You were there."

"There was a lot of anger, hate and—greed."

"In the old books, I read they also had sports and dancing."

"It was different. Dancing was for fun back then. Now, it serves a purpose—to entertain and show excellence. It didn't used to be so acrobatic."

"How about the clothes?"

"Clothing isn't that much different than when we came down here. The music seemed to freeze up there before the Reset, but even down here, musicians emulate what we listened to up there. It's a nostalgia thing."

"Is it true what they tell us in school? That the war killed everyone up there? That only coming down here for the Reset saved us?"

"You must not question what you are taught."

"Can I go to bed?"

"You need to have dinner with me and your father. You can't let him think the Chanelle incident bothered you."

"Great." Though I felt the opposite.

"We all have to play our roles."

I heard a noise outside in the hall. My mom placed her hands to her lips and went out of the bathroom.

I heard Sadie, the maid, say, "I picked up the fresh supplies. Dinner will be ready shortly." I wondered if Sadie was a "top-tier robot," like Chanelle or some kind of lower-tier robot. Sadie had always been nice to me. It was hard to think of her as subhuman. But then apparently so was I.

The next day, after school, I went to the lab with my mom. I wanted to know more about the process. What had the prior Natalias been like? I wondered if there was information about me on the lab computers.

"The DC said I was following in your footsteps. Could I look over the computer files on myself?"

My mom seemed hesitant.

"Really. Hasn't everything been uploaded to facilitate whatever will replace me?"

"Everyone's files have been uploaded, but I don't think it's a good idea."

"It might help me understand."

She opened up my computer files. I saw myself smiling as a baby. I guess I was able to get away with it then. These days, most babies do not smile. They were as controlled as the rest of us. Or maybe they were now replaced at birth.

"Do you think I look like you or Daddy?"

"You have a bit of me in you, but you don't look much like him."

My records showed I was always ahead of other kids my age. I clicked on a button showing the dates of transitions. I saw myself at different stages of my life, but I didn't see any before and after photos of transitions. I asked my mom about that.

"Those may be among the confidential files. I am showing you everything I can."

Yesterday, I felt human. Now, I felt so empty. I had thought so many times about being a mother and now, I'd never be one. I might have a robot baby. But it wouldn't be real, and it would be killed to make way for the toddler.

"I have to get out of here!" I said.

That was when my dad walked in. "Hi, honey," he said to my mom. He turned to me. "Tomorrow is your big day."

"Day?"

"The transition. I assumed you were looking through your file. All your transitions have gone very well. Though they never seem as dramatic as I expect."

"Gradual changes," my mom said. "I've done extra transitions on her to make it more natural, more gradual, more like a regular girl. You know that. She's a prototype of that method."

"Make the next one more dramatic. Have you seen how great Chanelle looks?" he asked.

"She looks sophisticated," my mom responded.

"Her dad is very proud."

"He seemed to very much enjoy it."

"Maybe we can do it today. Why wait another day?"

"The replacement won't be ready until tomorrow," my mom replied.

"But I won't be sixteen for five months."

"You are doing so well on all subjects. Why wait?" Dad asked. He opened up a cabinet. "Nice."

I moved to see what he was looking at. I felt myself blacking out with my last memory being that of seeing my face, a little older, but it was mine.

CHAPTER 4

I woke up in my bed. Mom was next to me. Music was playing.

"I don't want to be replaced."

My mom stroked my hair.

"Is there a chance, any chance, we could go above?'

"Honey, the reports said that the entire upper surface of the Earth was destroyed."

"World War III?"

"You learned about it in kindergarten. We've talked about it."

"Yes. Up, we die. I'm going to die down here. Is dying free much worse?"

"I want you to trust me. Do you think I would ever let anything bad happen to you?'

"Not until Chanelle. My best friend."

"You barely knew the human Chanelle."

"Even if I am a robot, I have— Wait. Humans can't live above, but robots?"

"Robotic parts would stop functioning up there, according to the scientific consensus. The radiation would affect everything."

"You have access to all databases. You sure there's no chance there?"

She looked away as if she was worried about microphones. I knew there were microphones in all the houses, but I didn't know where specifically.

My mom turned off the music as sounds could be heard from the entry. I knew it was my dad returning.

"Eterra, I want to talk to you!"

She left the room to find out what he wanted.

"I don't want the new version glitching out like that."

He must be talking about my fainting. What is happening to me? That's twice in two days. Kalandro was right. I am defective.

"I've repaired the file. After the transition, she won't black out anymore," Mom said.

"Are you sure the transition will go smoothly tomorrow?"

"Of course."

The next morning, my dad took me to the lab. Inside, my mom said. "You're early. We won't be ready until later."

My dad patted me on the shoulder and walked out. "I'll see the new you when I get back, Natalia."

Not me, I thought. I rushed out the door. My dad was already gone and I had to find a way to escape.

"You need to return."

I turned towards the voice. It was my mom but not my mom. I could see the difference in her manner and the way she looked at me. Mom had been replaced.

CHAPTER 5

The replacement gripped me firmly and took me back to the lab.

"I don't want the transition. I don't care if they know I don't want it. I don't. Someone else will have my thoughts and knowledge, but that someone else won't be me."

"Have you gotten that out of your system?" she asked.

"No, I haven't."

I started for the door again. That's when my dad returned. "If Jason can do the honors, I can too."

"What did you do to Mom?"

"Nothing."

"Her old programming is having another breakdown," my not-mommy said. "I need to make sure the upload is free of those glitches."

"See to it," my dad demanded, starting to walk out of the room, again. "I'll be back and everything needs to be in order."

I hadn't seen him speak so sternly to my mom before. He paused. "I'd like to see the replacement, again."

My not-mom pulled out the replica of me with that horrible head on it. The face looked more mature than it had the day before, and the figure was more developed than mine.

She put it back in the cabinet and closed the cabinet door. "Now, I have work to do."

The not-mommy escorted my dad to the lab door. As she closed it, I grabbed a wrench from the utility closet and swung it at her, purposely missing her but forcing her back, again and again, until she was in front of the utility closet. I opened the closet door and with one more swing, she was in.

A few minutes later, my mom came into the lab through the door to what I knew to be an observation room.

"Mom, did you see?"

"Yes, honey. You need to relax."

"And Daddy wants to kill me, himself."

"I know."

My mom pulled out the shelf with the 'not-me' on it again and placed a blanket over it. She pushed the shelf back into the cabinet.

"You're really going to do this, Mom?" I started to cry.

She looked around. She pulled off my bracelet and smashed it. "I think the cameras and microphones are non-functional for the moment and I locked the observation room."

"Are you going to save me?" I was into hope.

"Listen, don't eat the apples."

"Apples?"

"Apples."

She went over to the computer cabinet, opened up the computer housing, moved some boards around and added an extra chip.

"Is that more of my upload? Mom, they're replacing you too."

"Don't worry. You need to be calm and unemotional. Please, trust me."

But I didn't. Not anymore. I headed for the door and tried to open it, while my mom checked the cabinet and closet areas. "Mom. Your replacement is in the closet. Don't open it!"

The lab door was locked. I had to find the key. My mom's lab was the only office with a metallic key as opposed to a key card. My mom was pulling something bulky, covered by a sheet, out of a different cupboard and lugging it to the far side of the computer desk. I saw the key on the computer stand. I went for it, but as I put it into the lock and turned, my mom took my arm, pulling me back.

"What's going on?" I asked.

"You need to know while the microphones are off," she said quietly. "You aren't an android. I've protected you, destroying duplicates each time. I couldn't let anyone suspect."

She handed me a device. "It detects radiation and air quality. Keep it with you at all times."

I pocketed it immediately. "I don't understand," I whispered, breathing a sigh of relief, learning I wasn't a robot.

My happiness was short-lived as the lab door opened and my dad entered. "Are you done yet?"

"I'm done," Mom said.

"I'm not going to let you kill me!" I yelled at my dad.

"I'm not going to kill you. I'm going to improve you. Why are you so emotional?"

"It's a glitch," my mom replied for me. "As some androids get ready for transition, occasionally an underlying protective program in their uploads goes off. I've removed it from her replacement."

"Good."

"I need you to sit on the chair," my dad instructed me.

"Do you really want to do this one yourself? Maybe the next one," my mom responded.

"No. I think it's time I took an interest in my daughter's future."

That's when it hit me. She was trapped. Even if she wanted to save me, my dad was going to make sure I died. I backed away. He grabbed for me, and I kicked him in the groin. That's when he went for the ax. "She won't remember this, will she?"

"No. But it will be better if she is calm. Give her a minute."

"I'm out of patience." As he swung the ax and I ducked, the computer blew apart and caught fire, spewing pieces and smoke all around the room. I moved away, tripped and fell to the floor.

Through the haze, I could see my mom lying unconscious on the floor, near what was left of the computer. The smoke thickened, and I couldn't see anything.

"Mommy," I called. A hand reached down and lifted me. Some kind of weird, almost translucent sack was placed over me as I was lifted up and carried out of the room.

CHAPTER 6

I had been hoisted over a shoulder as if I were weightless, carried down the corridor from the lab, and then placed on my feet.

"You need to be very quiet," my mom's voice said, but it sounded a bit off. She was wearing a see-through sack, too.

"Mom?"

"I'm taking you out."

"Out?" I knew it wasn't my mom's real voice.

"Mom, my mom's in the lab. She's hurt."

"She told me to get you out. She did this all for you."

"She planned the explosion?"

"She had to. Don't make it be in vain."

"I need to save her?"

"If she's alive, you'll both be executed if you go back."

I didn't know this thing that was pretending to be my mom. For all I knew, she could be leading me to my death.

My mother's words, "Trust me," came back.

"We're not invisible. Anyone can see us. I can see through this ridiculous thing."

"These coverings will make us invisible to the cameras—but not to real people. There are no microphones in this area. Let's go before someone sees us."

We went down corridor after corridor. She opened the doorway to the four-seat trams. I held the covering over me, looking out through it.

"We don't have a passkey," I said.

"I do." She activated the recall, and one tram was lowered to the corridor. We got in and she used her key card to disconnect the monitors and automatic drive, placing it on manual. A minute later, she turned down a road I'd never been on before and attained a velocity I'd only seen in speedway competitions. Only Directors had passkeys able to turn off the internal cameras on the trams. Her having one could be bad news for me. This could be a set-up—a last-minute adventure before my death.

As the vehicle bolted, I wondered if this was how races had been in the past, not AI-driven, but just wild speeding. I couldn't stop thinking of my mom. I was feeling disloyal, torn between Not-Mom's warning of a possible execution for my mom and me and my need to know my mom was okay.

We got out in an unfamiliar area, and she guided me to an elevator. I heard footsteps behind me and wondered if we had been tracked. I looked behind and didn't see anyone.

As she reached to tap a passkey against the elevator reader, I heard a familiar voice. "This is a restricted area. I don't think you're supposed to be here in those funny things. I'm going to report you."

It was Kalandro.

"Your dad killed your sister," I told him.

"I know. But you made it possible," he angrily growled at my not-mother, apparently misrecognizing her through the covering.

"You aren't a robot," I said.

"What?"

"You're human. You want to escape, too?" It was a risk, but also a hope.

"How?"

"Come with us," I said.

"I don't have another covering," Not-Mom countered.

"I'll come or I'll talk."

"Get under hers with her."

"Cozy."

"I don't like it either."

"That makes two of us," Kalandro said, snidely.

He got under my covering and put his arms around me, causing me to feel both icky and something else I couldn't decipher as we went up the elevator. My ears popped and my head hurt. After we got out, we proceeded through more corridors.

"Are you sure you know where you are going?" I asked Not-Mom.

"We can't go outside. It's radioactive," Kalandro warned.

"Shut up. I'd rather die free than live a slave. You don't have to come," I said. "I mean, I hate you, too. You only cared about your sister after your father killed her. He did it. Not my mom."

"I saw him. I was in the observation room."

"And you let him do it? You're sick."

"You were closer. You looked like you were going to scream. Not a good response for a robot. I guess you have special privileges since your mom is the replacement monster."

"Stop talking about my mom. I don't even know if she's alive."

"Isn't this her?"

"No."

"Would you two stop whispering? Someone might hear you. You're lucky that covering is muffling your sounds."

"Then who is this?"

"Not-mom."

"And your mom?"

"What business is it of yours?" I started to cry.

"You really are human," he observed.

"I am, and my mom was lying on the floor after an explosion, and I left her there. We need to go back."

"I have one overriding program, and that is to get you out safely. I'm very strong," Not-Mom said.

"Stronger than me?" Kalandro asked.

"Easily," Not-Mom whispered. "Now shut up."

We went up a staircase. And then, another.

"You know we are going to certain death," he advised.

"Then, don't come," I responded.

"I find this too challenging to turn back. Trying to survive the unsurvivable. A better chance than Chanelle had."

We exited on a corridor. Partway down, Not-Mom turned to the side and kicked down a door.

"I guess she is stronger than me," Kalandro confirmed.

We walked through the open doorway. There were all kinds of gears, switches, and several computer consoles. Not-Mom inserted something that resembled an archaic flash drive into one of the computers. She pulled a number of switches that were beyond my comprehension and then threw something into the room as she pushed us out and rushed us on. I could hear an explosion behind us. Everything went dark.

"Did you start the explosion in the lab?"

"Your mom did that. Part of my assignment involves taking out this section's power, tapping into the main AI processor and wiping out the surveillance circuits for the last twelve years, which I just did."

"My mom showed you how to do that?"

"She programmed me and created the backdoor to let me do that."

"I can't see," I said.

"I can." She replied, holding my hand through the coverings, as we continued down the corridor.

"Halt!" Lights from behind broke the darkness.

It was two security control androids, several feet behind us. They had their own lighting system that flooded the hallway. They apparently had the ability to see through the coverings. These glowing red robots looked nastier than any androids I had ever seen before. They had guns that were huge and aimed at us.

CHAPTER 7

I stood frozen, fearing our journey had come to an end. I had never before seen weapons like those pointing at us, but I was pretty sure they could finish us off and then some. These actually were the first guns I had seen in real life, but they looked even more ominous than the ones in the computerized picture books and videos of the terrible world above from before the Reset.

Not-Mom pushed us to the ground with the covering on top of us. Shots rang out. It sounded as if parts of the walls had been blasted out. Was I saved from the transition—only to die here with Kalandro and my mom's duplicate? As debris from the former walls fell on us, the firing stopped.

Everything had gone dark again. Something fell beside me. I was trying to get my bearings as Kalandro moved away from me. A minute later, something heavy tapped me. It was one of the guns.

Had the androids taken out Not-Mom? Were they about to finish us?

"Don't shoot us," I said to, I presumed, a security android.

"They're out for now," Kalandro's voice replied.

Next to me, I felt Not-Mom's body, crumpled on the floor. "Not-

Mom, are you okay?" She wasn't moving. "We need her to get out of here," I told Kalandro.

"I'll take her. Whatever knocked out those things may have knocked her out, too. As long as she doesn't need to be reset, she might come back."

"Let's get her away from those security robots."

"If the surveillance cameras are out, we can use this," he handed me a small flashlight and turned it on.

He next handed me the weapons dropped by the security robots and, without asking for help, picked up Not-Mom. We kept going in the general direction we had been traveling, away from the androids who had threatened us.

I was surprised by how strong he was. I was struggling with the oversized weapons.

We made some turns through several corridors and he sat her on the floor. I knelt down to feel her. Chanelle always had some amount of warmth and Not-Mom did too. I guessed it was to make them appear more human. She was breathing, but if she were an android, it was fake. Her ability to imitate human bodily functions meant her program was still functional.

"Not-Mom, Not-Mom, we need you," I whimpered, cradling her head. I couldn't feel any blood. But did robots bleed? Mom said they had fake blood. "Please wake up."

Kalandro smacked her face.

"What was that for, jerk?" I reacted.

She started to stir. I breathed a sigh of relief.

"I heard, in the old days, people would smack their cars to get them to work."

"Not-Mom is not a car."

"So, she has an alias, 'Not-Car.'"

"Very not-funny."

"Natalia. Are we where I collapsed?" Not-Mom asked.

Kalandro described the route we had taken.

"Good instincts."

"So did I guess right?"

"No. But close." She continued to escort us back a little and then further on.

"What was that—that took them down and knocked you out?"

"Not powerful enough to get past my memory shielding. Your mom created me special."

"She said I was special."

"Different special."

"If it knocked out power, how does the flashlight still work?"

"It's luminescent, not battery powered," Kalandro replied. "We'd better hurry before more of those security things show up."

I thought about how we were going to a wasteland, but it would be better for me than what we were leaving, no matter how aesthetic things below the surface were.

"You have a good life here. Were they going to transition you?" I asked him.

"No. The guys in the leadership program never get transitioned," he answered me.

"Your sister?"

"Girls aren't in the leadership program. They're either baby-makers, part of leadership, married to leadership or androids."

"In other words, your dad's a sexist, killing your sister, but not you."

"Our society didn't consider her valuable."

I felt angry. "What about before her first transition—when she was human?"

"I said 'our society.' I only found out about transitions after that."

"I found out about it when he chopped off her head."

"I hate robots."

"You hate me?" Not-Mom asked him.

"Not if you get us out of here," he replied.

"You didn't hate your sister either—even after she was an android. In spite of the nasty remarks, I know you cared about her. I saw you in the park that day."

"Your father was above my father. Maybe that's why you weren't changed."

"He wanted to transition me himself, today. My mother convinced him I was a robot."

"That's talent, tricking the Chairman."

"She put a removable wrist surveillance device on me and told me to avoid emotions."

"You weren't very good at that."

"Ha!"

"My sister would say you were trying out emotions. She thought that was silly."

"I wish I had just been trying. Everything would hurt less."

It hit me. "Your internal microphone, or do you have a bracelet? The AI has been able to hear everything we've said."

"Those are for robots, not humans. How did you fake it in school?"

"I studied."

"Would you two talk less?" Not-Mom advised.

We arrived at a point in a wall that looked solid. She pressed her pass card against the wall, and it opened.

"My mother programmed that for you?"

"She did. This is my purpose."

Inside was a round chamber with a ladder. We followed her to the base of it. "There is an electrical defense, independent of the main power. I'm going to take it out and then permanently close off this portal. I'll have to do it quickly while I still have my programming."

"Permanently close? How?"

"After I take the charge, race up there quickly." She ascended the ladder and used her card to open a hatch on top. Hundreds of sparks flashed from the opening onto her and then went out. She moved down a few rungs on the ladder as we rushed up. "Don't touch anything but the ladder and the ground above. Now!"

She pulled me up past her on the ladder. Kalandro followed, guns in hand, as she also lifted him up above her. She then pressed something on a pendant she was wearing.

"I don't understand."

"Go!"

"You can't go back down there," I told her. "Come with us. My father—"

"He's not your father."

"I knew it," Kalandro practically growled as we observed Not-Mom glowing. We waited until the glow went out.

"Not my father?" I asked and then saw that Not-Mom was visibly weak, barely hanging onto the ladder.

As I tried to reach past Kalandro to grab her, I heard her order "Go," as she fell from the ladder into the darkness.

I was about to go back down when Kalandro pushed me up and through the opening into the night, beneath a field of stars and surrounded by a wide-open space.

"I'm going back," I insisted, as he joined me on top.

"You can't. The field might reactivate."

"She looks like my mom, not yours. She saved both our lives," I said angrily, wondering how he could be so heartless.

He picked me up and started to carry me over one shoulder with the guns in the other hand.

"Put me down!"

"You're stupid and your hair is a mess."

"Old joke. Put me back on my feet. I want to go—" My words were silenced as an explosion blew through the opening behind us, and the ground around it collapsed.

CHAPTER 8

"They killed her?" I asked in disbelief as Kalandro rushed away from the area, continuing to carry me over his shoulder. He lowered me to the ground.

"I think she killed herself. She was talking as if she planned to die. She said, 'before my programming goes out.' I think the electrical circuitry was deactivating her and that pendant was a bomb."

Explosions continued, shaking the ground. Kalandro picked me up and began running, again, as the ground beneath where we had stopped collapsed behind us.

He continued running until we were at the edge of a cliff. It was dark and it was hard to make out our surroundings.

I pulled the radiation detector my mom had given me from my pocket. A panel lit up as I touched a sensor on its top. The letters "neg" were visible, along with a meter.

"This area isn't radioactive. I would have thought the whole planet was."

"Yeah. They lied, alright."

We were sitting below a giant apple tree. He got up and started to reach for the low-hanging apples.

"Don't," I said. "My mom warned me about the apples."

"The apples?"

"She said we couldn't eat them."

"I'm hungry."

"I am not going to be out here all alone. If you even start to take a bite, I'll punch you."

He came back to sit beside me. "So, you don't hate me."

"Of course, I hate you. I'd just rather have company I hate than no company at all," I said, standing up.

"I hate you, too. But you know what the closest thing to hate is," he remarked, rising to stand beside me.

I knew it was supposed to be love, but I didn't want to go there. He was mocking me. He had always mocked me and put me down. So, I kicked his knee and lay down at the edge of the cliff. "Maybe we'll find some safe food tomorrow." I couldn't see what was below the cliff but I suspected it was a long way down.

He picked up the radiation detector and pointed it at an apple. "It's not radioactive. I wonder if it's poison."

"Don't know," I said, finding I couldn't keep my eyes open. As I dozed off, I asked myself how I could sleep when my mom might be dead. But sleep I did.

―――――

The sun hurt my eyes as I woke. As I re-closed them, I could still see the bright image. In the underworld, the yellow ball in what we called the sky had never hurt my eyes.

A breeze swept by my face, cool and refreshing, with multiple scents blending together. I wondered if it was safe to breathe them in.

"I'm thirsty. If we can't eat the apples, I still want water," Kalandro complained.

Now that it was day, I could see we were sitting by a big drop-off. The sky was blue. "What is that smell?"

"Dirt?" he guessed, picking up a handful.

"It's more than that." I looked down. "Look at the lake below. It's larger and bluer than the ones in the underworld. And the rivers going into and out of it are wider and swifter than the ones below."

"Duh. You think I'm blind? I've been looking at it for the last half hour. Do you still have that radiation detector?"

I pulled it out of my pocket and pointed down at the lake. "Not radioactive from up here. But we're a distance, maybe a couple hundred feet above it." I checked the air quality and it read, "Excellent."

"How do we get down there?"

"We climb."

"Climb?'

"Climb. You're supposed to be athletic. It can't be any more dangerous than the climbing walls back home."

"They aren't this high and my skill was basketball."

"We could walk for miles until the trail is easier or until you find some basketball hoops. It looks like there is a narrow path over there," I pointed.

We moved over to the start of a downward trail. The path was so narrow, we had to walk sideways. It wasn't steep, but it was uneven and difficult to maneuver. I regularly checked the radiation readings while trying to avoid stumbling over stones. The radiation wasn't increasing.

As I continued walking, a stone under my foot gave way. I tried to stabilize myself, but found I was slipping even more, about to go down the cliff. Kalandro reached for me. In desperation, I reached back for his hand, but in doing so, I threw myself even more off balance. I was falling.

CHAPTER 9

I prepared for the worst. Would I be crushed by falling from this height? The lakes back home weren't surrounded by cliffs and I had only jumped from short diving boards into swimming pools in the past. Fear rushed through me.

My feet hit the water first and I went down, down, down, down. I held my breath, afraid I would soon take in water.

When my descent stopped, I pushed myself back up to the surface and took a deep breath. The water was cold but not freezing.

I had lost Kalandro. *He must have gone back up the cliff.* I looked for a safe place to get out. That's when I saw him in the water, not far from me, yelling and panicking. I swam over to him.

"I'm going to drown!" he sputtered as I helped him keep his head up. He didn't know how to swim.

"Relax. Let the water carry you. Lie on your back, it's easier." I pushed up his body into a back-float position. His head went back and he almost started breathing in water. I pushed up his head. "Keep your head up on the water, like it's a bed."

"I can't do it," he complained as he succeeded in doing just that. "I'm afraid."

"You're in the leadership program. Didn't your parents or the servants teach you to swim?"

"No."

"Then just stay on your back for now." Eventually, I got him to turn over and do something resembling the breast stroke. It turned out that he was left-handed. I hadn't paid attention before. My mother was left-handed as well.

There was a sandy bank on the far side of the lake from where we fell in, but it was quite a swim. I was almost surprised when we made it. I lay down in the sand and found it clinging to my body.

"I swallowed some of the water," he said. "Was it radioactive?"

I pulled the radiation detector out of my pocket. It was glitching on and off. "I think it's waterlogged, but it doesn't appear to show any radioactivity."

He looked upset.

"What's wrong?"

"I dropped the guns."

"Don't worry about it. I don't think those things are going to follow us up here."

"Where is here?"

"I wish I knew."

"How do we get out of here?"

Next to the sand was another high cliff. I didn't see a trail up. The cliffs were pretty high up on both banks.

I looked at Kalandro. He seemed like a different person. Instead of the insulting, self-assured egotist, I saw a vulnerable, uncertain, even helpless boy. If I didn't watch out, I might start liking him.

"I'm hungry," he complained.

"Look," I pointed. "Fish. If there were a problem with the water, they'd look sick or two-headed or something. Maybe when the detector dries, it will start working properly again."

"Isn't the fallout supposed to have lasted for about two hundred thousand years?"

"More. Maybe this area somehow escaped," I speculated.

"They said the fallout would have covered the planet—even the areas that weren't hit. Maybe that detector is malfunctioning."

"The fish seem to be doing well and some of them are pretty large," I observed.

"Large?"

"Not large enough to eat us."

I couldn't believe how skittish he was. There was something charming about it, making him less hateful. I told myself when we got away from this area, he'd turn back into his usual disparaging self. "How come you were always so mean to your sister?"

"I told you. I don't like robots."

"But then, you were sad when her last robot self was axed."

"She still had a piece of the sister I once loved."

"Loved? That's something I never considered you capable of."

"There's a lot you don't know about me."

"Why did you come up here?"

"To get away from my dad. Did you see the glee with which he killed Chanelle's robot? One day, he could do that to me."

"But you're in the leadership program."

"That's no guarantee."

"I don't even know who my real father is. I guess I'll never know."

"I might."

"You?"

"I heard a rumor about my father and your mother. When my mom died, everyone was so sorry for him. I wasn't. He was so cruel to her before he died."

"And you blame my mom without any evidence that she was involved with your dad? Besides, your sister and I were almost the same age and we are or were both younger than you."

"According to the rumor, after your mom was involved with my dad, she married the Chair and then my dad and mom got back together, but he was really cruel and mom was always crying over the mean things he shouted at her."

"I can't imagine my mom being so loose that she'd get involved with someone like—" I didn't finish the sentence. "Did you hear this rumor from other kids?" The thought disgusted me. I told myself it was nonsense from an idiot.

"No. My dad had me playing with other kids at a party and I went out of the kids' room and heard some of the adults talking. They said he had a wandering eye and messed with a lot of women but liked your mom the best. I saw some of those women after Mom died. I hated them."

"They say that sons turn out like their fathers. Are you going to be a womanizer who is cruel to your wife? I feel sorry for whoever you wind up marrying. And as unlikely as it is, if you are my brother, which I doubt, I will nail you if you do that to my sister-in-law."

"Go ahead. I've never dated. Every time I look at a girl—even a girl android—I think of how awful my mother must have felt. Dad was grooming me to be like him."

"You're off to a good start. I can see why they put you on the Youth Leadership Council. Nobody else was as capable of uttering the nasty insults you came up with."

"I don't want to be anything like him. Not ever. I figured, if I played along, he wouldn't kill me and I'd find a way to be free."

"I don't think anyone down there is free."

"On that we agree."

I shook my head.

"Aren't you hungry?" he asked.

"Starving. But I'm going to play it safe. Look, a squirrel." A little squirrel was climbing up a tree. "It's adorable."

"Food."

"You're going to eat that sweet little squirrel?"

"I eat meat."

"Don't you dare try or I might feed you to—no, you'd give him indigestion." I thought about Chanelle. "Your sister used to always eat lunch. I wonder how the androids eliminate it."

"The same way as the humans—except with internal tubes and whatnot," he said.

"All the time I grew up, my dad, or the guy who called himself my dad, thought I was a robot. He never knew I was human."

"How did your mom explain you only having subtle or normal changes?"

"Apparently, she made it appear I had more transitions than most

—an experiment to see if subtle changes worked as effectively as more extreme ones."

"My sister went through those extreme changes, apparently also known as real transitions."

"When I was younger, I just thought Chanelle was having growing spurts. But I did notice she treated me less warmly with each transition."

"They don't want warmth. You might develop a conscience. What they are doing is psychotic. In the leadership program, we were told to report anyone showing emotions. They would be dismantled and rebuilt."

"But you didn't report me?"

He looked at me but didn't give me an explanation.

We stood up. "Let's get out of here," I said.

"Where are we going?"

I put my hand into the water. "That way," I said, pointing in the direction I had seen the river snaking down through the hills. As we walked downstream, the beach narrowed.

Everything started shaking and I heard the crackling sound of trees bending or breaking. I had to stabilize myself to keep from falling.

"Watch out!" He yelled, grabbing me and throwing me to the ground and dropping down next to me.

"What—"

A tree fell where I had been standing. The shaking continued.

"Do you think that has anything to do with a chain reaction from that explosion?" I asked.

"I don't know. If it prevented security droids from coming after us, it's a good thing," he said, lifting his voice on the last word as another tree fell to the other side of us.

Rocks from the cliff behind us tumbled. The water was choppy and splashed onto the shore over us as the violent shaking continued and I wondered if the ground would open up and swallow us.

Kalandro started to stand and then fell on me. I tried to move him off. Kalandro had gone limp and heavy and was hard to push off. Then, I noticed, blood, dripping from his head onto me.

CHAPTER 10

I managed to roll him off me. The side of his head was bloody. I put my head against his chest. His heart was still beating, but the unconsciousness and blood frightened me.

I tried to wake him. "Kalandro? Kalandro!"

There was no response.

I took off my over-shirt and wrapped it around his head. "Please, don't leave me. I don't really hate you. Please, come back."

I slapped his face a couple of times, not knowing what to do to wake him up. Slapping had awakened Not-Mom. I hoped I wasn't making it worse or causing new problems.

"Oww."

"You're awake."

"Yeah. What did you do to me?"

"I think a rock hit you. I've been trying to wake you."

He reached up to his head and felt the shirt.

"Your head is bleeding. That was the best I could do. I need to get you help. I think I can make some kind of raft by using some of the vines over there to tie around the fallen logs."

"Where did you learn to do that?"

"From a book I read. Do you think it will be too much for you to raft down the river?"

"I'm feeling a little dizzy."

"Concussion. Remember, Toby Woods got one when he fell on the basketball court. We all heard about it."

"They almost took him out of the game. But then he came back by halftime—totally healed."

"I was surprised by his amazing recovery. That must have been some fast medical work."

"Or maybe he was replaced. He was an important player. Do robots have concussions?" he asked.

"I don't know, but my mom said that everyone's memories are backed up, uploaded into the closed system in the Bio-Enhancement Lab."

"I wonder if a robot crashed or the real Toby died and was replaced?"

"Or was killed. Remember, they expect perfection. You might have a concussion."

"Shade my eyes and see if the pupils contract when you unshade them. That was in one of the banned medical books."

"We aren't in direct sunlight, but I can darken your face some by leaning over you."

I tried several times to change the lighting. I could only shade his eyes a little. "I'm not doing a good job but I think your pupils are responding properly. I can't be sure."

I started trying to gather the logs. He got up and started to help.

"You need to take it easy."

"And leave this to you? You're a girl. How likely is it that you won't mess this up?"

"At least, I can swim," I said.

"Ha-ha. I'm feeling better."

"Just don't bleed on the logs. You wouldn't want to contaminate them with your elitism."

"Or your obnoxiousism."

"Me?"

"You said it yourself. You hate me, too."

"And I meant it." *I must have been out of my mind to say I didn't when he was unconscious.*

With some difficulty, we managed to tie some logs together. They weren't even in size, but I hoped they would provide us with a platform to ride on. We used branches lying on the ground as oars and pushed the raft into the water.

"Which way?"

"Maybe you do have a concussion. The same as before. With the flow."

"It works," he said as the river casually carried us downstream. "I guess you can do something right."

I glared at him.

"That looks ominous," he said as we rounded a bend and the current picked up speed.

There were some trees leaning into the left side of the river and some thicker branches on the right in our path and I couldn't see any of the river past that point.

"It's a cliff."

"Waterfall. Let's row towards the right," Kalandro advised.

We tried but to no avail. Cold water splashed up from the oars onto us as fear swept over me. Our oars and strength proved insufficient for the task. The river was in control as we were being swept, full speed, toward the fall. I wondered if this would be the end. I tried to grab onto a branch on the left, but failed as the raft started to upend and drop. I screamed.

CHAPTER 11

As I looked down the waterfall, I knew these could be my last seconds of life. But I had no regrets about leaving. I was free. Maybe death would be an adventure like the up-above.

As I took what might be my last breath, a hand pulled me up. Kalandro had latched onto a branch with his other hand. I reached out and grasped a wispy branch that I was afraid would break. The roughness cut into the flesh on my hand.

Kalandro lifted himself onto his branch. It was thin and flimsy but somehow it was strong enough to allow him to rescue me. He lifted me beside him as I waited for it to break under our weight, as it bent towards the river. We carefully moved to the trunk and then across another branch to the shore.

I was cold and wet but alive and safe. Part of me wished anyone else, someone who liked me, had saved me. *I am alive. What difference does it make who rescued me?*

"Thank you. That's the second time you saved me."

"I think we're about even now." He almost smiled and then frowned.

I stood up and whirled around. "Up-above is wet, dangerous and even beautiful; nothing like we were taught in school. And we're not dying."

"We were taught it would be a grey, burnt-out, desolate place where nothing could grow and the air was unsafe to breathe. Maybe we're in an oasis and moving toward the devastation. We could set up our new home here."

"And you still believe anything we were taught?" I didn't wait for an answer. "Let's go on. If we glimpse the bad part, we can stop."

"Unless it's too late at that point."

"Let's go," I insisted.

On shore, we climbed to the bottom of the waterfall and continued following the river.

"The raft survived," I observed. "Look. It's stuck on that rock in the river. Those falls and rapids are no good for hard rafts."

"How did you know about making a raft?"

"I had read about pre-World War III rafts in school in our history books. I used to wish I had lived back before the Reset—in spite of being taught that the nuclear war was a good thing. It eliminated the terrorists—even though society had to go underground. Part of me would have rather lived side by side with the terrorists, vandals and fire-starters than in the underworld. We have vinyl and rubber rafts in the rivers down below. Same principle—except I doubt those rivers are natural," I said.

"They aren't. They have teams of people working on the waterways."

"Of course. And don't forget Water Adventure is one of the most fun." It was a park in the underground with small waterfalls and soft rapids where the Elites, as they liked to be called, such as my dad, and their families sometimes hung out. I noticed that none of the worker class ever made use of them. I guessed they weren't assigned to enjoy themselves.

Like Kalandro, I was hungry. I felt queasy about the idea of killing a fish to support my life form. It wasn't just an objection to eating fish but rather to killing any living thing. Food had always been provided for us. There was meat below, but it wasn't alive. I knew we could survive a few days without food, maybe longer, but it didn't make my stomach feel any better.

Along the side, we saw some black berries. I wasn't familiar with this fruit.

"I don't know about you, but I'm not going to die hungry," he said.

My detector was working again and showed no problem with radiation or the air quality.

"I wonder when we're going to get to the radioactive area," he pondered.

"Probably when we get close to the river's end."

"Then why are you taking us downriver? Do you have a death wish?"

"Would you rather go uphill? I wonder if people used to play in this river. Don't!" I reacted as he put one of the berries into his mouth.

"If this is poison, then poison it's delicious." He started eating more and more berries. "Eat."

"Somebody has to take care of you when you're dying."

He grabbed his throat and then collapsed.

"Kalandro, Kalandro, I told you not to eat those!"

A smirk appeared on his face.

I smacked his shoulder. "You."

He broke out into a laugh. "Seriously. These are not poisonous. Take one."

When I didn't react, he added. "Okay. More for me."

After he had eaten a couple dozen, my hunger got stronger. I laughed. "You should see your face."

He looked at his reflection in the water and saw that he had berry juice covering his face.

"You look better like that."

He waved a fist at me.

Watching him continue to happily eat didn't help my hunger. "Rat," I said, taking one. "If I die, you have to be the one to bury me."

"Bury?"

"My mom said that above they used to bury people, rather than incinerate them."

"In the ground?"

"In the ground, and you're going to dig me a grave if I die."

I plopped the berry into my mouth. I didn't want to admit it, but he was right about them being delicious. I had a few more. I figured, with all he had eaten, he'd show symptoms faster than me.

"I need a bathroom break. You can't look," I said as I went behind a bush along the shore.

"What makes you think I would want to look?"

At least, I had running water for a bidet and for cleaning my hands.

As I pulled my pants back up, I saw eyes looking at me. They were big black eyes attached to something very white.

"Hello?"

It barked.

"What is that?"

"I think it's called a dog, a real one, not an android," I replied.

I came out from behind the bush and the white dog followed me.

"It doesn't look like any of the dogs I've seen before."

"We don't have these below. He's, no, she's, very cute."

"It's wild. It might attack us."

"I think she wants to lick us." I knelt down. The dog put her paws on my shoulders and licked my face.

"Yuck," Kalandro said.

"Let's keep her," I responded.

"Keep?"

"We need a name for you." I thought for a minute. "I miss my mom. I'm going to call you Eterra."

"You're giving it your mother's name!"

"That way, I won't feel so alone."

"You're not. I'm here."

"But you're a jerk. Between you and the dog. I like her."

"I don't know why I saved you. You prefer the dog."

Eterra went over to the berries and started eating them.

"Now her instincts I trust." I ate more, as did Kalandro.

We stuffed our pockets with berries to eat as we continued on our way. I wasn't all that hungry anymore, but Eterra liked the berries and continued eating.

"I wonder if she belongs to somebody."

"Maybe somebody who's dead. Maybe she ate her last owner."

I rolled my eyes. "If you're going to hang out with me, you have to be nice to my dog."

"Half an hour ago, you didn't have a dog."

"And now I do."

I picked up a stick and tossed it. Eterra ran and caught it. Then she came back. I held out my hand for her to return it. That she didn't do. I picked up another stick and threw it. She dropped the first and ran to catch the second stick and then came back and gave it to me.

"I didn't realize dogs could be so much fun. With a dog, who needs a boy?"

"Didn't you pass your sex education classes?"

"Yes. Apparently, even android girls are expected to have sex at some point." I thought about Chanelle's latest look. It was probably the kind of look men liked. "I want to be one of those religious people with the black outfits."

"Nun?"

"I read about them in a history book. They are celibate. That way, I don't have to worry about guys."

He gave me a thumbs up. "Finally, you got something right. What guy would want to have sex with an emotional freak like you?"

"I'm not an emotional freak, and I'm the same age as Chanelle." I started to argue, but then realized she wasn't that age at all as she had been replaced repeatedly.

He ignored my comment. "And you don't care for boys?"

"Look at the offerings. There's you. Yuck. Then Charlie Doran. Super yuck. And Colby Sharitan. Triple yuck. And a bunch of guys who make security robots look desirable by comparison."

"What kind of boy do you want?"

"Handsome, charming, says nice things, fights for me and is willing to risk everything anytime I'm in danger. A hero type."

"I want a girl. Who—" He paused, looking at me as I went back to playing with my dog.

I didn't care what kind of girl he wanted and didn't ask him to continue.

"I'll just say it. A girl who will listen to me and trust my judgment, someone who is pretty but not vain, mild-mannered, compliments me all the time and is eager to please me."

"If I see a doormat, I'll send her your way. One thing is for sure."

"What's that?"

"We'll never wind up together."

"You're right about that," he said.

"Come on, Eterra, let's keep going."

I glanced at him. Something was troubling him.

"Okay, out with it."

"It's nothing."

"Nothing?"

"Nothing."

"Good," I said, walking on.

I started thinking of the guys I knew back home. Was any of them like the one I described? Robert Horton came to mind. He had golden blond hair, close to my own color, a little longer than most boys', green eyes, and a nice smile. Every time he saw me, he always seemed to brighten up as if I were the most important person in the world.

Robert's father was a big shot in the government, a former pharmaceutical director before society went below. Supposedly, he sold the world on important creations they claimed saved everyone. I suppose the kind of diplomacy involved in presentations and salesmanship was part of Robert's training, but I always felt really warm and happy inside whenever I saw him. Just thinking of him brought a smile to my face.

I saw Kalandro glaring at me. He always knew how to destroy my moods and make me angry. Below, anger was not allowed, though our fathers sounded angry with each other at times when I'd almost walked in on their private conversations.

"Thinking of me?"

"What an ego. Never. Actually, I was thinking about Robert Horton."

"That loser?"

"That loser could have any girl he wants. He's nice and sweet and good looking, you know, all the things you're not."

"Dandia Hartford is my dream girl."

"Her? She doesn't have a brain in her head. She must be a really defective robot. I guess she would be just your type. In fact, if she winds up here, I'll perform your marital ceremony, myself, and get you off my back."

"I'm not on your back."

Eterra barked and then something landed on me, something with claws.

CHAPTER 12

The claws scratched through my clothes into my chest and arms as I unsuccessfully tried to push the thing that looked like a cat away from me. It was strong and wiggly and snarling at me. The pain was almost overwhelming. I feared I'd be its dinner.

Kalandro was trying to pull it off me, but as he did, I fell back and it came with me. Eterra grabbed the creature by the back of the neck and flung it into the river.

It came back at me as I was checking myself over. I had scratches, excruciating scratches, but no bites. Kalandro picked up a branch. The animal gripped its teeth into the branch and Kalandro flung it all the way across the river.

I hugged Eterra. "Thank you, my friend. You saved me."

"What about me?"

"You did great, too."

"But I take second place to a dog."

"Sorry, but she was quicker."

"Maybe we ought to name her Lightning."

It occurred to me that I had never actually seen lightning. I had read about it. I wondered if there was still lightning up here.

"What if everything we were told about life up here was a lie?

Maybe all our history was just made up. Maybe there was no cherry tree and nobody named George Washington."

"Hey, anyone doubting the cherry tree story is a conspiracy theorist," Kalandro objected, eyeing me as if I were from outer space.

"It's gospel in our history books. Do we have to swallow everything our books say completely?"

"Remember what we learned about people who questioned the narratives before World War III. They were violent and had to be locked up and executed."

"But what if they were right and the truth was killed with them?"

"You sound like those heretics we read about."

He was condemning me for just posing questions. I was glad he wasn't my type and never would be.

"You're part of what I hate about our society," he griped further.

"Me?"

"You refuse to condemn your mother, who facilitates the killing of kids and copying their brains into robots. If she didn't create the robots in the first place, my sister might still be alive."

"Someone else would be doing the work she does in that case. At least, I never saw her execute anyone. The only one I've ever seen kill anyone, human or robot, was your dad."

"My sister, yes, but what about the ones where you didn't watch? And who killed my real sister?"

I had no answer to that. I had so little knowledge of my mother's work. I wished I could speak with her, again, and find out the truth. I couldn't believe that the person who had given me so much love could have ever harmed a child.

I silently whispered a plea to my mom, wishing she could respond. "Please tell me you didn't do that." She had said she hadn't killed anyone. I wanted to believe that, but she had lied to me about virtually everything my whole life. I just hoped that that one statement was true.

I leaned down and hugged my dog. I was glad I had given her my mom's name. Like my mom, she was a giver and a protector. *She would never harm a child,* I kept telling myself.

"Those scratches look nasty," Kalandro said, acting as if he cared a little.

I leaned down and used river water to rinse them. There was a small amount of clotted blood, but the flow had stopped.

"Let's keep going," I suggested.

"Now, you sound more like an android."

Kalandro's words reminded me of all the hate he had spewed over the years towards me and my mother. The sooner I could get away from Kalandro, the better.

We continued walking. Eterra was sure-footed as we moved over pebbles in the shallow water, where it went all the way up to the bottom of the cliff.

Kalandro bent down for another drink. "This tastes better than any of the water we have back home."

I had accidentally swallowed some of the river water but not a lot. I took a double handful of water up to my mouth and gulped. I didn't want to admit he was right about anything. But he was about the water.

"I'm tired," I said. "There's a place over there where we can relax."

We sat down on a narrow sandy beach. I laid back and closed my eyes.

Kalandro shook me awake. "We have to get out of here. Flash flood."

I was having trouble seeing but as my eyes came into focus, I saw a huge wall of water approaching from upriver.

CHAPTER 13

I picked up Eterra and started to run.

"Put her down."

"Never."

"We won't make it with you holding her."

Eterra was barking and squirming. She freed herself from my arms and ran towards the cliff. As I followed her, I saw she had gone through an opening in the cliff wall.

"If we go in there, the water will cover us and we'll drown," Kalandro warned

"I trust Eterra." She was waiting just past the opening for us.

I rushed in, followed by Kalandro, who threw up his hands. Off to one side, there were steps I climbed as quickly as I could. Kalandro followed me. The water flooded in. We continued sprinting up the stairs as the water rose below us. Eventually, the water level stopped rising.

As we got to the top of the cliff, we could see a large building, made of bricks and plaster. I didn't see any people around it. As we approached, I was able to read a plaque that read, "History Museum of Culture, Politics, and Inventions."

"This is some kind of history museum," I said.

"Duh, you can read. I guess you learned something in school."

"How is this building standing? Everything is supposed to be dead, pulverized, radioactive. Yet, we haven't found anything radioactive since we've been up here." I shook my detector, wondering if it was really working.

We opened the unlocked door and walked in.

"Lights. The radiation must be powering the place," Kal said. "We need to get out of here."

"If you prefer the flash flood, you can go back to the river," I replied, strolling through the museum.

I was amazed by all the exhibits of inventions and history I had never seen before in real life. We followed the invention of various forms of transportation in pictures, exhibits, replicas and signs containing plaques with written stories.

"I thought I was familiar with history, but this was different than in our history books. Mostly, our books showed massive polluting machines that looked ridiculous and clunky." I walked past the airplane section, looking at the pictures and reading the descriptions and history of flight. "Imagine, from their small beginnings, airplanes got so big and fast they could eventually fly around the world."

"We have drones and high-speed aerial trams for distance travel below. We're highly advanced."

"Ours don't go all the way around the world, and how can we say aerial when they stay underground?"

"If you hadn't seen the sky up here, you wouldn't have thought that?"

"I thought that below. I just didn't feel safe saying what I thought."

"You know what else could fly around the world?"

I knew he was talking about the nuclear bombs. "Not going there," I said.

"That's the next series." There was a gunpowder exhibit with a commemorative sign. It contained pictures and descriptions of TNT, dynamite, nitroglycerine, and various early and more developed nuclear bombs. Some of the smaller explosives were in glass cases. "They better not go off," Kalandro commanded, as if he were threatening the devices with his voice. "Let's get out of here."

"But how is this not dust and why do these exhibits look maintained?"

Kalandro shrugged. There were pictures of the damage done in Hiroshima and Nagasaki. "That was nothing compared to when the final war came. The bombs were so much bigger when our parents went underground."

I noticed a plaque commemorating the creator of dynamite with the creation of a peace prize that was given each year to the most deadly warmonger in the world. "Why would they give a peace prize to warmongers?" I asked.

"Like we were told, they were degenerates."

There was a section on personal weapons, which included swords, maces, rifles, guns, cannons, and what were called assault weapons.

"Whoever put this together did not like guns, judging from the signs," Kal noted.

I knew my dad or my not-dad had a gun. I had seen him pull it out of a drawer in his office to check it and put it back at times. But his gun looked nothing like the ones in the museum.

There were pictures of Presidents with their names underneath. "Why is the picture of Trump defaced?" I asked.

An X, that went through the fabric, was scratched into the painting of Donald Trump.

"He was a dictator, not a President."

"That's what our history books say," I noted.

"Maybe this is the propaganda they warned us about. Trump was supposed to be some Orange-headed Russian who tried to use Russian forces to coup the government of the United States. Eventually, they put down the coup and sent him back to Russia."

With Kalandro looking over my shoulder, I skimmed through a book, sitting in front of the exhibit, which stated that Trump was popularly elected and had support from both the left and the right, but he kept none of his campaign promises, upsetting people who had voted for him. Apparently, he had said he would free some guy named Julian Assange in his first term and then didn't and that he would be a peace President and was anything but.

"The history books up here must be really screwed up," Kalandro commented.

"Maybe. Or maybe ours are."

"We have the best researchers and historians in the world."

"But our scholars don't have access to this library or anything other than the standard approved computerized history books," I pointed out.

My attention focused on a series of framed pages Kalandro was reading. "Preposterous," he said. "None of this is what they taught us in the Youth Leadership Program. Now, does any of this make sense, Natty?

"It's Natalia to you. This page shows officers taking selfies with people in the National Capitol. Underneath is a label saying, 'Violent Capitol Insurrection.' If you read the page, it says those who did the insurrection brought no weapons and were let inside by the Capitol Police. The only one killed was a female Marine veteran who was one of the insurrectionists. A Capitol Policeman shot her as she was walking inside the building."

"Look at that picture of an insurrectionist with horns. It says he came to bless the chamber and was escorted into the various rooms by the Capitol Police, who unlocked doors for him."

"Is this some different definition of insurrection than we were taught?"

"Must be."

We went to another exhibit. "Why does it say 'Ukraine heroes' under a picture of people wearing swastikas? I thought our country fought against the Nazis." Kalandro queried.

"Next to it is a picture of a check for fifty trillion dollars from the U.S. Treasury to Ukraine, the place where that army with the swastikas was from. I don't think it's a real check, though," Kal observed.

"It looks like it was put there to symbolize money given to them over a period of time. It doesn't look authentic. The plaque lists various amounts given to them. There's a statement that the money was diverted to private jets, yachts, homes and to war contractors but says there was never an accounting for what was actually done with the money." I noted.

"Who would believe that?" Kal asked.

"And this one has a picture of Congress voting to grant a white guy named Bibi trillions to shoot and blow up brown women and children in a place called Palestine and to give people in Bibi's country the health care for all that Americans dying in the streets lacked. It shows Democratic and Republican members of Congress joining together to call brown babies 'terrorists' and giving a standing ovation to the child-killer."

"Maybe all these stories were fake. Maybe Trump never was President and no shaman entered the House chamber to bless it," Kal suggested.

"The picture labeled 'Shaman' looks authentic, but who would dress up like that? It must be altered. For once, you may be right, Kal. Maybe this whole history museum is fake. And what is Palestine? It's not in our history books."

"I think it's what Sagat called 'misinformation', and 'disinformation,'" Kal postulated.

"Where is Eterra? Eterra! Eterra!" Panic went through me at the disappearance of my dog.

I rushed from room to room until I found her in a little office, curled up next to a body lying on the floor.

CHAPTER 14

"Don't touch him," Kalandro warned. "He could be radioactive."

I checked. He wasn't. He also wasn't breathing and I couldn't feel a pulse when I kneeled down to check. I leaned my head towards his chest as Kalandro grabbed my shoulder.

"You crazy? He could be diseased."

I knocked off Kalandro's hand and listened to the man's chest. Nothing. He felt cool to the touch.

Eterra looked sad. "I'm sorry, girl. You knew him, didn't you?"

She kneeled with her front paws near the body and howled.

"We should get out of here," Kalandro advised. "He looks a hundred. Maybe being above aged him. He could have been our age when he came up here."

There were no old people down below. I wondered what had happened to anyone older than our parents' generation. Down below, replacements were available for body parts and organs, including skin, that wore out or were damaged. Maybe the older people had been rejuvenated or become robots.

On the office desk, I found a California ID card. "His name was Ottis Malone. According to the card, in 2022, Mr. Malone was eighty-five. That would make him about one-hundred and eight if he just died."

"How could anyone live that long up here?"

"I don't know." I looked at Eterra, who was lying on the floor, looking devastated. Tears were coming from her eyes. "I didn't know dogs cried."

"That's because android dogs don't have tear ducts."

I looked at the old man. "We need to bury him."

"We?"

"Do you see anyone else around?"

"We didn't come up here to bury people."

"It had been a tradition up above before the Reset. There is a picture of a graveyard for Presidents in the exhibit hall. According to the sign on the desk here, he was the curator of this place. That's very impressive."

"Curator of a fake history museum? Big deal. He wasn't a President."

"Look at the awards on the wall from various historical societies. Besides, I think Eterra would like to see him laid to rest. I wouldn't want someone to just leave me if I dropped dead."

"Down below we'd—"

"I know. But we're not down there, and I think the burial idea is nicer than burning what's left of a person to oblivion. That's what Hitler did in World War II—even in our history books."

"That doesn't mean we have to bury some stranger we never met in real life."

"Let's see if we can find some shovels."

We went outside and found a shack with tools. I pulled out some shovels and looked for a good place to dig. I pushed the shovel I was carrying into the ground. It was soft.

"I'll do it," Kalandro gripingly offered.

"You trying to show off your gentlemanliness?"

"You'd slow me down, and I want to get out of here."

I went back inside. "Eterra, we're going to have a memorial. You might not be able to speak English, but you can speak your sentiments in dog speak." I picked up a piece of paper from the desk and read it.

Looking around the museum, I found a kitchen with glass containers of food and water.

After a little more searching, I went outside, where Kalandro had dug a grave deep enough to bury the deceased and cover him with dirt.

"I found this. It's a First Aid kit."

"It might be dangerous."

I tore open a packet and put a little towel against the area of Kalandro's head that had previously been bleeding.

"Oww!" he screamed. "I told you that was dangerous!"

"It's to sterilize the wound. Here's an antibiotic cream."

"No. I don't want it."

Before he could object more, I had pushed it out into his scalp and was rubbing it in."

I pulled out a roll of gauze and wrapped it around his head, over the wound, several times. Then I cut it and tied it off.

"If I die, you're digging my grave," he griped.

We went inside. I took the nameplate from Ottis's desk to put in his grave. I looked at plaques on the wall, commemorating his years of service. He had started working at the museum eighty years before. The dates showed a ten-year gap in his service. Eterra followed us out as we carried Mr. Malone, the paper I'd read and the nameplate from his desk.

"Let's cover him up and be done with it."

"I think we're supposed to have a service."

"Service?"

I rushed over to a garden that had some flower bushes and picked some red and pink flowers. I put them down on top of Mr. Malone, along with his nameplate.

"I'll start. I never met Mr. Malone but he was a great man, according to all his awards. If more men had studied and remembered history, maybe there would have been fewer wars and the world would be much different now than it is. From Mr. Malone's dog's love for him, I know he was a good person who will be missed. Nothing can take away his contribution to the world. Mr. Malone wrote these words and left this paper on his desk. Perhaps he had planned for it to be read now in his memory. May we always remember his great example.

"'*If I have one true love, it's history. He who forgets the past is bound to repeat it. May this museum keep it alive. Ottis Malone.'*"

Eterra started barking as if to say her piece. I looked over at Kalandro and was surprised to see tears in his eyes.

"I didn't know you, and I don't know if I agree with your history, but I do believe you cared about the world and that's what is important," he said. He wiped his eyes, as if to hide his tears. I could tell Kalandro was holding back more tears. This was a kinder, more caring side of him I had only gotten a glimpse of once before—after his sister's robot was killed.

I went over to Kalandro and kissed his cheek. "Thank you."

"Don't get emotional on me, Natalia."

Kalandro packed down the dirt on top of the body. I went into the office and took down a marble plaque for excellence and put it over the grave as a marker.

"It's getting late. Maybe we should stay here tonight and continue our journey in the morning," I said.

Kalandro nodded. I had an ulterior motive. I wanted to know more about Mr. Malone's history. We looked for the source of electricity and discovered the building was powered by solar energy. I checked the food for radioactivity and it was negative. Kalandro refused to eat any of it. I decided to try out a jar of peaches. It tasted okay.

I took a nice warm shower and it felt so good. Unlike below, Mr. Malone didn't need any kind of nuclear energy to run lights, as he had the sun itself.

I stayed up practically all night reading various history books. I liked the feel of the paper books and wondered why we didn't have any below. In one of the books, I read about the dangers of nuclear energy and about all the people who had been injured working at nuclear power plants. It included pictures of mass contamination from Hanford and meltdowns that included Santa Susana, Chernobyl, Fukushima and Columbia, a near meltdown at Three Mile Island and a disaster at Limerick. Below, we used nuclear power. *Our people* called it "safe power." We had fusion plants and were told that those were safe.

However, we were also told that there was no waste. Were we somehow pushing our disasters above ground through a vent, or were the service workers burying them in a way that could contaminate lower-class or robotic workers?

"Our people," or were they? I didn't want to be one of those people anymore; people who were blind and controlled and doing what the leaders wanted.

The books told how the government had tried to end motherhood, separating mothers from children, sex trafficking little kids around the world, forcing them to live with sexual predators and sterilizing boys and girls. It had created scamdemics and told people it was dangerous to have dinner with their families.

In them, I read the underground cities were created so the "elite" could survive the genocidal depopulation of a nuclear war while leaving the populace to die. *But how was there a nuclear war up above when nothing seems radioactive?* The government and the military industrial complex had all the nuclear weapons, not the people. The government that undoubtedly sent its intellectuals, the creators of that nightmare, down below to survive the nuclear holocaust had to have been the very ones responsible for it, not the people left to die, who didn't have access to the catastrophic weapons.

I wished Ottis had lived longer so he could tell me about the people living above ground. Was it just him or were there others who survived Armageddon?

There were books about customs, etiquette and people helping other people. In some of the pictures, people were hugging. Kids were hugging, too. They looked happy, as if hugging was natural. I wished I had lived up here when people hugged. Though it was long ago, my body remembered the warmth and feeling of my mother hugging me as a young child.

There was so much more I wanted to learn but exhaustion hit me and I dropped off to dreamland on the floor.

In my dream, my mom was singing words, but not the original ones, to a tune similar to Braham's Lullaby. It felt more like a memory than a dream. The rhyming and cadence were off, but maybe that was intentional.

"It was faked.

Poisoning.

Global Reset is here.

Up rising

When it's safe

To be up there in years.

Beware those below.

No injections. They do kill.

Find Selini Andrews.

She will be there for you."

My dream drifted to images of nuclear war, people being vaporized, and whole cities being destroyed. I wanted my mother back. I started screaming for her.

"Hey, she's not here," Kalandro's voice came through, as he shook me into wakefulness.

"My mom sang me a song. I'm supposed to find Sel, something: Selma, Celanie, I don't remember."

"Only you would think a dream was real. We should be getting on."

"What if there is nothing else but this?"

"Then we'll come back here. We won't know unless we check out more of the above."

"Now, you want to go further. If anything happens to us, do you think anyone will miss us? I don't know if my mother is alive. Your sister is an android, and your father—" I shuddered.

"He might be your father, too."

"That would make me your sister or half-sister."

"I could think of worse fates. You give me more grief than my other sister, but maybe that's what human sisters do."

"Your father was so gleeful with that ax. I don't want him to be my father. I'd rather a janitor or groundskeeper they failed to replace was my real dad. My father or rather pseudo father, was ready to kill me, too, but he thought I was already a robot."

"If he thought you weren't his, maybe it was a revenge killing."

"Maybe." I paused. "I really cared about him until he was ready to kill me."

"My dad was always a creep."

"I don't want any of that creep in me."

"What you said at the grave yesterday was sweet, beautiful. I used to think you were just some obnoxious girl robot, but you're really very nice."

"Thank you. And you're kind of nice yourself—when you're not a jerk."

He put an arm around me. "Whatever happens, at least we'll each have someone to see this world with."

Until you go back to hating me.

He finally got hungry enough to trust the jars of food. I cooked a combination of sweet potatoes and spaghetti from the jars.

"This is actually pretty good. I think it's when you are starving that food tastes best."

I nodded. "When did you ever starve?"

"When I was practicing for basketball tournaments."

With Eterra at our side, we set out from the hill on which the museum sat into a valley.

"I don't see any roads nearby. I wonder if the bombs destroyed the roads but somehow failed to nuke the museum," I speculated.

"How are the radiation and air quality readings?"

"Fine. What are those red things growing in that field over there?" I asked.

"I hope they aren't insects," he said. I ran down into the field and turned around. I was surrounded by little red fruit with miniature seeds on the outside, set in short green leafy plants.

"They aren't insects," I said. "I read about these in the museum in a book about the Beatles."

"Beetles? We've gotten rid of those and other parasite plagues below."

"No. The Beatles were a singing group. I think these are strawberries. This is a strawberry field. Food."

Eterra was already indulging in the strawberries. Kalandro picked one up and ate it. "These are delicious."

I tried one. "Super delicious." I filled my pockets with them. I whirled around again. "This world is beautiful and tasty," I shouted. "And we were always told up-above was a bad place, torturous."

We continued on.

"The food here is much better than at home," I enthusiastically declared.

"I kind of miss that prime rib my dad used to bring home."

"I don't. I'll take strawberries over prime rib any day."

We kept walking. Soon, we were in a field of what looked like wheat. We had that below but not as big and bountiful.

"Do you think it grows naturally?" I asked.

"Somebody must be in charge. I hope they don't replace kids and workers with robots like below?"

"That would be bad. We'd better hold in our emotions and not tell anyone we're human—until we know. That is, if anyone is alive up here."

"I almost wish we could go back down and tell everyone how beautiful it is up here," he said. He looked thoughtful. "But then they'd call us defective and have us replaced."

"I don't ever want to go back down again—except to rescue—"

"What are you two kids doing in my field? You're disturbing the plants." It was an angry-sounding older man.

CHAPTER 15

We'd been so distracted that we hadn't seen him approaching. From the anger in his voice, I suspected he was either a defective robot or a human.

"Where are your parents?" the man asked. He was wearing grungy, blue, rugged-looking clothes. They resembled pictures I'd seen in the museum of something called denim. Everything back home was pristine. So, I guessed he probably wasn't from there. I looked at my own clothes, which were also pretty dirty.

"We didn't mean to harm your plants. We were just walking along, hoping to find people," I responded.

"Are your parents in town?" His voice grew softer.

"There's a town?"

"Where are you from?"

"Here and there," Kalandro replied.

"That's not an answer."

"How far is the town?" I asked.

"Riverhill isn't far. I'd take you, but my truck broke down, and I'm waiting for parts to fix it. They should come in tomorrow."

"If you just point us in the right direction, we can walk," Kalandro suggested.

"It's a long enough you won't make it there by dinner."

"Dinner. Is the food good?" I asked.

"So-so," the man said, flipping his palms upward. "How old are you?"

"Fifteen."

"I'm sixteen," Kalandro threw in.

"Ah, you came out in the fields to make some nooky."

"Nooky?" I asked. "Is that a type of food?"

"You don't know what that is? Are you Russian?"

"Russian? I don't know any Russians," I said. The thought of Russians scared me. Our history teachers had said they wanted to kill all Americans and take over our country. I hoped they wouldn't find us.

"No, we're good kids," Kalandro assured him.

"The Russians are good, too. They often bring me supplies from the city."

I looked at Kalandro. Maybe after the war, the Russians had taken over. I didn't want to offend this man by insulting his friends. If he or his friends found out we were descended from Americans and not Russians, what would they do to us?

"It was very nice talking to you," I said.

"You didn't give me your name. I'm Roy."

"I'm Natalia."

"You are Russian."

"No. I'm Natalia."

"Natalia is a Russian name."

"It's not." *I slipped up. I should have pretended to be Russian?*

"Okay. Your friend is—"

"I'm her brother. Kalandro."

"You have some interesting names. Maybe Miss Holiday can take you into Riverhill."

"Miss Holiday?"

"She's just down the road a bit. Can you ride a horse?"

"Horse?" I had seen pictures of horses. They had some down below, too. They were used for recreational games, like polo.

"Do you play polo?" Kalandro asked.

The man laughed. "No. I leave those games to the young and fit. Come back to the house, and then I can take you over to Miss Holiday's."

We started walking over to him. I was concerned about his Russian friends. I didn't want to go to a Russian city where they might discover who we were. Maybe they would string us up or shoot us once they found out we weren't Russian.

As we walked, I saw a large fenced-in field of sheep, meandering around. I had seen photos of sheep before but never in fields. Below, sheep were wrapped in wire so our society could get their meat and wool. Those pictures had looked so cruel. But I'd been told not to discuss my feelings about them.

A tiny sheep grabbed my attention. "It's so cute."

"You like lambs. Baby sheep?"

"Lambs? That's a lamb?"

"I'll never eat lamb again," Kalandro quietly said.

I went over to pet the little baby and apologize for what the people below did to little lambs like him. Kalandro followed me but wasn't watching the ground. He slipped and fell into a muddy pool of water. The mud splashed all over him.

I couldn't help but laugh.

"You're the first person to fall into the sheep-dip," Roy said.

"Don't," Kalandro warned me off as I prepared to help him. "You'll get your outfit muddy." His comment stunned me. He was confusing, almost talking like he cared.

Roy pulled Kalandro out and picked up a towel lying on the fence. I looked at it. It was dirty but cleaner than Kalandro was. "You can shower back at my place and put on some fresh clothes."

One of the sheep screeched and fell to the ground.

"Radiation poison!" I exclaimed in fear as I felt blood rush to my head. *Will I die writhing on the ground soon, too?*

CHAPTER 16

I looked at my detector. Nothing around me, including the sheep, was radioactive.

"She's not radioactive," I notified them.

Roy laughed. "Of course not. She's pregnant. She's about to give birth."

We watched as he started to calm her as he waited for the lamb to appear.

I screamed as the head came out.

"You've never witnessed a birth before?"

I shook my head.

"You're in for a treat. At least it's not a breech birth. They're not as safe. Give me the other towel on the fence."

"What is that stuff around the baby's head?"

"It's the sac. When it breaks, we have to make sure the lamb is breathing all right. Normally, ewes give birth standing up, but this mom is tired out."

He pulled the lamb's front legs out and then the back legs. The sheep was lying on its side and the man put the lamb next to the mother's head. She started licking the lamb, particularly its face. The weird covering over the baby came off and the lamb started bleating. Roy put the lamb's mouth around a nipple on the mother's underside and it started sucking.

"Why does it do that?" Kalandro asked.

"All babies need their mother's milk. You must not spend a lot of time around babies. Are you the only children in your family?"

"She's my younger sister," Kalandro said.

"Then, you must not have paid attention when your mother was nursing her."

About an hour later, we were headed to Roy's house. Mud was caked on Kalandro. I had to keep myself from laughing every time I looked at him. Roy sent Kalandro into the shower and put some clothes in the bathroom for him. He also handed me some clean clothes. "Miss Holiday may have some clothes closer to your size. With these, you'll have to roll up the legs and sleeves."

They didn't look like any of the clothes we had down below. They were a bit raggedy, like the man's, but they looked soft. I could see and feel the seams in the clothing, something that would never have passed muster back at home. I thought about his remark about rolling up sleeves and legs. Our clothes were tailored to be exact fits. I would have laughed if I had seen someone in rolled-up clothes below and wondered if they were going to a costume event.

Roy invited me into the kitchen and offered me some strawberry pie.

"Yes," I said. It tasted delicious—especially the crust.

"So, what brings you here?"

"My mom sent me."

"Is she meeting you in Riverhill?"

I didn't answer. "I'm surprised she just sent you into the country when you didn't know where you were going." He looked at Eterra. "And this little fellow."

"Eterra. She's our dog."

"American Eskimos are great dogs. She reminds me a little of the dog old Ottis had. He's the curator of the history museum, a little to the northwest near the river. He's over a hundred now."

I didn't say anything. I didn't want him to think we stole Ottis's dog. We didn't have anyone to ask for permission to take Eterra.

"She's really nice."

"So how long you fixing to stay in these parts?"

"I don't know."

"Your mother didn't tell you?"

"I thought this area was radioactive."

"I hope not. Everyone had to move away for about ten years until we cleaned up the area and the rains finally washed away the poison. No radiation. Except for Rancho Seco, and that was closed before I was born."

The lullaby started to come to mind. I remembered a couple of words: "poisoning" and "faked," which I blurted out loud.

"That's right. We thought they were going to start World War III, but instead, they poisoned the food, the air, the water, and everything they could. Only those of us who were using bottled or filtered water and eating hot-house organic foods survived."

"Poisoning, not nuking."

"That's it."

"And the ones who poisoned you are down below?"

"And they better stay buried under a thousand feet of dirt."

CHAPTER 17

That's what my mother was trying to tell me—when she sang that lullaby to me. The war was all faked. Why fake a war?

"But people went underground," I pointed out.

"The Elites running the world did. They thought we'd all die from the poisons and then they could come up years later and reclaim the planet."

"All the Elites?"

"The leaders of all the countries were in on the plan. Mexico, Cuba, Venezuela and Russia and most African nations didn't follow through. They didn't want to kill their populations. Most Americans who survived did so by migrating to Latin America, Africa or Russia. A great many returned and quite a number of Russians and Africans moved here as well. Even after the poison was cleared off the lands, people had created new homes elsewhere and many didn't want to move back. I could have stayed in Mexico. It would have taken less work than creating this farm, but I missed California."

Kalandro came out of the bathroom dressed in the farmer's clothes. I felt like laughing but held it in. He looked so silly in them. "Your pants are too big." They looked as if they would fall off.

"I'll get you a belt."

As Roy went off to get a belt, I told Kalandro. "There was no nuclear war. It was all a lie."

"What? That can't be true."

"It explains why nothing is radioactive. My mom even sang me a lullaby. I remember the words now.

"It was faked; poisoning; global Reset is here. Uprising when it's safe to be up there in years. Beware those below. No injections. They do kill. Find Selini Andrews. She will be there for you."

"No nuclear war?"

As Kalandro spoke, Roy came in with a belt.

"What's with you kids?" He chuckled. "Did you take a history class on Hiroshima?"

"I need to find Selini Andrews."

"Is she your mother?"

"She's the person my mother sent me here to see."

"Maybe Miss Holiday will know her. I'll tell you what. I'll ride Candy, my mare, over to Miss Holiday's to see if she can help you out. You're welcome to eat whatever you like from the refrigerator.

"It's not poisoned?'

He laughed. "You kids made my day. The poisons have been gone from this area for over six years. After the rains took a lot of it away, we worked to clean and restore the fields and the groundwater. Food and water are safer and cleaner than they've ever been in this state."

"You should have some of this strawberry pie. It's delicious," I told Kalandro after Roy left.

He joined me in digging in. "You aren't kidding. I hope Roy won't be mad when he sees we've eaten the whole thing."

I opened the refrigerator. "This looks good. I think it's sweet potatoes."

When we finished those, I started feeling guilty.

Roy returned with a woman. She had a sweet, warm smile on her face and red hair that ran down her shoulders. "What beautiful kids you are."

She reached out and gave me and Kalandro each a hug. He had a sour look on his face, but I enjoyed it. "You hug here?" I asked.

"I'm a hugger. I hope you don't mind."

"I love it," I said.

She gave me another hug, this time a longer one. "Let's call your mother so she doesn't worry. Maybe she can tell us where to find Mrs. Andrews." She looked at Kalandro. "Could you give me your mother's phone number?"

"My mother's dead," he replied with a troubled expression on his face.

She looked taken aback. "I'm so sorry. And before she passed, she sent you to find Mrs. Andrews?"

"Could you give us a ride to town?" I asked.

"But you don't know where you are going?"

"We'll be okay," Kalandro said.

I wasn't so sure. In spite of Roy's positive attitude regarding the Russians in the area, I had a gut fear reaction, thinking about them. *What if they discover who we are and kill us?*

"How about if I take you home, let you stay with me overnight while I call my phone tree and see if anyone can locate your Mrs. Andrews?"

I looked at Kalandro. "I suppose that would be alright."

"Roy said you might want some clean girl's clothes. These are stretch cotton and will cling to you. I think they'll fit." She handed me a blouse and pants.

"Thank you." I went into the bathroom and changed.

We thanked Roy for the food. Roy had bagged Kalandro's dirty clothes and handed me a bag for mine.

"I can wash them for you when we get home," Miss Holiday offered.

"Thank you, Miss Holiday," Kalandro and I replied.

"Call me Claire."

"Claire," I repeated.

We didn't have an actual plan. At least, we'd have a place to stay for the night and we wouldn't have to walk to get into town. She might even help us find Mrs. Andrews.

She had a big green Ford she called a minivan. She suggested we sit in the middle of her car and made us wear seatbelts. "The middle seats are always safer." She put a harness and a seatbelt on Eterra. "There are minimal roads in this area. During the cleanup, a lot of blacktop was found to be contaminated and removed. This road is the main one they rebuilt to our farmlands. We've thought about building more roads, but the area is mostly just farms."

As she started the car, I asked, "This car doesn't drive itself?"

"Manual cars are safer. Self-driving cars used to get into accidents with pedestrians and were banned long ago."

"How is it powered?"

"Gas?"

"Isn't that dangerous?"

"I hope not. It's more environmentally sound than electric."

"Are you sure?"

"Long ago, our government overthrew other governments to steal their lithium for the toxic batteries that ran electric cars but they took more energy than gas cars." Miss Holiday explained.

"What about nuclear?"

"That's very dangerous. I guess you haven't studied that in your history classes."

"Santa Susana, Chernobyl, Fukushima, Columbia, Limerick?" I recalled from the museum.

"That's right. We still haven't been able to clean up the radiation from Columbia and Limerick. It will be quite a while before anyone returns to Washington State or Pennsylvania and the eastern states nearby."

As she drove towards her home, and I looked at the colorful countryside, a warm feeling energized me. The sky was blue, but it looked natural, rather than like a picture. There were wispy clouds in the sky. The grass was green and I could see multi-colored flowers, green and flowering trees, some with fruit on them.

We were happily traveling along when a noise shook the car and it was as if it were thrown off balance.

The car careened off the road into a ditch and started rolling over, landing upside down. Kalandro looked fine as he unfastened his seatbelt. I unfastened Eterra's and my seatbelts. Kalandro and I climbed out with Eterra bouncing out behind us.

"Miss Holiday!" I called, looking into the front seat. She wasn't responding. "Claire!" I sniffed. "I smell something."

"Gas," Kalandro observed.

Kalandro helped me open the driver's door. Balloon-type bags had opened up in front of and to the side of Miss Holiday. Unlike us, she wasn't wearing her seatbelt. We pulled her out into the road. Let's get her away from that gas smell. A minute later, the van exploded in a ball of fire.

CHAPTER 18

We moved her down the road away from the fire.

"This is why gas cars are banned down below," Kalandro pointed out.

A big red vehicle with flashing lights was coming toward us. It emitted a loud, high-pitched noise. I jumped up and down, waved at it and it stopped. Men got out and worked to put out what remained of the fire.

"She's hurt," I said, pointing to Miss Holiday.

"The paramedics are on their way," a man in a Fireman uniform said. We didn't have those below as there were no fires there—except in my mom's lab.

"She said the car was safe."

"I suspect, after the tire blew and it hit the edge of the ditch, the gas line ruptured and the fire was ignited by sparks from the engine, following the crash. The odds of that happening are minuscule."

We waited until another vehicle with more flashing lights and weird noises arrived.

Miss Holiday was placed on a cot and then into the vehicle. They let us ride with her. The man who checked her out said, "Her vitals look good. We don't know the extent of the head injury. There's a special trauma unit for head injuries at Valley Hospital in Sutter Springs. It's a little further than Riverhill and better equipped for emergencies than University Hospital."

"Head injury?"

"She's unconscious." He looked more closely at Kalandro. "You've been injured too." He made Kalandro lie down. "I'm sorry, but the dog can't come."

"She has to come. I need her," I said.

"Oh. A service dog."

"She serves me."

"No problem."

As the ambulance drove off to take us to the hospital, we heard that loud, high-pitched sound again.

"What is that sound?"

"The siren. We want to get to the hospital quickly without any accidents."

The man who had been talking to us stayed in the back and kept checking Miss Holiday and writing on a clipboard.

I didn't like the idea of going to a hospital. "My mother said hospitals used to be terrible places."

"That was long ago. We got rid of the CDC, and doctors are free to use their best judgment with patients these days."

"That's awesome." I had no idea what the CDC was.

"What's her name?"

"Claire Holiday. Will she be alright?"

"I believe so but they'll know more at the hospital. And you?"

"Natalia."

"And your brother?"

"Kalandro."

"Nice names."

"Thank you."

He continued writing. "What is the name of your service animal?"

"You mean dog."

"Right. Service dog."

"Eterra."

"I think you should get checked out, too," he told me. "You may have some injuries that aren't showing up yet."

At Valley Hospital, they put all three of us on stretchers, with Eterra next to me on my stretcher, and wheeled us in. They checked over Miss Holiday and took her to something called ICU. As they were going to wheel off Kalandro, I said, "I need to be with my brother."

"This is Emergency. You'll each have a private room for your exams, but if you have to stay here, maybe we can get you a two-bed room together."

"The dog," a woman in a blue and white striped outfit reacted.

"It's a service dog. The girl's," the man from the vehicle told her.

Eterra lay across my lap as they took me into a room and someone checked me over. The nurses seemed nice as they took my temperature and told me they liked my dog.

"Is there someone at home we could call to pick you up?"

"No. Nobody."

A doctor came in. "I'm Steve, and you are a lucky girl, Natalia. You have some minor scrapes and bruises, but there won't be any scarring. Your brother's head injury isn't serious. Your mother is injured and unconscious. We believe she'll recover. However, it will be a while before she can go home."

"We'll be okay," I replied.

"Would you like to see your brother?"

"Yes. Please." He had me sit in a wheelchair and took me into Kalandro's room. There was a bandage on Kalandro's head, better than the one I had put there.

The nurse and doctor went off to speak to each other. Kalandro looked happy. "They did some stitches. My first ones. They said the hair would grow over it."

"Good. Let's get out of here."

Doctor Steve came back. "Is there someone we can call for you?"

"Selini Andrews," I said.

"Who is she?"

"A friend of my mother's."

"Do you know where she lives?"

"No."

"How about her number?"

"I don't have that either."

"I can call in a government worker to find a place for you."

"No government," Kalandro replied. "We'll be okay."

"If you don't want us to call in a government worker, would you like to stay with me and my wife until your mother recovers or we locate her friend? This isn't standard procedure, but we have a couple of extra rooms."

"My dog?"

"She can come too."

He listened to an announcement over a speaker on the wall. "I'll be back."

The nurse turned to us. "I can find a room, here, for you two until the doctor's shift is over."

"Why is he doing this?" I asked her after he left.

"He's a very nice man. He and his wife recently lost their baby and he thinks having children in the home will make her feel better."

"Is his wife sick?"

"Just sad."

"I'm sorry they lost the baby. Maybe we can help find him or her? Or was it a robot?"

"Robot? No." The nurse shook her head as if trying to make sense of my question before continuing. "It wasn't a missing kind of loss. She miscarried the baby."

"Miscarried?"

"It didn't survive to birth."

"I'm really sorry."

I didn't know if my mother was alive. Not-Mom had exploded. Kal's mother and sister were gone. Mr. Malone had died. Steve's wife had lost her baby. Death was all around. I hoped Miss Holiday would survive.

"We'll stay with the doctor. You don't need to call the government," Kalandro said.

The nurse brought us food and drinks and let us watch TV in one of the hospital rooms.

"What's that?" I asked, pointing to the warm, nice-smelling desert.

"Apples."

"We can't eat apples."

"I'll bring you something else, then," the nurse said and then went out.

"If we can't find Selini Andrews, we'll have to find a place to live and food to eat."

"Maybe I can get a job," Kal replied.

"Me, too. Mom said they used to kill people in hospitals. I hope they don't kill Miss Holiday."

"The guy in the ambulance said it's different now. Have you noticed that most of the people we've met up here are Black?"

"So? There are Black people down below."

"But not many. I wonder if they were immune to the poisons."

"Or maybe they were too smart to trust the leaders," I speculated.

"I bet you're right. Claire said that Africa was one of the safe places others migrated to. It refused to poison its people."

I went into the hall to see if I could find the doctor. A bed was being rolled down the corridor with a sheet over a figure on it. "What happened to her?" a nurse asked.

"She died of an overdose," a guy in a white coat answered her.

Below, androids dispensed drugs and only a malfunction would result in an overdose—though I understood that years before people had taken their own drugs. As I looked at the corpse-carrying bed on wheels, a burst of fear washed over me. This was a hospital, something I had been warned about.

I noticed a tag hanging out from under the sheet. It read, "S. Andrews."

CHAPTER 19

I ran back into the room and burst into tears. "They killed Selini Andrews."

"What?"

"I saw her. She was dead. They overdosed and killed her."

"We'd better get Claire out of here."

I picked up Eterra and we ran to the desk. "What room is Claire Holiday in?"

"Who are you?"

"We need to see her."

"Oh, you're her children, with the dog."

"Please, we need to see her."

The nurse had an assistant take us up to the third-floor nursing station, where another nurse took us to her room in the Intensive Care Unit. Claire was asleep. Cords and tubes were connected to her.

"They're replacing her," I whispered to Kalandro. "We need to get her away before they kill her." I tried to shake her shoulder. "Please wake up. They killed Selini Andrews. We need to get you out of here before they kill you, too."

Kalandro started to move the bed as I prepared to pull out the wires.

"You can't do that!" a nurse ordered. "She's connected to machines."

"Please, don't let them kill her," I begged.

"We're going to make her better."

"We like her the way she is."

"She's unconscious and needs to rest until she recovers."

"Or dies? Miss Andrews came here and was overdosed to death."

"Oh. I remember that case. She came here because of an overdose. We tried to save her."

"But you didn't and she's dead."

"We can't save everyone, but looking at your mother's chart, I can almost promise you she's going to be fine. Her EKG and her EEG are normal. There's no skull fracture. Her brain just needs time to recover from the bump."

"And they won't replace her?"

"When we move her out of here, the bed will be open for another patient."

"But it won't be her—not the real her."

"She'll be awake and in another room."

"And you promise you won't let them kill her?"

"I promise. I will protect her with my life." I wasn't sure if she was saying that to placate us or if she was being honest.

About that time, Doctor Steve walked in. "I heard you were worried about your mother. All indications are that she should be fine. She's in a mild coma, but all her signs look good."

"When will she get to leave?"

"After she wakes up and is fully recovered. It could be a few days or a few weeks. Don't worry. As soon as she is able to go, we'll send her home." He turned to the nurse. "Cindy, I've finished my shift. So, I'll take the kids off your hands." He turned to me and Kalandro. "You're going to like my place. We'll pick up some food and a bed for your dog."

"Really?"

"Really."

I was reluctant to leave, hoping they were telling the truth and that the Claire we knew would recover.

I turned back to the nurse. "You promise she'll still be the same her when we come back?"

The nurse appeared puzzled and looked at Steve before answering. "I promise."

———

The doctor had a smaller car than Claire's, but it was big enough for Eterra and the rest of us.

"If you have the key to your home, we can stop by and pick up some clothes for you."

I shook my head.

"Then, how about we stop by a store and pick up some clothes you like."

"Sure," Kalandro said.

Steve had us pick out a bunch of clothes at a store.

"It says 'All clothes: one-hundred percent cotton, silk, wool, hemp and bamboo' on the wall," I noted.

"The government has banned clothes with microplastics. We have studies showing they do brain damage. That's probably an old sign."

Next, we picked up some supplies for Eterra.

"Why do you think he's getting us so much stuff?" Kalandro whispered. "Do you think my dad told him to watch us until he arrives to —" He didn't have to finish. I knew Kalandro was going to say, "kill us."

"Maybe. But why would he buy us clothes if he's going to let them kill us?"

"What's your favorite food? Do you like pizza?" Steve asked.

"Sure. I've had that at home," I said.

"I bet you did."

"We can top it off with some chocolate almond milk ice cream."

"On the pizza?"

"After."

"Healthy ice cream?"

He paused as if trying to make out our question. "Of course. Toxic chemicals have been banned in growing food for six years."

"He's really being nice to us," I whispered to Kalandro. "Maybe he's just a nice guy. I like him."

"I do too, but remember all the people we knew who were nice and betrayed us. If he does anything that scares us, we run."

"There's something else off here. Everyone is treating us like little kids—doing so much for us— even the way they talk to us."

When we got back into the car, I asked. "Why are you being so nice? It's not like we're two or three."

"Since they moved the age of consent up to twenty-one, everyone has been more respectful of the youth."

"Twenty-one? Why did they do that?"

"The government orchestrated or allowed bad things to happen many years ago."

"Like what?

"Before the poisoning, the leaders sent teenagers off to die in wars for profit, pressured them into unwanted operations, injected them with deadly poisons and even encouraged euthanasia for depression. We decided never again and to guarantee protection for the youth from the government until they were twenty-one."

"Did any of that happen to you?"

"No. I had good parents and most of my youth was after things changed."

"Was there any opposition to raising the age?"

"Yes. There was a concern about a loss of youth rights. So those above the age of twelve but below the age of twenty-one are allowed to refuse medical procedures. However, to accept them, doctors have to get the consent of parents. Kids can still drive at fifteen and own a car at fifteen but they cannot be sent off to prison under twenty-one."

"And other rights?"

"Voting at fifteen. Drinking at twenty-one. Didn't you learn this in school?"

"So, children are treated nicely here."

"They should be everywhere. Also, before the age of twenty-one, parents can't throw kids out on the street or send them to behavioral modification programs. There used to be a lot of homeless teenagers.

Kids had awful experiences in Gulag camps and schools. After the Reset, Gulag programs were banned altogether."

Up here, they were also calling it the Reset. I wondered if those who went below told them what they were planning but nobody listened.

Steve picked up a mushroom and pineapple pizza and went into another store for the dessert while we waited in the car.

"They still have voting up here," I remarked to Kalandro.

"And drinking is at twenty-one? I guess he's talking about alcohol or teens would die of thirst. Since I was twelve, my dad has sometimes given me alcoholic beverages with dinner."

"I've never gotten any."

"Maybe alcohol and androids don't do well together. You said he thought you were an android."

"Did Chanelle drink?"

"No."

"But androids can process food and beverages. We used to have lunch at school."

"They apparently wanted the girls to be like real girls in most ways."

"Chanelle looked really pretty after the last change," I recalled.

"At sixteen, girls generally work and are assigned a mate."

"If babies are androids, what are the breeder girls for?"

"For any leader who wants a real baby. They have to perpetuate the line. Some of the wives can't have babies or don't want that part of the experience. The guys in Future Leaders aren't robots. If they get out of line, they leave the program and—"

"Are replaced?"

"Probably."

A woman rushed to greet us when Steve opened the door.

"This is my beautiful wife, Katerina. Natalia and Kalandro."

"I'm so glad Steve invited you. The house has been a little empty."

Steve hugged her and gave Katerina a kiss. Up here, hugging seemed common. I wished that custom had been brought below.

"I'll show you to your rooms." She said as she led the way.

She escorted us to a blue room she said was for Kalandro and then me to a pink room. I wondered if there was some significance to the color scheme. Stuffed toys covered my bed. Eterra pranced into the room and picked up a little stuffed bear in her mouth. I had seen pictures of stuffed toys in books, but we were told attachment to such irrelevancies was part of the depravity above.

"I hope this is acceptable to you," Katerina commented. For an adult, she seemed very placating and somewhat timid.

"Eterra seems happy," I observed.

Katerina showed us the bathroom where the linens were kept. "By the end of dinner, I can have the pajamas Steve got you washed."

The pizza was delicious. We had several slices and then two bowls each of almond milk chocolate ice cream.

Eterra also ate some pizza, ignoring the official dog food Steve had purchased for her. "I guess she's used to human food," he said. He looked at the empty pizza box. "You must have been hungry."

We nodded.

Katerina showed us where the refrigerator was. "You can come in here any time you're hungry or thirsty. This is summer vacation."

"Isn't summer June 21st?"

"The school season is different than the calendar one. The schools here let out for vacation early. You're on vacation too, aren't you?" Katerina asked.

"Yes," Kalandro said.

"Do you prefer Kalandro or Kal?" Steve inquired.

"Kal is fine."

I looked at my maybe-brother. I had never tried shortening his name—except to tease him. Somehow, Kal seemed to fit, though.

"You look like you've been starving. If you want, I can make you some more food," Katerina offered.

"That would be great," Kalandro said.

She pulled some spaghetti with mushrooms out of the refrigerator and heated it up.

She also gave a plate of spaghetti to Eterra. "When I was a little girl, I had a dog and he loved spaghetti."

"It's delicious," I said, gobbling down as much as I could as quickly as possible. "Look, Eterra loves it too. Her bowl is empty. Have there been any more wars? I mean, since years ago?"

Katerina looked surprised by the question.

"They were probably studying the wars in school," Steve presumed.

"What school did you go to?" Katerina asked.

"We didn't—" I started to say we didn't go to one here.

"Homeschooled." Katerina assumed. "That's often the best way."

Steve answered my question. "People thought there was going to be a big war when I was a little boy. But then people started dying off from injections and poisoned food and water. The government dropped poisons from the sky that killed a lot of people."

I shuddered. Ottis had mentioned that, too.

"Not anymore," Katerina reassured us. "Don't frighten the child."

"That was over long ago. When the warmongers left, and it was safe to return, we cleaned and recultivated the fields and purified the waterways. A lot of areas had to be torn up to remove toxins deeper down and purify the groundwater. The chemical-free rain helped. Soil was imported from safer countries. After that, we planted chemical-free food."

"No injections." I thought about the lullaby.

"No more poison ones," Steve said.

"The bad people are coming back," I warned.

"I hope not," Katerina responded. "It's so peaceful, now."

"Where did you hear that?" Doctor Steve asked. "About the bad people."

"My mother," I replied.

"She was probably just preparing you in case the worst happened," Katerina said. "But I've been told we're safe."

"Do you have any robot people?"

"Robot people?" Doctor Steve asked.

"Like replacements for real people."

"We don't replace people."

"I bet she's watched some of the old horror movies," Katerina surmised.

"If any robots come here, we'll protect you," Steve assured us.

"The robots are mostly nice. It's the people chopping off their heads who are mean," I said.

"You should write a book. You've got quite a vivid imagination," Katerina complimented me.

"A book? Me?"

"Yes. Document all your thoughts. I bet people will love to read it."

After the after-dinner snacks, we went into the living room.

"Do you play an instrument?" Katerina inquired.

"Harp," I said.

"Maybe we can pick up your harp," Katerina told me.

"Some band instruments were just donated to the Valley Hospital. Maybe they'll let me borrow the harp," Steve told her. "How about you, Kal?"

"I mostly play basketball."

"Would you like to go to the park after I get home from work tomorrow and play some basketball?"

"That would be fun."

"I dance and do gymnastics," I informed them.

"Those are excellent skills," Steve said.

Katerina brought us some more bowls of the almond chocolate ice cream. Food seemed to be a big deal up here. We usually only had one dinner a night back home.

As Katerina went to the laundry room to check on our clothes, the doorbell rang. Steve answered it.

When the man walked in, I recognized him right away. It was Kal's and Chanelle's dad, Jason Denton.

CHAPTER 20

I screamed and dropped my bowl of ice cream.

Kal grabbed my hand and we ran. Eterra followed. We found a door on the far side of the kitchen and rushed through it like lightning to the backyard. If there was a gate, it wasn't on that side of the house.

"It was all a trap," I shrieked. "And I bet they did kill Selini Andrews."

Eterra jumped into my arms and the three of us started over the fence, but the doctor managed to grab our legs. With us kicking back to try to free our legs, he still managed to pull us down. An image of an ax swinging at my neck filled my mind.

Katerina ran out. "Please, don't run away. I don't know what frightened you."

"Please, don't let Mr. Denton kill us!" I cried.

"You mean the man who came to the door?" Steve asked.

"He's here to kill us!" Kal exclaimed.

"He is an undertaker. He only buries dead people," Steve asserted.

"After they've been replaced, you mean!" Kal yelled.

"I saw him kill Chanelle," I said.

"So did I! He chopped off her head," Kal exclaimed. "Please let us go. We won't cause any harm if you let us go."

"I'm not going to let anyone kill you," Katerina responded almost convincingly, but I'd learned not to trust adults.

"Let's go in and talk it over. If you want to leave after that, we'll drive you wherever you want to go," Steve promised.

"He won't let you. He'll probably kill you, too, if you try to help us."

"You didn't see the big red S under my shirt." An almost smile crossed Steve's face. I didn't know if the smile was because he was tricking us or if he felt he could handle things. I looked at Kal, who shrugged. "I can take him if he comes near either of you."

We went in, hiding behind Steve and Katerina.

"Would you tell the kids your name?" Steve asked the man.

"Jay Fenton."

"He's lying," Kal countered. "It's Jason Denton."

"He was my cousin."

"Cousin?" Kal asked. I could tell he didn't believe the guy any more than I did.

"But he's not here. I haven't seen him since the poisoning."

"Did you look alike?" Steve asked.

"People used to think we were twins."

"Did he have violent tendencies?"

"He was a warmonger. He was running a weapons manufacturing operation for the government. I assumed he was dead, but I hoped he was in one of those bomb shelters." He held his palms up as if to indicate he was flustered.

"If you hear from him, let me know. Don't mention anything to him about the kids. They seem to be very frightened of him," Steve advised the man.

"Show me your left arm," Kal demanded, clearly no more convinced than I was.

"What?" the man responded.

"He has a snake on his left arm."

"You mean a tattoo?" Steve asked.

Kal nodded.

"I remember when he got that," Fenton said. He rolled up his left sleeve. No tattoo.

"It's better if we wait until tomorrow to talk about the funeral service," Steve told him. "Nice of you to drop by."

"Sorry to have frightened you," Jay told us as Steve escorted him to the door. "So, you've seen my cousin?"

"No," Kal lied. "Don't know him."

As Steve closed the door, he turned back to us. "They say everyone's got a double. I've known Mr. Fenton for about five years. He's been running a funeral home here in Sutter Springs. We normally don't have to lock doors, but I'll do so tonight."

Katerina turned me to face her. "I promise. I won't let anyone hurt you."

"He's arranging a funeral for a former patient. I told the family I would contact him."

"Are you feeling any better?" Katerina asked.

"I don't know," I shivered. Seeing the man had been unnerving. I wondered if he could have had the tattoo removed. I knew they had quick procedures for repairing or replacing skin below. I wasn't about to let my guard down. And despite Kal's lie, we had given ourselves away.

"How about you take a nice shower and get into your bed clothes," Katerina suggested. "A good night's sleep always helps me feel better."

I went into the shower room, feeling very uncertain.

Katerina brought me the cleaned pajamas. "I'll guard the door. If anything is off, I'll grab you and we'll run," Katerina assured me. "The towels are in the cupboard."

The warm water felt wonderful. I hadn't had a good shower since I left home. The shower at the museum was nice but this was nicer. After I towel-dried, I put on the new pajamas and went outside. Katerina placed Kal's pajamas on the counter and he went in to shower.

"Now I'll watch the door for your brother."

"May my brother and I stay in the same room tonight?"

"You're really scared, aren't you?" Katerina asked.

I didn't say anything.

"Steve, can you set up a cot in Natalia's room for Kal to stay there tonight?"

"If that makes them feel safer."

Steve followed through, setting up the cot. When Kal came out from his shower, he said he liked the idea too. "Thank you, Doctor Steve."

"Just Steve."

Steve and Katerina tucked us in. "If you get scared, our door is across the hall, the first door before the living room."

"Thank you."

After they left, I asked Kal. "Do you think we can trust them?"

"I don't know. I don't trust that Fenton guy. He reminds me too much of my dad. Let's see if we can hear what they are saying about us."

We heard the couple turn out the lights and go into their room. We tiptoed to listen at the door.

"Do you think we should contact the police? It sounds like they witnessed a horrific crime," Katerina said.

"The police would put them through the third degree. Let's see if we can get them to open up to us."

"They're such sweet kids, but they are really scared. They need lots of love. I wish we could keep them."

"They belong to Miss Holiday."

"Maybe she knows about the people who scared the children."

"I'm wondering about this Mr. Denton. Maybe he is still alive. After he couldn't warmonger anymore, he might have gone on a killing rampage. I'll see if I can find out something about him tomorrow."

"Do you think we can trust Jay?" she asked.

"I'm not so sure now. Until tonight, I absolutely would have said 'yes.'"

I signaled for Kal to come back with me to my room. We lay on our beds. "I don't think Steve and Katerina would hurt us. They seem nice, and they want to help us."

"I concur. Maybe, up here, a lot of people look like people below. I still don't trust Mr. Fenton."

The door opened. It was Katerina. I sat up. "I just wanted to make sure you were comfortable. Would you like anything? Hot chocolate?"

"Sure," I said.

She closed the door and came back a little later with two cups of hot chocolate. I had never tasted such good hot chocolate.

"Thank you for being kind. I didn't mean to cause trouble," I said.

"I understand. You were frightened. If you witnessed something really bad, let us know and we'll do our best to help. I promise we're here to protect you and keep you safe."

"I believe you," I said.

After she left, I turned to Kal. "We told them, he chopped off Chanelle's head. Does she think we imagined it?"

"Maybe."

"At least, she's more willing to look at what is happening than the women down below. They were all complacent. Maybe because so many of them were fixed, or rather replaced."

"And they treat us almost like babies up here. They shop for us and want to protect us."

"Up here, being a teen is like being a toddler down below."

"We need to fit in better," he advised.

"I like it. We only had a few years before we had to conform. I was so young, I barely remember those years. Now I get to experience what I missed."

The bed was so comfortable, I dropped off to sleep easily after finishing the hot chocolate. It was as if my mother were reaching out to me in my dream.

She touched me and looked into my eyes. "I swear I didn't kill anyone. I did what I did to keep you alive. I couldn't tell you, or my husband would have had you killed immediately."

"He's really not my dad?"

Her image drifted away.

"Mommy, mommy, I want you back."

My dream drifted to the explosion and seeing my mom on the floor. "No," I screamed. *"Mommy, Mommy!"*

Kal was shaking me, and Eterra was licking my face.

Katerina ran into the room. "Are you alright?"

"Just a dream."

"About your mother?"

"I don't know if she's alive."

"Steve says she'll be alright. Would you like me to call the hospital to check on her?"

"You don't need to. I'm feeling better now."

She closed the door.

"Everyone thinks Claire Holiday is our mother," I said.

"I get that impression."

"Should we tell them?"

"If we told them, they'd ask who our real mother was. What do we say? Would they even believe us? They didn't believe us about my dad or Mr. Fenton or whoever he was."

"He didn't have the tattoo and he claimed your dad was his cousin."

"That would make him my first cousin once removed. They'd make us live with him if I told them Denton was our dad."

"We don't know your dad was my dad."

"I'm sure of it."

"What if my real dad is someone good, someone like Steve, who doesn't kill kids to replace them with robots? I don't want my dad to be a killer."

"I wish mine weren't."

The next morning, we had pancakes for breakfast. "All the food here is delicious," I said.

"Thank you," Katerina replied, smiling. "That makes me feel really good."

"I'm sorry we were so weird last night," I apologized. "I think I just had a dream and thought it was real."

"My sister sometimes has nightmares," Kal backed me up. Apparently thinking the same thing that had occurred to me, he whispered to me, "He could have had the tattoo replaced with fake skin."

"Anything wrong?" Katerina asked.

"I was just telling her I wish we had had pancakes like this before."

"So, everything's okay?" Steve checked. "You had quite a day, yesterday, with the accident and your mother being in a coma."

"Can we see her?" I requested.

"Maybe this afternoon, Katerina can drive you over there. But I don't know if she'll be awake."

"That's fine. Maybe we can sit by her bed for a while and see if she wakes up." She was injured trying to help us. I felt guilt over what had happened to those who had tried to assist us: Mom, Not-Mom and Miss Holiday.

There was another reason Kal and I wanted to see her. Before breakfast, we had decided to plead with Miss Holiday not to tell them she was not our mother. We didn't want people trying to find out who we were or even worse giving us to Mr. Fenton and wind up being raised by him or being sent back below.

After Steve left, we asked if we could use the computer. The computer was old-school, archaic, but we searched until we found Jay Fenton's information.

"Look," I said. "He really does own a funeral home." I saw Kal relaxing a little.

"Maybe he was one of the people who did the poisoning, and he's planning to bury the dead so that our dad can come back up."

"Stop saying he's my dad."

"Why? Because he's a lower rank than your not-dad?"

"I don't want either of them. I want a nice dad."

"I'd like a nice dad, too, but, I'm stuck with the child-killer I've got."

"I remember Chanelle being a lot different when she was younger. Maybe something awful happened to her and my mother simply built the replacement. Everyone's intellect is uploaded—even the humans."

"You're still excusing your mom?"

"My mom wouldn't kill a child. I know it. Her job was to build the computers—not kill kids."

"But she killed computers."

"They weren't kids."

"She was part of it."

"I dreamt she talked to me last night, and she said she didn't kill anyone. I believe her."

"You believe a dream? Dreams are imagination."

"Selini Andrews was real. Do you remember your mother?"

"She was sweet. I hated my dad for making her cry."

"Are you two kids having fun?" Katerina asked, opening the door. "That's a picture of Fenton's funeral home. So, you are verifying his story."

"We are," Kal confirmed.

"He said he had a cousin named Denton, Jason Denton was it? I'm going to try to look him up," I told Katerina, trying to make light of our freak-out the night before. "But first I want to look up something else."

I quickly did a search and found a page for the World Economic Forum. It showed that years ago, Not-Dad was calling for a transhuman revolution, complete with total monitoring of society, redirection of wealth to natural leaders, transference of all knowledge into Artificial Intelligence and an end to physical problems and death, courtesy of replaceable bodies. I guessed he got his wish for the kids and the service personnel. But the Elites retained their bodies. I wondered if they had computer backups for when they died. I knew replaceable parts were available.

"It looks as if you have computer skills," Katerina complimented me.

"I'm not used to a computer like this one, but it's nice," I replied.

"We don't use it for anything fancy. It works for us. We could arrange to give you kids laptops if you wind up staying with us for a while."

"Why are you being so nice to us?"

"I always wanted kids, and well, even if it's for just a little while, it feels good to have you here."

"Maybe you'll have some kids in the future."

"I hope so, but at least this is good practice. When I do have kids, I hope they will be like you."

"Like us?" *After all the trouble we've been, why did she want kids like us?*

"You're both polite, sweet and intelligent."

"Thank you," we both said in unison. Katerina looked as if she was going to start crying. We stood up and I put my arms around her. To my surprise, Kal hugged her as well.

"Maybe you are the one who needs love," I told her.

"I'm just sentimental."

She went out of the room. "Don't tell her you were thinking of building her a baby," Kal said.

"What? Of course not. That's cruel. I was thinking that she could still have children. Just because she lost one baby doesn't mean she can't have more. Your parents had two kids."

We continued on the internet and found some links to pictures and information about Jason Denton.

"Those pictures of my dad are when he was a lot younger."

"Look. Here he is pushing the depopulation idea, saying there are too many people. He called the masses, 'useless eaters.'"

"He's probably one of the ones who poisoned everything."

"Would you like to go to the park?" Katerina asked, opening the door, again. "They have a basketball court where you could practice basketball. Fresh air is good for you."

"That would be fun," Kal replied.

"I've washed the rest of your clothes. Steve got you some sneakers you can wear. When we get back, I'll heat up an extra pizza Steve got for you."

Yep. Food really seems important to people up here. How are they not fat?

In the park, another boy was shooting hoops as Kal walked over to the court with Katerina and me, loosely following.

"I'm Roger."

"Kal."

"You want to play against each other?"

"Sure."

"A merry-go-round," I observed, turning away from the court.

I had seen pictures of one in a book, but we didn't have one below.

"Would you like me to push you on it?" Katerina asked.

"Yes. It's a centrifuge."

"It is."

As she turned it faster and faster, I held onto one of the bars, threw my head back and laughed. Eterra ran in circles around the merry-go-round, counter to the direction we were going, barking excitedly. I was enjoying this life more and more. I remembered my mother whirling me around in her arms when I was really small. I wished she were here to see me.

After I got off, I went over to the swings. Chanelle and I used to sit on the swings at the park near my former home. The purpose of the swings below was to develop our leg muscles. Katerina gave me a push and I went high in the air. Eterra lay down a few feet ahead, watching me.

"Your dog is very devoted to you," Katerina said.

I smiled. She really had become my dog.

A boy about my age started swinging on the seat next to me. "I'm Brad."

"Hi."

I took another look at him. He reminded me of Robert Horton. He smiled at me. "Playing hooky?"

"Hooky?"

"From school."

"No. I—"

He laughed. "It's summer vacation."

"Oh."

I guess that made a difference. Underground, there was year-round learning. Apparently, teens up here made jokes and didn't mind being kids. Maybe, I could be me.

"You're Brad Fillmore, aren't you?" Katerina interjected.

"Yes, Ma'am. I live across the street from you."

"I should have gone over to meet your family. You just moved in a few weeks ago, didn't you?"

"Uh-huh. We were a block away before. You're Katerina, correct?"

"Yes."

"And your daughter?"

"Natalia," I said, not wanting to discuss my family.

"I'm having a party at my house tonight. Would you like to come?"

"I don't know. She's had a lot going on," Katerina said.

I turned to Katerina. "Maybe I could go for just a little while?" The idea of seeing kids my age excited me. I was curious about what teens were like above.

"Will your parents be supervising?"

"They'll be there if that's what you're worried about."

"Then, that will be fine."

"It will start at eight."

Kal came over with his new friend.

"Your brother can shoot," Roger remarked.

"Can Kal come?" I asked.

"Sure. The more, the merrier."

"Come where?" Kal inquired.

"To the party tonight," Roger chimed in. "I'll be there too. Bring a swimsuit. They've got a really nice pool."

Later, as we were devouring the pizza back at the house, Steve called. Miss Holiday was waking up but was extremely groggy. She didn't know she was supposed to be our mother. *What if she tells him she had just been giving us a ride before we got to the hospital?*

As we rushed into Miss Holiday's room, we could see she was awake and smiling. Some wires were still attached to her but most of the tubes had been removed.

"We've been having a nice discussion about you," Steve said.

Oh no! We should have come earlier.

CHAPTER 21

"I'll let you talk," Steve said, leaving the room.

"What did you tell him?" I asked, nervously.

"More importantly, what did you tell him? That I'm your mother?"

"They assumed you were our mother. We found out Mrs. Andrews is dead and there's a man in town who looks like a horrible man we once knew and we just don't want to be put on the street or sent to the government," I rambled on. "But now Steve knows and he'll probably throw us out or call the police on us."

"Wait. That's a lot to take in. So, your mother's friend is dead, and you're all alone without anyone to help you?"

"Yes." Tears were starting to fall from my eyes.

"Someone needs to give you a home. You kids are great and I enjoy your company, but I think you'd be better off with the doc and his wife. He was saying how much they are enjoying having you. He was talking about how special you are."

"But now, they won't want us anymore."

"I didn't blow things for you. When he called me your mother, I figured you had a reason for telling him that, and I played along."

"You didn't tell him?" Relief went through me. I brushed my tears away.

"I didn't tell him."

"Thank you, thank you." I bent down and gave her a hug.

"I'm going to be in here for a while, and then I'm going to need some rehab, but you should consider telling Steve and his wife the truth. Eventually, they'll find out. They'll expect you to come with me when I go home."

"By then, maybe we'll have things figured out," Kal predicted. "Thank you."

"Thank you, so much, Miss Holiday."

"Claire, remember? I guess you can also call me 'Mommy' for now."

I hugged her again. Surprising me once more, Kal hugged her too.

Steve knocked before walking back in. "I see you two and your mother are making up for lost time."

"You said they could stay with you for a while. I want to make sure I'm fully recovered before they come with me. After all, I'm alone."

"We'll make sure someone comes in to assist you if you need help. The kids are welcome to stay with us as long as you like."

Things were starting to improve.

"I think you'd better let your mom get some more rest," Steve advised.

"Remember to be good with the Drakes."

"We will," I said. I gave her another hug.

Katerina was waiting outside. "I bet it was good to see your mother."

"She looks so much better," I said. "And she said we could keep staying with you if that's alright."

Katerina smiled. "We'd love to have you."

"Thank you."

The truth of the matter is, we didn't know where else to go.

Katerina took us back home. We went to the computer, again, to see what we could find out about Selini Andrews. There was a picture. She was apparently very outspoken and an accomplished scientist. There were lots of pictures of her with her daughter, Tarinda.

"Maybe Tarinda knows something," I suggested.

"Here's one of those phones they are using. Let's see if we can find a number for Tarinda." The daughter's number was, in fact, easy to find. We dialed it and someone answered.

"Tarinda?"

"Who wants to know? I don't normally answer, but I was about to make a call."

"We're calling about your mother."

"In that case, I couldn't care less. Call someone else." She hung up.

"Look at these pictures of Mrs. Andrews and Tarinda. Selini looks so devoted to her daughter, so proud of her, and Tarinda treats her like that?" I fumed.

"Tarinda'd love it in the underworld. No feelings," Kal grunted.

"If I had a chance to find out how my mother was doing or to see her again, I'd jump at it."

"Are you thinking of going back?"

"Not after what Not-Mom said would happen if I did. I certainly wouldn't want to do anything that might risk harming Mom, but I wouldn't refuse information about her. I wonder if Tarinda even knows her mom died."

"I guess not everyone up here is nice."

"Not Tarinda. That's for sure."

Katerina knocked on the door to the den.

"Come in," I said.

"It's your house. You don't have to knock," Kal pointed out.

"I thought you might like privacy. You liked the spaghetti last night and so I'm making some more. I forgot to mention, Steve was able to borrow a couple of laptops for you from the hospital and—" She paused and smiled a broad smile. "They loaned him a harp."

"That's great." I jumped up, whirled around and then caught myself, with a gut feeling that I was doing something very wrong. But up here, showing emotions wasn't a fault.

"I've seen you play. You're good," Kal told me when Katerina left the room.

"It's so nice up here. The food is delicious. The water even tastes good. Nobody's trying to make robots out of us. We have friends!" That was the best. "And she didn't freak out when I got excited."

"But if they find out who we are, who knows what they will do to us. I've been looking at the things that were written about people like our dad and your fake dad. Most everyone up here hated the people who went underground. Some said they'd kill them and their descendants if they got their hands on them."

"Was that recent?"

"No. It was written about the time of the poisoning."

"Online, I saw a book and a movie about people going underground during a war and leaving others above ground," I informed him.

"What's it called?"

"*Time Machine* by H.G. Wells. How come we didn't read it down there? According to this site, it's an old book, written back in 1895."

He searched and found it. "Maybe it was too close to reality. They didn't want us to know about it." He looked around some more. "Here. The video is available online."

"They didn't have videos in 1895—according to our history books."

"They lied to us about everything else. Oh, this movie was made in 1960."

As we watched the Morlocks, I cringed. "That's not what we're like."

"Dad is worse."

The movie was terrifying. I cheered as the Eloi killed the Morlocks and but felt odd doing it. "You and I don't look like that. They're ugly. Well, maybe you." I smiled.

"Everyone looks human below—even the non-security androids. Everyone just acts like a robot—at least, compared with the people up here. The book was written before androids. H.G. Wells probably had no idea of how advanced the warmongers would get by the time there was a final world war."

"But there are other differences," I said. "The people up here are more self-sufficient than the Eloi and the Morlocks don't want to take them below for food—I don't think." A horrid thought overcame me. "Is it possible, we—"

"No!" he sternly cut me off as if knowing the end of my question. "Also, we weren't in dark caves. There were underground sunlamps for the farms. The artificial sky looks sort of like the one up here."

"But we didn't see the food being processed. Do we really know?"

"Let's assume we didn't, so we don't throw up. If anyone came below, they'd off them. The under-people are monsters. Look what they did to Chanelle," Kal reminded me.

"I wonder if people up here will want to kill us when they find out we're Morlocks," I fretted.

"We aren't Morlocks."

About that time, Steve came home and we started to come out of the den.

"How is—Mom?"

"She's improving. She's looking forward to your visit tomorrow. Now close your eyes," Steve said. He guided me through the living room. "Now open them." Standing before me was a beautiful full-sized harp.

I threw my arms around him. "Oh, thank you! Thank you!" I next hugged Katerina.

"Your mother said you didn't have your own harp and she wanted to get you one. The hospital loaned me this one but said they'd let me purchase it if you like it."

"It's beautiful."

"It's used. It was donated to the hospital. Now, for both of you." Steve pointed to the couch. Before us sat two foldable computers. They were different than the little expandable holographic computers we used to carry to school in our pockets but we had left those behind. Down below, only certain stationary computers were full-sized and had solid screens.

"Awesome!" Kal declared.

"I asked your mom if I could borrow the key to pick up your things. Apparently, it was left behind in the accident. I called the towing yard and they said they'd look."

I glanced at Kal. What would we do when they discovered we didn't have any clothes at Miss Holiday's house?

As we sat at the dining room table, Stave asked us, "Now, how did your day go?"

"We went to the park and made new friends. We were invited to a party tonight," I replied.

"A party?"

Katerina explained. "Brad, the boy across the street is having a swim party. I picked up some swimsuits for Kal and Natalia on the way home from the hospital. His parents will be there." She turned to me. "I'll watch Eterra during the party if you want."

"Thank you."

"It looks like you're getting off to a good start here," Steve noted.

"We saw *Time Machine*."

"The original?"

"I guess. It was a very old movie."

"Did you like it?"

"Not really," I said. "It was all wrong. I mean if the people underground were advanced, they wouldn't be looking like monsters and eating people up here, and people up here aren't mindless like the Eloi."

"A deep thinker. A well-reasoned analysis," Steve complimented me.

Brad opened the door as we arrived, escorted by Steve. "Natalia, it's great to see you."

"It's great to be here."

"Hi, Kal. Roger's been eager for you to show up."

"Looks like a good party. I'll see you later, kids," Steve said as he turned to leave.

"Your Dad came with you to check things out. Your parents must be the protective types."

"Sort of."

"Helicopter parents."

"You mean they fly." I guessed that's what he meant. I'd read about helicopters in history books and at the museum.

"I mean, they hover around you and check up on you."

"I guess."

Roger came over to us. "Hey, Kal. Glad you made it."

"Catch you later, sis," Kal said as he walked off with Roger.

"That banner says 'Happy Birthday.'" I pointed to the message that ran across the living room.

"That's right. It's my birthday."

"I didn't get you anything. I'm sorry." Even back home, we would exchange birthday gifts. I thought of the locket I'd given to Chanelle. I had also planned to give her a box of hair ribbons after her transition, but they seemed inappropriate with her new look.

"No need. My gift was seeing you here. He leaned towards me. I've been taking inventory and you are the prettiest girl here."

I smiled. "That's really sweet." He was a lot nicer than the boys I had known back home.

"My parents made lots of food and treats, but I spiked the punch."

"You put spikes in the punch?"

He laughed. "You're a kick. Let me guess. Are you fifteen, sixteen?"

"Fifteen, almost sixteen."

"When is your sixteenth birthday?"

"October eighth."

"After the start of the school year. We should have a big party. Do you like birthday parties?"

"I like yours so far."

"You're a Libra. I'm a Gemini. Geminis and Libras are supposed to be perfect friends."

"That's good. Friends are great."

He took me to the backyard where people were standing around the swimming pool. There were several pizzas on a nearby table. "What kind of pizza do you like?"

I picked up one with mushrooms.

"I like mushroom pizza too." He grabbed a similar piece. "Do you like movies?"

"I saw *Time Machine* today."

"That's a really old one."

"I didn't like it. Do you think that's how things are?"

"Morlocks and Eloi?"

I nodded.

"I'm smarter than the Eloi. I can pick my own fruit." He laughed.

"How about the Morlocks?"

"All I can say," Roger remarked from behind us, apparently having eavesdropped. "Is that if something comes up from under the ground, I'm killing it."

"Isn't that close-minded?" Kal asked him. "It could be something good coming up from underground."

"Nothing good ever comes up from under the ground."

"Potatoes," Brad commented.

"Nothing good that's breathing ever comes up from underground," Roger clarified.

"His father is part of some kind of vigilante group. They think the warmongers are going to come back and we'll have to fight them."

A terrified scream broke the peace. It was a girl with pink hair, staring directly at me.

CHAPTER 22

"I think Harris slipped her some acid," Roger speculated.

"Acid?" I asked.

"Obviously some bad stuff," Brad replied. "Somebody better calm her down before my parents call off the party."

Roger went over to the pink-haired girl, put his hand around her mouth and then carried her out.

A man and woman, who had apparently been hanging out upstairs, came down the staircase. I assumed they were Brad's parents. "What was that?" the woman asked.

"Just a girl trying to act out a scene from *Psycho*."

"*Psycho*?" I inquired, almost under my breath.

"Another really old movie," Brad informed me.

Roger returned and quietly told Brad. "I put her in my car and she passed out. I think she'll be good when she wakes up."

"We need to find the stash or whatever she got before someone else goes bananas," Brad pointed out.

Roger looked around. "You don't think he would have spiked the whole punchbowl, do you? Look at the crowd."

People were making weird motions and walking funny.

"I'll dump the punchbowl. See if you can get some people to round up anyone who's affected and take them home," Brad looked at me. "Excuse me." He went over to the punchbowl and poured out its contents. Then he poured in some fresh punch. He returned to me. "I'm leaving the booze out of this one or they'll accuse me of being the one who put the acid in it."

"What kind of acid?"

"You've lived a sheltered life. Makes sense with your parents escorting you to parks and parties. It's lysergic acid diethylamide, LSD."

"I've read about that. Wasn't it used in mind control experiments by the CIA?"

"You're informed. It was an MK Ultra thing. Where did you read about it?"

"At a museum."

"I like museums. There's a cool history museum over near the river."

"The one run by Ottis Malone?"

"Yeah."

"He died."

"That's a shame. I didn't hear that. He was a cool old man. I used to go over there and white-water raft down the river."

"Over the waterfall?"

"Not that part. I don't have a death wish." He smiled as I laughed. "How long ago did Ottis die?"

"Recently."

"Sad."

"Would you like to go with me to a science museum tomorrow?"

"Yes." I clearly had so much more to learn.

"I'll pick you up at about two P.M."

"That would be great."

"It's a date then."

"I heard this was a swim party."

"Nobody's gotten in the water yet. You want to be the first?"

"Sure."

I pulled off my overclothes, jumped in and started swimming. The backyard pool was warm like the ones underground. Brad joined me.

After swimming for a few minutes, we stood up in the shallow end. "This is fun," I excitedly said.

"You're a pretty good swimmer."

"Thank you. So are you."

"Does your brother swim?"

I looked around but didn't see him. "I taught him, but I don't think he likes it."

"Talented girl, and you look great in a bathing suit."

"Thank you."

"Do you know how to save someone from drowning?"

"Sometimes."

"Help, I'm drowning." He ducked under water. I reached down and pulled him up. We both started laughing.

"Oh no," he groaned.

"What?"

"My parents are bringing in the birthday cake. It's kind of embarrassing."

"Why?"

"You're right. Parents are great—especially when they foot the bill for parties."

I laughed. We got out, dried ourselves with towels from a stack sitting on a chair and went back inside. Kal and Roger joined us.

"Where were you?" I asked.

"There's a game computer with a big screen in the den."

Everyone sang "Happy Birthday." Brad's parents cut the cake and went back upstairs.

"They like it upstairs," I commented to Brad as my brother and Roger grabbed a couple of plates and took off with their pieces to another room, again.

"I asked them to hang out up there during the party."

"They seem nice from what I could see of them."

"They are. So are your folks."

Another girl started screaming and fell into the pool.

"I should have collected all the glasses," Brad said as he ran to rescue her. I jumped back in, too. We brought her onto the deck. She was unconscious.

CHAPTER 23

I heard the word "paramedics." I guessed they were on their way. We had learned CPR, though we never used it. I guessed it was taught in case an elite person collapsed down below. Kal came over and helped.

I noticed most of the party-goers were standing around, looking worried with furled brows and frowns, expressions I never saw back home. Below, everyone would have gone about their own business without checking back on the person's condition.

The girl opened her eyes.

"You know some useful skills," Brad said.

"I thought everyone was supposed to learn this. Are you alright?"

The girl lay on her side, looking at me and coughing, but not speaking.

We heard sirens and a minute later, paramedics rushed into the house. Brad's parents ran down the stairs.

"What happened?" the mom asked.

"Drowning girl," Brad explained.

The girl sat up. "I'm fine. Could I have another drink?"

"I think you've had enough," Brad responded.

"I'll take her home," Roger said, before the paramedics could react to the drinking reference.

"I've a feeling I'm going to be in for it," Brad muttered.

Brad's mother was looking at him in dismay.

"You can never tell who comes to these parties or what they took before they got here," he told her and then smiled sheepishly.

Everyone went back to talking.

Steve and Katerina rushed inside. "Is everything alright?"

"It's fine," I assured them. I turned to Brad. "I'll see you tomorrow."

"Looking forward to it."

"What's this about tomorrow?" Kal asked as we walked across the street with Steve and Katerina.

"He's taking me to a science museum," I responded, excitedly.

"We promised Mom we'd see her," Kal whispered, "Brad thinks Steve and Katerina are our parents."

"We'll go in the morning to the hospital. He'll take me in the afternoon," I said.

"I don't know if I like the way he hangs around you," Kal remarked in an irritated tone, reminiscent of the one he had sometimes used with me and his sister below.

Katerina related, "I checked with some of the other neighbors. They all said Brad is a nice boy."

"I think your sister will be safe with him," Steve assured Kal.

The next morning, we went to the hospital. "People are starting to ask me questions about my kids," Claire told us.

"What did you say?"

"That I was groggy and couldn't answer any questions. An old friend named Jack came by and I had to tell him to pretend you were my kids."

"Did he?"

"Yes, but he's looking forward to an explanation."

"We're making friends. Steve and Katerina are so nice. They got me a harp and both of us laptops, and we really don't want to be taken away by the government," I went on.

"It's fine for now. But eventually the truth will come out." She had said that before. I hoped that "eventually" was a long time from then.

"Maybe by then, we'll figure things out," Kal responded.

Steve knocked and came in. "Are you and your mother having a nice conversation?"

"Yes. We were telling her how wonderful it is at your place."

"I was having a lot of trouble managing these two youngsters on my own before the accident. Maybe they could stay with you for a while—even after I get home. It will take me time to get myself in shape to have them back."

Steve seemed taken aback. "Of course. They can stay with us for as long as they like. They are such nice kids."

"The best, but I don't want them to feel bad when they see me trying to be my old self."

"You'd be surprised how well kids adjust."

She didn't respond to him.

"I love you," she told us. "Now, go have some fun."

"Yes, Mom," I said, hugging her. Kal hugged her as well.

Katerina was out in the hall. Steve turned to us. "I'd like to talk to Katerina for a minute. Maybe you can get some hot chocolate." He gave me some change and told us where a machine was.

"This is archaic," I said as a woman assisted us in putting our coins into the machine. Taking our hot chocolate, we went down a corridor that intersected with the one where Steve and Katerina were conversing. I moved close enough to hear them without being seen.

"I don't think their mother wants them. She actually seemed relieved they were staying with someone else," Steve told her.

"She's recovering. How can anyone not want those kids?"

"Don't get too attached to them. Eventually, they'll have to go home."

"I understand that. They're teens, and even if they were ours, teens often leave for college, right?"

"Not so much as when we were kids. I remember during the plandemics, families broke up and kids hated their parents and vice versa. These kids have a mother and one day, they'll go home. You are still recovering from the loss of our baby."

"Even if they move out, they'll still be family."

"You sure you can handle it?"

"They're already family."

I went back to Kal and whispered what I had heard. "She must have really wanted that baby. We need to be there for her."

"I wish they were our parents."

"I like them too, especially the hugs, but I want my mom back."

"Maybe if we found someone who knew Selini Andrews and liked her, we would know why your mother wanted you to see her."

When we got home, I prepared to go to the museum. Brad knocked on the door. I was dressed in slacks and a white stretch shirt that showed off my figure. Katerina had me carry a jacket in case it was cold in the museum.

"You look great," Brad complimented me.

"She does," Kal noted.

"Where will you be going?" I asked, noticing he was also dressed nicely.

"I thought I'd get a ride to the museum with you two. I love science museums."

Brad glared at him.

"That's a nice idea," Katerina acknowledged. She handed each of us some cash. "In case you need anything."

"I wish my parents were that helpful," Brad said. He looked at the harp. "Do you play that thing?"

"Some."

"Would you play a song? I never knew anyone who played a harp before."

"Alright." I went over to it and played a section of Beethoven's Ninth.

I was so focused on the harp that I didn't notice any reaction until I heard Katerina and Brad cheering and clapping. Kal was moving his hands in a fake clapping motion.

"You liked it?"

"That was amazing," Brad commented.

"It was beautiful, honey," Katerina said.

I had never received that kind of reception back home. Of course, my mom always liked what I did, but these were people I barely knew.

I hugged Eterra and made her promise to be good while I was gone. "Do you mind watching her, again?" I asked Katerina?

"I love dogs. Before you arrived with Eterra, I was thinking of getting one for myself."

***

The museum featured numerous hands-on exhibits. In one section, we put electrical circuits together, built a pulley and made it work. In another, we made volcanoes and even created a small earthquake. The astronomy section was fun. The stars below looked different and they didn't move. Mostly, they were just random dots in the sky—instead of part of constellations. I had imagined stories behind the positioning of the stars below, but those stars didn't fit into any of the four seasons I saw here.

In an outdoor section, we constructed miniature rockets that actually flew.

We moved on to a section with an image changer that showed what our faces would look like if we had parts of them altered.

"I like your face exactly the way it is," Brad said.

"Don't you think it's a little round?" Kal asked, coming up behind us.

"No. It's not round at all," Brad countered.

"Aren't there some exhibits you'd like to see by yourself?" I asked Kal.

"I'm enjoying the tour."

"What tour?" I asked.

"He's acting more like a jealous boyfriend than a brother," Brad whispered.

"We used to hate each other. I think he's just trying to harass me," I lightly replied.

"Oh. It's like that. Maybe we should get him a girlfriend." Brad looked around. "Ah, I ought to introduce him to Jennifer. She's Roger's sister. She wasn't at the party last night. Jennifer!" Brad called to a very pretty girl with long red hair. "I've got someone for you to meet."

Brad made quick introductions and asked Jennifer if she'd like to join the threesome.

"Sure. I was here with some friends, but they won't miss me. They're into their own thing."

Up close, she was taller than me. Her eyes looked like dazzling blue diamonds. Brad didn't seem to notice how pretty she was. He kept looking at me.

Kal looked between me and Jennifer, perhaps sizing up the differences. Maybe this would get him to stop following us.

It did. After a little while, Kal and Jennifer went to a quantum physics exhibit while Brad and I headed over to a biology section. He showed me how blood types are determined. We checked our own blood with small pricks. I turned out to be A negative. I hadn't checked before. I did know my mom's blood type, though. She was O negative, though for some unknown reason she wanted everyone to think she was A negative.

Brad wanted to see the robotics section. It frightened me a little. "Robots aren't real kids. You just think they are," I reacted.

"Of course not. They're robots. AI is banned. Robots just do things we program them to do."

There was a picture of some of the scientists who had excelled in robotics, historically.

"She looks like you." It was a picture of my mother, younger looking than when I last saw her, though she had retained her age well. "Look, it says that it was believed she died sixteen years ago. That was about the time of The Great Reset."

"The Great Reset?"

"It was when the leaders and fat cats went underground, poisoning everything in an attempt to kill the world. My dad said everyone thought World War III was coming, but it was just a distraction."

"What if they are planning to come back?"

"You think they'd still be alive, living below ground all these years? Those people needed servants and a subclass."

"Robots for the subclass," I said.

"Maybe. They wanted to put chips and trackers into us."

I was still staring at that picture of my mother when I noticed the name, Eterra Stafford. I had thought Stafford was my mom's middle name. It must have been her last name before she was married. There was a tribute below it.

"To my best friend:

You were the kindest, smartest most caring person I ever knew. I will miss you forever.

Selini Andrews"

Below that was a picture of the two of them with their arms over each other's shoulders, like Chanelle and I used to stand when we were very young, maybe two or three.

"Isn't your dog also named Eterra?"

"Yes. It's not an uncommon name."

"The only Eterras I've heard of are this woman and your dog."

That's when someone yelled, "Eterra," at me. It was a man. I didn't know who he was, but if he knew my mother, then he knew I escaped. I ran.

"Wait!" Brad called, taking off after me.

The man seemed to be running after me, too. The man was fast.

As I turned a corner, he caught my arm. "Eterra. Your mother is Eterra."

I screamed.

CHAPTER 24

Brad punched the man in the face. Security came and started to ask what was going on. I ran. Brad chased after me, and I knew others were following me as well.

I heard the man yell, "Wait, wait! I need to talk to you!"

I couldn't let the man catch me, know where I was staying or who I was. It hit me that, by running, I had fully given myself away.

Outside, Brad caught up with me. Kal and Jennifer rushed to us.

"What happened?" Kal asked.

"For a minute, I thought they were going to arrest me for hitting the guy," Brad said.

"What guy?" Kal asked. "Did somebody hurt you or Natalia?"

"No." I had to be careful what I said in front of Brad. "Some man started yelling at me. I got scared."

"He chased you, yelling as if you were a long-lost friend or a ghost of a long-lost friend. I bet it was because of your similarity to that picture."

"Picture?" Kal asked.

"There was a picture of a scientist who looked a lot like Natalia."

I said the first excuse I could come up with. "Steve, or rather my dad, says that a lot of people look like other people."

"I'm sure that's true," Brad acknowledged.

"The night before last, we mistook a man for someone else," I informed him.

"Do you think you're related to this Eterra?"

"Is that the scientist?" Kal asked. I shook my eyes at him, hoping he'd pick up on my hesitance. "What did this Eterra do?"'

"She was into robotics," Brad said. "She also had a background in biology and physics and was using her knowledge to humanize robots. That's not allowed anymore."

"Imagine, humanized robots," I said, flatly.

"They were pretty close to perfecting that when the Reset happened," Brad pointed out. "Let's go somewhere and get some espresso or do you like slushies?"

"Sure. That would be nice." I didn't know what they were, but any distraction would be good.

"Isn't a slushy a really old drink from our great-grandparents' time?" Kal asked.

"And it's back," Jennifer replied.

As we got in Brad's car, I was still shaking.

"Are you cold?" Brad seemed concerned.

"No. It's summer—almost."

"Are you still frightened?"

"I guess I'm not used to people chasing me."

"I hope they arrest that guy," Jennifer said. "There's no telling what he wanted to do with you."

"My sister is used to people being a little calmer around her. Yelling always frightens her."

"It frightens me too," Jennifer said.

"Jennifer, what about your friends?" I asked.

"Oh, I told them that I was going to hang out with the three of you. My brother was telling me about this great guy he met at the park. I guess that was you, Kal."

"We met at the park and threw some hoops together," Kal confirmed.

"He wants you on the high school basketball team next year."

"Maybe."

"Do you play sports?" she asked me.

"I swim."

"She also plays a harp like an angel. Listening to her is like being in heaven."

"That's a sweet thing to say," I responded. "My brother mostly puts me down."

"Brothers do that," Jennifer remarked. "There ought to be a law against them."

"I agree."

"Against what?" Kal asked.

"Brothers," Brad said. "I'm glad I'm not a brother."

"How long have you been playing harp?" Jennifer asked.

"Ever since I was a little girl. It was just one of those things I did."

"There's an orchestra at school," Brad informed me. "My parents checked the high school out before I enrolled."

"You think they'd want me?"

"Want you? They'd feature you."

"Kal, why don't you say nice things like that?" I asked.

"I'm a brother, remember?"

Everyone laughed, including me.

Brad drove us to a lake where we sat on the shore and drank slushies from a stand. I got one that was strawberry flavored. Brad ordered some bread, and we crumbled it into little pieces and threw it to the ducks.

"They're so beautiful," I admired.

"So are you. I bet all the other girls at school will be jealous," Brad said.

"Me? Jennifer is beautiful."

"I guess she is. I've watched her grow up and she's just Jennifer. I like the way you look."

I glanced at my brother and Jennifer. They were laughing together. "My brother seems to really like Jennifer."

"She's a nice girl," he said, looking at me.

"She's very friendly. Everyone I've met here is."

"Here?"

"I mean, since a couple of days ago, when I started meeting more people."

"Were you a hermit before that?"

I laughed off my fear of his figuring things out. "No. I was just more reserved."

"I'm glad you came out of your shell."

Jennifer and Kal came over to us. "I have to get back," Jennifer related. "I have to do some babysitting tonight."

Brad dropped off Jennifer. "It was great meeting you," Kal said.

"Same here."

Brad dropped us off in front of the Drakes' house. He walked me up to the door. "I had a great time."

"So did I."

"Except for getting chased, I bet."

"You were really courageous to hit that guy."

"Protecting my girl."

Kal cleared his throat.

"See you tomorrow." Brad started to lean towards me.

"It was fun," Kal said, sticking his hand between me and Brad for Brad to shake.

Katerina opened the door.

"I hope you had a nice time."

"Wonderful," I replied.

"You have a beautiful daughter."

"Thank you. You keep complimenting me."

"Just telling the truth."

Inside, I asked Kal, "What was that all about?"

"What?"

"You were like a shadow."

"I was mostly with Jennifer. I was hardly a shadow. She's quite a girl. Very, very pretty."

"Jennifer?" Katerina asked.

"Roger's sister. The guy I played basketball with yesterday."

"She's really nice. And she says brothers should be *illegal*," I gloated.

"I'm glad you're making new friends."

"They want Kal to join the school basketball team and me to join the school orchestra."

"I hope you can stay that long."

"My mom said it would take her a long time to recover."

"I didn't think she was hurt that badly."

"She's feeling badly enough that she wants a lot of rest, a lot of alone time."

"Are you okay with that?"

"We don't want to be a burden to her," Kal said.

We went to my room. "If that guy from the museum catches up with us, we're cooked," Kal remarked.

"As long as we stay away from there, we're probably safe."

This time, Steve brought home some mushroom ravioli.

"You have the best food here," I said.

"You seem to like Italian," Katerina responded.

"Would you like Japanese tomorrow?" Steve asked.

"Isn't that where Fukushima hit? Isn't Japan radioactive?"

"Most Japanese food you'll get here isn't from Japan. It's just Japanese style."

"Good. I don't want anything radioactive," I noted. "I don't mean to be rude."

"Stating how you feel isn't rude," Katerina countered.

There was a knock at the door. A woman strode in past Steve. "I'm from Social Services."

"Do you have a warrant? Otherwise, you need to leave," Steve reacted, firmly.

"My mother told me about them," I whispered to Kal. "Before the Reset, they would take kids from good parents and send them overseas to be raped, boys too."

His eyes widened.

"We want to go to our rooms," Kal said.

"We'd like to talk to you," the woman asserted.

"My mother told me never to talk to strangers," I countered.

"I'll show you my ID, so we won't be strangers."

"I don't want to see your ID. I want to go to my room," Kal sharply stated.

"Me, too."

"You need to leave," Steve insisted.

"Is this usual behavior for them? Fear of strangers?"

"They've been socializing a lot. They have friends. I guess they just don't trust adults they don't know," Katerina responded.

"That's good policy," Steve commented. "They are less likely to be whisked away by a stranger. Good day."

"That's what we are checking out. There is no record of Claire Holiday having had children."

CHAPTER 25

"You believe her?" Kal shouted. Before Steve could respond, we went into Kal's room with Eterra and shut the door.

We opened the window and crawled outside. In the backyard, we climbed over the fence with our dog. Once next door, we went out through the neighbor's gate and snuck over to Brad's place.

"Hi. I wasn't expecting to see you so soon," Brad said, seeing me and Eterra as he opened the door.

Kal walked up. "Or you," he said more flatly.

"Can we come in?" Kal asked.

"If we tell you something awful, will you help us?" I hesitantly inquired.

"Son, you didn't finish your dinner," his mom called from another room.

"I'm not really hungry," Brad responded, loudly.

"I didn't see you had company," his mother said, coming to the entry. "I'm Janet, Brad's mother. I saw you at the party last night. You're Steve and Katerina's kids, right?"

I nodded.

"I'm going to take my friends upstairs to my room," Brad informed her.

"I can bring up some dessert."

"Knock."

"If you wish."

Up in Brad's room, I opened the subject. "Can you keep a secret—even if it sounds ridiculous or makes us sound horrible?"

Brad pretended to zip his lips. "I'm pretty sure you aren't mass murderers. Are you going to tell me you're from outer space and are planning an invasion?"

"Try inner space."

"Like the movie?"

"Like *Time Machine*. Except we're not Morlocks. We're not monsters. We're kids."

He sat down. "This is getting interesting."

"At least, he's not running for a gun," Kal observed.

"I'm not going to shoot you."

"My mom is Eterra Stafford Cambridge. That man today recognized me or her and he knew I was her daughter."

"You're not Steve's and Katerina's kids?"

"Steve works at a hospital where Claire Holiday, a nice lady who gave us a ride was taken after we were all in an accident, and he thought she was our mother. She couldn't take care of us, and so Steve and Katerina became like our parents. But now Social Services has realized the woman didn't have any kids and we're in trouble. They might take us away and find out who we really are."

"And then?"

"Social Services sex traffics kids."

"I've heard that. And your mom?"

"My mom may have given her life to help me escape from down there. I hope she's alive, but I don't know."

"Sixteen years ago?"

"No. Less than a week ago. Down there, a lot of kids aren't kids; they're robots. Babies are messy."

"Are you robots?"

He didn't believe us, I didn't think. I kept on. "No, we're humans. My dad was going to kill me and replace me with a robot—except my mom saved me and I learned he wasn't my real father."

"Kind of like when Lawn Moosk, or whatever his name was, wanted to chip and upload everyone's brains?"

"They did that. My mom was useful to them and she was married to the Chairman. So, she stayed a person and killed the replacement robots instead of me, each time I was to have a growth spurt. They called those transitions."

"How about you?" he asked Kal.

"They didn't try to replace me. The servants and most of the children are replaced. A lot of us are groomed for leadership. My dad is Deputy Chairman. But he chopped off my sister's head."

I continued, summarizing how we escaped and how Miss Holiday came to be taking us to meet Selini Andrews.

"The friend of your mom's from the picture?"

"Right. But after the accident, when we were in the hospital, I saw Selini dead in the hallway."

"Are you sure?"

"A name tag was attached to a bed with her body."

"After Steve and Katerina agreed to take us in, we thought we were safe, but now Social Services has figured out that Miss Holiday didn't have any kids," Kal related.

"This story is so wildly unbelievable that's it's got to be true or at least partly true. We all heard that the Elites went underground."

"They'll kill us if they find us, and a couple of days ago we saw a man who looked like his dad," I looked over at Kal.

"Our dad, I think."

"The robot told us my dad wasn't my dad before we got out and he thinks his father is my real father."

"So you're maybe half-brother and sister."

"Correct," Kal replied.

"Social Services is over there right now?"

"And they can't find a birth record on us."

"You might have come to the right source. I'm not saying I believe absolutely everything, but my dad works in Vital Statistics, and I know a backdoor into the records."

I looked at Kal and back at Brad. "Are you saying you can help us?"

"Now, this woman they think is your mother is Claire Holiday?"

"That's right," I replied.

He started typing on his computer. "I see. This is part of it. She was never married. So now it's going to turn out she was married to a Jeff Jackson and they had two children before he died. She had her name changed back, but Jackson is on your birth certificates. However, it was at an out-of-the-way place not too far from here, called Placerville, formerly the seat of El Dorado County. A lot of the records in Placerville were destroyed when everyone moved away after the poisoning—except your birth certificates, which are among the few still available."

I looked at Kal. I had thought Brad would help us get away or hide, but this was much better. "But what about digital ID?"

"You had that below?"

I nodded.

"It was banned right after the Reset. It was used to target anyone questioning the government narratives and was part of why the Reset couldn't be stopped. Non-compliers were starved to death or subjected to government raids."

"Below, nobody questioned what we were taught," I noted.

"Even in the Youth Leadership Program, it was dangerous to question the government."

"I'm printing up a bio on Mrs. Holiday. You were with her when she left the country and returned. I'll slip a copy of the bio and birth records into an envelope and sneak over to Valley Hospital tonight and get it to her. Here is a copy of your birth certificates with a replica of the official seals from that time and a copy of the bio. Memorize and destroy the bio. Your original birth certificates will be available on a search of the Placerville records."

"Do you do this often?" Kal asked.

"Some of my friends like to drink and they need to be older to do so. Unfortunately, the poisoning didn't destroy most public records. So, I sometimes help and make a little money on the side."

"We didn't bring any money with us."

"I'm not asking for any. We're friends. And you don't have to worry about trusting me. I'd get in as much trouble as you if the truth came out."

"I don't know what to say. Thank you," I wanted to throw my arms around him and give him a hug, but I didn't know if that was acceptable for girls and boys.

"If you aren't who you say you are, you have to be pretty scared to come up with a story like that. If you are telling the truth, then you definitely need help."

"Thank you so much," I said.

"Thank you," Kal threw in.

"Now, who is this guy who looked like Kal's dad?"

"His name is Jay Fenton. He's a funeral director. He claims to be the cousin of Kal's dad."

"I'll see what I can find out about him. The important thing is that he doesn't put two and two together like that guy in the science museum. The museum guy wasn't Fenton, was he?"

"I never saw him before," I replied.

"Let's see if we can get back before we're missed," Kal encouraged.

"They'll probably figure it out when they go into your room."

"I locked the door," Kal said.

As we started to return, I saw the lady from Social Services leaving. She and Steve appeared to be arguing. As soon as she left, we snuck back, retracing our steps, climbing over the fence with Eterra and into Kal's window.

Katerina was knocking on the door. "Please come out. We want to help."

Kal came out and handed her our folded-up birth certificates. "I had these in my pocket during the accident and forgot about them. They're the only record we have." She unfolded them and handed them to Steve, who had come up beside her.

"That explains it. Holiday is listed as a maiden name on the certificates. I'll get these to Social Services in the morning and tell them to leave you alone."

Katerina hugged us. "It's going to be alright, kids. I told you we wouldn't let anyone hurt you."

I could feel my heart beating fast, very fast. They had us eat some of the ravioli and then Steve got us some hot chocolate.

Katerina took me into my room and read me a story until I fell asleep. I remembered my mother doing that when I was little. The story Katerina read to me was a fantasy story about a girl who wanted to be loved but believed she was unlovable, only to discover that she had been loved all along.

"I like it here—except I've heard bad things about Social Services."

"Before the poisoning, they used to be involved in trafficking children and doing horrible things to them. I don't know if they do that now, but I didn't like that lady who came to the door," Katerina related.

"Neither did I," I said. "I don't want to talk to her. Not ever."

"With those certificates, you won't have to. We'll see to that."

I said a silent thank you to Brad. I wondered if Robert Horton would have been so kind. I really liked Brad. The *Time Machine* had a story about love. Maybe the way Brad was helping me was a form of love. I knew being around him made me happy.

Later, Kal opened my door and whispered to me. "You awake?"

"I am. Now, do you like Brad?"

"He's great. But he's still not the guy for you."

"Did I say he was?"

"You act so giddy around him."

"I've never had a boyfriend before."

"Boyfriend? All the more reason not to let yourself get carried away with him. He's probably had a lot of girlfriends, and other girls know how to do things to impress guys."

"What kinds of things?"

"I don't know. Maybe what the android girls do. I haven't had any girlfriends."

"So, you're guessing. And I'm not giddy. Just happy."

"You were practically singing his praises all yesterday, today and this evening."

"He saved us, and he saved me earlier today, too. I wonder who that man in the museum was."

"I don't know, but we need to avoid him. He could blow our lives wide open."

"I know. He could expose everything, and if he's tied to the underworld, he could drag us back, and we'd never get to see our new parents or friends again."

"Parents? So, you don't miss your mother anymore?"

"Every night I dream about her. I'd give this all up in a moment to have her here with us."

"If she were here, the others would follow, and we'd soon be dead."

"I know, but she loved me more than anyone. Katerina is wonderful, but she's not Mom. We have a special bond that nobody could ever replace."

"I understand. I miss my mother too."

"Do you believe we'll see our mothers after death? I heard someone talking about that in the hospital."

"Nobody below talks about after death. They talk about living forever."

"They replace parts if they go bad. Most of our leaders are partially robots—even if they aren't fully robots."

***

The next morning at breakfast, I asked Steve, "How often do people die in the hospital?"

"Very rarely. Medicine has changed since the poisoning. People are eating healthier. Doctors now focus on keeping people strong and fit rather than just helping when they are critical. We no longer treat people like science experiments. Cures that were suppressed have been rediscovered. Also, we're no longer going along with the germ theory. That was used to slaughter millions during the plandemics and their aftermath."

"The plandemics? I read something about those at the museum."

"Some very bad people created a virus that wasn't that dangerous, but they used the excuse to kill millions of people with lockdowns, deadly masking, ventilators and very poisonous drugs like Remdesivir and mRNA vaccines. Millions of people who didn't die right away from the mRNA died later from heart attacks, turbo cancer, and other horrible diseases for which we've now gotten cures, but in some cases, the brain damage was permanent. After people showed how compliant they could be, the government kept creating new plandemics."

"That sounds horrible."

"We think it was all a plan for depopulation."

"What happened?"

"Many top doctors wouldn't go along with it, and they saved lives in spite of losing their medical licenses."

"Why did they lose their licenses if they were saving lives?"

"Because the AMA was in the hands of those trying to kill off large sections of the population. That's why it withheld and hid life-saving treatments for things like cancer. They knew how to stop cancer in the 1940s, but for close to a century, they suppressed the knowledge and just let people die."

"That's horrible."

"Part of it was profit. Big pharmaceutical companies made more money off people being sick than well. We've changed the profit structure such that drugs that don't make people well are no longer recommended and any company making them has to pay for the medical care of anyone injured or not helped by those drugs."

"That's great," Kal replied, enthusiastically.

"But they said our Mrs. Andrews died of an overdose."

"I think that is the murder the police are investigating."

"Murder?"

"They think someone poisoned Mrs. Andrews with a plate of drugged spaghetti."

"What happened?"

"I don't know if the kids—" Katerina started to say. She looked uncomfortable with the discussion as if she felt we were too young to hear it.

"We want to know. It's important to us," I assured her.

"There are safe limits on some drugs. From the talk around the hospital, Mrs. Andrews was about to leave her husband and break up their business, leaving him broke. He made her spaghetti and she died later that evening. The ambulance arrived too late to save her."

"Did they arrest the husband?"

"They have circumstantial evidence, but they need more. There are pictures of him doing some bad things with other women at the couple's home."

"Did he kill them?"

"No, but he did bad things with them. He took the family funds out of the bank account right after she was poisoned and died indigent, with him refusing to foot any bills for the funeral. These days, the government picks up the tab when that happens."

"Can't something be done?"

"Normally, he'd be required to reimburse the funeral expenses, but the money is hidden."

"The spaghetti?"

"The husband threw it out and scrubbed the plates."

"You're frightening the children," Katerina complained. "This will give them nightmares. Most people here are good people."

"No. We need to know the truth. She was our mother's friend," I insisted.

"Then, maybe you know her children," Steve surmised.

"We've never met them."

"I'll see if I can get their information so you can talk to them. But don't discuss the theories we were just talking about. It might upset them."

"Of course. We'd just like to speak with them," I replied.

"Even though they're teens, Natalia and Kalandro need to be protected from that kind of talk."

"I'm sorry. Katerina is right. Sometimes I get carried away. I've helped train new doctors and sometimes I forget who my audience is."

"I'm glad you told us. We want information. There is so much we have to learn," Kal said.

"I thought you knew everything," I whispered to him.

"Just more than you," he responded, but this time, I got that Kal was teasing.

In Kal's room, after Steve went to work, I expressed my confusion. "The bio I saw online only mentioned one daughter."

As Kal pulled out his laptop, Katerina knocked to notify us Brad had arrived.

We told Brad what little we knew about Selini Andrews.

"Maybe the husband who killed her was the guy who was chasing you at the museum."

"Maybe he thinks I have evidence and wants to kill me."

"But you don't have any evidence. We didn't even know Selini. Just her name," Kal pointed out.

"Maybe he saw me at the hospital. That's where I saw her body."

"Your father works at vital statistics. Her death certificate should be there, shouldn't it?" Kal asked.

"If it's completed. They may be doing a full autopsy—especially if they think he killed her—and that could take a week."

"I got a phone number for the daughter. Her name is Tarinda."

I took him to my online source. He did a few clicks. "Here's her address."

"Let's go," Kal said. "If you'll drive us, Brad."

"Of course."

"I'll clear it with Mom, or rather, Katerina," I said.

Katerina approved our drive to the lake. We didn't tell her about Tarinda. She gave me and Kal each a hug and offered to make us lunch.

"I'll take them out to eat," Brad offered.

Katerina gave us some lunch money. We thanked her and left.

"She really cares about you. She's better than most real moms."

"I know. I'll have to pay her back someday when we have money," Kal said.

"We'll pay her and Steve back double," I upped Kal.

A little while later, we were at Tarinda's apartment building. She was in a high-rise in downtown Riverhill.

Brad told security that Tarinda was his sister and had been expecting us. The security guard was a female, and she seemed to really like Brad. She called Tarinda at the fake number he gave her. Nobody answered. The guard confirmed the apartment number. Brad continued flirting with her, or at least I thought that was what he was doing. She authorized the elevator to take us up to the fifth floor. "You'll have to wait outside the apartment."

"That's fine. I'm sure my sister will let me in when she returns."

On the fifth floor, I asked, "We wait in the hallway?"

"I've got a master card—not the former credit kind. It opens ninety-nine percent of electronic locks."

"How do I get one of those?" I asked.

"By having me order one for you. These are theoretically illegal. It might not work." But it did. "I got a fake ID for a guy whose dad works for the agency that makes these."

We went inside and waited. Brad went over to the refrigerator. "She's got a lot of junk in here and look at all that alcohol."

"Do drunks hate their mothers?" I asked, recalling the phone call.

"Drunks usually hate everyone. I'm going to order some food to be delivered. We might have a bit of a wait."

He ordered avocado sandwiches.

"My mother told me how delicious avocados tasted, but I was never able to get any below. Is this bread poisoned?"

"Farmers don't use glyphosate anymore, like the corporate farms did before the poisoning. It's healthy bread."

"Good."

"Something is troubling you."

"It's that Tarinda was so mean on the phone."

"Maybe something else was going on. If she's mean again, the heck with her."

"What do we tell her about ourselves?" I asked. I looked at Kal, who had been unusually quiet.

"How about we tell her we came by to offer our condolences about her mother. Your mother was a friend," Kal suggested.

"But what if she recognizes me from my mom's picture?"

"From that many years ago? Laugh it off. Tell her she is delusional. But don't give her your address or anything that could sell you out—in case she is an awful person," Brad advised.

Brad opened a cabinet. "Look at all these old singing and dancing awards. They're from long ago, before I was born."

"I guess she somehow turned into a snob. Too many awards."

The sandwiches arrived, along with the slushies we ordered.

"This avocado sandwich is delicious," I gushed. I looked at Eterra. She had quickly finished her sandwich and looked ready for more.

"Mine too. Your mother told you about these?" Kal asked.

I nodded. "I didn't know they still existed."

"I guess you missed out on a lot down below. What is the tech like?" Brad inquired.

"The computers are easier to operate and less clunky. There isn't any, what you call, hacking. Everyone pretty much does what they are supposed to do. Nobody seems to rebel."

"Sounds like the robots fit right in. So, the other girls were mostly robots?" Brad asked.

"Judging from what they did to my sister, the daughter of the DC, probably most of the kids are robots."

"But they didn't change out the guys in the Youth Leadership Program and my mom let my dad think I'd been replaced."

"Perhaps your fathers were misogynists," Brad speculated.

"You mean guys who hate women?"

"Or think they're superior."

"That would explain the way Dad or Not-Dad treated Mom. It was as if he expected her to cooperate with him at all times—though she was a top scientist." I turned to Kal. "I don't know about the brother/sister thing. I always thought I was an only child."

"Unless I'm your brother."

"Maybe you can tell from a blood test," Brad suggested.

"To see if we have the same blood type?"

"The odds are you do, unless you each have your mothers' blood types, instead of your dad's."

I relaxed on the couch and had almost fallen asleep when the door opened.

"Who let you in?" an angry, stern voice asked.

"I guess I had a key," Brad reacted. "Maybe one of your friends gave it to me."

"I didn't invite you. And what is that disgusting creature?"

"My dog." Eterra came over to me and jumped onto my lap.

"Get her off my couch. Now!"

"She's good company, very polite, and she doesn't put others down," Brad responded.

"We just wanted to offer our condolences about your mother," I explained.

"My mother?"

"We're so sorry about what happened to her," I said.

"You've said it. Now go."

"Dad said he thought she was poisoned," Kal finally spoke.

"It's none of my business."

"Your mother is none of your business?" I asked

"Why should she be? I have my own life."

"You owe your life to your mother, and that's all you can say? She's none of your business." I retorted.

"Is there money coming to me?"

"My dad says there's no money." I was virtually seething. "You don't care about her at all. You're awful!"

She shrugged. "I know where I've seen you before. That friend of hers from the picture."

"Did you know her friend? I've been told I look like the friend, but I don't know her. I'd like to meet her."

"I hear she's dead. You've said your piece."

"You are the coldest person I've met here. Did you take cold lessons?" I asked.

"So I'm a louse, and I'm fine with it."

"You most certainly are a louse," Brad agreed. "My friends' dog is nicer and prettier than you and so are fleas."

She glared at us. I was a bit dismayed, thinking the prettier comment was over the top.

"We were wondering if you had some old papers of your mom's so we could find out more about that friend of hers," Kal threw in.

"If I had old papers of hers, I'd burn them. It looks like you've eaten my food."

"Your food isn't this good. We ordered out," Brad responded as we walked to the door.

"I have things to do, and I don't have time for you. Bye." She looked at Eterra and scrunched her nose.

"Bye," Brad said as we moved into the hallway. She slammed the door in our faces before Kal and I had a chance to return the goodbye.

***

After we left the building, I sadly said, "We didn't learn anything except she's as mean in person as she is on the phone."

"We learned something else," Brad said.

He opened up a phone. "We have her phone book."

"Her phone?" Kal asked.

Brad smiled and nodded. "No surprise. Her mother isn't in here."

"These phones are so funny," I said.

"What are yours like?"

"Ours were three-dimensional. We'd tell the phone who to call and a hologram of the person we were speaking with would pop up."

"I bet the computers were also three-dimensional with images extending out like a holodeck."

"Holodeck? Most screens were holographic. My mother didn't like using three-dimensional software—except when she was demonstrating her results. I don't think she liked people watching her work. There was an observation room."

"That's where I was when my dad chopped off my sister's head. "

"Chanelle was my best friend. Now, I don't have a best friend."

"I'm your friend," Brad said. "And Jennifer likes you. Roger said you were all she talked about last night."

"Me?" I asked.

Brad nodded.

"What about me?" Kal inquired.

"I think he said she mentioned you, too."

"Girls."

"I guess you're only used to robot girls. Real girls think for themselves," I chided.

Kal looked upset. I knew he was thinking of Chanelle. Before we could get to the car, I heard my name. "Natalia."

I turned. It was the man from the museum.

CHAPTER 26

"Get away from me. I don't know you and I don't want to know you."

"But you know your name." The man was tall and slender with light brown and grey hair.

"I recognized your voice. You're the guy who grabbed me at the museum."

"Only to talk to you."

"What do you want with Susie?" Brad asked him.

"Susie?"

"Yeah. Susie's my neighbor. She and I have been friends for a long time."

"You look like someone I used to know."

"This Eterra person? You called me that yesterday. Now, you're calling me another name I never heard of."

"We have to go," Brad announced, taking my arm and pulling me away.

"Wait. Please." The man took out a pen and wrote down a number. "If you want to talk, call me. My name is Robert, Bob."

"I don't know any Eterra or Natalia, and I'm not who you think I am," I responded.

We went down a side street to where Brad had parked. The man didn't follow. "I don't trust him either," Brad said.

"How did he know my name? I was born below. He shouldn't have known my name unless he was down there, too."

"You think he is after you? Maybe he's waiting for you to slip up and admit who you are?"

"I don't know."

"You're not going to call him," Kal strongly advised.

"Of course not."

I tore up the paper and tossed it in a trash can.

"I live right across the street. If someone tries to drag you back, I'll find a way to stop him."

"Thanks, Brad, you're really nice."

I had Brad take us to the hospital to see Miss Holiday. The staff let Eterra accompany us. I heard a nurse say, "Service dog."

Miss Holiday looked more awake and smiled as we entered the room.

"It's good to see you kids. They let you bring in your dog."

"They've classified her as a service dog," I informed her.

Miss Holiday reached out and petted Eterra as my dog put her paws on the bed. "She is certainly making me feel better." Her expression turned to one of seriousness. "That social worker was here. She told me, if I didn't admit you weren't my kids, she'll have me arrested."

"What did you tell her?"

"I didn't have to. Steve walked in and showed her your birth certificates. He told her he'd have *her* arrested if she came by my room or his house again. The only problem is I didn't have any kids in Placerville."

"A friend has connections and he printed those birth certificates up," I whispered.

"A friend?"

"Someone we met at the park. He's a really nice boy."

"You make friends easily."

"Most everyone here is friendly, but there's this scary man who keeps trying to speak with me. I think he may want to hurt me."

She looked concerned. "You should tell the police."

"We can't. For starters, I don't know who he is."

"But he's scary?"

"To me, he is," I said.

"To me, too," Kal added.

"Be careful. You're right. Most people are really nice—except that social worker. She was terrible."

"Did you get the confidential envelope Brad left here last night for you?"

"I meant to open it."

"It has copies of the birth certificates and a short bio. They may assist you if the Social worker comes back."

"Your friend must be very talented or connected."

"Both."

Brad was waiting for us in his car. "How is Miss Holiday doing?"

"Fine. That social worker threatened her, and then Steve threatened the social worker."

"Then, those certificates helped?"

"Did they! You saved our lives." Again, I was so overcome with gratitude, I wanted to hug him, but I worried it wasn't appropriate—even though people tended to hug freely up here.

"When someone saves another person's life, he has to make sure that the person he saved stays safe."

"You're saying we need to let you keep saving us?" I asked.

"Exactly. Consider me your guardian angel."

"Gee. Thank you for being my guardian angel," Kal replied.

Back at home, Katerina had baked an apple pie. It smelled delicious. "Apples. I can't eat apples."

"Oh. I'm sorry. You're allergic?"

"Yes. Allergic."

"I have some cherries. I could make you a cherry pie."

"You do so much for us. Maybe I could help you cook or do something around the house."

"Why don't you join me in the kitchen, and we'll make a cherry pie together."

"Mind if I do some Internet?" Kal asked.

"Go ahead. We can handle this," Katerina replied.

"It's interesting you two are allergic to apples. Toward the start of the poisoning, they injected a high dose of a lethal toxin into the apples that instantly killed thousands. Still, the government insisted the apples were safe. After that, it was found that everything was poisoned to some extent. Most people trusted the government and kept eating apples and other toxic food. The only ones who survived were the people who ate organic fruit, mostly home-grown, but the water and air still weren't safe. So, my family left as well as Steve's. I met him in Venezuela."

"Venezuela?"

"The President, there, had his army block the poisoning. He had Russian missiles to stop the poisoners when they tried to take over."

"Handy. I had heard that Venezuela was a bad place."

"It's an educated place. People there were always having informed discussions. They welcomed anyone from America who needed help. I learned Spanish as a young child."

"I guess most of what I learned about Venezuela was a lie."

"Don't blame your mother. There used to be a lot of propaganda, and honest speech was censored before the Reset. Did she leave the country?"

"I-I think I blocked a lot of stuff out." *Stupid, I should have read the bio.* Brad had said something about leaving the country, but it slipped my mind.

"Maybe I shouldn't have brought it up."

"No. I want to learn about everything."

"So, did they get the poison out of the apples?"

"The poisoned trees were chopped down and new organic apple seeds were imported when the soil and water had been purified and were safe. Apples are now better than ever. It's too bad you and Kal are allergic."

"It is too bad. But I'm looking forward to the cherry pie." I had to be consistent, though now I yearned for a piece of apple pie.

Cooking with Katerina was a blast. We had had food synthesizers and androids, like Sadie, at home in the underground that did all the cooking. A robotic cleaning service did the housework. The cleaning maid came in during the mornings, worked faster than any human and left the house clean in almost no time.

Sadie was always proper and polite and said nice things to me and Mom. But this was so much more enjoyable than letting a computer, prepare the food—even if it was a polite and friendly computer. I wished my mom could experience this. I was a terrible cook, though. I got flour all over me and baking soda in my hair.

Katerina laughed. "Do you plan to eat the food or wear it?"

"I'm sorry. I'm making a mess. I'll clean up your kitchen." I knew she didn't have the robotic maid service. I had seen her do her own house-cleaning.

"It's fine. You're adorable. You've never cooked before, have you?"

"No. But this is so much fun."

"Did you have fun at the lake?"

"The lake is lots of fun. We went to see Miss, or rather, Mom. She said that Steve threw the social worker out of her room." *I have to stop almost giving myself away. Why am I doing that? Is it guilt over my real Mom?* I ached inside at the thought of her on the floor.

"He called and told me about that. If she comes back to the door, I'm not to answer. He also called an attorney who said he'd file a complaint if we heard from her again."

"A complaint?"

"The attorney said the best defense is a good offense."

"I've heard that. My dad used to say that."

"Your dad. Where is he?"

"I don't know. I mean, he died right after I was born." I thought that was what Brad had said.

"Then, how do you know?"

"Mom must have told me."

Another slip-up. I had loved my dad, or the man I thought was my dad, until he was ready to kill me. At least, Steve wasn't going to chop off my head.

"That cousin of Mr. Fenton's: Steve looked into him. Apparently, he vanished around the time of the poisoning. Some thought he may have gone underground to avoid the war that didn't happen. But you saw him alive up here hurting someone?"

"Maybe it was just a bad dream, like after watching a bad movie."

"You were pretty frightened."

"I was. But I guess it seemed as if my dream was coming to life."

"Did Kal have the same dream?"

"Maybe. Perhaps we saw the same movie."

"With all you've been through, it must be tough for you to go to a new place and adjust."

"I like it here. You and Steve are wonderful. And, soon I'll be sixteen."

"That's right. Your birth certificate says June Seventeenth. That's in a few weeks."

"It's no big deal." And it wasn't my real birthday.

"Sixteen is a really big deal. Your brother is sixteen now, isn't he?"

"Yes. What's wrong?"

"I was just thinking that in a couple years, you'll probably go off to college."

"I hadn't thought about it."

"It's better now than when your mother was younger. Back then, they had stopped teaching in the universities and started indoctrinating. Now, they've returned to teaching. Same for the secondary schools. You said you were homeschooled."

I nodded.

"We can fix up some records for you if you want to go to the high school here. You mentioned joining the orchestra."

"That would be fun. Do you think the other kids would like me?"

"You've already made friends. I understand Brad and Roger are pretty popular. Roger's sister is a cheerleader. They'll help you get settled in. But let us know if you have any problems."

"Will that be soon?"

"It will start in August."

"August?"

"Here, the schools run from the middle of August through the start of May."

I heard the door open.

Steve came into the kitchen. "I see you've got a helper today."

"We just put a cherry pie into the oven," she said.

"How long does it take to cook?" I asked.

"About half an hour. Years ago, they used microwaves that cooked very fast."

"But they were unhealthy. A lot of people got sick and didn't know why," Steve pointed out.

"My mother threw ours out the window," Katerina recalled, smiling.

"Smart woman," Steve said.

I went into the living room and froze. In front of me was a miniature killer robot, like the ones shooting at us down below.

CHAPTER 27

I screamed and then realized that was a bad move. Before I could plan a course of action, Kal was out of his room, pounding the robot with a chair.

As he did so, the robot said, "Hi. My name is Robbie. My name is Ro-o-bb-eeeeee." Then it collapsed.

Steve looked at the mess as Kal continued smashing it. "I killed it. I saved you," he said.

"You saved her, but you killed the toy I bought you. You said something about robots, and I thought you'd like this."

"Toy?" Kal asked.

"But it looks like—it looks so real," I said.

"It's fine, honey. Maybe we can put it back together," Katerina responded.

"Don't," I said. "Please don't."

"Okay. No robot," Steve assured us.

"I'm sorry I broke your toy. I thought it was here to attack us," Kal apologized.

"It's only a model," Steve said.

Katerina looked at me.

I was still shaking.

"I guess they're making toys scarier these days."

"I didn't mean to frighten you," Steve put his hand on my shoulder and looked reassuringly into my eyes. "I'd never do anything to hurt you."

"I know. I'm sorry. I didn't know it was a toy."

"You're right. It did look scary. Next time, I'll find something more friendly-looking."

"You don't need to give us presents. You've been so nice. We just like being here with you two."

They both gave me a hug. Kal came over and we had a group hug, my first and it felt great. If I ever had to go back, hugging was what I'd miss most.

"Nice job of protecting your sister," Steve told Kal. "Now we know we can count on you if somebody dangerous ever comes to the door."

"They sold this at a toy store?" Kal asked.

"This is a really old model. Apparently, the original designer was someone named Eterra Lancaster."

I wondered if Lancaster had ever been my mother's name or if it was a different Eterra.

Katerina insisted we have dinner before enjoying the cherry pie. This time we had broccoli and mushrooms smothered in vegetable Bolognese sauce.

"I've never had this before."

"And it's healthy," Katerina said.

"Is the cherry pie unhealthy?"

"It's healthy, but it's dessert, and it's best to have dessert after dinner."

"Oh."

I could see why. The cherry pie was so sweet that I didn't want anything else after eating my two slices.

After dinner, I went with Kal to his room. He had discovered a picture of my mom working on a project. Next to her was Robert, the guy who had been chasing me. It didn't mention his name, but he and my mom were smiling.

"He knew my mom. That's what he wanted to talk to me about. Do you think he's from up here? Or was he also working with my not-dad and did my not-dad send him up from down below?"

"You tore up his name and number. I guess we'll never know."

"My mom really was pretty."

"She looks a lot like you. You are essentially acknowledging you're pretty."

"You think I'm pretty?"

"I didn't say that."

I looked down. *Boys*, I thought.

"Alright, you're pretty. In fact, if you weren't my sister, I'd ask you out on a date."

"You would?"

"But you're my sister and a rat, as far as I can tell."

"A rodent? I read about them at the museum. We don't have rats in the underground. But I used to hear my mom use the term as an insult."

"Jennifer was telling me about a big rat they found in her kitchen. Roger took a broom to it."

"He killed it?"

"I think so. She said it was a mess. Roger threw it out and they haven't had any since."

"Thank you for killing the robot for me."

"No problem. Next time you want me to kill a toy, just tell me."

I laughed. "I thought it was the real thing. Do you think this Robert wants to take us back? Mom didn't tell us to look for Robert, just Selini."

"Maybe Robert was a bad guy and she didn't want us to find him. That's why she didn't mention him."

"He could be nasty, like our dads or our not-dads, chopping off kids' heads," I speculated.

"If we see him again, we shouldn't take any chances. Let's pretend that we don't know anything about Eterra."

"He knows my name."

"Maybe there are other Natalias. Maybe some of them look like you."

"Brad told him my name was Susie. Let's keep it that way if we see him again."

The next morning, Katerina said she wanted to take us somewhere special. She drove us to a parking lot by a field. The area looked familiar.

"There's a really nice history museum near here. It's a bit of a walk but a nice one. They no longer have any roads going directly there. I heard you say you like history museums." She led us over to the place where we had spent the night.

The door was open. There was a policeman there. "Ottis, the owner, died and is buried outside," the officer said.

We didn't say anything.

"That's terrible," Katerina replied.

"We don't know who buried him," he continued.

"What did he die of?" she asked.

"Maybe old age. He was about one hundred and eight or nine."

"Lots of people live older than that now," she responded.

"At least, he wasn't alone when he went. Someone took the time to bury him and put a name plaque over the grave," the officer told her.

"Then you don't expect foul play?"

"There is no sign of violence. Expensive relics and cash were left in the museum."

I looked at Kal.

"Maybe we should go," I said.

"That's not necessary," the officer assured us. "It's a free museum. Look around."

We walked through the museum, looking at the exhibits. I pretended to be seeing it for the first time, as did Kal. Katerina suggested we go outside to look at the river. We went above the stairs, where we had climbed five days before.

Below, standing next to a security robot with a gun aimed in our direction, was Kal's dad. Or was it Mr. Fenton?

CHAPTER 28

Kal pulled me back. "We need to get out of here."

I hadn't realized the officer was behind us. He stepped around and forward to see what was going on but turned to watch us as we grasped Katerina's hands.

"What?" Katerina asked.

"Now!" Kal demanded as we turned to run towards the car.

"Wait, there's Mr. Fenton," she said, apparently not seeing the gun. Maybe she thought the killer robot with a gun was another toy.

"No. Run!" I insisted.

"I guess you folks are in a hurry," the officer said.

"Big hurry," I uttered as we whizzed away, both of us pulling Katerina with us.

"You kids are fast," she remarked.

She pulled out her key. The car wouldn't start at first. "Hurry," I urged. I heard what sounded like a couple of gunshots in the background and then an explosion. That's when the car started and we were out of there.

"What's going on?" she asked.

"We'll tell you when we're closer to home."

She didn't stop until the car was in the driveway.

"Could you put it in the garage?" Kal suggested.

"What's going on?" she asked as she pulled into the garage.

"Let's get into the house and close the garage door," Kal advised.

Inside, she asked, "Are you still afraid of Mr. Fenton?"

"I don't think that was Mr. Fenton. I think it was Mr. Denton."

"The guy you dreamed was an ax murderer."

"He is a murderer. He killed Chanelle," I said.

"Who is Chanelle?"

"She was a robot," I explained.

She turned to Kal. "Like the robot you killed last night."

"No. She was a human robot, and he killed her."

"Is this from a movie?"

"It's real life, and that man is very dangerous. If he finds us, he'll kill us," Kal explained.

"Why?"

"Because he wants to turn me into a robot," I expounded. "And that thing with him was a security robot, not a toy. I know it sounds crazy, but it's true. You said you'd protect us, but to do that, you need to believe us."

"Katerina, call Steve, and without sounding suspicious, find out if he knows where Fenton's been today?" Kal encouraged.

Before she could do so, Steve called and Katerina put her phone on speaker. Katerina asked if he had been in contact with Jay.

"He's been at the mortuary all day. They've had several funerals today. I hope you didn't go by the history museum, like you planned?"

"Why?"

"A police officer was shot there today and there was an explosion. So far, they haven't found any witnesses. Apparently, the officer shot something that exploded before he died. A large projectile went through him. They're still looking for it. An unidentified man was found under the rubble. They had to get protective gear to dig him out. There was a lot of radiation in the area."

"Is he alive?"

"The officer isn't. I don't know about the other man. I heard he was in critical condition at University Hospital."

After the call, she sat back on the couch, looking confused.

"Radiation? Why would they bring radiation up here?" I asked Kal. "Your—I mean Mr. Denton—wouldn't want to be exposed to radiation."

"They were planning a small number of new security robots with radioactive cores—for remote exploration, but I didn't think they had built them yet. That's what we were told in the Youth Leadership Program."

"And the officer hit the right point on the security robot to make it explode," I guessed.

"Of course, he could have brought a device to spread radiation spikes in case we had made it up here so he could discredit claims of no war. The radiation would prove us liars."

Katerina looked at us. "Alright. I'm ready to listen."

"Do you think he saw us?" I asked Kal.

"No. I think we pulled back before he spotted us, but I think he may have tracked us to the museum."

"You were there before?" Katerina asked.

"We're the ones who buried Ottis. We found him dead, and felt he needed a burial."

"And your mother?"

"She was driving us the next day when she got into the accident," I explained, avoiding the subject of parentage.

Katerina looked like she was taking it all in. But I wasn't sure if she believed us or thought we were just fanciful.

I called Brad as Katerina was trying to digest the information. He came over. We told him what had happened.

"Katerina, you can't tell anyone what you saw today," he told her.

"Nobody would believe me. Does your mom know about Mr. Denton and the nuclear robot?"

"We haven't told her yet," Kal replied

"And anyone we tell will be in danger," I explained.

"They're right, Mrs. Drake." Brad concurred. "If anyone asks, you spent the day at the lake. You didn't go near the museum. The news said the officer was dead, and there were no witnesses."

"He was a really nice man," I lamented, feeling awful about what had happened to the officer.

"This Mr. Denton must be a psychopath," Katerina said. "If he survives, he should be tried for murder."

"There are more where he came from," I added. "That's why we can't let anyone know we were there today."

"He was after you?"

"We think so," Kal said.

Leaving Katrina on the couch, we went into Kal's room. "If they tracked you to the museum, do you think they'll track you further?" Brad asked.

"How were they able to track us?" I asked Kal.

"The locater," Kal murmured.

"Mom pulled my bracelet off and threw it out. All my monitoring devices were in there."

"You got a removable one?" Kal pulled up his slack leg. He pointed to an area above his ankle. "I understand they implant them here. I can feel it right against the skin."

"I never had one of those," I said.

Kal felt my ankle. After also feeling my wrist, he related, "Some have it here. You're right. She didn't chip you. Your mother designed the implants. She must have been preparing for your escape for a long time."

"Does yours have a microphone?"

"Only the robots had those."

We followed Kal into the bathroom, where he found some pointed scissors in a drawer. He felt around the implant area and then stabbed himself next to it.

"Kal!" I silenced my scream as blood spurted out.

"I guess you're not a robot," Brad responded to the blood.

"They have blood, too, but not real blood." Kal grimaced as he pulled out something that looked like a pinhead.

"Give that to me," Brad said. "I'll drive it miles in the wrong direction and then destroy it."

Brad and I fixed up Kal's leg with some supplies from the cabinet.

As Brad left, I asked Kal, "Do you think that will do it?"

"Let's hope so. And Sis, please control the screams. Just because you're up here and can have emotions, doesn't mean you have to overdo them."

"I've never been able to control them the way my mom wanted me to. I'm lucky they didn't change me out before."

Katerina was still sitting silently on the couch as we returned to her.

"I should tell Steve," she told us.

"It will be easier for him to deny everything if he doesn't know anything," Kal pointed out.

"But I told him we were going to the museum."

"You changed your mind," he suggested.

"I've never lied to Steve."

"It will be safer for you and for him," Kal advised her.

"I'll wait to tell him and think about it for a while."

"We love you and Steve, and we don't want to get you into trouble. If you want us to leave, we will," I said.

"No. If you are in danger, I just need to know how to protect you."

"The best way to keep us safe is to let things stay the same as they were before we went to the museum," Kal advised.

"I'll make dinner tonight. Just tell me how," I said.

"I'll help you," she offered.

"One second," I said, as Kal went into the bedroom. I had to speak with him. "Your father might die."

"He killed my sister, and I'm sure he would kill both of us if he caught us. Better him than us."

"Even though my father would have killed me, it would hurt to see him dead. I know you're angry at him, but is this how you really feel?"

"Yes." He said it resolutely, but I didn't believe him.

"If you need to talk, I'm here." I gave Kal a hug. "Remember, I might be your sister and we're both strangers in a strange land." I smiled, recalling a reference to a book with that title I had seen in the history museum.

I joined Katerina in making the dinner. About the time we finished, Steve was home.

Katerina was visibly still shaken but seemed to be trying to act peaceful.

"Is everything alright?"

"We're not the easiest kids to live with, but Katerina is wonderful," Kal said.

"She is," I added and then hugged her. "I'm sorry I gave you such a rough time earlier."

"It was me. I'm just not used to teenagers."

"What happened?"

"It's not important. They were telling some stories, like tall tales and they frightened me."

"Imagination is good. I guess you may have to tone down the stories around Katerina."

"We learned that."

––––––––

The next morning, Katerina looked exhausted.

"You didn't sleep?" I asked her.

"I kept thinking about yesterday. Maybe you were mistaken about what you saw and what he was doing there."

"How often do you see exploding robots?"

"We've banned androids. There was too much talk before the poisoning about uploading people's brains. Those of us who survived wanted to go a different direction that was more people-oriented."

"Wise move. What about the toys?"

"Those are toys, programmed to say and do cute things. But where do these other robots come from?"

"Below. From the people who left."

"And how do you know this?" It was as if she had turned out

much of the conversation she had heard, or maybe she was too deep in confusion to understand what we were talking about.

"If we told you, you and Steve would be in more danger. We've already put you in too much danger."

"I'm not worried about danger to me."

I hugged her. But I sensed she was worried about Steve.

"If this is real, are others here?"

"Maybe. That's why nobody can know we're here. If it turns out we're putting you in danger, we should leave."

"I'm not going to let you two kids brave danger on your own. It's our job as parents or even foster parents to protect you. You are the future."

"My brother's sixteen and I'm almost sixteen."

The doorbell rang. It was Brad. We went into Kal's room.

"Roger and Jennifer are at my place."

"You didn't tell them."

"No. But I think we can trust them. If we're going to protect you, we need a team of lookouts and researchers."

"I don't know," Kal said. "I barely know them."

"I've known them for years. They are good at keeping secrets and being there when someone needs them."

"Roger wants to kill anything from underneath," Kal reminded him.

"Exactly. Which is why he'll want to protect you from the under-world killers."

"But we're from down below," I pointed out.

"You're teens. You didn't create the poisoning. You escaped from those who did. It's sort of, 'The enemy of my enemy is my—'"

"'Enemy.' I watched a *Dick Tracy* movie last night and that's what he said," I noted.

"That was a movie. Usually, the sentence ends with the word 'friend.' Roger and Jennifer like you."

"You don't think they'll try to kill us?"

"What if we float a theory and see what their reaction is? If they want to go out and kill the hypothetical kids, we won't tell them."

"I like it," I said.

"I'm not so sure," Kal fretted. 'It's agreed that if they say anything to indicate they hate the kids in the hypo, we don't tell them?"

"Deal."

***

"What's this all about?" Roger asked, as we entered Brad's room. "Oh. Hi, Kal. Want to shoot some hoops?"

"Sure."

"And maybe we can go swimming," Jennifer addressed me.

"Better than shooting hoops," I replied.

"That's your opinion," Roger contended.

"But first, I want to tell you about this story I invented as a backdrop for a video game," Brad informed them.

"I'm listening," Roger said.

"These really bad people went underground, but they don't look like Morlocks. They look like ordinary people, and they replace anything that breaks with mechanical parts that look real."

"I see."

"But they are evil and they don't like kids. So, they have robot kids, and they kill them off each time they are supposed to age."

"That's ridiculous. How do they perpetuate the species?"

"Certain ones are allowed to remain real kids, like future male leaders and some of the females. Two human teens escape to avoid being turned into robots, and the bad guys will kill them if they find them—even if it means coming above ground to do so. The goal of the game is to save the kids."

"This is really cool. I want to play," Jennifer enthused.

"I'm in, too," Roger stated.

"What do you think the first step should be to save the kids?" Brad asked.

"Get them a human army," Roger suggested.

"But in this world, kids don't carry around AR-15s or cannons. They have to find other ways and they have to worry about anyone betraying them. Who can they trust?"

"How old are they?"

"Fifteen, sixteen," he said.

"Fifteen's old enough for a license. That means they can drive cars into the bad guys. They can also do electrical experiments on them."

"The bad guys also have killer robots."

"You came up with this yourself?" Jennifer asked. "You're more creative than I realized."

"I had some help." He looked at Kal and me.

"You dreamed this up?"

"So are the teens good or bad?" I asked.

"Good, if they are escaping the people below," Roger said.

"I told you he'd be cool."

"With the game?"

"It's not a game," Kal confessed, glancing at me for reassurance.

Roger started laughing. "That's a good one." He looked at us. "You aren't laughing."

"That guy at the museum," Jennifer interjected. "Does he have anything to do with this? The one that chased you?"

"He knew who I was. I don't know how. Maybe he was Selini's husband and he murdered her and now he wants to kill me."

"Selini?" Roger asked.

"A friend of my mother's."

"A friend of Mrs. Drake's?"

"My real mother is Eterra Stafford Cambridge."

"You're the daughter of Eterra Stafford?" Jennifer asked. "She's a legend."

"And you?" Roger looked at Kal.

"My dad was Jason Denton, but I think he was also Natalia's dad. Before we left, we found out her dad was not her dad, and there had been a rumor about her mother and my dad."

"So, your dad was a faithless jerk?" Jennifer asked.

"He killed my sister. My other sister. He chopped off her head. But she was a robot, then."

"Was she born a robot?"

"I don't think so," I said. "She used to be a lot different. I think at some point, she was replaced by a robot. My mother built the robots, but I don't think she killed anyone. She pretended I was a robot but told me I was real before she had a double of herself help me escape."

"Do you believe us?" Kal asked.

"The whole thing is absolutely insane and totally unbelievable, which means nobody in their right mind would make it up," Roger remarked.

I looked at Brad, who had stated almost the same thing.

"But what if you think you're human and you really are robots?" Roger went on.

"Then they wouldn't be trying to kill us," Kal replied. "They told us you guys had been nuked and there was nothing alive up here."

"Surprise," Jennifer glowered. "So, we have superheroes for friends —unless this is a belated April Fools' joke."

"It's not April," I noted, feeling confused. "We aren't superheroes. We're just ordinary kids."

"Who needs us to help protect them from the underground creatures," Brad related.

"Yesterday, we were at the history museum by the river," Kal said.

"When that explosion happened and the officer was killed?" Jennifer asked.

"My dad killed him, I think," Kal said. "He was accompanied by a security robot with a gun aimed at the top of the cliff when we looked down. We moved back and the officer moved forward. We didn't see the actual shooting. I gather either my father or the robot shot the officer and the officer shot back, blowing up the robot who was with my dad. My dad was the one they dug out of the rubble."

"Isn't he in critical condition?" Jennifer asked. "Your father."

"He can stay that way. He killed my other sister."

"Chanelle was my best friend. I didn't realize she was a robot until after his dad chopped off her head and my mom pushed me out of the room. Then I saw her later, and she was all different."

Jennifer cringed. "You saw it. How awful. Even if she was a robot."

"We both saw it," Kal replied.

"Did she spark?" Roger asked.

"Most androids have parts that emulate human parts. The security robots and special project robots are built differently," I explained.

"So how do we know you aren't robots?" Roger asked.

"I'm too emotional," I said. "My mother kept telling me to hide my emotions. I thought it was because emotions were disapproved of. And Kal was arrogant and angry all the time."

"Wasn't I nice, sometimes?"

"Not that I can recall."

"How about when you turned three and I gave you a birthday present?"

"What present?

"The cricket. It was the only one I ever saw down below."

"I thought you gave it to me because you wanted to terrorize me."

"You had told Chanelle you wished you had a pet. I thought it could be your pet. You screamed, and your dad or the guy you thought was your dad squashed it."

"I'm sorry. I didn't mean to freak out. I thought it would eat me."

"Crickets do look scary," Jennifer said. "So, if they find you?"

"I was about to be killed when we escaped. The exit was blown up during the escape and I didn't think we'd be followed."

"My dad and that robot got out anyway," Kal pointed out.

"The explosion caved in the whole ground around the exit. How did he get through?" I queried.

"Maybe there was another exit or the robots dug out the area."

"Of course, we'll help," Jennifer said. "This is the most exciting thing that's ever happened to me."

"Eterra. You named your dog after your mom," Brad noted.

"I loved my mom. Last time I saw her, she was lying on the floor after the lab exploded before her double took me away. I don't know if she's alive. The double said if I went back, they'd kill us both."

"You say your mother had a double?"

"An android she created for the purpose of rescuing me."

"What caused the explosion when you left?" Brad asked.

"I don't know. I think my mom caused the one in the lab and mom's double may have set the explosion at the exit to save us. I'm pretty sure the double blew herself up in getting us out."

"And you?" Roger asked Kal.

"Would you stick around after you saw your father chop off your sister's head?"

Jennifer grabbed her throat.

"If they try to invade here, whose side are you on?" Roger asked.

"Not theirs," Kal definitively stated.

"But if my mother's alive, I want to save her. She couldn't have been happy there. She lied to them about me and protected me, and she had to watch everything she said because they were watching."

Roger, Jennifer and Brad each put out their right hand and stacked them one on top of each other. Kal and I put ours on the pile.

"From now on, our first priority is to protect each other and to stop any invasion from the underground," Roger declared.

"Agreed," Brad said.

The rest of us repeated, 'Agreed.'"

As Brad opened the door for Kal and Roger to go to the park, Kal closed it quickly.

"What is it?" Jennifer asked.

"The social worker!"

CHAPTER 29

We quickly explained the situation to Jennifer and Roger.

"I'll handle this," Jennifer said. She called Roger's phone. He answered and put it on speaker. Jennifer put her phone in her pocket, allowing us to listen as she walked across the street. We watched through Brad's bedroom window.

She went right up to the woman. "You don't look like you belong in this neighborhood."

"I'm working."

"It doesn't look like anyone is home. Are you working as a burglar?"

"You've got quite a mouth on you for a little girl."

"And you do a lot of talking for a burglar."

"I'm not a burglar."

"Are you sure? Because most people wait until someone is home before they hang around their house."

"Someone is inside."

"If I saw a burglar outside, I wouldn't open the door either. I should probably call the police and tell them that you are trying to break into a house in the neighborhood."

"I'm not trying to break into the house."

"Then why don't you leave until someone invites you to come in?"

"Did these people take you in, too? Do you live here?"

"No. I don't live here, but have you ever heard of a neighborhood watch committee?"

"There isn't much need for those in this area."

"With burglars casing places, there so is a need. Now, I'm going to leave and call the police. You can explain to the police what you are doing." Jennifer walked off down the street.

The social worker looked around, rang the bell again and then left.

When Jennifer returned, we rushed downstairs and everyone high-fived her. "Chanelle and I used to do that," I said. "After she was replaced, she said it was childish."

"Jennifer, who was that you were talking to?" Brad's mother asked coming out of the kitchen. "I saw you out of the window."

"A very mean woman. I think she's a kidnapper who tries to pick up kids."

"Stay away from her. I'll notify the neighbors to be on the lookout for that woman."

"Her license plate is V109UTID and she drives a white Razor VIII."

"How very observant. Thank you, Jennifer."

After Brad's mother left, Brad asked me. "Now, did your mother have any other friends besides her dead friend?"

"She didn't mention any to me. In fact, she told me to go to Selini Andrews in a lullaby, maybe so I wouldn't ask about her in front of my dad or my not-dad."

Roger and Kal went off to the park while Jennifer, Brad and I swam in his pool.

"You're pretty good," Jennifer complimented me. "When school starts, do you plan to try out for the swim team?"

"I hadn't thought about it. I guess I might as well. I'll be trying out for the orchestra."

"When Miss Holiday recovers, will you have to leave with her?" Brad asked.

"I don't think so. I don't think she wants kids. She likes kids but not to live with her."

"Good. Then you can stay with the Drakes."

"I hope so."

"Your dad's back," Brad's mother told us.

We got out of the pool and changed back into our street clothes. On the way out, we thanked Brad again.

"I brought you a present you might like better than the robot." He pulled out some AP Calculus and Physics books that had practice exams at the end. "If you study these, you might score high enough to get into the college of your choice. Colleges used to base admission on something called a SAT I. They've eliminated that and now they base admissions on grades and AP scores."

Kal glanced through the physics book and I looked at the problems in the calculus book. I went down each page telling Steve the answers until he told me to stop. "Don't you need a pencil and paper?"

"Why?"

"Because most kids need a pencil and paper to figure out the answers."

"But, if I know the answer, do I still need one?"

"You're very gifted."

"Not really. I always thought I was a little slow." My mom had insisted I study extra hard, probably so nobody would notice I wasn't AI.

"More like a mastermind."

"Did I do something wrong?"

"No. You've been getting them all of them correct."

Kal went to the back of the physics book and started taking the test.

"It's easier if you study the materials first."

"Don't need to. These are fun questions."

I turned to the practice test at the end of the Calculus book and started filling in the answers.

When I finished it in about ten minutes, I gave Steve a hug. "Thank you."

He looked puzzled. We went into our rooms and began researching colleges. Apparently, after the poisoning, Harvard, the university my not-dad attended, was burned to the ground. The same happened to Yale and Stanford. My mom's Massachusetts Institute of Technology was still there.

As we were looking at the information, Steve opened the door. "You two really are geniuses. Not only did you finish in probably the shortest time on record, but you got one hundred percent without even looking at any of the instructions and without any scratch paper for calculations. I bet you could get scholarships to any university you want."

"We like it here."

"I like having you here. You can pick a local university." He changed the subject. "You are probably wondering why I'm working so many days. Long ago, before you were born, they were removing licenses from good doctors while rewarding those who took bribes and did bad things to their patients. After the poisoning, we remedied the situation, but doctors who cared enough to do research and use the safest methods to preserve lives were in higher demand. There is a lot of need for doctors now. I often donate my free time to doing research at the hospital and reviewing data. If you want, I can take more time off."

"You don't have to do that for us," I said. "I like that you are a good doctor. I think Katerina misses you during the daytime, though."

"I'll talk to her. I can cut my back my days this month, and maybe I can put in for vacation and spend more time at home next month."

"I think she'd like that."

He closed the door.

"Why did you say that?" Kal asked.

"Just a feeling. Katerina seems lonely, and I think she wants to feel needed. It would make her feel better if she saw more of Steve."

"Did you ever make that suggestion to your not-father?"

"No. Mom was busy with her work. I got that working made her feel important."

"Killing kids?"

"Programming the various groups of robots and working on artificial organs for humans."

There was a knock at the front door. We peered out from Kal's bedroom door towards the living room. When Steve answered it, Mr. Fenton came in.

"My cousin is here," he said.

CHAPTER 30

"Denton?" I asked, coming into the living room and trying to stay calm.

"They said a guy they brought into University Hospital yesterday is my cousin."

"Is he okay?" Steve asked.

"Far from it. He's in isolation in a coma."

"I'm sorry," Steve said.

"I thought he was underground or else dead."

"He must have been up here all along. I suspect all those underground people are dead. How long could they live down there?" Steve asked.

Katerina came in from the kitchen and dropped the plate of macaroni she was carrying. "I'm sorry. I don't know what's gotten into me today."

"I'll help clean up," I said.

"You kids knew he was alive, didn't you?" Fenton asked.

"Us? No. We just saw a picture of him somewhere and thought you were him."

"You said more than that."

"Bad dream. After we saw that picture, each of us had a nightmare."

"These kids could be psychic. You ought to have that checked out," Fenton said. "They may be indigo kids."

"Indigo kids?" I asked.

"Very advanced," Steve replied.

He escorted Fenton to the door. After Fenton left, Steve turned back to Katerina.

"All right, what is going on?"

I looked at Katerina and I knew she was going to break.

"We were at the museum yesterday, and Fenton's look-alike was there with a robot. We left before the shooting and explosion but we heard the sound when we got to the car.

"Did you tell the police?"

"No. The children were afraid, and we came home."

"Katerina wanted to say something to you, but we begged her not to tell anyone," I explained. "After those dreams, we were afraid."

"We should call somebody."

"We left the scene and somebody died," Katerina fretted. "I knew we shouldn't have left, but it was awful."

"It will be okay. I guess we'll just let it go—unless someone else saw you there."

"Nobody else was there," I said.

"You can't let kids get you to do something wrong," Steve told Katerina. "Kal and Natalia, I know you were afraid, but it's our duty to call the police when something like that happens. We already have a social worker breathing down our necks. She's claiming I'm violent for throwing her out of your mother's hospital room. As it is, I think the authorities have figured out who shot who at the museum."

We nodded. "I'm sorry," I told him.

"You all relax. I'll make a fresh dinner tonight," Steve offered.

"Thank you. I'm sorry about the dinner," Katerina said.

"No problem."

Katerina turned to us. "I'm sorry," she whispered.

"It's alright," I assured her. "At least, you didn't tell him the rest."

"He wouldn't have believed it."

I thought about how Roger and Brad had said it was all unbelievable.

"We don't want to cause trouble for you and Steve."

"I'm not going to tell him about you being at the museum before, but I'm not going to lie to him again."

"Of course," I said.

———

The next morning, Roger, Jennifer and Brad took us back to the science museum. We wanted to find out as much information as we could about my mother.

I was staring at the picture when somebody behind me cried. I turned to see a face I recognized, though it was older than the picture. "Selini Andrews!"

CHAPTER 31

"You're alive?"

She looked at herself. "I hope so."

"But I saw a dead woman in the hospital with the name S. Andrews attached to her."

"Did you see her face?" Brad asked me.

"It was covered with a sheet."

"Was that Susan Andrews?" Selini inquired.

"I guess."

"I heard about her. She was my former husband's sister-in-law. I bet her husband did kill her. Violence runs in that family."

"Did you know her?"

"I never met her. She married Marty after I divorced Mack, my ex."

Shortly afterwards, we were all in the museum cafeteria having lunch. "Your mother and I were best friends for as long as I could remember. She was so sharp and so capable."

"What happened?"

"That awful man, Stan Cambridge, insisted she join a robotics team because of her talent. She refused and he threatened her with something. Next, I knew she was gone and the poisoning happened. I didn't know if he killed her or if she was safe, but I knew she wouldn't have gone with him willingly. I came to believe she had refused him, and he had killed her. But she lived and had you."

"Stan Cambridge was married to my mom. He is the Chairman of the Western Region down below. He was my father, or I thought he was."

"I'm sorry. I didn't realize you were raised by him."

"You're right. He is an awful person. I didn't realize how awful until just before we left. Do I really look like her?"

"So much. The resemblance is uncanny. Is she alive, well?"

"Last I saw her, she was lying on the floor after the lab explosion. I never saw her again. I was taken above and told we'd both die if I went back."

"They had replaced the workers and most of the kids with robots to serve the Elites," Kal said.

"And we think they're looking for us. Mom created a double for me and Mom's double blew up herself and the exit when we escaped, but we saw Kal's father the other day. He was following our path and he had a killer robot with him."

"I was the one with the tracker. They might not know about you," Kal said. "Unless my dad saw you."

"Then you are in danger?"

"A policeman shot the robot and it exploded. My dad is in a coma," Kal said.

"Are you okay?" she asked Kal.

"Sure. My dad chopped off my sister's head. I don't like him."

I shuddered as Kal said that. I was starting to wonder if he kept repeating it so he would keep hating his dad. My dad or my not-dad was going to kill me and still a part of me loved him.

"We met Tarinda," Brad said.

"Oh!"

"She's mean," I noted and then wished I had bitten my tongue.

Selini'a expression turned from happy and excited to sad. "She may have been having a bad day."

"That's not it. I don't mean to hurt you, but she's the meanest person I've met here. She's even meaner than Kal used to be."

"I'm sorry. I thought you were a robot, like Chanelle."

"Robot abuser," Jennifer teased.

"Why do you let Tarinda treat you so badly?" Kal asked.

Selini looked like she was going to cry. "I shouldn't talk about it."

"Kal, maybe this is a bad time," I warned.

"That's not it. I don't know why she is the way she is," Selini lamented.

"I'm sorry," I said. "We've been trying to understand what people are like up here."

"She's unhappy about her childhood. It was rough. Her father beat me, especially when I would demand things for Tarinda. She didn't like watching."

"It sounds like you were the one who had it rough," Jennifer said.

"I shouldn't talk badly about my daughter. She's a good girl."

"The cat's out of the bag," Brad said. "That's an expression my mom uses. We've seen Tarinda and she is not a nice person."

"In fact, she is downright cruel—especially towards you," Kal added.

"Sometimes, it hurts, but I don't dare tell her how much her words and actions—"

"Hurt you," I finished. "She has everything I'd love to have back, particularly a caring mother, and yet she's awful."

"Tarinda feels I shouldn't have given birth to her while I was married to her father, but he didn't become violent with me until I was pregnant with her. I loved her so much. I would have done anything to keep her safe and happy, and I made that my number one goal while she allowed me in her life. She's angry she had to grow up under those oppressive circumstances."

"Oppressive? Does she have any idea what the rest of us have been through? She was never in danger of being killed by her father and replaced with a robot. She's got a mom who is alive and really nice. Does she care about anything but herself?" I realized I was projecting myself onto Tarinda, wishing I had my mom back.

Tears started to fall down Selini's cheeks.

"I shouldn't have gone on like that. I'm sorry I upset you," I said. Once again, I had spoken without thinking.

"You didn't. She was sweet when she was little."

Jennifer chimed in. "I bet you were one of those moms who didn't let her fail at anything. You let her dictate your schedule and decide what was important for both of you, working everything around meeting her needs, and treated her like a queen."

"How do you know?'

"My mom did the same. Except I really do love her. If she needs me now or in a hundred years, I'll be there. I have entitled friends who are a lot like your daughter, not caring how much their mothers do for them. They feel they deserve more and blame their mothers for their own shortcomings."

"I've spoken to other women who have been abused. Watching abuse does have an impact on kids," Selini related.

"My dad respects my mother. That may be why Roger and I still love our mom." Jennifer smiled, almost looking wistful. "Mom even got us trophies when we lost competitions and made us think we won."

"I did that too."

"Are you up to adopting a son?" Brad asked.

"If the judges had been neutral, she'd have won on her own."

"And what else? Did you keep her from getting into trouble when she messed up?" Jennifer asked.

"That's a mother's job. Didn't yours?"

"She did, but we didn't turn on her. We really loved her and wanted to please her. She always protected us if we let her. It wasn't as if we committed any crimes or got into any car accidents."

Selini looked down.

"Car accidents?" I asked.

"I didn't want them to go on her record. I switched seats with her to make it look like I was the one driving. It's my fault she never learned to take responsibility for her mistakes."

"And she blames everyone else, including you, for anything that has gone wrong in her life," Jennifer surmised. "I have friends who rag on moms who do everything for them, and I don't understand their animosity."

"Was the difference your father being a good guy?" I asked Jennifer.

"That and we finally convinced my mom to let us fail," Roger said.

"Roger, I was the one who convinced her to let us fail."

"That was really rotten of you, Sis."

"Why did you want to fail?" Selini asked them.

"Because I wanted to know what it felt like and how to deal with it. I knew I'd grow up and my mom wouldn't be able to cover for me forever," Jennifer replied.

"I really blew it."

"You did it out of love," I told Selini. "How were you to know she'd turn on you? My mom did her best, too and I would do anything to have her back. My father turned out to be really horrible and it didn't make me love her less."

"Your father?"

"I don't like to think of him as my dad anymore. Besides, her double said he wasn't my dad. If my mom is dead, it's my dad or sort of dad who is responsible for it."

"What you've been through. I can't imagine any child having to live through that."

"It helps that I found you. Now I know why my mother wanted me to meet you, given what good friends you were."

"Best friends. I am so glad she survived and had you. I hope she is still okay."

"When it's safe, I want to rescue her. Even with the wretched conditions under which we lived, we made each other happy. I could tell she didn't like her life. She said she had a special friend she missed. But she never mentioned who. She sang me a lullaby, telling me to find you."

"It's funny. We both married monsters. I hid how bad I had it, and I didn't know she would wind up going through an unhappy marriage of her own. I know she would be proud of how you turned out."

"I didn't realize Dad was a monster until he almost killed me. But I know she was afraid to say anything negative or explain things to me.

We were being monitored. I am so glad you survived the Reset. You escaped the poisoning by—"

"Bottled water. Filtered air. Food I grew myself. I also moved away when it started getting bad. It's a long story. I had Tarinda and a husband and I focused on making sure they were safe."

"I read a little about it in the history museum, and some nice people told me more. What about the apples?"

"In the scientific community, we knew they'd been vaccinating some food and most of us avoided that. When they stepped up their plan, they poisoned the apples with a high dosage of ModRNA or Modified RNA, inclusive of the metal particles that interacted with 5, 6 and 7g. The people who ate them and didn't die off immediately were remotely controlled to kill themselves and others. That was just the start of the mass poisoning, though they'd been doing it for years in smaller ways: chemtrails, fluoride, genetically-modified organisms, pesticides and herbicides. To survive, I and others had to leave the country. Enough awake non-compliant scientists and doctors survived the Reset that, when we returned, we were able to restore the environment in much of the country and some other places that had gone along with the WEF agenda."

"World Economic Forum?"

"They openly spoke of their plan for depopulation and turning humans into robots, but most people thought repeating their exact words was a conspiracy theorist thing. The sleeping masses died."

"If your daughter would only open her mind to learning of all you went through to protect her," I said.

"She used to have an open mind. Some of it is that she's acquired some close-minded friends. She now rejects anything I say, looks for the worst possible interpretation and blindly believes everything her friends tell her. I don't know how to break through that."

"I'm sorry. It's terrible she treats you that way."

"If I treated my mother that way, my dad would break his own rule about not spanking me," Brad said.

"She's a bit old for that."

I hugged Selini and she hugged me back. "You're not my mother, but being around you brings her back."

She hugged me again. "If what you tell me is true, it may be dangerous for you to hang around me. My relationship to your mom is well known. They might try to use me to find you."

"I realize that. But I want to learn so much more about my mother."

"I will be on the lookout for anyone coming up from below. In the meantime, will you all promise to protect Eterra's daughter?"

"With our lives and fortunes," Brad said.

"You sound like the three musketeers," Selini commented. "If you need me for anything, here is my phone number." She wrote it down.

When we left the museum, I said, "I hope I didn't put her in any danger."

"I think she was worried about the reverse. If you knew to find her, then others looking for you might know to find her to locate you, " Brad pointed out.

We picked up my dog and Brad drove us over to the lake. I was playing catch with Eterra when a voice said, "You named your dog after your mother?"

CHAPTER 32

It was that man again. I ran.

He called, "Please. Just let me talk to you." As he continued forward, Jennifer tripped him and we ran to Brad's car. Eterra ran after us and jumped onto my lap.

"Who was that guy?" Jennifer asked.

"The one who keeps showing up. Now he's at the lake. Eventually, he'll find us," I worried.

"And we'll be ready for him," Brad assured me.

On the way home, Jennifer asked, "Who do you think he is?"

"I don't know. Did you know everyone on the leadership council?" I asked Kal

"He wasn't in my classes. He's not a youth, maybe one of the Elites. I don't recall him, but the region is the whole country and then some. He could have lived outside Plathorya."

"Did you know that up here they still have elections?" I asked Kal. "According to what I read in the history museum, they never stopped having them—though there used to be a lot of election fraud before the Reset."

"The counsel below claimed that they were subject to Russian influence and responsible for chaos and depravity, that the fairer system was to let leaders choose leaders," Kal explained to our friends.

As we walked home from Brad's, the next-door neighbor said, "zdavstvujtye," or something like that.

"What?"

"Russian for hello," he said in clear English.

I backed off. "You're Russian?" I asked the neighbor.

"Da. There are a lot of us in the city."

"There are?" I asked.

"I'm Nick."

"We need to go inside," Kal responded.

"Nice meeting you, Nick," I said, not wanting to offend him.

"The Russians really did infiltrate," Kal remarked, once we got inside.

"Maybe our leaders were right. Maybe, they are running the elections here."

"What's happening, kids?" Katerina asked.

"Russians. They're all over the city," Kal warned.

"I know. They're good people."

"But didn't they steal elections and try to overthrow our government?" I asked.

She laughed. "Where did you hear that? Though I will admit they were smarter than we were. Their leaders didn't poison their populations. The result is that there are more of them alive than us."

"There really was no World War III in Russia?" I inquired.

"There was no World War III anywhere."

"But didn't we have bigger, better bombs?"

"My understanding is that Russia had more powerful bombs and more of them but didn't want to use them and always pushed for peace and sanity. From what I was told, their leader agreed to the poisoning to prevent a real war but then didn't follow through."

"Then they tricked our leaders into poisoning everyone and going underground?"

"The collective world leaders in the West were willing to kill us all. They didn't have to poison everything. Are the people you're afraid of relatives who went underground? Is that what this fear is all about?"

I nodded. "I was afraid you'd hate us if you knew."

She hugged me and then Kal. "What they did isn't the fault of anyone but those who wanted to depopulate the planet."

Later that night, I was awakened by a tap at the window. It was Brad. "You and Kal need to come with me."

"What's going on?"

"You need to come downtown."

"I'll get my brother."

I dressed and ran to get Kal. "Brad's outside. We need to go downtown."

After we escaped out of our respective windows with Eterra and went to the street, we hopped in Brad's car. Jennifer and Roger were already there. Brad informed us that something had been dug up. It was a countdown timer.

"I don't understand," I said.

"Someone found a chip in the rubble where the robot blew up. It had the coordinates of this location. A group of college students dug under the gazebo in the park to see what was there," Roger explained.

"How did the college students get involved?"

"One of the investigators was their professor."

"So, it led them to this clock?" I asked.

"Countdown timer. The seconds count down to two weeks from today. What does that tell you?" Brad inquired.

"I didn't hear anything about something happening two weeks from today and why is the timer buried up here?" I asked Kal. "There was talk about one day reclaiming the planet, but the radiation was supposed to last for a couple hundred thousand years."

"But that was a lie, maybe designed to keep us from getting curious," Kal pointed out. "They just needed to wait for all the poison to be washed away from the land, water and air."

Brad parked and we joined the crowd.

"My guess is the zero point is when the underground monsters are going to try to come up," a guy in the crowd said.

"Left alone, most of the poison might have been mostly washed out of the soil in a decade and a half. But our society came up with methods to clean it faster. If not for the advances in soil renovation, there would still be traces up here and it would not have been safe to resettle," Brad related.

"Maybe it's not an invasion—but a signal for a secondary extermination plan," someone else in the crowd speculated.

"If so, it's something we need to stop," I said.

"For sure," Brad agreed.

"What could they do to wipe out any remaining people but not delay their coming up?" I asked.

"Earthquake?" Jennifer speculated.

"But that would have underground implications," Roger pointed out.

"What do you think, Kal?" Brad asked.

"I'm trying to recall some of those meetings my dad took me to as a kid. There is something really familiar about this, but I don't remember. We didn't discuss it in Future Leaders while I was there."

"Now it would be helpful if you were a robot," Brad said. "We could just restore your memories."

"Aren't there drugs that help people remember things?" Jennifer asked.

"Our dad has a ton of those in his cabinet. Ginkgo biloba, vitamin E, caffeine," Roger said.

"You want me to take vitamins and caffeine?" Kal asked.

"Maybe hypnosis."

Brad took us home. I tried to sleep, but the timer kept popping up in my mind.

The next morning, right after breakfast, we went over to Brad's place. Roger was there. He had studied up on hypnosis and planned to hypnotize my brother.

They tried pendulums, sleeping pills, vitamins and spirals, but nothing seemed to have an effect in bringing back his memory about anything connected with the date. The sleeping pills started to make Kal drowsy. He laid down and kept tapping his face to stay awake.

"Now, let's go over what you know," Brad said to me. Brad began to summarize what we'd told him. "There was a council running everything. They blamed Russians and degenerates for World War III and you were told everything above was radioactive. They were replacing people with robots down below. Robots! Do you think they plan to send robots up here?"

"They certainly have enough of them."

"They could turn everyone up here into an android servant—well, the ones they considered useful and necessary." He paused, thoughtfully, for a few seconds. "If I were a bad guy, I'd send a force that wouldn't be harmed if there was still any danger—just to check it out. Then I'd send the most human of the androids and finally the real humans."

"Why don't the underworld people below have cameras up here?" Roger inquired.

"Maybe they did," Brad said. "Maybe they are watching us now or the cameras got destroyed by the rain and the re-cultivation of soil. The buildings have almost all changed. One of the few buildings still standing is the old history museum. The cities are all different than they once were."

"Russians. There are Russians here." I still got shivers when I thought of what I had been taught about them.

"A lot migrated here," Brad continued. "They aren't the enemy. They aren't political. There are more Russians than Americans alive today because their government didn't poison them. If they wanted to take over, they have the numbers, but they have no interest in doing that."

"Will they stand with us?" Kal asked, sitting up.

"I'm sure they will, but they are really peaceful and mind their own business," Brad said.

"So, everything we were told about them was a lie." Kal shook his head.

"Apparently," Jennifer noted.

"Let's say an army of robots is coming up here at the zero hour. How do we stop them?" Brad asked.

"How do we recognize them?" I followed up.

"What did you notice that was different about the androids from humans down there?"

"They didn't show emotion and they weren't as fun."

"How about a computer virus?" Roger suggested.

"They have to have a way to upload it to the computer brain," Kal noted.

"Once activated, the humanoid androids are closed circuits. They can download their experiences, but they don't have any ports. I think the headpieces pick up their thoughts like a radio transmission when they download the memories. I don't think things can be uploaded the same way—but I could be wrong." I wished I had a better answer. "My mom kept most of the procedures to herself."

"There has to be a way to upload things into their brains after they've been activated," Roger said.

"You want to open up their heads? I don't know if you can. They look like regular people. They replace them when they need to evolve or get older. Even in sports, there was no way to tell they were androids from looking at them or touching them," I expounded.

'What about EMP devices?"

"I don't know. They are banned down below. You could try those," Kal said.

"An EMP device?" I asked.

"Electro-magnetic pulse," Kal responded. "It can knock out the computers. Only the leaders are allowed to have them."

The discussion was getting me tired as well. I laid down as Eterra put her head on my chest. I tried to stay awake but dozed off.

My mother was back in my dreams with her song, but there was a second verse this time:

"The mindwash. It is easy and it's all done by sound, leaving all mindless zombs, with no protection around. You can save them all still, but be well aware, replacements are here to replace lives up there."

I sat up. That's it. There was a second verse to the song. I sang it. As I did, Kal, remarked. "She must have been planning your escape all along. That doesn't rhyme and the cadence is all wrong, you know."

"Sound? We know our government used soundwaves to program real people in order to win wars, like in Iraq and elsewhere," Roger said. "And those COVID vaccines and the later ones had metal particles that were activated by five, six and seven G. Most of the survivors didn't get them or took antidotes."

"Earmuffs," I suggested.

"We can use sound suppression earmuffs, but what about everyone else. How do we get them to put on earmuffs? I don't even think I could get my parents to do it," Brad said.

"When they get deafened?" Jennifer asked.

"They'll probably use a frequency below the conscious hearing threshold," Kal said.

"What about sound deflectors?" Roger suggested.

"Do you know how to build one of those? And what if they surround us with the frequencies from every street corner?" Kal asked.

"Maybe their plans will change with Kal's dad being near death. Maybe they'll hold off," Jennifer suggested.

"Have you ever known the Elites to back down or hold off? My mother spoke about how the people tried to get them to back down when they were pressuring Russia into World War III," Brad said.

"And then World War III all turned out to be a lie," I responded, thinking of how much of what I learned had been a fabrication.

"They might have countdown timers elsewhere," Roger noted.

"If they are planning to come up in Europe, they deserve it. It's still toxic. So are the areas around the nuclear power plant disasters," Brad contended.

"What if we went to the hospital where Kal's dad is staying to find out his real condition?" Jennifer suggested.

"He might recognize us." Kal frowned. "If he didn't before."

"I'll find a disguise for you too. I have a lot of old Halloween costumes," Roger said.

———

The next morning, Katerina offered to watch Eterra, and didn't even ask why.

Kal was made to look really old. Brad grayed Kal's hair and Robert attached a fake beard. Brad and Roger worked with some fine-point black markers to make it look as if Kal had some wrinkles. If the dad were awake, I'd stay out of the room as he would have recognized me.

We went to University Hospital and asked to see Jason Denton.

The nurse at the front desk said, "We've no record of a Mr. Denton."

"The man who was brought in from the explosion. Mr. Beeks—" Roger pointed at Kal. "Here, is investigating the radiation surrounding the incident. We can't let that get out of hand."

"We can only let family in."

"I'm his niece," Jennifer said.

"Family. That's different. The register says he was discharged."

"Discharged? As in he walked away?"

"Apparently," she said.

CHAPTER 33

I froze. *What if he is still looking for us?*

"He would have called my parents to pick him up and they didn't get a call," Jennifer told the woman at the desk.

"What's your name?"

"Denton," she said.

"Maybe you can go upstairs and speak with hospital operations. Except the secretary is out for a couple of hours. You can wait in the cafeteria."

"He wasn't discharged to the morgue, was he?" Kal asked.

The receptionist looked indignant. "This is a modern research hospital. People come here to get well, not to die." She paused. "Nobody has died here in some time."

We picked up some food and sat down in the cafeteria. "We need to protect Kal and Natalia," Brad contended. "If he's loose, he'll try to turn them into robots."

"If he does, I'll pick something up and throw it at his head," Roger declared. "If they could chop off this Chanelle's head, their necks must be vulnerable."

"The humanoid androids are built like humans," I asserted. "But not the security androids. Security robots are mostly metal. I only saw them briefly at times and they were very different. Some look really scary."

"The question is whether my dad is after us or simply here to check out the above world," Kal said.

"Either way, we need to know what he's up to," Roger reasoned.

"Are you two kids the ones who were inquiring about the man they brought up?" someone from behind me asked. I turned. I didn't recognize the man.

"Who are you?"

"I'm from the university. What do you know about the man?"

"That he was with some kind of exploding robot," Brad said.

"And where did you hear that?"

"It was all over the news."

"I don't recall the news mentioning the word robot. I think the news used the world device."

"I guess we assumed it was a robot," Roger clarified.

"Androids are illegal. You told the woman at the front desk, his name was Jason Denton. Where did you get that name?"

"I don't know," Kal said. "I guess we heard it or read it somewhere."

"Then he's not your uncle?" the man asked Jennifer.

"Why all the questions? For all we know, you're the one who blew him up," Brad asserted.

"Why are you questioning kids anyway?" Roger asked.

He looked at Kal, who didn't look like a kid.

"You were the ones who came here to see him."

"We're curious. It's for a science project at school." Brad said.

"Isn't this vacation time?"

"We were hoping to put together a device like the one he had with him to impress the teacher when school resumes."

"You are hoping to put together a radioactive device?"

"Was it radioactive?" Kal asked. "I read that radiation projects were banned."

"So what's with the disguise?" the man asked Kal.

"Disguise?"

The man tugged on Kal's beard and it came off. Kal snapped it back into place.

"That's an assault and battery," Jennifer accused.

"How about you simply tell me the truth about your connection to the incident?"

"What makes you think we're connected?" Brad asked.

"You've gone to a lot of trouble."

"I don't know you. We're doing a science project and we want to know more about that man."

"Mr. Denton?"

"Right."

Something in the man's pocket buzzed. He pulled out a cell phone and looked at it. "I'll be right up." He turned to us. "I want to finish this discussion later."

"We need to get out of here," Kal said when the man left. We started to leave when we saw someone starting to pick up a tray at the counter. Mr. Denton.

CHAPTER 34

Brad saw me trying to hide my face. "That's him?"

"Or his cousin," Kal said.

Our friends got up and Jennifer, not so accidentally, knocked Fenton's or Denton's tray up to his face as we and our friends rushed past him.

"Sorry," Jennifer said in racing by.

We moved quickly out of the cafeteria while he was wiping himself.

The receptionist we'd spoken to earlier called to us as we rushed by the information counter. "There you are. A man was just inquiring about Mr. Denton. He said he was a cousin."

"Fenton?"

"Yes."

"He's a bad dude. Beat up a nurse in front of us. If he comes back, don't talk to him," Brad said.

"Wait. Someone from the university wants to speak to you. That's where they transferred the man you were asking about."

"Which university?"

"Sacramento Institute of Technology."

In the car, I said, "I thought Sacramento had been wiped out in the poisoning."

"But the university is named after the old city that used to be in this area."

"Is the state government still around here?"

"The local government is in Sutter Springs. The President and Congress operate out of San Diego."

"The capital used to be Washington, D.C."

"The Southwest is where our parents and their parents initially rehabilitated the land," Jennifer explained. "D.C. and some of the states in the east still aren't safe because of the Limerick disaster."

"Do we go to the university?"

"We don't know which department," Jennifer pointed out.

"Maybe the Industrial Design or the Biology Department," Roger suggested.

"Let's try both of those for starters," Brad said.

"Are your universities open on Saturdays during the summer?" I asked.

"Summer school is popular and Saturday classes are almost as full as weekday classes," Brad replied. "That way, students can take off during the week to go surfing."

"Wasn't that a beach sport in Southern California?" I asked. "I read about that—"

"In the History Museum?" Jennifer asked.

"No. Down below. They said the surfers were stupid and were probably the first ones hit with the bombs."

"I'll have to watch for falling bombs next time I surf." Jennifer chuckled.

Brad parked in the university parking lot.

Kal removed the beard and wiped away the wrinkles. "I feel like I've lost a hundred years."

Brad and I checked out the Industrial Design Department while Kal, Roger and Jennifer went to the Biology Department.

We started with the department chairman's office. "We're here to see the man and the device you had transferred over here from the hospital."

"I don't know what you're talking about."

"All the students are talking and everyone wants to see them."

"This is the wrong department. If you are interested in a device, you might want to go to technology."

"Thank you," I replied. As we exited the building, the other members of our group approached us.

"Nothing," Roger said. "You?"

"Nothing, but the department chief suggested tech," Brad informed them.

The chairman of the Tech Department was out. We decided to look in the labs. In one room, they were working on creating electricity from water. In another, they were building cars. "Move over, Detroit," I said.

"Even before the Reset, nobody was manufacturing cars in Detroit anymore. China, Korea and Thailand had taken over most of the car market," Brad expounded.

"My mom said something about Japan," Jennifer responded.

"It got nuked by Fukushima. They told everyone it was safe, but the Japanese car companies started sending away their work when other countries started refusing radioactive cars," Brad told her. "Though they did their best to cover up the problem for years."

A third room was locked. Brad pulled out his card and crossed his fingers. It worked.

On the table was Mr. Denton's head or parts of it. There was enough to recognize him. Kal went over to him. "He's a robot. But look, he's not a quality one. Under the missing eye, there is what looks like tissue mixed with metal. He's a human-looking security robot."

"Part of the advance crew?" Brad asked.

"Maybe. It's got some copies of human parts, but the humanoid robots below don't have this mixture of metal with the tissue material." Kal said. "It's unnatural."

"A natural robot? An oxymoron," Brad commented.

Roger looked at Kal. "You know this from—"

"Leadership."

"I saw some of my mom's work with building workers and he's right. It's not the same materials. I wonder if it's a new process or if it's just for this android. The humanoid robots did not have security robot parts."

"The humanoids are only one group," Kal reiterated. "While they imitate real humans and are almost identical, physically, internally and externally, security robots are different. Some look fierce, like the toy Steve bought and the ones that tried to shoot us as we escaped, but most others look more benign. Apparently, for whatever their plan is, they are making security androids look human on the outside, making them less vulnerable and more dangerous."

"Let's get out of here," Kal advised. We started out the door.

A woman entered, blocking our exit. "Who authorized you to come in here?"

"We were looking for the room where they were working on new forms of energy," Brad lied. "The door was open."

"I'll have to talk to my assistant about that."

"What's that?" I pointed to the table.

"It's confidential."

"Are you creating robots?" Jennifer asked. "I heard human-emulating robots were illegal."

"This one was destroyed the other day in an explosion. I've never seen anything like it. It looks human but isn't, and it's got a programming that we haven't been able to find the key for," the woman said.

"Looks like a complicated project."

"I shouldn't have told you that. You didn't see this."

"Certainly, Professor Patterson," Jennifer said, looking at the instructor's nametag. "You are a real inspiration. Or at least, everyone says so."

"Thank you."

We started to leave and then saw the man from the cafeteria. We turned down the hall away from him and moved into the room where they were working on generating electricity.

A professor and the students turned towards us.

"Oh, I guess this is the wrong room too," I said. We rushed out, and the man saw us.

CHAPTER 35

We ran. Brad looked back and noticed the man go into the electrical room, maybe checking on what we were doing at the university. We were already around a corner, peeking back as he rushed out of the room, turning in our direction.

We bolted down another corridor, turned a corner and hid in large empty hallway lockers. I heard footsteps going by. The man from the cafeteria was speaking to someone. "They were in the electronics room and you don't know who they were?"

"I never saw them before." The footsteps moved on in different directions.

After a while, I heard a locker open and there was a knock on the lockers. "Coast clear," Brad whispered. The rest of us got out and raced for the nearest exit.

We went back to Brad's place. Katerina was there. "Did you kids have a nice outing?"

"It was very interesting," Kal said.

"We like science, as you know. We were checking out some new forms of electricity." I added.

"Brad is such a genius," his mother said.

"I took Eterra out for a walk. She missed you," Katerina told me.

"Mind if I bring her over here?" I asked Brad's mother.

"She's already playing in the backyard."

"That's great."

***

After lunch, we went up to Brad's room with Eterra.

"So, they are sending humanoid duplicates with security robot parts, accompanied by real security robots to check things out," Roger surmised.

"That guy who was chasing us seemed more like an inquisition officer than a professor. But who was he inquiring for? I wonder if the first two radioed back with their findings," Brad said.

"There wasn't much time between when we saw my dad's double and when we pulled back. I don't know for a fact he actually saw us," Kal reiterated.

"He may have had an internal monitor," I said. "He probably did. If they saw me, Mom could be in extreme danger." *I can't think that. It would be too awful.*

"Do you think your real dad was a robot?" Brad asked Kal.

"No. He took too much pleasure in chopping off my sister's head. His double's probably like your mother's double." Kal said, turning to me.

"It seems likely. But my mom's double was nice. She saved us. She didn't chop off anyone's head. But then there was that big explosion. I don't know if she was carrying explosives or if they were packed into her."

"Your not-mom was pretty sturdy. The lab explosion didn't stop her and neither did the device she threw that knocked out the security robots."

"The device briefly knocked her out too. Maybe it was timed to activate after she threw it. The lab explosion was a small one; it was mostly smoke and some fire—I think. I survived. That's why I'm hoping my real mom survived too."

"And your not-dad wouldn't suspect your mom if she appeared hurt in the explosion."

I looked up. "Please let her be alive and safe."

"Who are you saying that to?" Kal asked.

"I don't know. I'm just hoping that something in the universe grants my wish. We were told that God didn't exist down there, but I can still hope."

"So what's next?" Jennifer asked.

"We need to speak to Claire Holiday. She's supposed to be our mother. Besides, she's really nice," I said.

As I sat next to Brad in the car, he kept turning his head and smiling at me. In the backseat, while Roger looked deep in thought, Kal and Jennifer were smiling and laughing about something. That was good. I had never seen him so friendly with a girl before.

As we all entered Miss Holiday's room, we were in for a surprise. "Roy," I reacted. I should have expected that the farmer who had introduced us to Miss Holiday would come to see her.

"I'm sorry I didn't visit before. The oddest thing. These people here think you're Claire's kids. I tried to explain to them that she was just giving you a ride."

I looked at Miss. Holiday and then back at Roy.

"It turns out that we need to pretend to be her children. There are some really bad people after us," I explained.

"Did you tell the police?"

"They might not believe us," Brad responded.

"Who believes kids?" Jennifer asked.

"And we don't have any parents," Kal said. "The doctor and his wife have taken us in, and we're safer that way. Please tell them you're mistaken."

"I can, but I've already spoken to some social worker."

"The social worker? If you see her again, tell her you confused us with another family."

"I already told her Claire doesn't have any kids." He thought a minute. "I'll say she kept her family secret from me and finally told me about them. I didn't know her that well."

"That might work," Kal said.

"Is everything working out for you with Dr. Steve and his wife?" Miss Holiday asked.

"They're wonderful. They would like us to stay there long-term. Without any parents here, that's perfect," I said.

"I don't want to do anything to cause trouble, but I don't want that social worker arresting me."

"If we stick together, nobody will be arrested," Kal assured her.

Steve walked in. "What's this about Miss Holiday not having children?"

"It was me," Roy said. "I thought she wanted to keep her kids a secret. I said the wrong thing, thinking I was protecting her. You can see how much the boy looks like his mother."

"Now that you mention it. His eyes are very similar," Steve agreed.

"She has her father's eyes," Miss Holiday said.

"Your mother is doing well," Steve informed us.

"I just need someone to help with the kids. They are wonderful, but I just don't have the energy for two teenagers."

"Maybe you could sign over some kind of temporary guardianship paper to us so we could enroll them in school and other activities until you are able to care for them. Your daughter plays the harp beautifully, and they have a nice orchestra at our school."

"I know she'd love playing in an orchestra. Wouldn't you, honey?"

"Yes. Yes. Absolutely."

"I'd like to talk to your mother about arrangements. Maybe you could go down to the cafeteria."

"Our friends gave us a ride here, and I think they need to get back," I said. "We'll drop by tomorrow, Mom."

Kal and I kissed her on the cheek and she gave each of us a hug.

"Now be good with the Drakes. I shouldn't say that. I know you will." As we were leaving the room, she told Steve, "They're such great kids."

Down the hall, we were stopped by the social worker and a policeman. "You're coming with us. The jig is up."

CHAPTER 36

The officer started to grab me. I kicked him below the belt as Eterra jumped up, knocking him back, and we moved past him as Kal pushed the social worker out of his way. The officer caught up with us. "That's an assault on a police officer."

"If you were a police officer, you wouldn't be trying to kidnap my friends," Jennifer said.

"We have to take them in. We need to know who their parents are," the officer replied.

"Their mother is inside." It was Roy.

"You told me she wasn't their mother," the social worker declared.

"I said what? Maybe you've gotten too much sun."

"You say their mother is inside?" the officer asked Roy.

"Yes. These are Claire Holiday's children."

"We have birth certificates," Kal said, reaching into his pocket. He looked at me. I remembered he had given our copy to Katerina.

"I think you handed those to me," Brad said, pulling an extra copy out of his pocket.

"As you can see," Kal continued, "She was briefly married. Notice the maiden name is Holiday."

"And your mother is inside?"

"She has assigned temporary guardianship to the doctor until she recovers," Roy said.

"That's all a lie," the social worker countered.

"The guardians are Steve and Katerina Drake. I was there when they were discussing the guardianship. I've known these kids and their mother since they were little," Roy continued.

The officer took the social worker by the arm. "You'll have to explain your filing of a false police report."

"But they're lying. All of them."

"It looks to me as if you are the one lying," the officer said. He guided her outside to a police car, put her in the back and drove away.

"That was close," I breathed. I turned to Roy and hugged him. "Thank you."

"Claire is a dear friend. Anything for her."

Kal shook his hand.

"Let's go back to my house and strategize," Roger suggested. "It was nice meeting you, Roy."

"Like your mother said, 'be good.'" Roy smiled.

I hugged him, again.

Jennifer had a live menagerie. Eterra chased Jennifer's rabbit and then played with it as her Belgian Shepard watched. Brad brought his laptop out of his car and he and Roger worked side by side on their computers.

"We're looking for any other strange occurrences, explosions, people who could be robots, subliminal sounds coming from anywhere," Brad said.

"Your mother was into robotics. Did you learn anything about robotic assembly from her?" Roger asked.

"Enough to know that the Denton we saw was a really messed-up robot. Even the regular service robots had insides emulating ours."

"If they notified Fenton, he must have had some identification on him. I wonder if Mr. Fenton is also a robot," Brad pondered.

"Steve said he'd known him for years."

"I guess it's unlikely, then."

By the time we left Roger's and Jennifer's, everyone was flustered. We were up against some sadistic, shrewd people, and we couldn't be certain of their plans.

Brad walked Kal, Eterra and me home. As Kal went inside, Brad pulled me back. "I'd like to take you on a real date tonight. Maybe a movie and dinner. Wait until the last minute to tell Kal. He's great, but I'd like to take just you on the date."

"That would be great. What about Jennifer? She said she likes movies."

"She and Roger are doing research tonight."

"Should I be doing research?"

"If the world's going to end, let's have some fun first."

"I'll have to tell Katerina."

Katerina okayed it.

"Why do you suppose he didn't want Kal on the date?"

"You've never been on a real date before, have you?"

"No."

"Just remember, you don't have to do anything you don't want to do."

"Of course not." Her comment seemed silly.

"Let me help you fix your hair."

My hair was naturally curly but by the time she finished, I had long ringlets falling down over my shoulders and halfway down my back from a ponytail on top of my head. She wrapped a ribbon around the top of the ponytail and the strands draped down through the shorter curls that framed my face. She helped me into a white satin and silk dress with a blue waistband.

"I look nice like this," I said, standing in front of the mirror.

"You are beautiful."

"I always thought I was plain. Jennifer, she's really pretty."

"In a different way. I love your long golden hair."

"Don't guys prefer red hair?"

"Some guys. Others like blonds and some like brunettes."

"You are beautiful without red hair. Your dark hair goes with your eyes. I didn't mean to—"

"It's fine. I knew what you meant."

"Nobody but you has helped me get dressed since I was a little girl."

"Do you mind?"

"No. I actually love it. It's like having a big sister."

She hugged me.

I went into the living room. Kal stood up, open-mouthed. "Hi," he said, staring at me.

"Hi. Katerina thinks I'm beautiful."

"You look sensational tonight."

The bell rang. It was Brad. He was dressed up, too. "Wow. I thought you were stunning before."

"Are we going out?" Kal asked.

"You're having dinner with Steve and me, Kal. We're looking forward to discussing your day," Katerina intervened.

"Brad?" he asked.

"We'll see you when we get back."

After dinner at a restaurant, he took me to a comedy about a bungling investigator who was always chasing after a female cop who kept beating him up until they were locked in a room with poison gas. Then they fell in love.

"Do a lot of romances here start with people hating each other?"

"No. Just the opposite." As we sat there, he put his arm around my shoulder. The theater was a bit cold, and his arm was warm and it felt good to have an arm around me.

Afterwards, he took me out for a slushy, and we laughed about all the situations we had escaped in the last few days. It felt great to laugh about my fears. It was easy to relax around Brad. But he was always looking at me, and something about that made me feel a little awkward. When he drove me home, he stopped the car and I started to get out.

"Let me." He opened the door. This was the third time that had happened that evening. I wasn't used to guys opening doors for me, but it seemed nice. When we got to my doorstep, I said goodnight and thanked him for the wonderful time. He leaned in and kissed me.

CHAPTER 37

This was a first. I'd never been kissed by a guy before. It was sort of like the one in the movies but quicker. It felt weird, but I liked being liked. I kissed him back the way I had seen in the movie we watched. I had never been kissed like this before but I had seen my dad, or not-dad, kiss my mom. But that had always seemed yucky to me. This didn't feel yucky.

Brad looked happy, and so I guessed I did it right. I smiled, not knowing what to say or do.

"I'd like to take you out again."

The door opened and Kal stood there with his arms folded. "It's kind of late, isn't it?"

"It's not a school night," Brad said.

"We don't want to wear out our welcome with Steve and Katerina," Kal scolded.

"I'll see you tomorrow," Brad softly said to me. "Goodnight, Kal."

Inside, Kal asked, "What was that all about? He's not one of us."

"And it's a good thing. Who wants to hang out with someone from below? Been there. Done that. Everyone but your sister and Robert was cold and uncaring and the underground stole Chanelle's warmth."

Kal looked bothered.

"I mean, you and I are friends now, but most of my other friends or sort-of-friends were robots and not all that warm," I went on.

"I know what you mean. Too many of them were cold as if their hearts had been ripped out, and most of them had been."

"They replaced their hearts but not with real ones."

"And you still defend your mom."

"And you are still pushing that line? I don't believe she killed anyone. She just made robotic replacements."

"And killed robots that looked like you."

"At least she didn't kill me. That's what my dad or whatever he was wanted to do."

"He was the Chairman. He was running the show."

"Only for the Western Region."

"Which included the whole USA and Canadian underworld."

"I know you hate my parents, and I don't feel the same way. I'm going to bed." I stomped off to my room.

Katerina came in to see me as I was taking off the dress. "I thought I heard you come home."

"Why is Kal so mean?"

She laughed. "Brothers are like that. I think his heart is in the right place. He was really worried about you tonight. He practically paced a hole through the floor. He wants to protect you."

"Protect me? He's the last person I want protecting me. To him, I'm just a sister he would rather not have. My mother protected me, but she liked me." I recalled how angry he seemed when he told me that his father had cheated with my mom.

"Steve says your mom is really nice."

"Yes." I fretted, feeling as if I had almost blown it.

"Are you upset that she isn't having you come home right away?"

"No. I'm fine with that. She needs her rest."

"I'm still having trouble believing the story you told me after the history museum."

"I know. It does seem pretty unbelievable. You can pretend we never said anything if it makes you feel better. Call it our imagination."

"That's like unringing a bell."

"How do you unring a bell? Reverse time?"

"If that's possible. Mostly it's an expression that means you can't undo or unlearn certain things."

"You're really sweet. My mom and I didn't talk about stuff like this. It's probably because she was afraid people were listening. She put messages into songs."

"Songs?"

"Like Braham's Lullaby or something that sounded a little like that. She was scared and she would have done anything to protect me."

"Scared of the robots?"

"Of anything bad happening to me."

"We have that in common. Wanting to protect you."

I hugged her. "You have been so kind to me. You are so much kinder than anyone I have known before. All my old friends were refined, controlled. You are real."

"Thank you. Sometimes I feel I'm too emotional."

"I like that. That's how we can tell who is real and who isn't."

The next morning. I left the house to go to Brad's. As I crossed the street, I saw Bob, the man who kept showing up. He'd found me.

CHAPTER 38

My stalker, Bob, was in a car two houses away from the Drakes' house, looking at me.

Kal rushed out of the house. "Wait, Natalia!"

Darn. He'd called my name right in front of the man. I knocked on Brad's door and rushed inside as Kal followed.

"Why did you call my name? Didn't you see him?" I scolded Kal as he followed me into Brad's house.

"Who?"

"The man who keeps showing up. Now he knows where I live."

"Where was he?"

"The car, two houses down."

Brad rushed out. "The car's gone."

"He'll be back," I said, pessimistically.

"Katerina suggested going to church today. I wanted to let you know."

"Church? Didn't churches turn out to be scams where people were lied to?" I asked.

"It makes sense that those who tried to kill off the billions of people while escaping to safety are atheists," Brad commented.

"They don't believe in some omnipotent power, if that's what you mean," I said.

"Maybe because they think they are superior to such a Power or are themselves gods. Do you see them that way?" he questioned.

"Killing and lying are not superior," Kal stated.

"Everything else they said was a lie. That probably was, too," I acknowledged. "When did she want to go?"

"Steve's at work and she said we were late and would have to leave right away to catch the service," he noted.

"Maybe we can check it out another time," I said.

Brad called Roger and Jennifer, who came over. "We need to take turns watching their house."

"How about if I spend the night at your place—slumber party?" Jennifer asked.

"I could too. That is, if Steve and Katerina say yes," Roger offered.

"And I'll watch from here," Brad said.

At lunchtime, we all went to see Katerina and sold her on the idea.

Miss Holiday was fine when we visited her that afternoon. She had signed over some temporary guardianship papers to Steve and Katerina. "I don't know if I was supposed to tell you. Steve will probably tell you about it tonight. Look surprised."

"We will."

As we left, Brad asked, "How many entrances do you think the underworld has?"

"I only know of the one," I told him. "And the ground over it caved in."

"Could you find it again?"

"It's way upriver. There is a lake above the river and it's not far from where we got out."

Back at Brad's place, he showed us a map and we identified the lake.

"There used to be a road that didn't go too far from there. They've been planning to build a new highway to the lake. Have you driven any off-road cycles?"

"Not so far," Kal said as I shook my head.

I've got some binoculars we could use to see if people or robots are coming up through it, but it's a considerable hike.

"There might be other exits they are using," I said.

"I think there are," Kal related. "But we were told that going out any of the exits risked major contamination and that they were all sealed. We don't know if they dug through the cave-in or if Robo-dad took one of the other exits," Kal pointed out.

"That's true."

"How large is the underground?" Brad asked.

"Across the continent in all directions. There are trains and trams interconnecting the different communities, but the Administration and Power Center are located in Plathorya," Kal said.

"So they could have popups everywhere. I bet your mother chose that exit in the hopes that Selini Andrews would be near," Brad guessed. "Maybe they were originally from this area."

Despite her earlier concerns about our safety, we went over to Selini's place. Brad located the address through a search of voting records. Our friends kept a lookout below while Kal and I went up to her place.

"It's dangerous. Especially if they are sending up robots or people," she warned.

"Denton was a robot. We don't know if any real or fake people came up besides us," I said.

"Advance scouts or were they looking for you?"

"I don't know. There's a man who keeps following me."

"You think he's one of them?"

"I don't know but he knows my name and my mother's name."

"He could be one of the Elites from the underground or an android. Stay clear of him. Stan knows your mother and I were close. They could come here looking for you, and I don't want you caught."

"What about you?"

"I don't have anyone right now. I won't tell them a thing, and they can't make me."

"They could kill you."

"At least, I got to see my best friend's daughter again."

"What about Tarinda?"

"She doesn't care about me. She probably never did. Maybe it's good my daughter won't have anything to do with me. That will probably keep her safe."

"You deserve better," I said.

"Sometimes you give all your love to someone, and it's not enough. Be careful when it comes to giving your heart. I lost out twice, once with the man I married and the second time with the daughter I loved more than my life."

"Selini, you have a lot to live for. My mother may even be alive. We need you. I need you. Please take care of yourself."

She hugged me and then Kal. She looked at him and again said, "Take care of our little girl."

I felt funny being called a little girl.

"I will," he said.

That night, Steve asked why Jennifer and Roger kept looking out the front window.

"Brad's across the street. He is doing science experiments, and he said he'd flash his light if he had success," Roger lied.

"I'm so glad you kids are into science," Katerina said.

"Did you hear any more about that guy they took from the history museum to the hospital?" I asked Steve.

"I tried to check on it, and the government has blocked access to the information. There must have been some government operation going on that day."

"You do a lot of work with prosthetics, don't you, Doctor Drake?" Roger asked.

"Some. You can call me Steve."

"Steve, do you think it's easy to build an android that looks human and upload its brain?"

"I know Moosk wanted to do that before the poisoning. Now, there are laws against that. It turned out Moosk was part of DARPA and the Reset."

"You can make parts, but you are not allowed to make whole humans?"

"Where does it stop?" Jennifer asked. "At a hand, an arm, a leg?"

"We can do a great deal with parts, but, as I said, we don't reconstruct whole humans. If they lose a limb, we can replace it. Also, we have artificial organs, but there is a limit to how much of a person we will replace. I think there is a ten percent rule."

"So if I'm in an accident, you might have to decide between my arm and my heart."

"We'd choose the heart in that instance. We might be able to do the arm too. But we are not allowed to do the brain. Years ago, people who were unable to do any cognitive thinking for themselves were elected to posts like President and Senator. Chips made their brains functional. The people behind them gave the real orders and were responsible for the poisoning. We now make sure only real individuals, who can think for themselves, are elected to be leaders."

"Smart," I said.

"Are you thinking of becoming a doctor, Roger?" he asked.

"I don't know. I don't like blood."

"I don't like blood at all," Jennifer groaned.

"There are different areas of medicine, but to get through medical school, you can't get away from seeing blood."

"How about you, Kal? What do you think you want to be?"

"Maybe a doctor like you. I guess I'll have to get used to blood if I do."

"You'd make an excellent doctor. You are very gifted and ethical."

"Thank you. That's the first time someone has ever noticed or said I was ethical."

"It's the most important quality for a doctor. Unethical doctors cost us a lot of lives during the plandemics."

Later that night in my room, Jennifer asked me, "Are you and Brad an item?"

"Item?"

"He took you out on a date last night."

"We went to dinner, a movie and dessert."

"He must really like you."

"I guess."

"He's really great. You are so lucky."

"He likes you, too."

"He's never taken me out on a date?"

"Maybe you should tell him you like him."

"Would that be okay with you?"

"Sure."

"Did he kiss you?"

"Yes."

"I bet it felt great."

"I'd never been kissed by a boy before. I don't know how to compare it."

"Did it feel like you were in heaven?"

"Heaven?"

"Like the universe exploded?"

"Why would I want the universe to explode?"

"I meant, did you like it?"

"It was fine. Am I supposed to feel something special?"

"When a girl is kissed by a guy she likes, she wants him to continue kissing her."

"Oh. I guess it would be alright if he kissed me again."

"But, alright if he didn't?"

"I don't know. I guess that would be fine, too. But if he were to stop liking me, that would make me sad."

"So, you like him, but you aren't in love with him."

"Love is what I felt for my mother. I don't know if I will ever feel that for a boy."

"It's different with a boy. You want his arm around you. You want to be with him all the time."

"Is there something wrong with me?"

"Maybe you aren't ready to fall in love, yet."

"Do you think I'll feel this love you described someday?"

"Probably. A lot of people don't find love until they are older."

"Oh."

That night, nobody tried to break into the house, and Brad didn't see anyone either.

The next morning, the car with my stalker was in front of the house next door.

CHAPTER 39

"If I go out, he'll see me," I fretted.

"Leave it to Roger and me," Jennifer said.

Roger and Jennifer went out and spoke to the driver. He drove off.

"What did you say to him?"

"I told him where you would be this afternoon."

"Why?"

"It's an abandoned building. You aren't going to be there. We are."

That morning, I played with Eterra as she jumped over boxes and rolled over. Katerina cut a watermelon into slices and gave me and Kal each one. Eterra gobbled my piece immediately. Each time I got a new one, she considered it hers.

The bell rang. I looked out the window, fearing who might show up next. It was Brad.

"What's happening?"

He looked inside to make sure Katerina wasn't in the living room.

"She's in the kitchen."

"We have that man tied up in an abandoned warehouse. We're doing an interrogation."

"Interrogation?"

"He says he's not a robot and that he doesn't mean you any harm. But he won't tell us who he is. He insists on telling you."

"I wonder if he'll explode when he sees me."

"If he's really a robot, he might. It is a risk. He is tied up and we won't let him hurt you. If you want, we can blindfold him so he can't see you."

"I like that idea."

Kal spoke up behind me. "I don't like it. He could have a self-detonating device on him that goes off the moment he hears your voice."

"We can't leave him tied up forever—unless he's a bad guy. That would be cruel and a crime," Brad pointed out.

Kal and I agreed to go with Brad to where Roger and Jennifer were holding the man.

The warehouse looked as if it hadn't been used in a long time.

"They once used this to store food but now they have better locations," Brad explained. "They'll probably demolish it and build something else here."

I went over to the now blindfolded man. "What do you want?"

"Natalia?"

"I'm asking the questions. What is your name?"

"Bob, Robert Lancaster. Before the poisoning, I knew your mother."

"Did you know her husband, Stan Cambridge?"

"I knew your mother. Did not care for him."

"But she married him."

"He shot me, and she thought I was dead. I went to tell her I was alive, but before I could, he dragged her down below. She wouldn't have gone with him voluntarily." I could hear anger in his voice, but I didn't know if it was for my not-Dad or just an act.

"Why did he take her?"

"For her expertise and because he had always wanted her."

"And I should believe you, why?"

"Because I'm telling you the truth."

"How did you know my name if you weren't down there?"

"I found a way down. At that time, she was already married to him. I didn't want to put her in any danger. They were watching her. I just wanted to make sure she was safe. I've always regretted not rescuing her."

I could hear the sadness in his voice. I couldn't tell whether he was a good actor, like in the movies I'd seen, or if it was real.

"Why did you care?"

"She is important to me. She is a good person—too good to be forced into that society."

"So, you were down there—in the underworld?"

"I went there to make sure she and you were alright. I pretended to be a robotized worker so I could keep an eye on her and you. When I saw you. I knew."

"Knew what?"

"Who you are. I also know your mother would never have turned you into a robot."

"How do you know that?"

"Because she loved you. You were her world. I stayed there, keeping an eye on you as long as I could."

"You stalked her, too? Were you working for the Russians?"

"I'm an American."

"But you managed to leave there. They let you out?"

"When I was close to discovery, I fled up here the same way I got down there."

There was something about him that nagged at me. I backed away from him.

"Do you believe him?" I asked the others.

"His story makes sense if it's true," Jennifer said.

"If he knew my mother, Selini would know of him."

"Let's go ask her," Brad suggested.

"Thank you for being my friend," I said, giving Selini a hug.

Roger and Jennifer had stayed with Robert while Brad, Kal and I went to see Selini.

"It's a pleasure." Her voice was sad, maybe missing my mother or Tarinda.

"Did my mother know a Robert Lancaster? The man who has been following me claims he's him."

"It's impossible. Lancaster is dead. Stan must have sent this imposter."

We went back to the warehouse. "I was told conclusively that Robert Lancaster is dead."

"I'm not dead."

"Did my dad send you?"

"No. He would have killed me if he knew I was alive."

"What do you want with me?"

"I just want to make sure you are alright and to tell you I will do whatever is necessary to protect you."

"Or confiscate me. I don't believe anything anyone who has been below says—except Kal and my mom and she didn't say anything about you."

"She thought I was dead. There were monitors everywhere."

"If you came down later, you knew there was no World War III, and yet you didn't let me know. You didn't rescue us—because you are part of it. I don't believe you. I'm alright, where I am right now. You found out what you want to know."

"I want to help you."

"You can do so by leaving me alone, permanently. Will you stop following me and stop showing up where I show up?"

"If that's what you really want."

"That's what I really want."

"Then, I'll abide by your wishes."

Brad drove me and Kal home. "Do you believe him?" Kal asked.

"People will say anything when they are tied up and blindfolded," Brad replied. "If he follows through and leaves you alone, that's a good sign."

———

At home, I laid down for a nap. Eterra curled up next to me on my bed. I started dreaming. But was it more than a dream?

My mind shifted to a night when I was crying. I was really young, maybe three or four. Chanelle was supposed to stay at my place, and she didn't. I went outside to the park where we often played and he was there. He was younger, but it was Lancaster. His eyes were kind and he briefly smiled as he saw me and then looked around.

"What's wrong?" he asked.

"My friend stood me up. She forgot to come over and she's not here."

"Maybe there are extenuating circumstances."

"Extenu—"

"Something beyond her control. I can't imagine anyone being mean to a sweet girl like you. I bet your mother is proud of you."

"She says she is."

"Are you happy?"

"Yes, but not now."

"What can I do? I know." He pulled some paper out of his pocket and made a flower.

"It's pretty. It looks like a real one."

"A pretty flower for a pretty girl. But a fake flower isn't as good as the real thing. Just remember your mother loves you and you deserve good things. Your friend will come back to you."

"You think so?"

"How can anyone stay away from you?"

"Who are you?"

"A friend."

I examined the flower. When I looked up, he was gone.

I woke up. Was it just a dream? No. It was too vivid. It felt like a memory. It actually happened. But who was he? Was Not-Dad now having him watch me or was he telling the truth?

Our friends arrived and we went into Kal's room.

"Are you feeling better?" Kal asked.

"I remembered that man. He was down below."

"Was he one of them?" Roger inquired.

"I don't know. He was nice to me, and then I didn't see him again, I don't think."

Jennifer interrupted my thought. "I was thinking about something you said. Your mother went down below a little under sixteen years ago. You hadn't been born at that time, right?"

"I guess."

"If she knew that man enough for your not-father to want to kill him, maybe he's your real father."

"Mr. Lancaster!" Kal angrily retorted. "No. That's ridiculous."

"The toy robot. Wasn't it created by an Eterra Lancaster?" I asked him.

"Your mom was making human robots, not toys." He started pacing.

"My mom never mentioned any prior marriages or relationships. Must be a different Eterra. And Selini said the real Robert Lancaster was dead. This guy is alive."

"He said that he was shot and your mom thought he was dead. Maybe Selini didn't know he survived," Jennifer suggested.

"He's a liar. He's *not* your father. He's probably working for your not-father." Kal insisted.

"It could be that the real Lancaster died and this man hoped to gain my confidence by pretending he survived and is him. He might figure my mom mentioned Lancaster. Even if he is who he said, maybe after he went down, he was replaced and didn't know it. Maybe his programming includes convincing me he's my friend or my father in order to bring me down." I felt conflicted. I wanted to ask the man more. "Is he still at the warehouse?"

"We let him go. He swore he'd stay away from you."

CHAPTER 40

"I told him I wanted him to stay away, but now I want to ask him more questions."

"Maybe we can look him up," Brad said as he, Roger and Jennifer took off. "He said his name was Robert Lancaster."

I looked at Kal. His face was red as if he were angry. "He is *not* your father."

For some reason that didn't make sense, Kal's reaction mattered. I wanted to reach out and hold him, but I didn't.

Kal went into his room and slammed the door. I knocked.

"Go away."

I knocked again and then just walked in.

He looked sad. "You are my sister! Jennifer is wrong."

"Why do you want me to be your sister?"

"I lost my other sister, and now I have you."

"But I could be your friend. Isn't that just as good?"

"No. Friends go away." He looked as if he was about to cry.

"I'm not going away. We're together in this because nobody else can really understand who we are and what we feel."

He paused. "You're still my sister. I want a sister."

Kal's face was slightly contorted. The last thing I wanted was to hurt him. "Fine. Of course, I'm your sister."

I gave him a hug. He wrapped his arms around me. I felt a sense of belonging, not alone, knowing there was someone who understood what I had gone through. "No matter who comes into our lives, we're a team, forever," I said.

"You mean it?"

"I mean it."

I wasn't going to talk with him about Robert Lancaster, anymore. I needed to forget the man—especially if it caused Kal so much pain. If Lancaster were my father, he should have rescued me years ago. My mother risked her life to get me out. He abandoned me and my mom, down there. I didn't owe him anything.

As we were eating a late lunch, Brad returned and informed us, "I've been researching Robert Lancaster. Here's a picture of him from eighteen years ago." It looked like the guy in my dream and was clearly a younger version of the man who had been chasing me.

"He was telling the truth about who he is." I sighed.

"He is. And he's alive."

Kal went back into his room and slammed the door, again.

"He's upset. He thinks he's losing another sister. I'm the only family member he has left—the only one who's not a murderer."

"Sounds like you were a step up from his family."

"He never liked me before we left the underworld."

"Maybe he changed his mind when he got to know you.

"And just when he had lost his family, he found a new sister and he doesn't want to lose any more family."

"How about, if instead of sweating out the future, we just spend the rest of the day relaxing. Get your swimsuit. We can go swimming in my pool."

I knew we were on a timetable, but Kal was becoming more and more important to me. Right now, what I most wanted was to see the boy I had once hated happy again.

We went to Kal's room. He was lying down, staring at the ceiling.

"I'm inviting you to a private party at my house," Brad said.

"I feel like staying in my room."

"As your sister, I'm telling you to get on your swimsuit and bring something you can wear to play basketball."

"So now you're my sister?"

"That stuff about Lancaster was all wild speculation. Of course, I'm your sister. Maybe after Mom went down there, she was so depressed that she turned to your father. Everyone says she didn't want to go down there. And just because he may have known my mother doesn't mean Lancaster is my father."

While swimming at Brad's, I let all the worries about saving the world disappear for a few hours. He seemed to have gotten over his fear of water. I teased Kal, splashing him. We played something called Marco Polo, a water tag game Brad's mother had taught him. I watched the way Jennifer looked at Brad. She really liked him a lot.

"Brad," I said.

"Yes."

"That date the other night was really fun."

"Maybe we can do it again tonight or tomorrow night."

"I was thinking that Jennifer probably hasn't seen that movie. I hate having her miss out. Is there a chance you could take her to see it?"

He had an odd look about his face. "Roger might object. He's really picky about who his sister dates."

"Maybe the four of us could go to a movie tonight," I said. "It might cheer Kal up. And you don't have to pay for us."

"Can we see a different movie?"

"We can see whatever movie you like."

I realized that I hadn't visited Miss Holiday since the incident with the social worker. I asked Brad to take us over there.

She was relaxing in her bed, not connected to any monitors or IV drips. She smiled as she saw us. "The doctor says I can go home tomorrow. They are going to send a nurse to assist me at the house."

"That's great. You've been so kind and supportive," I said.

"You're the best fake mom I've ever had," Kal complimented her.

As we got ready for the movie, Kal seemed reluctant to go.

"You like Jennifer, don't you? She'll be there."

"She's nice," he said, but without any enthusiasm.

"Do you think she might turn out to be the one for you?"

"The one?"

"Jennifer says that when you are with the right person, you want to be with them all the time."

"She's okay. She and Brad aren't like us. I think we should focus on saving the world, not matchmaking. Don't pawn me off on Jennifer so you can hang out with Brad. You and I should spend more time together, strategizing."

"All four of us will be there, hanging out. If you get any ideas about stopping our fathers or not-fathers, I'll be there."

Part of my plan was to get Brad and Jennifer together, but I had to be sure Kal wasn't in love with her.

At the movie, Brad sat between Jennifer and me. Kal was on my other side.

"Jennifer, wouldn't you rather sit on the other side of Kal?" Brad asked.

"I'm fine here," she said.

My plan was working.

We went out to eat afterwards. I had to get Brad and Jennifer talking about something they both liked. "You two are into science, aren't you?"

"I am always curious," Jennifer said. "But I'm concerned about calculus. I have to take AP Calculus next year."

"It's easy," Kal said.

That wasn't part of my plan. "Brad, have you taken AP Calculus?"

"I took it last year."

"That's great. Maybe you can tutor Jennifer. You probably remember some of the test questions."

"Sure. I can help you," he told Jennifer.

"I love the way you both have been doing so much to help me and Kal. It's great to have friends like you."

"I also want to save the world," Jennifer said. "All this makes me feel like a superhero."

"Me too," Brad said. "Of course, I also want to help you while saving the world." He took my hand. I squeezed his and moved my hand away.

"Jennifer, you are so smart and good at dealing with people, like the way you spoke to the social worker and the policeman." I gave her a high five. "You're a great friend for anyone to have. And your hair is so pretty. Maybe you can show me how to do my hair like yours."

It occurred to me I might be getting obvious. I backed off. They were playing some songs I assumed were modern. Brad and Jennifer started tapping the rhythm. "Can you sing the words?"

They did.

"Wow. You two could be music stars."

"Us? I don't know as we're that good," Jennifer demurred.

"You are," Brad told her. "You've got a great voice. And Natalia could back us up on her harp."

"That sounds more like guitar music. Do either of you play guitar?"

"I do," Jennifer said.

"I do drums," Brad threw in.

"Perfect. If you listen to the music, those are the main instruments you hear."

Jennifer and I went to the ladies' room. "I know what you're trying to do, but why? I thought you liked Brad."

"I just think that you like him more. And you two have so much in common."

"I do like him, but I don't think he likes me more than as a friend."

"Of course, he does. I'll keep working on him. He'll realize how great you are in no time."

She smiled and gave me a hug. "You're a true friend."

"I want to be. I owe you."

"Thanks to you, my life's gotten really exciting."

Brad dropped off Jennifer first. Kal and I walked home from Brad's.

"That was weird."

"What?"

"The way you kept complimenting Jennifer."

"She reminds me of—" I stopped.

"Chanelle.'"

He looked at me.

"How Chanelle might have been if her personality hadn't changed."

When I went to sleep, I kept seeing Lancaster's face, not as it was that day but as it was when I was a child. I started tossing and turning, worried I had really messed up. I opened my eyes and stared at the ceiling. I had so many questions. I'd blown up that bridge. Selini was sure he had died over sixteen years ago, but did he? The picture was him. How long had he been below and was he a good guy or a bad guy? Being below didn't make someone evil or I would be evil.

Jennifer's other questions nagged at me. Why didn't I feel an explosion when Brad kissed me? Why didn't I yearn for more? Maybe I was a defective human.

I was more exhausted than ever in the morning. If only I could find Lancaster without hurting Kal.

Before Kal was up, I ate a quick breakfast and then ran across the street to ask Brad to take me to Selini's. When I got there, I told her what Lancaster had said and that he was the guy in the picture.

"A lot of people look alike. Are you sure he isn't an android?" she asked.

"He doesn't seem like one. Also, I remembered him from when I was a kid, down below. He looked younger then. He was kind when I was crying, and he made me a flower. Jennifer thinks he might be my father."

Selini didn't say anything at first. "If your Robert hadn't been killed, Stan never would have been able to take your mother below."

"I've got to find Bob, so I can ask him some more questions, but I told him to stay away from me permanently, and he agreed. If he were a bad guy, he'd still be hanging around me."

"I wish I knew what to tell you."

"Could he be my father?"

"See if you can verify his identity before you get attached to him." That was a non-answer but it made me think the answer might be "yes."

We went back to the science museum, the first place I had seen Mr. Lancaster. There was no sign of him.

"He promised not to see you again. He's probably avoiding the places you frequent," Brad said.

"I wish I hadn't made him promise. But don't tell Kal that. It hurts him to think I might not be his sister."

"The students from school are having a mid-summer vacation dance. Would you like to go? If the world is going to end, we might as well live it up in the meantime.

"How can you stay calm?"

"Panicking won't help. I think better when I'm relaxing."

"Why don't we all go? I don't want anyone to feel excluded, and besides, together, we might come up with an idea to save the world."

"You're very sweet. I noticed how you were trying to make Jennifer feel included last night. Not a lot of girls would do that for other girls."

"She is amazing."

"You miss your best friend?"

"I miss who I thought she was. Jennifer looks a lot like her: red hair, blue eyes and freckles. Chanelle was taller the last time I saw her. After her transformation, her freckles went away. After each transition, Chanelle became more and more reserved and controlled." I smiled at Brad. "You look a little like this guy named Robert Horton that I knew. He was really nice."

"Did you ever date him?"

"The first guy I ever went on a date with was you."

He smiled. "That makes me feel special. That's odd. Usually, red hair runs in families. Neither you nor Kal has red hair."

"I don't remember their mother, but Kal's dad doesn't have red hair. When Chanelle was little, her hair wasn't red."

"When did it turn red?"

"When she was about four. The transition! It was part of the transition." I started to cry.

"What?"

"It's just that most of the time, she wasn't real."

He put his arm around me. It felt comforting.

"Thank you for being my friend." I jumped. "The timepiece. Something is going to happen in a little over a week, and we don't know what for sure."

"If it's robots, we know they are vulnerable. The policeman at the history museum effectively killed two of them with one shot."

"You saying we need to all get guns and shoot them and hope it's robots we are shooting?"

"No. I'm saying they are not invincible. There was a movie, *Independence Day*, that also had a countdown timer. The good guys found the vulnerability in their computers. But those running the show below are human, not robots."

"I was wrong about my best friend. I could have been wrong about everyone—except my mom and Kal."

"Either way, they're more vulnerable than the space aliens in the movie were."

"I wonder if the university has any answers."

"The one where the guy chased us?"

"We can create a cover story for the professor. We're with a group of students who saw the countdown timer. We saw the story about the explosion and then asked questions. That led us to the hospital and then the university."

"He nailed us for having information that wasn't in the news, and we said it was for school. I'm sure we can concoct something."

"Let's go for it."

We went back to the university. We looked into the lab. The guy who inquisitioned us in the cafeteria wasn't there, and the robotic parts were gone, too.

"I wonder if he put Denton back together," I speculated.

"That would be dangerous for us all. Makes Frankenstein's monster look like a flower child."

We turned to leave, but our way was blocked.

CHAPTER 41

"Well, well, well, returned to the scene of the lies?"

"I wasn't lying to you. We saw the countdown timer. Someone at the dig-up there suggested there was a connection to the guy in the hospital, and we thought we'd investigate. We're just curious high school students," I lied, rather smoothly.

"Your interest seemed like more than that."

"I'm fifteen," I noted.

"I'm sixteen," Brad stated.

"Where is the guy with the phony beard?"

"Tony is just a student," Brad replied.

"Tony?"

"Tell me about the robot."

"The one you called Denton?"

"It was a made-up name," I said.

"Odd. A silver nameplate that came out of the debris said Jason Denton."

"Then that man in the crowd was right. We thought he made up the part about Denton that night when everyone was looking at the countdown timer," Brad covered.

"Man?" he questioned.

"He was an old man who said he was around at the time of the poisoning," I continued the lie.

"But enough of our answering questions," Brad said impatiently. "We want to know what is going on with that robot we saw in the lab."

"Confidential."

"So is our information, but we were forthcoming."

"What did you say your names were?"

"You haven't even given us yours. No more information until you tell us what you know," Brad countered.

"Brenden Marsh, Mr. Marsh to you."

"And in answer to our question?" Brad demanded.

"A man named Fenton insisted that Denton was his cousin."

"Was he able to claim the body?" I asked.

"No, because, as you know, there was no body. I was told you saw the head."

"Do you think the underground is planning an invasion to match the countdown timer? A robot invasion?"

"You watch too many movies."

"Preparation is the key to survival," Brad said.

"And if there is an invasion, you need to be prepared," I warned.

We left, refusing to give him any more information unless he gave us his. Had we satisfied him that we were not tied to Denton? I didn't know.

As we left the building, I noticed him following us. "If we go to our car, he'll run the plate," Brad warned.

"What do we do?"

"We walk and pick up the car later. Want lunch?"

We went into a cafeteria. By pre-agreement, I went to the ladies' room and climbed out the window.

Brad was outside. "He was watching the restrooms from the inside after you left and so I made it look as if I was there for a work shift and took off through the kitchen."

"Smart."

Watching my back, I ran to the campus library while Brad hid out near the cafeteria to watch for the man leaving.

I picked up some books and waited at a table for Brad, who wasn't long in arriving.

"I've been looking at sci-fi books on people coming up from the underground. Most are pretty ridiculous. But this book looks like it might be about stage two of the Great Reset. It mentions robots and a countdown."

Brad glanced through the book. "The author is Graham Woodly. He lives somewhere in the area. The publisher is over on Sierra."

He went to the photocopier and copied the cover page. We were very careful when leaving to make sure nobody was tailing us.

"What about the prof?"

"Went back to the classroom."

<hr>

Our next stop was Sierra Street.

"We don't give out our author's addresses," the woman at the front desk said.

"But we are working on a very important project for school," Brad professed. "With some of Graham's ideas, he could really help."

"He writes fiction, not science or history. If you have a phone number, I'll give it to him. If he's interested, he'll give you a call." She looked through her card file and then began typing a text on her phone.

"Please. It's important that we talk to him now," I said.

She glared at me. "Everyone claims their requests are important. He may or may not call you back. What are your numbers?"

"Never mind." I wasn't giving out any personal information.

"All we seem to get are dead ends," I said as we left.

"Not quite. I have an address. When she looked him up, I saw the file card."

"Double smart."

We went to the address. It was an apartment building. There was no answer at Graham's.

I knocked on his neighbor's door. A woman answered. "I don't know his name," she related. "He's not very neighborly."

"Do you have any idea when he'll be back?" Brad inquired.

"I see him every now and then. He comes in, picks up some mail and leaves."

"Do you know where he goes?"

"I mind my own business, but I don't think he lives there."

"You don't?" I asked.

"He only comes in for about ten minutes on the days he's here and then he's off. He's never here at night."

"Very secretive," I said to Brad as we were leaving.

"Maybe he really does know something."

At home, Kal was fuming. "Where did you go? Why didn't you take me?"

"It's good you didn't go. We went to the university. The prof who chased us was interested in us but wouldn't tell us anything," Brad said.

"And he asked about you in particular," I added.

"What did you tell him?"

"That you were Tony, a high school student."

"He could have captured you, followed you."

"He tried, but he didn't get very far," I said. "We also found a book by a Graham Woodly. He seems to know what is going on, but his book is fiction and he is keeping his whereabouts secretive."

"There is something really off about the prof. Did he act like any professor you've seen before?" Brad asked.

"No. Well, not like any from the underground," I said.

"Nor the above ground. He seemed more like an investigator."

"He did."

"Do you think the government knows what the underground is planning?" Kal queried.

"Isn't that their job?" Brad asked.

"If they are prepared, maybe we don't need to do anything," I said.

"Like those not part of the elite were last time. Do you want to take that chance?" Brad asked.

While we went to the hospital with Katerina and helped Miss Holiday get back to her home comfortably, Brad worked with Roger and Jennifer to find out what they could about Graham Woodly.

Miss Holiday's house was nice, but smaller than Steve's and Katerina's and surrounded by a farm. We tried not to act like we had never seen the place before.

"Roy has been doing double duty, taking care of his farm and mine," she said.

"This is partway to the history museum," Katerina noted. "I used to go there all the time. I liked Otis. He was always so full of information."

I thought about how we had buried him, privately, without anyone there.

"Maybe we can have a memorial service for him," I suggested.

Kal poked me, maybe afraid we'd be outing ourselves. We hadn't told Miss Holiday or Roy about burying Ottis.

"I think it's a wonderful idea," Miss Holiday said. "I'll call Roy and see what he thinks."

Katerina hugged me. "I am so proud of you, talking about a memorial service for that sweet caretaker."

I wondered if she had forgotten all we had told her about burying him. Maybe she was trying to dismiss it because our story was too ridiculous.

"Before we leave, we should pick up some of your clothes," she told me and Kal. "How about you run to your rooms and grab some?"

CHAPTER 42

"That's an excellent idea," I said, trying not to show any nervousness.

"Oops. I had asked Mrs. Cramer to pick up some things for charity and she said she had taken all the things I had put into the laundry room. I hope she didn't take your clothes while I was gone," Miss Holiday covered.

Kal looked at Katerina. "Let's hope not. We'll check."

We went out of the living room and started opening doors in the hope of pretending we had looked in our rooms. We opened one door and it looked like a bathroom.

We opened another door and went inside. "We need an excuse."

"How about the clothes are too poor?" Kal suggested. "We feel better in the new clothes Steve and Katerina got us."

I opened a closet. "Look."

There were clothes in what looked like Kal's size inside. We picked up a duffel bag and put some in it.

We went into another room with a closet containing clothes that looked like they'd fit me. We added those to the bag.

We returned to the living room. "Some of our best clothes are still here. With what Steve and Katerina have gotten us, we're all set."

While I gave Miss Holiday a hug, she whispered, "Roy found those at a second-hand store yesterday. Good thinking on his part."

After I pulled away, she said more clearly, "Roy has called some of the local farmers and other friends who used to visit the museum. We're all going over to Roy's and then walking together to the museum."

At Roy's, we were greeted by others who remembered the curator. Roy put Miss Holiday on a horse so she wouldn't have to walk. The rest of us walked over to the grave and placed flowers around it.

"I have an uneasy feeling about this," Kal whispered.

"Me too. It's as if someone is watching us."

"Make sure we're hidden in the middle of the crowd."

"That's what I've been doing so far."

Several of those who knew Otis said a few words about what a wonderful person he had been and how much he had contributed to the community. I wasn't the only one who had to wipe away tears.

Afterwards, we had refreshments at Roy's.

"We need to rush out of here before someone points out Miss Holiday doesn't have children," Kal whispered. So far, the subject hadn't come up. The neighbors seemed to assume we were with Katerina, but we'd already been taking too many chances. At points, where it looked as if someone would inquire, Roy or Miss Holiday would change the subject.

"Katerina, we need to get back. We have a date with Brad that we forgot about," Kal advised. "I don't want to rush you."

"Talk of death makes me a bit queasy," I added.

"Oh, I'm sorry." She went over to Miss Holiday. "We need to leave."

"That's fine." She looked over at us. I had a feeling she was a bit relieved too.

We each gave Miss Holiday a hug and were off.

Shortly after we arrived home, Brad dropped by to ask us to come over to his place.

"We've been researching Mr. Woodly, and we think it's a fictitious name, but we have another address he's used. It's at a convenience store.

"You think he lives in a convenience store?" I asked.

"No, but from the photographs, it looks as if there is an apartment above the store."

"Let's go," I said.

"What if he knows so much because he's one of the people from below and is setting a trap for the curious?" Kal asked.

"Kal, if we hang out scared, we aren't going to save the world."

"Okay, but we need to take precautions."

"What would you suggest?"

"Park down the street and have an exit strategy."

We didn't see an outside entrance to the apartment. But inside the outer door to the convenience store, there was a staircase. We walked up it and knocked at the door. We waited. Someone looked through a peephole.

"We're not going away until you answer," Jennifer announced. I liked her. She was bold and courageous.

"You are awesome, Jennifer," I said, making sure Brad heard me.

Finally, the door opened. We didn't wait for an invitation. We marched in.

"Enter," the man responded, sarcastically.

"We did. Thank you," Brad replied.

"What brings you marching in unannounced?"

"Your book, *When They Come Up*."

"That was a bust."

"Not with us," Brad said. We sat down on his couch.

"Have a seat." He glared at us, looking like he could hardly wait to be rid of us.

"They found the countdown timer," I said. "And two robots came up from below and exchanged gunfire with a policeman at the museum, only to be destroyed. How did you know?"

"I didn't."

"You wrote about it," I asked. "Are you a prophet?"

"I guess I might be. Things just come to me and I write them down."

"And what is the plan of the robots? Are they going to take over? Are they going to kill us all?"

"They weren't expecting anyone to be alive."

"And now that they have found people alive?"

"You said they were killed? Did they relate to others that there were people alive up here?" Woodly asked.

"Who knows," Kal said. "Their remains weren't forthcoming with information."

"Did they have a backup plan in case people were alive?" Brad asked.

"The robots are armed," he acknowledged.

"Does the countdown timer relate to an armed robot invasion or some kind of new poisoning?" I inquired.

"They don't want to poison themselves. The poisoning was to be temporary—long enough to kill off the above population."

"And you know all this how?" I asked.

"It just comes to me."

"I see. Did you ever live down below? Is that how you found out?" Kal asked.

"If I did, I couldn't tell you." He smiled. "It's a fiction book."

"You said that," Brad noted.

"Okay. What color were the rainbows?" I asked.

"Rainbows?"

"Down below."

"Like any other rainbows. They were all colors of the spectrum."

"You're lying. But how do you know about the underworld?"

"Lying! How dare you!"

"The rainbows were nothing like that," Kal said.

"You're wrong."

"And how would you know that?" Kal asked.

"You got your information from somewhere," Brad said. "Now we're going to reveal you as a fraud if you don't tell us your source."

"I wrote a fiction book. It came out of my head. I never claimed any of it was real."

"You and I both know that you didn't write it as a fiction book. Someone fed you that information," Kal accused.

"You're kids, and you don't have the right to speak to me that way. Get out!"

"We're going to give your name and address to the next set of robots we see if you don't give us your source," Brad threatened.

"You think that scares me?"

"We'll see," Brad said. "We'll be back tomorrow. We want to know your source." He turned to us. "Let's go."

Going down the stairs, I asked Brad, "We're just going to leave him? What if he's not here tomorrow?"

"There's a back exit from the building. I figure he'll next go to his source or call him. If he goes to the source, we can follow him. If he calls him, the source may come here. Kal and Natalia, you are the only two who could recognize someone from below. Natalia, you stay out front with me and Kal, you stay out back with Jennifer and Roger. Rog, call me if he goes out the back, and I'll do likewise."

We agreed.

We got some snacks from the store. I waited near the front while Brad brought his car closer.

An hour later, he was still inside. I knew that Steve and Katerina would be expecting me home soon. We were about to leave when Jennifer called Brad. "He's on the move."

Brad drove around to the back alley and she pointed to a garage. "Woodly went in there."

A few minutes later, a car drove out and we followed. It went from Riverhill to a high-rise apartment building in Sutter Springs. We started to follow him inside. A doorman said, "Halt? Who are you visiting?"

"Our daddy, Mr. Woodly, just went up and we were supposed to follow him," Jennifer said, looking like she was about to cry.

"The five of you are siblings?"

"These two are our cousins," Brad said, pointing to Kal and me.

"I guess you can wait downstairs until your daddy comes back down."

"But we are supposed to join him."

"I'm sure he'll return when he sees you haven't come up."

The worst part was that we didn't know which apartment he had gone to.

We wound up leaving. As we did so, Roger complained to the guard, "Dad will be so upset when he finds out."

"Stay. I'm sure he'll return for you."

"Just sit here? How boring," Roger responded.

We went out to the car. A while later, Woodly left the building. We followed him, but he only went back to the convenience store.

"What do we know?" Roger asked.

"We know that Woodly is getting his information from someone in that building," Kal surmised.

"We'll have to watch it tomorrow. We have to get Kal and Nat home," Brad pointed out.

As Kal and I started to cross the street, Brad pulled me aside. "Tonight's that dance."

"We're all going, right?"

"There will be one guy out?"

"Won't there be others there without dates. Maybe Kal or Roger will find someone."

"Roger will have to. He's not likely to dance with his sister."

"Brothers and sisters don't dance?"

"It's just weird."

When Steve and Katerina asked us how our day went, Kal responded, "Brad drove us around and we got to see more of the city."

I told them about the dance.

Kal looked unhappy until I told him that we wanted him, Roger and Jennifer to come. "There will be other girls there," I said.

"That will be nice," he replied, looking happier and then sad, again.

I asked Katerina, "Is it really that weird for brothers and sisters to dance?"

"There are a lot of brother/sister dance teams."

"Really?"

"Yes."

"So Kal and I could become a dance team."

"You can."

"But I need to know the dances teens do here."

"I think there's a show where there are dance competitions." She looked at an online guide. "Here's one." She turned on a wall monitor in the living room.

I went into Kal's room. "Katerina said there are a lot of brother/sister dance teams and she found a show with current dances. Want to see if we can do them?"

"I don't know."

"Come out and look."

The couples in the video were doing lifts and flips as part of their dances.

"That's competition level. Most dancers do more basic moves. Maybe I can find another show," Katerina said.

"That's okay," I said. Dancing below normally included gymnastics but the flips we were watching looked like baby moves.

We did our best to imitate the people on TV, adding in more age-appropriate flips, but our rhythm was off. We would have met extreme disapproval over that below.

"That's good," Steve said.

"It's awful. Our timing is off," I admitted.

"I couldn't tell, and those flips you did were amazing."

"They're kids' moves," Kal said.

"With those flips, you could almost compete in the Olympics," Katerina gushed.

"Olympics?" I'd heard about those. "Aren't the Olympics those old games where our government used to ban other countries that said "no" to our country's economic and military positions?"

"That was before the gap following the Reset. There's no banning, anymore, and now only girls compete in girls' sports and only boys compete in boys."

"Makes sense."

"Prior to the poisoning, boys were winning girls' sports, girls were getting injured and killed by the boys competing as girls. Most girls didn't have a chance," Katerina said.

"And who won the boys' sports?"

"Boys."

"So, girls basically had no rights when it came to sports."

"Society is much saner now," Steve acknowledged.

I reflected back on what I'd heard my dad say about women losing all their rights. Maybe that's what he was talking about.

Kal and I finally got into sync.

Katerina had me wear one of her long formal dresses. Once again, she did my hair.

"You always make my hair look so good."

"It's not me. Your hair is beautiful."

Kal kept staring at me after I came out of my room.

"What's wrong?"

"Nothing."

Our friends came to the door. "Wow," Roger reacted.

"Jennifer is the real wow," I said.

"She does look nice. You look more beautiful every time I see you," Brad said.

"I'm just me," I responded. "If I looked like Jennifer, Katerina wouldn't have had to do my hair."

"My sister's a natural beauty," Roger remarked.

"She is," I agreed.

"Would you like to get going?" Brad asked.

The dance was on the shore of a nearby lake, making my outfit totally inappropriate.

"I wish you had told me my dress wouldn't work," I told Brad.

"It looks so good on you. I didn't want you to change."

The dress helped with my plan. I pretended to trip and injure my ankle so I couldn't dance and had an excuse to talk Brad into slow dancing most of the night with Jennifer. But at the end of the night, he picked me up and carried me to the car, something that was not part of my plan.

Brad dropped Kal and me off at the Drakes and drove our other friends home. "Do you think he'll kiss her goodnight?" I asked Kal.

"Jealous?"

"Just the opposite."

"Your foot is better," he observed as I walked towards my bedroom.

"I guess it was just temporary. Bad timing. If I were still at the dance, I could slow dance with Brad."

"Maybe, next time." He stomped to his bedroom.

Katerina, who was watching, came into my room and said, "He's jealous."

"But he's my brother."

"Not of Brad. Of the fact that you have someone and he doesn't."

"Oh. Actually, I'm working on matching Brad up with Jennifer."

"Matchmaking isn't that easy. The people have to have something in common."

"They have a lot in common. They both like science, music, dancing, swimming and checking things out."

"You're a skilled dancer yourself."

"They did a different type of dancing tonight," I said. "And I got him to slow dance with Jennifer, but I don't know if it worked."

"A lot of times when kids grow up together, they start taking each other for granted. It's sometimes much harder for them to get together than people who have just met."

So, how to get Brad to stop taking Jennifer for granted? But it might not happen with a week left before a potential invasion.

CHAPTER 43

The next day, I was preparing to go over to Brad's, but as I went into the kitchen to grab breakfast, I could see that Steve was dressed very casually. "What's happening?"

"I've decided to take a few days off."

"Oh. Oh, that's great. What are you and Katerina planning to do?"

"We thought we'd take you and Kal to a carnival?"

"Carnival?"

"Today, the carnivals are more exciting than even some of the big theme parks used to be. Lots of wild rides and lots of fun."

Kal came into the kitchen. "Steve and Katerina are going to take us to a carnival with fun rides."

"Wonderful," he said, stiffly, though I suspected that wasn't what he wanted to do.

"Before I forget," Steve said. "I got you each a cell phone. That way, we can keep in touch with you. Don't worry. We don't use 4, 5, 6 or 7G if your mother warned you about the old days."

"Good."

Brad came to the door. We invited him in for some breakfast and told him the plan.

"Roger, Jennifer and I are going to research a book. I love sci-fi books." I knew what he was talking about.

"Me too," I said. "Maybe later this evening, you can tell me all about the plot."

"Will do."

As I said goodbye to Brad, he responded. "Last night, I had a wonderful time with you."

"I mostly just sat there."

"Looking beautiful."

"Thank you."

"Steve got me a phone." I showed it to him and he punched his number into it.

Kal handed Brad his phone. Brad did likewise with it.

After he left, Katerina said, "It may take a while. He seems very infatuated with you."

"That means attracted, right?"

"But if he goes too far, I'll pull out my set of golf clubs," Steve remarked with a smile.

"What does golf have to do with dating?" Kal asked.

"You'll know when you become a father."

They didn't have carnivals below. I could hardly wait to get on the rides. I thought about how Eterra would have liked some of them, but Steve and Katerina had talked me into leaving her at home. They had roller coasters that fell off the track in mid-air and dropped right back onto a new track. They turned us upside down and whirled us around.

"I've never had so much fun," I told Steve.

"With all the gymnastics you do, I thought this would be your thing," Steve replied.

There was also a splash ride where we descended down a windy waterway, with water splashing all over us, drenching our outfits. It seemed as if the water was especially aiming at me. At the bottom, I jumped out of the giant rubber cup we were sitting in and into the water. I laughed and saw Kal chuckling too.

"Hey," an attendant yelled at me. "You can't." I dove underwater and his words disappeared. Next I knew, Steve had jumped in and was pulling me to the side.

"They have strict rules here."

"Sorry, but that was fun."

He laughed. "Sometimes, the rules are for the birds."

I looked up. "The birds are really beautiful. We didn't have any where I used to live." As soon as I said it, I knew I had screwed up.

"I would think there would be lots of birds on your mom's farm," Katerina said.

"I guess they were afraid she'd get angry if they ate the crops," I lied.

"She probably has scarecrows," Steve surmised.

As we passed a house of horrors and mirrors, Kal tried to pull me in.

"We'll let you two go in alone," Steve suggested.

"Great," I said, figuring that Steve and Katerina might want alone time.

As we got inside, we saw ourselves surrounded by mirrors. Then I thought I saw a familiar figure in a mirror. One second it was there and then it was gone.

The face came into view again. "Brad!" I called. As I started to rush towards the figure, I smashed into the mirror.

I turned. The lights went out. Kal took my hand and pulled me onward. I tried to keep up with him, but our hands got separated. If I were an android I could have seen in the dark. They had better vision than humans. I wondered how we were supposed to navigate this place. I tripped over something and a hand clasped mine and guided me somewhere. I hoped it was towards the exit.

"Kal?" I asked. There was no answer. He was being really quiet. Something felt off about his hand.

"Kal?" He still didn't say anything as he continued guiding me.

We kept walking in the dark. "Why are all the lights out? I mean, we can't see the horrors or the mirrors if the lights are out."

Something was placed around my neck. It was some kind of

jewelry. I touched it. There was something warm about it. "Thank you," I said. I hadn't seen Kal buy me a gift.

I felt a hug.

A second later, the lights went on and I was alone. Kal rushed over to me. "Where did you go?"

"I thought I saw—Never mind. The mirrors were distorting everything."

The lights went out again and Kal held my hand tightly as we found the way out.

"We were wondering if you were going to spend all evening in there," Steve said.

"Hardly. They cut the lights," Kal informed him.

"Would you two like some snow cones?" Katerina asked.

"Yes," I said.

"There's something off," Kal commented.

"My brother worries," I said. But something was happening to me. I was feeling loopy.

Kal ran back to the exhibit. "Kal?" Steve yelled. We all followed, or rather, Steve followed, and Katerina pulled me along with her.

"Honey, what is it?" she asked me.

"Everything's fine," I said.

"Did you have something to drink?" Katerina asked.

"Snow cone. We were going to get a snow cone."

I heard my speech get almost slurry and I felt like I had to hang onto consciousness.

Kal loudly asked the man at the entrance, "Who turned out the lights in there?"

"We're checking it out. It was some kind of power failure."

"You didn't cut the lights on purpose?" Kal asked.

"No."

Katerina had me sit on a bench. "Wait here, honey. I'll help rush Steve with those snow cones." She leaned over me. "Are you alright?"

I nodded, but I felt barely conscious.

I found myself standing up and walking. It was as if my legs were moving, but I had no idea where I was going.

"Natalia, where are you going?" The voice sounded familiar. The name Kal floated through my mind, but I couldn't even recollect what that name meant to me. Someone took my hand. I twisted and pulled away. I didn't know why, but I had to go somewhere.

I started moving very fast. I thought I heard someone call my name, again. "Natalia, where did you go?"

Again, the word Kal came to mind. *What is a Kal?*

Next I knew someone grabbed me. I was in the air and someone was carrying me over his shoulder. I wasn't afraid. Suddenly, I was released. Through a blur, I saw my grabber's head on the ground. Sparks were flying from around it, but I had a feeling I knew him, and was supposed to go to him.

I started to the head and something or somebody smashed it. The electronic sparks increased, blasting brighter and wider. I could see electrodes on the ground. I had to put his head back together and stop the sparking, but I was barely conscious.

Wet stuff started pouring out of my eyes, but I couldn't figure out what was running down my face. Part of me felt the sparking person on the ground was important to me. Or was he?

"Miss." I looked through a blurry fog. It was an officer.

Someone else picked me up and ran with me. I didn't know what was going on, but it seemed as if we stopped somewhere dark as I heard footsteps, lots of them, going by.

"I think she went this way." It sounded like the officer I had seen through the fog.

In the distance, I heard the voice that I associated with the word Kal calling for me. I tried to answer, but my vocal cords wouldn't work. I blacked out. As a whiff of consciousness floated through my mind, I sensed I was in the backseat of a car. I was practically foaming at the mouth, like an epileptic, but I didn't think I was epileptic. What could be going on?

CHAPTER 44

Next I knew, I woke up on a park bench.

"Why don't you want her to know?" It was Selini's voice.

I sat up. "What happened?" Everything was swaying a little and then it settled down.

"They found you," she said. "Do you remember what happened?"

"What? I was like epileptic." There were no epileptics down below, but I had read about them. "I was out of it, almost controlled, like a robot. I'm not a robot, am I?"

"No. They controlled you with this?" She held out a necklace, hanging from a plastic pen. "Where did you get it?"

"I don't remember. I think I was at a carnival tonight."

"This needs to be put somewhere safe until we find out who is behind it."

"Why are you here?"

"Someone called me and told me you were in danger."

"Who?"

"I was asked not to tell. But it's nobody to worry about." She looked apologetic.

"What's going on?"

"I need to run some electronics on this. Call Kal and your friends. You are going to need them here."

I looked around. We were close to the science museum. "Why are we here?"

"Tell them to meet you here. Do you trust me?"

"My mother trusted you."

"I'll take that."

"Someone saved me?"

"That someone wants to remain anonymous. I had to promise."

"Am I safe?"

"I don't know. We need to find out what this does." She put the necklace in a metal case.

She pulled a cuff off my wrist.

"Did he put this on too?"

"No, I brought the blood pressure cuff to check you out."

I was trying to grasp what was going on. I remembered that Steve and Katerina had taken Kal and me to a carnival. Before I had a chance to make any calls, Brad, Jennifer and Roger showed up.

"How did you get here?"

"You texted me," Brad said.

"I didn't text you."

"It's alright. I think I know who did," Selini confided. "Where is Kal?"

"I'll call him," Brad offered.

"Only have him come if he can get away without anyone noticing."

I realized I didn't have Kal's number on the phone Steve had given me. I wondered why I didn't but fortunately Brad did.

Brad started to help me up. I was wobbly. He lifted me and we went towards the museum. Selini had an access code to a side door opening on a staircase to the basement.

"It's going to be alright. We need to find out what this trinket is and what we can do with it."

We went into the basement, where there was a lab. "Your mother could have figured this out right away," she continued. "She was my friend and mentor. I can't guarantee I'll be as good. Do you know who put this on you?"

I shook my head.

She put the metal box inside a clear, thick container and maneuvered the instruments inside to open the box. As I saw the necklace again, I felt my throat. Someone had put that on me. *But who?*

The thing started sparking in multiple colors.

"When this was on you, you lost consciousness and started acting almost robotically."

"What? They have a way to turn people into robots now without an operation?"

"I guess they don't have to chop off heads anymore," Jennifer said. "They can just reprogram someone."

"But when it was removed, you returned to normal. It's only effective as long as you're wearing it."

"They found me."

"Somebody did."

"If I had been a robot instead of a person, what would this have done?"

"Let me try to have my computer decode the signal. It may take a while."

"I texted Kal that we were taking you home," Brad said. "I said you weren't feeling well and I took you somewhere for something to eat."

Brad's phone buzzed. "Steve and Katerina are worried about you. They've been searching the carnival."

"Whoever saw me probably saw Kal too. Do you think it's safe to go home? Could I be putting Steve and Katerina in danger?"

"If they know you are up here, they won't stop looking for you. Be very careful, and don't put on any more jewelry."

Brad tapped something into his phone. "I told Kal to make sure they aren't followed from the carnival."

"Roger and Jennifer, can you stay at my house tonight?" Brad asked. "We can take shifts watching their house."

On the way home, Brad texted Kal with more of the details but told him to keep it quiet.

At home, Steve and Katerina rushed over to me.

"You should have notified us right away," Katerina scolded Brad.

"I'm sorry. She was very dizzy and disoriented. Maybe her sugar levels were low. She's better now."

"I'd like to take you to Valley to run some tests on you," Steve said. "You could be hypoglycemic."

"You seemed fine when we went into the House of Horrors and Mirrors and then the lights went out," Kal said. "It was probably the optics. I've read that certain images can trigger reactions like this."

"That was mostly flashing images in cartoons," Steve remarked.

"I don't remember it at all," I said. "Maybe it was an allergic reaction to something. Anaphylactic shock. I read something about it at the museum."

"Let's get her to her room," Jennifer said.

"I can do that," Katerina offered.

"It's okay," Steve told Katerina. "They probably want to say good-night to her."

"Are you still hungry?" Katerina asked.

"Starving," I said.

I sat on my bed and Eterra jumped up and lay across my lap.

Jennifer looked worried. "Someone recognized you, but you didn't recall or recognize him or her?"

"Everything is so foggy."

"Inside the House of Horrors and Mirrors, you called Brad's name. After we got out, Steve was going to get you a snow cone and you started sounding weird," Kal recalled.

"Me?" Brad responded. "I wasn't there."

"But you were later."

"Yes, but not until much later. Someone rescued her and I don't know who," Brad said.

"The three of us were together until someone texted Brad about your sister," Jennifer informed Kal.

"I don't recall. Maybe I imagined I saw Brad."

Kal looked at Brad kind of funny.

"He was with us, miles away from the Carnival all day," Roger assured him.

"I wonder if the person who took you away was following you," Kal pondered. "Could he have been in that place when the lights went out?"

"If I remembered being there, I might know. And who carried me to the bench and called Selini? Someone must have rescued me from whoever put the necklace on me and took me away."

"Selini didn't know who called her?" Kal asked.

"She didn't want to say. I wonder if my mom got out. My mom! If she is still down there and they know I'm up here and escaped, she could be in danger." My not-father had no qualms about killing me. I had thought he loved or at least cared about my mom, but would he kill her if he learned of her betrayal? I had to hope for the best.

Katerina and Steve came into the room as our friends left. "We love you both. If something bothers you, please come to us. Don't be afraid of upsetting us," Katerina said.

"We'll take care of you. It's great that you have friends, but we are in a better position to figure out what's wrong and help," Steve advised.

"Thank you. I didn't know what was happening. I was so dizzy. I passed out, and when I woke up, I wasn't at the carnival."

"Did someone do something to you?"

"No!" I said, a little too strongly. The last thing I wanted was to endanger my new family. "I don't know what happened. But when I woke up, someone had texted Brad on my cell phone and he and the others arrived shortly after that."

"We need to have this checked out. Have you ever experienced any blackouts or seizures in the past?" Steve asked.

"Not that I know of. I think it was what Brad said, that I needed to get some sugar in me."

"Low blood sugar can do that."

"Maybe a movie would calm Natalia down," Kal suggested. "I'll see what I can find online."

The movie he found was *Future World*. It was apparently a sequel to something, but starting with the sequel meant we didn't have to watch a two-hour lead-in.

While we watched it, Katerina brought in a plate of spaghetti for each of us. I was hungry and devoured the whole thing quickly.

"I guess brainwashing makes a person hungry," I told Kal.

"I was hungry too," Kal said. "I spent half the afternoon and evening rushing around looking for you."

As the two main characters kissed to figure out they were them instead of their android doubles, I asked Kal. "Do you think that works?"

"What?"

"That you can tell the difference between an android and a person by kissing them?"

"Maybe. You kissed Brad. Did he feel human?"

"I guess so. I didn't have anything to compare to."

"Maybe we should try it—in case one of us is replaced."

"But sisters and brothers? Yuck. That's disgusting."

"For scientific purposes, just so we'll know if we are changed out."

I reluctantly agreed. He leaned in and kissed me. It didn't feel yucky at all. In fact, it felt great or rather awesome. I wound up almost breathless. I pulled away, somewhat freaked out, not so much from kissing my brother but from enjoying kissing my brother.

CHAPTER 45

He saw the expression of horror on my face and looked almost frightened. "I didn't like it either!" he reacted. "Super ick." He made a face.

Wonderful, not only had I kissed my brother, but while I felt incredible, he hated it. I had to save my honor. "Then we shouldn't ever do it again. Brothers aren't supposed to kiss sisters like that. I'm going to try to forget that happened so I don't throw up."

"At least, now we'll know. That is, if a *Future World* scenario ever happens."

"Let's hope it doesn't, so we don't have to resort to that."

"Yeah," he said, looking a little stunned. "So, you think I'm an awful kisser?"

"It's just the idea of kissing my brother, you know, eww."

He almost looked sad. "Yeah." He hesitated and then asked. "What if that guy is your father, and you aren't my sister?"

"Now you don't want a sister? You tired of me or something?"

"No. I was just saying—never mind."

I had nightmares all night after I got to sleep. *I kept dreaming of Chanelle's head being chopped off, and of Robert Lancaster, Brad and Kal. In my dream, they were all robots, chasing me around, trying to put a necklace on me to turn me into a robot. Then, older Chanelle was standing there, saying, "Why resist? You'll be happier this way."*

In one dream segment, I had to kiss Kal and found he really was a robot. My mother was standing at the door to the lab. "You weren't supposed to come back," she cried, as my not-father chopped off her head.

I woke up screaming and then crying. Katerina rushed in. "It's all right, honey. It was just a dream."

"It isn't. They're going to turn me into a robot, just like those men at the museum."

"You have a wonderful imagination, and it's a wonderful thing."

"You don't believe anything we said that day after the museum."

"What happened there was strange. Hopefully, they get to the bottom of it, but you can't let your imagination frighten you like this."

She didn't believe me. We had produced the birth certificates and anything contradicting that would contradict our own documentation. Yet, I had to protect her, Steve, my friends and my brother while remaining human myself.

My brother. I had a hard time taking my mind off that kiss. I wasn't supposed to like it. There was something sick about that. I didn't even like him that much. He'd been really mean to me and Chanelle in the underworld. I wished that kiss had never happened. It was messing with my mind.

I looked at my window. I wanted thicker drapes. I took a comforter and hung it over the curtain rod.

When I opened my eyes in the morning, the room was really dark. I adjusted my eyes and in the dim light, I saw Kal sitting on the floor watching me.

"How long have you been there?"

"I couldn't sleep. I heard you screaming and after Katerina left, I kept worrying. Finally, I had to come in here to make sure you were safe."

"I'm fine. Not worried at all."

"I can see the not-worry hanging over the curtain rod. You said your mother sang about sound. Do you think the necklace spoke to you below the threshold of your hearing?"

"I don't know. If it were talking to me, I couldn't hear it. Do you think whoever, whatever it was, just saw me or did they come looking for me?"

He shrugged. "You can't remember anything?"

"Sparks. I remember a smashed head and sparks and electronics on the ground."

"An android?"

"I guess. Did I kill the android or did someone else do it?"

"It was taking you away. Maybe you did. After you disappeared, a policeman was yelling that someone had broken an exhibit."

"If androids are illegal, it wouldn't be an exhibit."

"The officer could have been confused."

Brad came over. "I think we should retrace your steps up to where you lost consciousness."

"I either dreamed about or remembered an android."

"Let's go back there and find out."

"No. What if they are waiting for my sister?" Kal objected.

"I need to remember. If this helps, I need to do it."

"What if someone sees you again?"

"We'll all run interference," Brad said. "We need to know who is after her and why, and only she can tell us that."

"I agree with Brad," I affirmed.

After breakfast, I asked Steve if we could hang out with our friends.

"I'm off today," Steve said. "I thought we could do something together."

"How about you and Katerina take some together?" I replied. "You have been so busy with us that I think Katerina would like it if you did something special with her."

"We're a family now."

"What if we let you have some alone time this morning and then go somewhere, together, this afternoon?"

Steve turned to Katerina as she entered the living room. "Katerina, would you like to go out on the lake this morning?"

"If the kids want to."

"The two of us."

She looked a little flustered. "After the night Natalia had, I think we should be with her."

"We were also thinking of spending the morning with our friends and then joining you for the afternoon. I'll be alright," I said.

"Are you sure?" she asked.

"Yes."

"If that's what you want. I don't want to crowd you."

"You aren't crowding us. We'll be looking forward to seeing you after lunch," I said.

As we went over to Brad's, Kal asked, "Where did you learn about that alone time stuff?"

"My dad or not-dad used to want alone time with Mom."

"Yuck."

"I thought it was sweet back then."

The five of us returned to the House of Horrors and Mirrors. "It was pretty pathetic in the dark," Kal recalled.

"I don't think it's supposed to be dark in there," Brad said.

Inside, we examined the mirrors and looked for stray occupants.

"Wait! Move over there again, Brad."

He moved in the direction I pointed.

An image flashed in my mind. "That's it. In the mirrors. Someone had your color of hair and complexion and was about your size, but the mirror distorts. You don't even look like you in it."

"Then, what?"

"The lights went out."

"I took your hand but we got separated," Kal recalled.

"Someone put his arm around me, put something around my neck and hugged me."

"He hugged you?"

"It was dark. I thought it was you."

"There was something rigid about him when he hugged me."

"Then?" Brad asked.

"The lights came back on and he wasn't there, but I was really dizzy. It's coming back. They went out again after you found me, Kal, and stayed out. You complained to someone about the lights. Steve and Katerina were going to get snow cones. I sat on a bench. I was so dizzy. It was like I was functioning in a body that wasn't my own. I got up and heard, I think I heard, you call to me, Kal."

"I caught you and you got away from me and ran."

"Then someone picked me up and carried me over his shoulder. Was that you?"

"No," Kal said. "I couldn't find you after you broke loose."

"I was pulled away, and the someone was knocked down. I saw his head smashed in with sparks flying and pieces of his head broken off. I wanted to help him. I think I cared about him in some way."

"Then, you did recognize him?" Brad asked.

"Or it may have been the necklace. It's like a surreal dream with pieces missing. I remember there was a policeman shouting and someone carried me off. The next thing I recall was waking on a park bench near the museum. Selini was there and you three arrived right after that."

"Do you remember anything else?" Brad pressed.

"Selini had the necklace off me and told me that was the problem. I was groggy but awake. We went into the basement?"

Brad nodded. "Someone texted me on your phone. Selini said it wasn't her. Someone called her to be there."

"I was rescued by someone who didn't want to be seen. He or she told her not to tell."

"If the android is smashed, do you think the person reported back that he found you?" Jennifer asked.

"I don't know."

"You said you cared when your captor was smashed. Do you think it was your father?" Roger inquired.

"My not-dad doesn't look anything like Brad and he is not an android."

"An android could be a copy of a living person down there. Your mother had a double," Brad noted.

"She did. And Kal's dad had that double that was destroyed at the History Museum."

"You said I looked like someone you knew," Brad recalled.

"Robert Horton."

"Who is Robert Horton?" he followed up.

"A guy down there. He was in the leadership program with me," Kal responded. "Really quiet. I don't think he liked the program. You do look a bit like him."

"Was he an android?" Brad asked him.

"The leadership program was for real boys who were being groomed to be future leaders. The leaders weren't planning on being replaced by androids."

"Was it him you mistook for me?" Brad asked.

"It's possible."

"What if the androids decided to replace the leaders below?" Roger speculated..

"I saw that in a movie," Jennifer said.

"I knew Robert. He was nice. He didn't act like an android. Androids aren't supposed to show emotion or do weird things like play with flowers and he did," I said, defending him.

"Did he give you flowers?" Kal asked.

"He did. He was nice to me." That seemed to bother Kal.

"Then, maybe they are sending doubles of those below to check out what's above," Brad pondered.

"What about the necklace?" Kal asked.

"Whoever took you could have been programmed to use it to take someone below if they found people alive up here. Robert's double's brain recognized you and put it on you."

"If he was smashed before he could let them know about me, they still might not know. Mom and Steve and Katerina and all of you might be safe."

"That would be the best-case scenario," Kal reasoned.

"But they'll send more. We're approaching the countdown," Jennifer reminded everyone.

"This is a considerable distance from where we came up," I said. "Do you think there are more exits around the city?"

"Maybe," Brad said, concernedly. "The android was probably attracted to the electronics here and maybe something he had, such as the necklace, played havoc with the power."

"Hence the blackout. But why didn't it black him out?" I questioned.

"It might not have been an EMP that cut the lights. Some part of the android might have emitted signals that communicated with the computerized light system in the House of Horrors."

"If it could do that, maybe the next android will go to the power station and take that out."

"If you were the one checking things out for an invasion, where would you go to learn about our post-poisoning culture?" Roger asked.

"There's the history museum," I said. "And the university."

"We need to go back to your house," Brad said. "We promised Katerina you'd be back after lunch."

"Let's grab something to eat on the way back," Jennifer advised.

Roger looked around. "Let's make sure nobody follows if someone is watching here."

"This place is starting to give me the creeps," Jennifer stated.

"Tomorrow morning, we hit the university as incoming freshmen checking out the summer session," Brad proposed.

That afternoon, Steve and Katerina took us to an outdoor roller rink. "If you'd prefer, we can take you to an ice rink."

"I like warm," I said. "And I love the natural sunlight."

It took a little while to get used to it, with Kal falling on his bottom several times, but as skaters started dancing, we steadied ourselves and applied dance moves we'd previously learned on solid ground and somehow managed to stay upright.

Before we left, we were invited to apply for a summer job but hesitated to reply.

Steve told the manager, "We'll let you know."

That evening, while Steve and Katerina were preparing dinner, Kal and I went to his room. "I would like to help pay for our expenses. I hadn't thought about it before we were offered a job. They are doing so much for us and giving us what they call allowances for extra spending."

"You aren't thinking, Natalia. If we get involved in anything that shows us off, someone from below could be watching. We need to keep a low profile."

"Maybe we could find low-profile jobs."

Steve and Katerina had prepared mushroom and pineapple pizza.

Kal and I each grabbed several pieces. "We've been talking," I said. "We'd like to earn some money to pay for all the things you've been buying for us. You know, cover our expenses. And then, you wouldn't need to give us allowance money when we go out. Maybe we could be librarians."

"You don't need to worry about that," Steve countered. "Enjoy your youth. You'll grow up too soon."

"We still wouldn't mind getting jobs," Kal said. "But I really am not into skating."

"You were both sensational," Katerina effused.

"Did you see how many times I fell when I was trying to figure out what I was doing?" Kal asked.

"You're both naturals at so many things: math, basketball, harp, dancing, skating."

I knew she was building up our egos. Brad and others had talents we lacked. Below, I felt ordinary. Mom urged me to excel and now I knew she did so to disguise that I was human.

"We were also thinking that maybe we could tutor other students in math."

"That's an excellent idea. I'll contact the high school and have them add you to the list of private tutors," Steve said.

"Do we need degrees?"

"With your skills?" Steve asked.

That night, Kal and I decided to watch a couple more movies about robots. Most of the movies were older and portrayed robots in a bad light. I figured that the producers had foreseen what the Elites had planned and wanted to avoid that. The first one we saw was, *I Robot*.

"Do you think they included those three laws in the androids below?" I asked Kal.

"They probably coded some kind of subservience to the leaders."

I thought about the necklace. "When I had the necklace on, it was as if I wanted to do what I was directed to do, as if the necklace's choice was my choice."

"With those, if they don't replace people, they can program them."

"Except, the Elites want the latest model, taller, more agile and more ready for the duties they have planned. So, they'll probably stick with the robots." I thought of how busty Chanelle was after the change. I wondered if human males preferred large busts.

"Maybe those necklaces are slave necklaces for unwanted people up here. In *Time Machine*, people were programmed or trained to go below when they heard sirens, as if they had no free will. Maybe the people with necklaces will commit suicide with glee."

"I read in the museum that countries such as Canada encouraged euthanasia for individuals of all ages for all kinds of reasons: depression, bad grades, loss of a job, bills, dissatisfaction with family, vaccine reactions and so forth. Much of the Canadian population was killed off before the poisoning."

"Our parents and the people they worked with are sick," Kal said.

"My mom was nice. If my real father were yours, he wasn't nice."

His face looked a little fallen. "What if we aren't brother and sister? I'm not saying we're not. I'm just posing a hypothetical. If we aren't, would you still hang out with me?"

"Of course. Nobody has been through what we've been through. At first, I didn't like you, but now we're friends."

"Friends?" he asked with a sad tone.

But why would he be sad? Maybe at the thought we're not related. "Friends and brother and sister."

Brad tapped on my window. Roger and Jennifer were with him. I opened it. "Selini called. She's been observing the necklace, and it has some dangerous qualities."

CHAPTER 46

"Does she think it's damaged, Natalia?" Kal asked.

"She didn't say. I think she meant dangerous potentials," Brad expounded.

"We're going to go to the university tomorrow to see if anyone from the underworld has infiltrated. Does she think her analysis will be done by then?" Kal asked.

"I don't know. She wants to see us tomorrow at about noon."

"We've got a week before the countdown date."

"If nothing else, maybe Roger and I can create some giant EMP devices. Of course, that will stop cars and most computers from working. But it could stop a robotic invasion quickly."

"Come on in. We're watching robot movies," Kal suggested.

"Have you seen *The Terminator*?"

"*Terminator*?" Kal asked.

Brad went over to the computer and found the first one. "There are a number of movies in the series. Will Steve and Katerina mind if you don't get much sleep?"

"They're cool," Kal said.

"I would like some sleep before tomorrow," I said.

"We'll just watch the first one and maybe the rest another night," Kal said.

When *Terminator* arrived naked, I laughed. "At least, we didn't have to steal clothes."

"You aren't from the future," Roger pointed out.

"Who would want to be? Did you notice how gloomy it is at the beginning of the movie? At least down below, there are houses and parks, and people are in charge."

"Or they think they're in charge," Roger pondered. "What if robots took over a long time ago and that's why they're transforming every-one. Maybe the leaders just act human?"

"They didn't try to transform me. But I'm sure they'll try if I go back," Kal said.

"And my mom didn't transform me?" I pointed out.

"How do you know? Would you know if you were a robot?"

"Actually, no," I said. "They used organs that look like real ones. Not like the sparking guy or the fake Denton. If I wasn't told Sadie, our maid, was an android, I would have thought she was human."

"The robots that came to the history museum were security robots?" Brad asked.

"Had to be," Kal said. "As I said, the non-security ones don't have those metal parts. The humanoid robots are generally programmed with the brains of their mentors. I suspect, if my dad's robot was supposed to function as my dad, it had his memories, even though what was on the table in the lab was clearly parts of a security double. It's possible the one at the Carnival was programmed with the brain-waves of the person it was modeled after as well."

"You're saying with some of the robots or androids, we might not be able to tell—even from a medical exam—and with others, it's more obvious?"

"Yes," I said. "My mom was working on full organ models, programming them and so forth. Nobody else could do the full organ ones."

"You knew what she was doing?" Jennifer asked.

"I didn't realize they were killing people or kids. I thought it was to assist in the workforce or in case someone was too debilitated or near death and they wanted to save them by using the parts—in some cases, the whole body."

"And they transferred the memories like in *The Sixth Day*," Roger said. "That's another Schwarzenegger movie. I wonder if Arnie knew what they were up to."

"That was clones, not robots. But you bet he did," Brad said. "He had connections."

"If your mom died, do you think they would just replace her?" Roger asked.

"They might be able to do AI security robots without her. I don't know if they could continue the humanoid program without her. She refused to use AI and had a closed system computer. I don't think she gave that double that part of her scientific knowledge, and the double killed herself, anyway."

"Smart," Kal said.

"She probably kept critical details in her head as life insurance," Brad noted. "The problem with AI is it makes humans unnecessary."

"Then you can thank my mom for you being still human, Kal. If AI had taken over, the computers could have replaced everyone."

"But her double had some of your mom's brain. Her primary directive was to protect you during the escape. Your mom knew the schematics and how to get around the AI," Kal recalled.

"I don't believe any of the uploads contain everything. Remember how Chanelle changed every time they aged her? It was as if part of her was missing. I just thought she'd changed, but after I knew what had happened, I also realized that each time, she was too different to be the same person."

"It would freak me out if they replaced my parents," Jennifer said.

"Though it might be an improvement with you," Roger teased.

She slapped his shoulder. "It could only improve you."

"If you were designing the new Kal," Jennifer asked. "What would you change?"

"He'd be nicer to me."

"I am nice to you."

"Now."

"Kal, what would you change about Natalia?" Roger asked.

Kal looked at me. "Nothing."

"Hey, Kal, that's a crime against brothers," Roger said. "We've got to stick together."

"I wouldn't change anything either," Brad said, looking me over.

"I don't know," I said. "I think Jennifer's hair is a prettier color than mine. If I were in charge of my changes, I'd change my hair color."

"I like your hair the way it is," Kal said.

"Kal, brothers aren't supposed to say that," Roger scolded. "Let me try. Your hair: disgusting. Your ears: super repulsive, and that forehead is a sign of low intelligence. I'd redo the whole thing."

"Thank you, Roger," I chuckled. "That makes me feel so good."

"Well, Roger," Jennifer said. "I'd change your teeth to locking snaps so I wouldn't have to listen to you and I'd change that dazed look to one of having a brain behind it. I'd straighten your hair and shorten your nose and when it comes to the ladies, I'd add an extra—"

"That's enough," Roger warned her.

Jennifer smiled at me and we high-fived each other.

"I don't have to worry that you are human, Jennifer. You're terrific and much more fun than anyone down there is now," I said.

I wished I could take that back, thinking about how Chanelle had changed from warm, bubbly and fun to reserved, complacent and polished. "Sorry, Kal," I whispered. "I—"

"It's fine. I saw the changes too," he said. "It's not the same, but I'm glad my current sister is real."

I gave him a hug.

"Rule number one," Jennifer said. "Sisters do not hug or kiss brothers."

"I'll remember that."

Friday morning, we decided to check out the university again. We wanted to find out what was going on with Brenden Marsh, if that was his real name. We decided to start at the records office.

"We need the profiles on the professors," Brad said.

"You think they'll just give us Marsh's record?" Kal asked.

"Of course not," Brad replied. "Jen and Nat, you distract the records supervisor while Roger and I try to locate the computer file on Marsh. I read a book called *Silent Deathfall,* where they pulled this off. But we'll have to vary the distraction in case they've read it, too."

"What about passwords?" Jennifer asked.

"Hopefully, he'll already have his computer open."

Jennifer and I walked into the records office. There were two people working there. A man and a girl who didn't look much older than me.

"I need to see why my profile doesn't reflect my AP scores," Jennifer said.

"What's your name?"

I fainted. "Lani, Lani!" Jennifer yelled at me. I felt hands all over me. "Get her some water and a candy bar. She's going into shock." Jennifer's voice sounded very convincing. Ever since claiming the blood sugar thing, we had read up on diabetes and hypoglycemia, and we'd learned that eating a candy bar was one of the ways to counter an overdose of insulin.

"Susan, go get the girl a candy bar and water from the snack counter," the man said. I was pretty sure he was still right by me, though I was faking unconsciousness. I heard the door open and close.

"My friend, poor thing. This must have been too much for her," Jennifer said.

"Has she done this before?"

"No, but hypoglycemia runs in her family."

"I'd better get her to the nurse's office. If she doesn't respond when Susan comes back, I'll carry her over there myself."

"She is breathing, isn't she?" Jennifer asked. "Oh yes, I can feel it."

As I was lying there, I reflected on my collapse a couple of days before. I wondered if this was what hypoglycemia really felt like.

"She isn't waking up. I need to get her to the nurse," the man said. His voice sounded worried.

"That might be wise. I'll let Susan know where you went."

I was lifted and carried out the door and down the hall.

Another door opened. "What happened?" I heard a woman ask.

"She fainted. Hypoglycemia runs in her family."

"Here's the candy bar and water." It was Susan's voice.

"Who's manning the office?"

"The other girl told me to bring the candy bar and water here."

"I'll go back there."

"Ow," I whined as I pretended to start to come to. "Where am I?"

"I have to leave."

"Wait," I said to him. "What happened? Why am I so dizzy?"

Susan opened the candy bar and put the end in my mouth.

"Thank you," I got out in spite of having my mouth full.

"Susan can fill you in. I have to get back to the office."

"I remember you, sir. You were the last one I saw."

"You fainted."

"Lie down and I'll check you out," the nurse said. "You can give me a report later, Sam."

"Sam, you were the one I was there to see," I coughed out. I was glad I had seen people choking and coughing in some movies. "I needed to speak with you."

"About?"

"It will come to me. It was really important."

"What is your name?"

"Lani. I'm getting dizzy, again."

"After you recover, you can come by my office and we'll discuss your problem. Susan, we need to be getting back. Nice to see you, Sandy."

"I'll let you know when she recovers."

"I haven't thanked you, Sam," I said.

"Now you have."

"Get better," Susan said.

The two of them left. I hoped that was enough time. I picked up the candy bar Susan had left beside me and finished eating it. "I feel much better. I must be having one of those low sugar episodes like my brother has."

"You need a full check-up."

"I have a doctor's appointment later today. Thank you," I said, getting up.

"Wait. You need to—"

"I have to rush or I'll miss my next class."

"I'm sure you'll be ex—" Before she could finish the sentence, I was out the door.

As I exited the admin building, Brad's voice said, "Nice recovery."

I followed him to a table in a food court, called Veggie Delights. Kal, Jennifer and Roger were sitting there, looking at Roger's laptop display.

Everyone was munching on sweet potato fries. I took a handful. "Did you find anything?"

"There is no listing for Brenden Marsh in the employee records. Apparently, he is on a special fellowship funded by a private investor," Brad elucidated.

"Investor?"

"WEFDP," he said.

"WEFDP as in World Economic Forum Depopulation Project?" I asked.

"Where did you come up with that?"

"My dad or not-dad mentioned it."

"The WEFDP was run by the board of directors that oversaw the setup down below and the end of everything above," Kal explained. "It's defunct now and the directors of that project are currently regional directors."

"Maybe not so 'defunct.'" Brad commented.

"Maybe they are still in charge of the security robots. No wonder Marsh was so interested in us and in the androids," I said.

"Look," Roger said. "There is another organization using that acronym: Western Educational Freedom Development Participation."

"So Marsh may be working for this other group or for the underworld," I debated.

"Maybe you weren't the first to return and discover that we were alive. Some secondary organization may have already been created to investigate," Brad pondered.

"At any rate, he isn't a regular professor. He's been here since last Friday, the day after the timer was discovered, and will be working with advanced honor students," Roger read.

"On underworld androids?"

"Why would a bunch of students be checking out androids they didn't know existed and aren't legal?" Kal asked.

"There weren't any students in the lab when Kal's not-dad's head was in there," I noted.

"Do you think the students are a cover?" Kal asked.

"Or maybe they're robot students, who sometimes hang out at carnivals," Jennifer suggested. "Even if the program started with real students, if the underworld got wind of it, they could have been replaced. We know at least three androids made it above."

"I managed to make a change in the student records," Brad said.

"You are not going to love this." Roger turned to Kal with a smirk on his face.

"What?" I asked.

"Marsh has seen you, Natalia and Brad, right?" Roger asked.

"Marsh has seen all of us," I pointed out.

"But he hasn't seen you as a short-haired brunette with glasses or me with shoulder-length dark hair and brown contacts."

"And?"

"You, Kal and I have been added to the list of honor students."

"Won't they wonder where we've been for the last week?" I asked.

"We are late arrivals. We will be arriving on Monday."

"What will we tell Steve and Katerina?"

"You are being considered for a special program at the university."

"Our names?"

"Abigail Wilson, John Cleveland and Thomas McKinley."

"Clever," I said. "Mixed historical names."

"Easy to remember," Brad stated.

"Did you find out what they are up to in the project?" Kal asked.

"That will be up to us to discover on Monday," Roger said. "I hear you are math geniuses, and I was in Brad's AP physics class last year. As for your other skills, you should do fine. You probably have skills nobody up here has seen."

"What will you be doing?" I asked Brad and Jennifer.

"We'll be monitoring you. You'll take transmitters and receivers with you into the classroom," Brad told us.

That afternoon, Brad took us to a shop where we were fitted with wigs. "These really do look natural."

"Wigs have improved over the years," Brad said.

"What about your eye color, Roger?" Jennifer asked.

"I have an appointment with an optometrist. Removable color contacts."

We went from there over to Selini's. "I'm only working at the museum after closing," she said.

"We're going to need tiny transmitters and receivers that can't be detected or turned into mind control devices," Roger submitted.

"I've almost cracked the code for the necklace. It not only speaks to humans but to computers. They've found a way to transmit information to the computers through inaudible sound waves. I'm still trying to decode the language. Maybe one of you could help me."

"My mom programmed androids."

"There must have been some kind of computer language she used to program the computers. This doesn't fit into any standard one."

"But humans don't normally speak computer," Brad said. "How did the necklace program Natalia?"

"There are dual tracks, which is making it more confusing. I'm trying to isolate the computer sounds. Natalia, could you teach me the computer code?"

"My mother could. I can tell you what I know of it." I asked for a pen and paper and went through the meanings of all the symbols on the code I had seen. "But I never dealt with a sound code."

"Maybe you are doing it backwards," Brad said. "What if you isolate the sounds that would affect a human brain and then see if you can translate the rest?"

"That might work."

That evening, when we went home, a man I had seen in the hospital was there.

"I want to take some blood samples from you, Natalia."

CHAPTER 47

"Why?"

"To check your glucose levels and insulin resistance as well as your potassium and sodium levels. I'm Doctor Connor."

After he finished drawing blood, he checked me out on a blood pressure monitor and on a pulsometer. "I want you to come to the hospital tomorrow for an EEG reading."

"I'm fine."

Kal and I went into my room with Eterra but listened through the door.

"I'm really concerned about Natalia. I'd like your permission to keep her in the hospital over the weekend," Doctor Connor stated.

"What's the problem?" Katerina asked.

"I haven't run the blood tests yet, but her heartbeat was slow and her blood pressure was very low. It could be temporary or something really serious in view of the recent incident."

"Serious? What do you mean by serious?" Katerina sounded scared. I was scared too.

"What's wrong with me? Do we have slower heartbeats down there?" I whispered to Kal.

"Don't worry, Natalia. A slow heartbeat is better than a fast heartbeat, and it's high blood pressure everyone is worried about. He did say it could be temporary."

"I don't want to undergo tests in the hospital."

Kal opened the window. "Shall we?"

I hugged Eterra, who was lying on my bed. "Don't let on that we left."

Brad drove us to the museum to see Selini.

She took her own blood samples and checked my pulse and blood pressure.

"The blood pressure is low, very low and the heartbeat is definitely slow," She said. She started to check it again.

I recalled being with Chanelle one day when we checked our heartbeats and blood pressure. She was a robot and had artificial organs, but somehow our heartbeats and blood pressure matched. I started to cry.

Selini looked at the reading and said, "I'm going to do another check in a minute." She touched the tears on my cheeks. "What were you crying about?"

"What if Mom lied? What if I am a robot, like Chanelle?"

CHAPTER 48

Selini shook her head. "I'm not concerned about that. I would like to do a chemical analysis on your blood myself, though."

"Androids have heartbeats and blood pressure. They have organs —at least the humanoid robots like Chanelle."

"And your mother had to hide the fact that you were human and not a robot. She could not have kept your nature secret if you had a normal heartbeat and blood pressure."

"You're saying her mother lowered those, but how?" Brad asked.

"There is a drug that has that effect. Back in the old days, they were suppressing a lot of cures and the government did its best to eliminate all traces of the flower from which the drug came, as it could have been used to cure a variety of diseases. But I know your mother studied it. The inventor called it 'Reversesave,' but then he died suddenly. The idea that the government wanted people sick concerned your mom and prompted her to do additional research into it. She probably gave it to you when you were down below. "

"But I've been up here a while."

"It continues working for quite some time after you take it. Your mother probably only had to give it to you once a month or so."

"Then, I'm not a robot?"

"No. There's another reason this isn't a surprise." She went over to the container with the necklace and attached a wire from it to a speaker.

It started going "Thumpa thumpa."

"What's it doing?"

"It's generating a heart rhythm, the same one the cuff had for you when you were wearing it. Last night, the necklace used that rhythm to communicate with your nervous system. After it was removed, when you got upset, your pulse and blood pressure went up. After you calmed down, they went down. A robot would maintain the same blood pressure and pulse rate since feelings don't impact its organs in that way."

"You are saying—"

"The fact that your pulse is variable is proof that you are human."

"Then all she has to do is make herself upset and her blood pressure and pulse will go to normal," Kal summarized.

"Not normal but closer to normal. Hospitals take vitals repeatedly. She can't stay upset all weekend. I suspect the Reversesave also helped mitigate the effects of the necklace. The trinket might have rendered someone without Reversesave totally unconscious."

"They want to run more tests on me. Will the drug show up?"

She wrapped a band around my arm.

"More blood?"

"I have a test that will detect the drug."

I was feeling like a pincushion. She put the blood into a device that spun it and a colored pattern appeared. She pointed at one graph. "There it is."

"The doctor took her bloodwork to Valley Hospital with him," Kal said.

"Steve has a key, doesn't he?" Brad asked.

"I don't know if he brings it home."

"Don't you have some kind of card that can get into places?" I asked Brad.

"We can try. It doesn't work everywhere."

"I'll do you one better," Selini said. She handed Brad a device that looked like a set of pliers but not quite. "Push the ends together when you want to disrupt an electronic lock. It works like a charm."

At the hospital, we looked at the exterior cameras. "How do we get past those?"

"That way," Brad said. He tied his hood up against his head and went inside. A few minutes later, he came out in a white coat, pushing a wheelchair.

Kal sat in the chair and I sat on his lap and lowered my head. Brad put a sheet that had been on it over me and most of Kal, partially covering his face. He rolled us back, turning away from the cameras and partially blocking Kal's face.

Inside, there were cameras too. Brad kept his head down as if he were focusing on his patient.

"Emergency procedure," he muttered as he went by the desk. Peeking out, I could see that the person on duty looked pretty busy and she barely noticed.

Brad turned away from the patient wings and moved towards the offices. "What was the name of the doctor?"

"Connor," Kal said.

He looked at a directory on the wall. "This way."

He took us to an office and opened the door with Selini's lockpick, with his back between the lock and the cameras.

It was dark inside. He turned on the computer. "If this doctor put the password in or under a desk drawer, he's stupid." He pulled out a little flashlight as he looked underneath. "Stupid."

He turned on the computer and started typing. "The blood was entered under your name. Now it's under the name of an elderly man with high blood pressure. The results of your tests are back and every-thing is normal. Let's change the blood pressure and EKG results here. See, this elderly patient now has the lower rhythm and pressure. I just switched them."

"What about the other patient?"

"The doctor will be relieved when he checks again and finds the patient has improved."

"But what if he needs assistance for high blood pressure?'

"It was high normal. And as he's in the hospital, they'll check it again, anyway."

"Kal, do you think you have that stuff in your system?" I asked.

"I didn't touch the necklace if it was communicating the rhythm. In the leadership program, we were told that we were different physically from the robots. They didn't need to hide our vitals."

"You say there were no girls in the leadership program?" Brad asked.

"No. Apparently, powerful girls had mostly been erased from society except when deemed important to the board of directors. Breeder girls were used as surrogates when the Elites wanted kids. Robo-wives couldn't have kids and some of the human women couldn't either or didn't want to."

"And when the kids stopped being cute little kids, off with their heads," I remarked.

"Was your mother who you thought she was or a breeder girl?" Brad asked Kal.

"My mother was my mother until she died. That replacement system was perfected after Natalia, Chanelle and I were born. They started with the youth and the help."

Brad went to the file cabinet. "I'm going to change Natalia's physical record as well. Easy. The doctor used pencil."

As Brad finished, the door started to open. We hid under the desk. The light came on. I figured Doctor Connor was in the room. I heard footsteps moving over to the side of the desk, under which we were hiding. I heard the sounds of something being picked up off the desk and the footsteps moving away. A couple of minutes later, the lights went out and the person exited the room.

"That was close," Kal said.

"Let's get out of here." Brad covered me and mostly covered Kal with the sheet again. "The camera isn't pointed this way," he said. Going by the nurse's station, Brad stopped.

"Sorry, I need to check on orders from the last doctor."

"Be my guest. I'm off duty. The next on-duty nurse should be here at any minute." The nurse who had spoken walked away.

"What are you doing?" I whispered as he went through some files.

"Making sure there are no tracks. Let's go."

A few minutes later, we were in a service elevator going down to the laundry room. We got into laundry bins and were wheeled out by someone who looked like a physician's assistant to the car. I knew it was Brad. Once in the car, he took off quickly.

"Tomorrow they want to run all kinds of tests on me."

"Refuse. Have them prove you need them," Brad advised me.

"But we're minors."

"I think you'll win this one."

That night, when I laid down, I slept more easily.

In my dream, Brad was kissing me. Why hadn't I liked it before? It felt sensational. Then he pulled away, and it was Kal.

"*Go away,*" *I told him.* "*Not interested.*"

"*Yes, you are, and you want to kiss me again.*"

"*No, I don't. I don't!*"

"Natalia, you okay?

It was Kal. "I don't want to see you."

"What?"

"Go away!"

"Are you mad at me?"

"No. I'm mad at my dream. I hate you."

"Natalia, what did I do?"

"You kissed me."

"Was it that bad?"

"The worst. Go away!"

The next morning, Steve announced, "We are going to the hospital."

"I don't want to go to the hospital. I refuse."

"They have ice cream there."

"Then you should eat it. I'm not going."

"Natalia. This is not optional," Katerina said.

"No!" I insisted. I went to my room, locked the door and laid down on my bed. Maybe if I stayed in my room long enough, they'd forget about it.

Eterra climbed onto my bed and sympathetically put her head on my chest and started licking me.

"Thank you, girl."

I got up and listened at my door. Kal was arguing with Steve. "My sister is fine. She's had lots of checkups, and she has always been fine. In fact, she was checked over following the accident."

"That was just a quick, cursory exam. You were the one with the injury."

"And we were both healthy."

"Doctor Connor was very concerned last night," Steve said.

"Did you see how upset she was that you didn't believe her when she said she was fine? She doesn't feel believed."

"It's not about belief. We already have Social Services after us. If they find out that we were told to take her for an exam and we refused, they might take you both away from us."

"They can't. Our mom signed the papers."

"There is still a concern about child abuse, and this could be viewed as neglect."

"Just like when parents refused to let girls become boys and vice versa?"

"That was different, and it was exposed as a depopulation agenda."

"How about when they forced parents to give kids poison vaccines and the kids died?"

"The people who did that are gone. We don't force medical treatment on anyone anymore."

"But you are forcing medical tests on my sister."

"If she goes to the hospital with me and she refuses, then I'll tell them I am standing by Natalia," Steve said.

I came out of my room. "If you will agree to back me when I say 'No,' I'll go with you."

"I'll go with you, too, Natalia," Kal declared.

"They also want to see you," Steve told him.

Kal rolled his eyes. "Why me?"

"To check whether there is a hereditary problem."

"I'm refusing, too."

"Even if your being tested would help Natalia?"

"I'll tell you what. You can test me instead of Natalia. That is the only condition under which I will be tested."

"Kal, you'd do that for me?"

"I'll do whatever it takes to protect you from those needless procedures."

I ran over to him and hugged him. "I love you. Uh, brother. I love you, brother."

"I think, if parents had stood by their kids as these two are standing by each other, when they were forcing medical procedures before the poisoning, things would have been different and a great many lives would have been saved," Katerina said.

"As bad as the Great Reset was, at least we got rid of those authoritarians who were forcing that stuff on us," Steve noted. "Medicine is different now."

"And yet, they are still trying to force exams on us," I pointed out.

"You are not undergoing any exams you do not want," Steve said. "But remember, we do want to find out why you passed out."

"Everything's been a big adjustment," I said. "You have been great. But after mom was in the accident, we saw someone who frightened us and crazy things are happening, like robots blowing up. Who wouldn't be feeling a little off?"

"Oh, honey. Of course, you've been through so much. What you need is a rest." Katarina turned to Steve. "Let's go to the hospital and tell them that Natalia feels fine and wants to wait for any tests. We don't want her to undergo the stress."

"You both wait here," Steve said.

"How about at Brad's?" Kal asked. "He has some ways to help us relax, like swimming."

"I'll walk you over and ask his mom to keep an eye on you until we come home from the hospital."

"You worked last Saturday. Are you working today?"

"I'm taking extra time off these days. I need to focus on our family now. I've worked so much overtime lately that they can't argue."

"I love living here with you," I said.

"Me too," Kal agreed.

After breakfast, we grabbed our swimsuits and Steve and Katerina took us and Eterra over to Brad's. They spoke with his mom before leaving.

We went upstairs to Brad's room. I noticed his mother watching us closely as we mounted the stairs. "I wonder what Steve and Katerina said to your mom," Kal commented.

"I wouldn't worry about it. My parents are cool. I knew you could stand up. If people had stood up twenty years ago, the Great Reset never would have happened."

"And the Elites would still be running your world," Kal noted.

"So many people were killed and injured by the jab, there was a counter-reaction after they left. Children are treated more like treasures now—especially since so many could not have children after being injected with the depopulation poison."

"Not to mention, the poisoning of the food, air and water," I recalled from my readings and discussions.

"Everything was designed to that end. None of us were to be left after the poisoning."

"They underestimated the people," Kal pointed out.

"There are some documentaries about what happened. Would you like to watch them? It might make it clearer," Brad offered.

"Sure," Kal said.

The first one Brad showed involved the lead-in to the fake World War III. We saw how the U.S. had stolen elections and had invaded countries as part of an elite theft and money-laundering scheme while pretending Russia had stolen elections. Our government engaged in or backed genocides and used mass censorship to hide the truth from the masses.

"This was all the lead-in to the fake war?" I asked. "And the leaders were all in on it, weren't they?"

"All of them, including the leader of Russia. There was an agreement to fake World War III and for the rich and powerful to go underground while everything above was saturated with temporary poisons. The jabs hadn't killed enough people," Brad said.

The next video showed leaders at the World Economic Forum talking about plans to chip and monitor everyone and to depopulate the planet. There had been some Georgia Guidestones that showed the plans. So they were blown up.

It showed the depopulation agendas: fake plagues, mandated lethal injections, removal of reproductive organs, genocidal wars and the nuking of America's northwest and Eastern US due to the GCC and Limerick disasters, the cutting of all the power lines, the mass poisoning and the disappearance of the world elitists, theoretically into their underground mansions.

But it wasn't all negative. A rebirth of compassion took place as people and children helped their friends and neighbors survive and move to safer zones. Russia, Mexico, Nicaragua, Venezuela, Cuba and much of Africa refused to follow the depopulation agenda. Surviving Americans had to leave the country. Interestingly, a lot of Palestinians, who were used to a reign of terror, survived and were able to retake their land.

Australia, New Zealand, Israel, Canada and the former European Union countries had been so badly wiped out that it was believed there were no survivors in those areas.

An effort was made to restore portions of the US, starting with California.

From the video, we learned that because the depopulation agenda has been so successful, anyone giving birth was honored and children were celebrated and cherished. The right of parents to raise their children, free from interference by the state, was respected.

"No wonder Katerina and Steve are so protective of us," Kal remarked.

"So why is there still Social Services?" I asked.

"It's archaic and there is a push to end any use of that agency to investigate parents or children. Surviving CPS sex traffickers were tried for crimes against humanity and locked up in this place called Guantanamo. That was years ago."

"But there are still Social Service workers," I pointed out.

"Current Social Service workers know this could happen to them if they try to follow in the footsteps of their predecessors. CPS Social Services is supposed to be monitored for any trafficking or abuse activities and the presumption is now always in favor of the parents over anyone trying to take away their kids."

"What about that woman who is after us?" I asked.

"She was arrested and unless she agrees to change her ways, she may wind up in prison."

"She seemed intent on proving we were lying."

"She'll have a hard time doing that from jail."

"You think so?" Kal asked. "Look?" He was peering out of Brad's second-floor window. "She's back?"

CHAPTER 49

"Steve was afraid they'd take us away if I didn't agree to the test. They were going to the hospital to refuse to let me participate. I should have gone with them. If I took the tests and we fixed the results, like we did last night, that woman wouldn't be back here."

"She's just sitting there in her car, watching our house," Kal observed.

Kal called Steve. He didn't answer. Kal left a message for Steve to call us back. I tried Katerina with the same result.

"Time for us to call in the hired gun," Brad said. He called Jennifer and told her about the woman. He turned to me. "She *was* the most effective at dealing with her."

"True," I agreed.

The woman got out of her car, took some pictures and made notes. A little while later, Jennifer came along. She dialed Brad and he put the phone on speaker. Our end was muted.

"I thought you had stopped burglarizing this neighborhood."

"Little girl, where do you live. I think you need to come with me."

"Not a chance."

The social worker whipped out some handcuffs as Jennifer backed away.

Leaving us his phone, Brad rushed downstairs to tell his parents that the kidnapper was back, trying to kidnap Jennifer. His mom called Jennifer's parents and other moms in the neighborhood and both of Brad's parents went outside as Roger raced down the street with a broom.

Roger aimed the broom at the social worker. "Away, kidnapper. Away. Be gone with you."

That sounded like a paraphrase of something out of old literature, but he was very loud. From all around, neighbors rushed out and surrounded the woman, yelling accusations at her. Roger's and Jennifer's parents showed up, as did the police.

"We should go out there too," I suggested as Brad returned to his room.

"Then she'd make you the subject. She has no case of any kind against Jennifer or her family."

"This woman tried to kidnap me," Jennifer yelled at the police. "She's a kidnapper."

"Our precious daughter!" Jennifer's mom cried.

"My sister, an A student on the honor roll, one of the most respected students in our high school and this kidnapper wants to take her away!" Roger shouted.

"We'll handle it," an officer said.

"I'm filing charges," Jennifer's father declared.

"Her father's an attorney and he's on the city council," Brad informed us.

Once again, the social worker was escorted away by an officer in the back of a police car. As the police car left, applause from the crowd could be heard as Jennifer's parents and brother comforted her and the neighbors surrounded them.

I heard someone say, "If anyone sees that woman in the neighborhood, again, call the police immediately."

Jennifer's father spoke out. "I'm getting a restraining order, and I'm going to ask that she be held without bail. I heard she tried to kidnap some kids from the hospital the other day and now my daughter."

Steve drove past the departing police car and looked at the crowd in front of his house as he and Katerina returned.

Katerina asked people what was happening. Jennifer's phone was still active, but as she disconnected it, I heard her father say, "A kidnapper tried to grab my daughter."

Oddly, I felt a little sorry for the social worker, which didn't make any sense, as she had targeted Kal and me. She should have simply accepted the birth certificates and left us alone. But she wasn't a kidnapper—except in the sense that Social Services had a long history of kidnapping children for forced sex with elites.

I turned to Kal. "Do you ever worry about the harm we cause others while protecting ourselves? What if that lady goes to prison?"

"It would do other kids a favor," Brad said. "If she went after you two like that, imagine what she is doing to other kids who don't have anyone to help them."

"I guess."

Brad went downstairs as Steve and Katerina came into the house with his parents. A minute later, he came up. "Now, we might have something to feel guilty about."

"What?" I inquired, feeling nervous. I hoped I hadn't caused problems for Steve at the hospital.

Before Brad could answer, Steve called us downstairs.

"Hi."

"You need to be careful. I understand there are kidnappers in the neighborhood."

Kal and I looked at each other and didn't say anything.

"Is everything alright?" I asked.

"Now it is, thanks to the neighbors and the police," Brad's dad answered.

"What happened at the hospital?" Kal asked.

It probably was not the best time for the question, as both of Brad's parents were there watching.

"Everything is fine. Doctor Connors's readings were confused. The Internal Medical Chief looked at the findings and said there was no reason for you to come in."

I felt relieved until Steve said, "Doctor Connor was suspended."

"Over me?"

"This isn't the first time he has over-reacted to a situation."

I looked at Kal. *We did this. We changed the results.* Brad was looking down. He reached out and put his hand on my arm and gave me a warm look as if trying to make me feel better.

"But he checked me over as a favor to you. Even if he made a mistake, it was a mistake. He shouldn't be punished," I said.

"Today, he pushed to have you brought in and that's when the internal medical chief checked over the results. He called Dr. Conner into his office and went down a list of prior complaints."

"But it was our situation that got him suspended. Couldn't you tell the chief that we aren't upset with Dr. Conner and not to suspend him?"

"It isn't up to me or you. It says a lot for your character that you don't want him suspended, but he was almost suspended over a complaint regarding a prior patient and this simply put him over the top."

"But we don't want to be what put him over the top," I said.

"I'm with Natalia. I don't want to hurt anyone," Kal backed me up.

"You aren't. He'll learn not to be so pushy next time," Steve replied.

"Could you let his boss know that we think he was a nice person and don't want him suspended?"

"I'll tell him when I go back to work tomorrow."

"You have to work again on Sunday?" Katerina asked Steve.

"Sorry. But not until the afternoon." He turned to us. "Would you like to go to church with us tomorrow morning?"

"Sure," Kal said. He looked at me. We had to find a way to make things right.

"How about the seven of us do lunch today?" Brad's father suggested.

"Is that okay with you kids?" Steve asked us.

Kal and I nodded.

"Can we go back up to Brad's room?" Kal requested.

"Have fun," Steve said.

Up in Brad's room, I urged, "We have to fix this. We went in there last night and messed things up for Doctor Connor. We need to undo that."

"You don't want to go through with the exam."

"We can change something else."

"He was a bit pushy over a one-time exam in the evening," Kal noted.

"Even Selini said my heartbeat was really slow and my blood pressure was low from whatever drug was in my system. Her blood test showed the drug."

"To a doctor who didn't know about your background, that would have been a red flag," Brad pointed out. "If it's a choice between him and you, I choose you."

"It shouldn't be a choice," I said. "Please, there has to be something we can do."

"Perhaps we can look up the people who filed the other complaints and get them to withdraw them," Brad suggested.

"That's a great idea," Kal said. "How do we do that?"

"Break into his boss's office and look at the disciplinary file on Doctor Connor," Brad suggested.

I looked at him. "You had fun last night. I saw you smiling a lot."

"It was exciting. Don't tell me you didn't feel it too."

"Actually, it was fun," I admitted. "Is there something wrong with us?" Maybe there was. I thought about all that had happened lately and aside from the fear, there was something really thrilling about it.

"I found it exciting, too," Kal acknowledged. "I think we thrive on danger."

"I've lived a relatively boring life until now," Brad admitted. "I did little rebellious things before but nothing like what we've been doing."

"That may be part of what sets us apart from the robots," Kal noted. "We don't conform to societal rules."

"Tonight, we save Doctor Connor. Tomorrow the world," I said.

"What about that author, Graham Woodly? Have we given up on him?" Brad asked.

"He's a liar," I said. "But he does know something."

"Or maybe he is bait to catch those of us who know more," Kal warned.

"He's pretty ineffective bait," Brad said.

That night, after dinner, we said we were tired. We went to our respective rooms, locked the doors and turned out the lights. I told Eterra to stay and watch my bed. I didn't want to put her in danger. Then, I exited through my window, joining Kal outside.

"This looks better than exiting through one window while making it look like we're watching videos all night," Kal said.

We first dropped by the science museum to see if Selini had discovered anything new about the necklace.

"I put in bits of the code you gave me and it started putting forth more information in code. Then I had it translated. The android must have been wearing it when he put it on you. He probably became a little lost after that."

"But he knew to carry me."

"There could have been something in his base programming that told him you were important."

"What were his instructions?" Kal asked.

"What we suspected. To report back on any survivors and bring back samples for return preparation."

"Return. Preparation. That sounds like an invasion," Brad speculated.

"Why did he pick me for the sample?"

"He may have recognized you."

"Robert Horton would have recognized me, but this was an android?"

"Was it his double? If he had any of Robert's brain, his double might have remembered you."

"Maybe you shouldn't go to that program on Monday. Someone else might recognize you," Brad warned.

"I'm going to look very different. Besides, Kal and Roger will be there and you'll be watching," I reminded Brad.

"I'm putting together monitoring devices," Selini said. "I'll give them to you tomorrow, Brad."

"There's one more thing," I said. "The person who rescued me?"

"It's better that you do not know."

"My mother? Is she up here?"

"No. It wasn't your mother. We'll talk later about it when it's safer."

From her comment, I gathered someone helped me but that someone or I could be in danger if we met. I wondered if it was someone from below or maybe a friend who was assisting Selini up here.

"Do you remember anything about your rescuer?" Brad asked as we left.

"No. Everything was too blurry."

Valley Hospital's Internal Medicine Chief was Dr. Martin KaKool. This time, we went to the Internal Medicine Department in the hospital. The door to KaKool's office was locked, but Brad was able to open it. We looked through the files on his desk. Connor's file wasn't there. We started to go through KaKool's file cabinets. One section was marked "Discipline." We searched that. There were reports about several doctors. But we didn't see a file on Connor.

"Look," Brad said, looking at one of the papers. "KaKool has just been appointed Acting Assistant Chief of Staff for the entire hospital, effective Monday. The current chief of staff will be on vacation."

"And his first act in prep for his new position is to suspend a very efficient doctor," I lamented.

"I guess his temporary position has gone to his head," Brad replied.

We opened a closet. I held back a scream as a falling body barely missed me. According to the name on his coat, it was KaKool. Dead.

CHAPTER 50

Brad and Kal took a closer look at the body on the floor. "Definitely dead," Kal said.

"We need to scrub our prints from the office," Brad advised.

"Prints?" Kal asked.

"Fingerprints."

"I figured, but do you think they'll accuse us?"

"He just suspended Connor over your sister's case."

There was a box of sanitary wipes on the desk and we each picked up one and started wiping. There was a large calendar on his desk with appointments scheduled in red. Connor had been listed for that morning with the number 3988 next to it.

"What do you think that is?"

"Maybe a file location," Kal said.

"It could be a locker number," Brad conjectured.

"Look at him. There is something weird about his head," I observed.

"He's dead," Brad said.

"No. I've seen that before." I looked at his temples. "He's been uploaded."

"What?" Brad asked.

"You're right," Kal said.

"It's what they do below so that they can enter a person's knowledge into a computer file. Someone wanted to know what he knew. In some cases, it leaves temporary bruise marks," I explained.

"There. On the floor. A watch," Kal said.

Brad started to pick it up and froze.

"What's wrong?" I asked.

Brad didn't respond.

Kal used a pen to pull it away from Brad and toss it onto the floor.

"What happened?" Brad questioned us.

"It's like the necklace."

Kal used the pen and a metal box that had contained medals on the chief's desk to enclose the watch.

"Maybe Selini can figure out something from this. But Brad didn't get Reversesave."

"Maybe it has a broader spectrum," Kal said. "Or maybe this device just freezes a normal person until someone kills him."

"Should we stuff him back in the closet?"

"The less we contaminate him or ourselves, the less they will find," Brad replied to me. "Leave him there."

"Where would they have lockers?" Kal inquired.

As we slipped out of the office, I heard a familiar voice.

"What's Steve doing here?" I asked.

Steve was speaking with a doctor down the hall. We quickly moved in the other direction, hoping he didn't see us.

"The cameras," Brad said. "We need to go to the security center to retrieve the video of our entry into the office."

"The other night?" Kal asked.

"We were disguised, remember?"

In the security office, we saw one person departing. There was one security guard left, nursing a coffee and occasionally looking at the closed-circuit screens.

"What do we do?" Kal asked

"I'd say we have the perfect tool," Brad pointed to the metal box.

With a pen, he flicked the watch onto the office floor near the guard. Hearing the sound of the watch landing, the guard reached down and picked it up. He seemed to freeze and then collapsed on the floor.

"I guess he had less stamina than you or even me," Brad said.

We went inside. Brad went to the computers and found the video files for the evening. He proceeded to erase them and set the cameras to pause for fifteen minutes. We retrieved the watch and prepared to leave.

"That's how long we have to get out of here." We started to leave, turning down a corridor to an exit. "Look, Steve is coming along the path we should be leaving on," I pointed out.

We rushed to the nearest elevator in the opposite direction and closed the door. "This one doesn't go to parking or the laundry room."

On the bottom floor, we stepped into the morgue.

"Get on your lab coats and get to work," a woman ordered. "I have been waiting all night for them to send some techs."

We took three coats.

"I'll be back in ten minutes. Make sure you fix the stupid spectrometer while I'm gone." She got into the elevator.

"Let's get out of here," I said.

"Wait," Kal reacted. "That number. 3988."

"You see it?"

"Not yet."

Rows of numbers, all starting with 39, were visible above metal doors on the wall. We followed along the wall to 88. The number was mounted above a door to a vault for a casket. Unlike the others, which simply had handles, this one had an electronic lock. Brad used his card, which failed. The lockpick Selini gave us opened it automatically, and a body rolled out.

"This body is not at all decomposed," I said.

"It's not human," Kal observed.

CHAPTER 51

Brad pulled the watch out of the metal case with the pen and touched it to the man, who sat up. Quickly, Brad pulled the watch away and the body collapsed.

"It's a robot?" I asked.

"Got to be. The tag said six weeks ago. No human who died six weeks ago would look this good," Brad said.

I looked at a note attached to the sheet that was over the body. "Attending physician: Max Connor."

"So that's why Doctor Connor freaked when he saw my results. Reversesave emulated a robot's responses and he thought I—"

"Was a robot," Brad finished.

Brad pulled out his phone and took a picture of the man and the tag. "We need to leave. We only have a couple of minutes left."

We closed the vault and found a door to the stairs. We managed to exit into the underground parking lot and rushed through it to Brad's car.

"I think we made it past the cameras in time," Brad said.

"So that person who tried to kidnap you was not the first robot to come up here," Selini said.

"There were also the fake Denton and security robot, more recently, but this was six weeks ago."

"If they sent four, they could have sent more. You say the only way to detect the humanoid ones without testing is by their neutral personalities?" Selini asked.

"Pretty much."

"So, Connor knows about the robots and thought you were one of them," Selini summarized our suspicions.

"What do you think deactivated the robot?"

"Maybe the tests. A CT scan might have had too much electromagnetic radiation for a robot to handle," Selini suggested.

"The record we erased last night indicated Connor wanted to do a CT scan on Natalia," Brad said.

"If that's what killed the robot—"

"Then he would have been willing to kill you if you were a robot."

"Are we sure the CT scan did that?" Kal asked.

"Something else could have killed him," Selini said.

"But the watch reactivated him. He dropped after we took it away," I pointed out.

"He was different than the one that kidnapped Natalia," Brad said.

"Whoever rescued me smashed my kidnapper's head, leaving metal parts and electrodes on the ground. He was more like a security robot or a limited-use robot. The man in the morgue apparently emulated a real human on the inside, which would have gotten him past the cursory exams."

"Connor is no longer working. Let's try to talk to him," Brad suggested.

"He suspects I'm a robot."

"But you aren't, and somehow, he found a robot on his own. We need to find out how he found the guy and what killed the robot."

"We're going to church in the morning with Steve and Katerina," I said.

"I got the address from his file last night. I can watch his place in the morning. I'll see if Roger and Jennifer can join me."

The next morning, we attended a non-denominational church a few blocks from Steve and Katerina's home. I was surprised when Brad, Jennifer and Roger entered the door. I looked at Brad's hand and followed the finger pointing off to the side. Connor was there. Could this be the reason he and Steve had bonded? Not only did they work together, but they went to church together.

After the service, we went into a lunchroom towards a line for a self-service food table. Doctor Connor picked up his rather full plate and turned, accidentally bumping into me and spilling his food.

"I'm sorry," he said. "And I apologize for the other night. I'll get you a napkin."

"I'll take care of it," Katerina offered, moving towards the table for some napkins.

"We're super sorry about the suspension, Doctor Connor," I said.

"Thank you."

"I think you've been working too hard. Maybe some time off will do you some good, Max," Steve told him.

I looked at Doctor Connor. "Let me help you get some more food," I said. "I seemed to have ruined your lunch."

The minister waved Steve over.

"I'll hold your space," I told Steve.

"No exams while we're gone," Steve teased Connor, half smiling.

"I don't mix exams with lunch."

Jennifer came up as Steve and Katerina moved away.

"I apologize for upsetting you," Doctor Connor told me.

"I'm not a robot."

"What?"

"I'm not a robot. My mother gave me Reversesave to lower my heartbeat and blood pressure."

"That's a mythical drug."

"Tell me about Dr. KaKool," Brad interjected.

"KaKool?"

"He fired or suspended you. That must have been upsetting."

Connor looked irritated. "I should be going."

"Did you kill him?" Kal asked.

"Are you crazy?"

"Maybe. Are you going to answer my question?"

"I'm not a killer. And what makes you think KaKool was killed?"

"You didn't kill 3988? How did he die?"

He started to push past us and Jennifer rushed over and blocked him. "We're not dropping this until we get some answers."

"I haven't killed anyone."

"But you kill robots," Brad said. "We want to know how."

"Was it the tests that killed 3988, or was it some device you know about?" I asked.

"You watch too many science fiction pictures." He moved past Jennifer and Brad.

"I've been there. My mother made the robots." I knew it was risky, but I could deny it later. *Who would believe him now?*

He turned back.

CHAPTER 52

"Tell us what you know," Brad said.

Connor wrote down an address. "Drop by this afternoon, and we'll talk."

"Here, Max," a woman said, coming up with two plates of food. "It looks like you lost your lunch."

He took it. "Thank you, Muriel."

Steve returned as Connor walked away. "The minister suggested you two might like to join the church's teen choir."

"He hasn't heard us sing."

"I mentioned that you play harp and he was very impressed. He said the church has always wanted a harpist."

"I'll think about it," I said.

"Less talented kids would jump at the opportunities you've been turning down."

"We just want to be regular kids, like our friends."

"I can understand that," Katerina said. "You'll have plenty of time for careers and hobbies as you grow up. You're still young."

I had come to realize how compressed our childhood had been and how we had been more like trophies for the parents who had us. Down below, we weren't all that special and had to work to keep up with others our age. Up here, we had to slow down to fit in.

―――――

After church, we went home. Jennifer's mom called Katerina and invited her over to her house, where her parents were having a meeting to discuss preparation for the school year.

"I don't know," Katerina said. "Natalia and Kal—"

"It's okay," I assured her, eavesdropping on her half of the phone conversation. "Our friends have invited us to hang out with them this afternoon."

"I'll be there." She turned to me. "I'm so glad that you've made so many good friends."

"Everyone here is nice—except that social worker. What's going to happen to her?"

"I don't know. I just hope we've seen the last of her."

―――――

Connor's apartment was in the same building we had followed Graham Woodly to.

"I discovered that when I looked him up in Vital Records this morning," Brad said.

"I don't think this is a coincidence," Kal remarked.

This time, we took Eterra. I was feeling guilty about not spending more time with her.

The security guard was apparently expecting us and ushered us into the elevator. "Apartment 505. Where is your dad?"

"Busy today," Roger said.

The guard did not seem impressed.

Connor offered us some lemonade. We politely declined.

"How did you know Graham Woodly?" Brad asked.

"He had a source that was giving him information for a book. But then the source started going into weird trances. So, I took the source to Valley Hospital for tests and everything stopped. His heart, his lungs, his brain, everything. Woodly was angry and filed a complaint, claiming I had killed Aaron with my tests."

"Woodly didn't seem like the kind of person to want to go on record with anything."

"He didn't report the person as his source but rather as a friend, and he gave a fake address for Aaron. Dr. KaKool didn't know what to make of it until Steve complained about your exam. Dr. KaKool looked at the record and claimed I had made the same mistake in your case as in Aaron's, who you know as 3988."

"But he probably really did have lower pressure and a slower beat if he was a robot."

"It was very similar to yours."

"That's because my mom wanted me to pretend to be a robot, but she didn't tell me what she was doing."

"Your mom was?"

"Eterra Stafford."

"*The* Eterra Stafford?"

"I grew up below. The servants, most girls and a lot of boys were replaced by robots. I would have been replaced, but my mom gave me Reversesave."

"That was a mythical drug, supposedly used to reverse the side effects of the deadly vaccines, but there was never any evidence it was real."

"The Elites stockpiled it until they had protected themselves from all the shedding," Kal explained. "Natalia's mom must have kept a stash for her."

"When did the robot escape?" I asked.

"Six weeks ago, he died. The first book in Woodly's planned series came out six months ago."

"We didn't hear anything about a robot escaping," I said. "We had cameras everywhere and even our houses were monitored. They even knew what we said at the breakfast table."

"From what Woodly said, Aaron was supposed to be doing some kind of hazardous duty. He was injured and could only remember certain details. He wandered above and somehow wound up with Woodly."

"Which is why Woodly didn't know about the rainbows. He either never asked or Aaron didn't remember," I said.

"Then he wasn't sent up. He came up on his own," Kal guessed.

"But what about the watch?" I asked.

"Watch?"

"We found it in KaKool's office after he was killed," I explained.

"Killed?"

"It looked as if his neck was twisted and broken," Brad said.

Connor shook his head. "He and I had differences, but he was a good person." He shook his head, again, and lowered it.

"I'm sorry. I would have expected his death to be known by now," I told him.

"When did it happen?"

"Last night, we found him. He was on the floor of his office."

"The cleaning crew should have reported it."

"Unless the killer came back and removed the body," Brad surmised.

"This watch."

"When we put it against Aaron, he sat up, but then he went back to being dead when we removed it," Kal related.

"I want to get in on these late-night adventures," Jennifer demanded.

"We think the robots will be invading, and we need to know how you killed Aaron," Brad refocused him.

"I tried electro-magnetic stimulation."

"What?" Brad asked.

"We sometimes use it to improve the functioning of certain areas of the brain, but he just went limp and everything stopped, his heart, his lungs, everything. We tried CPR, but it didn't work."

"Can we get a portable set of electromagnetic stimulators?" Kal asked.

"I don't understand," Doctor Connor responded.

"The robots will either kill all of us or take us down below. We found a coded necklace with instructions. That appears to be the plan," Kal said.

"Have you notified the government?"

"Do you think they'd believe us?" Brad asked.

"Probably not."

"There are multiple types of robots too. There are those that have the internal organs that match human ones and others that just look human but have mechanical insides and spark when hit. The one that put the necklace on me was one of those."

"What did the necklace do to you?"

"It made me dizzy. It has subsonic soundwaves that put human brains to sleep while working on the subconscious or so we've learned. I was going somewhere with the robot before he was smashed when someone rescued me. I don't know who."

"How do you know I'm not a robot?" Doctor Connor asked.

I laughed. "You're too emotional to be a robot. My best friend was a robot. She would express happiness but there was something neutral about that happiness."

"It was like she had the mannerisms and the voice but it wasn't the same as the real thing," Kal explained. "She was my other sister."

"So was Eterra your mother, too?"

"We had different mothers. I was in the Youth Leadership Program and being trained to be a future leader. They didn't mess with me. It was different with girls."

"How did you get out?"

"A robot was programmed to help us get out and then it committed suicide. If they find us, they'll kill us and replace us with robots or they'll just kill us," I informed him.

"What makes you think you can trust me?"

"Because nobody believes us as it is, and they certainly wouldn't believe you if you told on us. And those below would kill you for knowing too much. We're really your best friends," Kal clarified.

I high-fived Kal.

The one thing we weren't doing was telling Conor about Selini.

"Do Steve and Katerina know any of this?"

"Steve, no," I said. "We told Katerina some, but I don't think she believes us and is acting as if we never said anything. She thinks we've got great imaginations."

"People want to normalize everything. I tried to explain my findings about Aaron to Marty—Doctor KaKool—and he thought I had had a breakdown. To downplay it, I backtracked. When I pushed the exam with you for similar reasons, that was it. I was suspended."

"I'm really sorry about your suspension. I'm pretty sure Steve and Katerina will stand by you if you try to get your job back."

"Fortunately, it's just a suspension. It will give me some time off. It looks like you might need my help."

"Two robots blew up by the museum last week and the one that looked like our dad was taken to the university. The guy who took the body is in charge of a special student program and three of us are going to infiltrate. But if robots show up—" Kal said.

"You'll need protection."

"Exactly," Kal confirmed.

"Aaron was already damaged when I first saw him. I can't be sure that electro-magnetic stimulation would have that impact on a healthy robot." He chuckled and shook his head. "Healthy robot."

"An oxymoron," Brad noted.

"You know androids are illegal here because of the attempts of the World Economic Forum to upload people's brains and replace us with robots. That's also why we've banned AI—that and it was spying on everyone."

"Steve told us about that. But the authorities are not equipped to deal with humanoid and human-emulating robots. They look so real, who would believe they were robots?" Kal asked.

"The one who tried to kidnap you, what did he look like?"

"A guy named Robert Horton. But I only saw him briefly in a mirror. Robert is a similar size and has similar coloring to Brad's. But it wasn't Robert. He was in the Youth Leadership Program and I'm sure he was human."

"The government monitored everything and everyone. Do you think it saw you through his eyes?" Kal asked.

"I don't know. If it did, my mom could be in danger. And they'll probably send more to kill me."

"Your mom was, or rather is, a genius. I thought she died long ago," Doctor Connor said.

"Are you three going to be prepared for the infiltration tomorrow?" Jennifer asked me, Kal and Roger.

"The countdown timer is set for Thursday. Time is of the essence," Brad told her.

"But they could be in extreme danger. Marsh acted like a cat ready to pounce on our group," she replied.

"A controlled cat. He didn't actually pounce," Brad said. "He'd get thrown out of the university if he tried and they found out."

"Unless he killed the administrators and threw the bodies in the basement," Jennifer speculated.

"Nice image," Roger said. "Thanks, Sis."

"I'm going to show you some self-defense moves when we get home," Jennifer speculated.

"You do self-defense?" I asked.

"She learned from someone who used to train students in something called Krav Maga." Roger rolled his eyes.

"I know some self-defense, too," Brad said.

"If you have access to anything for electrical stimulation, we'd appreciate it," I told Connor.

"Wait, I know." He went to a cupboard

Inside was a blue and green hoop.

"The documentary!" I exclaimed.

He looked at me. "Documentary?"

"There was a little boy at a protest with a hoop like that."

"My parents took me to a number of protests when I was a kid. I sometimes brought my hula hoop."

"Do you have a picture from back then?"

He pulled out an old picture book of himself and his parents."

"You were the kid! You were in the video we were shown below." I looked at Kal and he nodded.

"A lot of protests were on video. I didn't know I was in a documentary."

Feeling an overwhelming sense of relief, I hugged him. "I thought you'd died in the war."

"I hope I'm still here." Connor pulled out a tiny box with some attachments.

"What's that?"

"It's a mini defibrillator. I specially designed it for a dog. My former dog had several cardiac arrests. Normally, you use it on the heart, but I can alter this to generate an EMP that you can touch to a head—"

"That's really small," I observed.

"I had a Pomeranian, one pound. I might be able to amplify the signal. Give me a few minutes. It will need a stronger battery."

After he finished, we thanked him, made sure it was off and Brad put it into his shirt pocket.

Jennifer wasn't kidding about knowing self-defense. If she hadn't been so good at her verbal skills, her physical abilities would have saved her from the officer and social worker.

Brad had a different style, but he showed us how to turn our opponents' strengths into weaknesses.

"I can't believe how fast you picked that up," Jennifer said.

"Down below, we were expected to learn skills immediately. I thought I was working hard to do as well as regular teens, not androids."

"And you kept up with them? So much for the superiority of AI robots."

"Your basketball skills will make you a star player when school starts," Roger told Kal.

"And I've seen you swim. You planning to be on the swimming team?" Brad asked me.

"Don't forget, she'll also be in the orchestra in school," Jennifer noted.

"School is going to be fun—" I didn't finish the sentence. The next half would have been "if we survive that long."

After we got back from Jennifer's, Steve was home.

"I want you to know how proud I am that you wanted to stand up for Connor after he tried to push you into an exam. Apparently, his readings were all off. His intentions were good, but he still made a mistake."

"Anyone can make a mistake," I said.

"Anything unusual happen at work today?" Kal asked.

"Not really. It was all fairly routine. I spoke with Dr. KaKool this evening and he said that they just can't afford any more mistakes on Connor's part. He wants Connor to present proof of retraining before coming back to work."

"Wait, you spoke to KaKool?" I asked.

CHAPTER 53

I worried that I might have shown my surprise but Steve didn't act as if he noticed.

"Yes. He came in on a Sunday."

"He doesn't usually?" Kal asked.

"No. He often works on Saturdays, but this is the first Sunday I've seen him there. I know you felt bad about Max, but this will make him a better doctor."

"KaKool added a retraining requirement to the suspension?" Kal asked, maybe to deflect from my reaction. "Will that be difficult?"

"No. There is an emphasis on quality medical treatment these days. Annual retraining is encouraged for all doctors."

"Oh," I said. "After tonight at Jennifer's, I'm really tired. Tomorrow, there is an advanced program for high school students that all of us are going to be monitoring at the university. It will assist us in deciding our career direction. Katerina, would you mind watching Eterra again?"

"Of course, not. She's very sharp and helps me feel cherished when you and Steve have to be away."

"I didn't hear anything about it," Steve said.

"It's voluntary. Brad is going to drive us to see if we are even interested in participating."

"You should get some sleep tonight," Steve recommended.

"I'm tired too," Kal said. He yawned.

"I'll bring your dinner to your room," Katerina offered.

"Maybe I should drive you to check it out," Steve said.

I looked at Kal.

"Our friends will all be going together."

We ate quickly and took the plates back to the kitchen. Then we locked our doors and waited until we heard Steve and Katerina call goodnight and go into their room.

"Goodnight," I called back as I turned out my light and went out through the window with Eterra.

Kal was already waiting outside. Brad was in his car across the street but two houses down from his house. We rushed over to him. Roger was with him. "Jennifer is covering for me," Roger said. "Mom is watching us like a hawk, and Jen is pretending to be watching a movie with me. When Mom conks out, Jen will go into my room, stuff my bed and lock my door."

"You have a key?"

"It's an easily disabled lock. Is there an investigation into KaKool's death?" Roger asked.

"The opposite. He's been replaced," Kal informed them.

"By another worker?" Brad inquired.

"By another KaKool," I explained.

"The guy we saw couldn't have recovered. His skin was turning blue and he had no heartbeat. He wasn't breathing," Brad said.

"I remember."

"And you are certain he was the real KaKool?" Selini asked as we recounted the events for her.

"We didn't check the identification in his wallet. He had a name badge on him."

"Could he have stolen it?"

"She's got a point. Maybe someone was impersonating KaKool and someone, maybe KaKool himself, caught the man and killed him," Brad suggested.

"That's better than the alternative," I acknowledged.

"Alternative?" Brad asked.

"That they killed him or somehow knew he had been killed and quickly replaced him. That would mean that they are monitoring us from below and constructing replacements almost immediately."

"Be careful. If they are monitoring us and know you're up here, you could be on a wanted list," Selini advised.

"I'm not sure you should be going to the university in the morning," Brad forewarned.

"I'd have to concur with Brad on this," Selini advised.

"Given that Marsh knows about the robots at the history museum, if this is a legitimate program, then it will likely just be a bunch of students trying to figure out whether they need to stop a possible invasion."

"You don't think Mash is an android?" Selini asked.

"He was cold as a robot, but I think he had a hot temper underneath that coldness."

"I got the impression he would have liked to have ripped us apart if he could have gotten away with it," Brad said. "And the way he glared at Natalia. Woo!"

"I don't like that," Selini said.

"Why would he hate me?" I asked.

"I don't know," Brad replied.

"Do you think this device Connor gave us will work?"

"Do you trust him?" Selini asked.

"I think so. He seems human," I said.

"This might work better," she said, pulling out some devices that looked like tie tacks.

"What are those?"

"They send out very strong electro-magnetic pulses. If that android Aaron was deactivated with an electromagnetic device, I would think these would do the trick," she said.

"Remember the device Not-Mom threw at the security robots that dropped them."

"I bet it was an EMP," Kal said.

"It even knocked her out, though she was away from it when it went off. Her memory was intact. Maybe Mom gave her something to protect her from full EMP deactivation."

"You have to tap these twice with two rotating fingers to activate," Selini said, showing the technique. "It's not easy to do by accident. Here's one for each of you."

"What do you think about Aaron? Could his memory chip have been damaged before his operating system went out altogether?"

"It's possible."

"There is another possibility we need to look at," Brad said. "What if they have been watching us for some time, replacing critical personnel, like Dr. KaKool?"

"It would have taken considerable strength to break his neck that way. He looked like a strong, sturdy person. A security robot could have done that," Kal responded. "But I don't think I could have and I don't think a regular humanoid robot could have done it either."

"I know I'm not strong enough to break someone's neck like that. I don't know if Jennifer could," I noted.

"What if it was an android we saw in KaKool's office?" Brad asked.

"When androids are damaged as opposed to destroyed or deactivated, the chips look for an alternate route around the damage. The skin does not turn blue. The man who was lying there was definitely a real person. We just don't know if it was the real KaKool," I responded.

"And if it was the real KaKool—" Kal started.

"Then Steve is in danger. He's working tomorrow," I finished.

"You changed the medical files so that they don't implicate you?" Selini asked for verification.

"That's why Connor was suspended," Kal said.

"Then the records show no indication you are from below."

"How do you unring a bell?" Brad asked. "Connor sounded an alert."

"Katerina says you can't," I recalled.

"Connor sounded it with the real Dr. KaKool, who is hopefully still the only Dr. KaKool," Kal said. He grimaced a little.

The next morning, Steve tried again to convince us to let him drive us to the university. He was making some good points. We were younger than the other university students and he wanted to make sure we were safe. As we were trying to figure out how to deflect his reasoning, Brad knocked on the door.

"We're all ready to go. We've got Roger's car."

I hugged Katerina. "You are wonderful, but we don't want to be the only ones who have parents taking them. That will follow us around when we start school next year."

"I understand," she said.

I didn't like lying to Steve and Katerina, but Katerina already couldn't accept the limited truth we had told her. I was sure she and Steve wouldn't believe the rest of the truth.

In the car, Jennifer and Roger did a make-over on Kal and me such that we didn't look anything like ourselves.

Brenden Marsh was at the front of the class when we arrived.

We kept our actions and expressions neutral and acted as if we knew what to do. Like the other students, we sat down at tables and worked on puzzles. First, Marsh put down pages of math problems which looked similar to ones we had had below, not the baby physics questions in the book Steve brought home. We paced ourselves to finish at the same time as the other students. Nobody looked particularly perplexed by the problems. To me, this was a sign that my classmates were from below.

Next, we were to put miniature human-resembling robots together and program them. I looked at Kal and Roger. I had thought these were illegal. One of the girls in the class looked my way and I refocused on her. She lowered her eyes.

Marsh spoke to her. "Cheating?"

"No."

"You?" he said to me.

"No. I'm finished."

"Record time."

He picked up my robot and said, "Speak."

The robot didn't speak.

"You were to instruct it to utilize language."

"Mama," the robot said.

"What crap?"

"It's a baby robot that says baby things."

"Does it also poop?"

"Actually, yes but not the smelly stuff—unless I have it process real food."

"Mama."

"Pathetic." He shook his head.

"If you had a baby robot, wouldn't you teach it to say 'mama' or 'dada?'"

"Maybe dada. Mothers." He huffed and shook his shoulders and threw back the robot.

"You don't like mothers?"

"You are out of line."

"Some kids don't have mothers."

"Which kids?"

"This one, for instance." I held up the robot.

"It could be assigned a parent. Mothers are overrated."

There was something weird about him and his freak-out.

"Why are we making robots if humanoid robots are illegal here?" I asked.

"So, you will know one when you see one."

I looked at the toy robot I had put together. It looked like a machine with plastic skin.

"You are disrupting the class," one of the students said to me. "Next project?"

I looked at the student, a girl about my age but with long dark brown hair, looking like she had been to a beauty salon. Her tone was very neutral.

"You missed the first five days of class. I didn't notice until I got a corrected roster. Where were you?" Marsh demanded.

Roger answered. "We were working on another project for WEFPD. We can't discuss it."

"I see. With students coming in late and some skipping class, we will all have to work doubly hard."

I wanted to ask him what we would be working on, but I had already called too much attention to myself.

Next, he pulled a box out of a closet. When he opened it, I saw the damaged head of Kal's not-dad.

CHAPTER 54

"Is this a human head or a robot head?" Marsh asked. He had covered up the metal parts but couldn't make it look human.

"Robot," Roger said.

"How do you know?"

"It is messed up, but it has no decay on it. Also, no blood, but you could have cleaned that up."

"It looks in bad shape. You say, 'no decay.'"

"The skin," I said. "Real skin wouldn't look like that after it had been sitting in a box with no preservatives."

"I have some star pupils here." He looked at us. "And being star pupils, I expect you can build a body for this head."

I was not my mother. Building a plastic-covered toy robot was one thing. There was no way I could build a body for Mr. Denton. I wouldn't want to if I could.

"Isn't it illegal?" Kal asked.

"This is a research facility. Who here thinks they could build a body for this head?"

Nobody raised his or her hand.

"You are to be protégés capable of doing anything, electronic."

"I can," one boy said.

"Me too," the girl who had tried to silence me joined in.

The boy, named Bryan, and the girl, named Koda, proceeded to assemble body parts but they looked more like wires and metal pieces attached to circuit boards. When they had assembled the body, they put on the head and flipped a switch. Nothing happened. They didn't seem to react with upset or rage at their failure. Finally, the girl spoke. "We would need the schematics upon which this robot was built."

"You're a mouthy little broad," he said.

He dismissed the class. Roger and Kal took off to speak with Koda and Bryan. I stayed behind to speak with Marsh. "Why do you hate women and mothers?"

"That is none of your business."

"Do you hate your own mother?"

"Yes, if that answers your question."

"What did she do to you?"

He seemed to freeze as if he was confused or going against some kind of indoctrination or programming. "She married my dad."

"Oh. And what else?"

"You ask too many questions. I'm going to check your chart."

"Of course," I said. "It occurred to me that you might be a robot, but you are too emotional."

"And how would you know?"

"If I were building a robot, I'd make him cold and unemotional. But then, wouldn't that be a mistake? People could tell the difference. If the goal were to make him fit in, it would make more sense to make him emotional so he couldn't be detected."

"Interesting theory, but it's just a theory."

"Right," I said. He leaned his head down to look at Denton's head. I swept my hand into my pocket and up as I walked past him, brushing against his head with the EMP, tapping it twice. He straightened up and then started to collapse. I pushed a chair under him and he collapsed into it. I swept the EMP around his skull in a circular motion. He closed his eyes and started to fall forward, hitting his head on the desk. I was hoping I hadn't killed him. But it was kinder than an ax.

He shook his head and then straightened up. He looked around. "What's going on?"

"You were teaching a class. You told us all to leave and I was about to leave."

"No, something else. I think I need a doctor."

"Are you sick?"

"Who are you?"

"Just a girl in the class. You were showing us how to make robots and you don't like mothers."

"I don't know why I don't like mothers. Mine was always there for me."

"And you said you hated her."

"Does that make any sense to you?"

"No."

Kal and Roger walked back in.

Kal whispered in my ear. "Those two kids were androids. Deactivated and in a closet. Brad and Jennifer are going to check them out."

I put my fingers to my lips.

"I remember going to this camp that the Unitee Church had and I was talking about how my mom was the only one who had ever been there for me. I was sent into a room for a massage. They put something over my ears and I fell asleep. After I woke up, I started doing horrible things to my mother and hating her."

"Is the Unitee Church a mother-hating group?" I asked Roger.

"They think the individual is more important than family. They do not support families."

"When was this?"

"Before the poisoning."

"You've hated your mother ever since?"

"And I—I don't know why."

Marsh was looking down with his lips trembling. I tapped the EMP against my hand behind my back to convey to Kal and Roger what I'd done.

"The robots were deactivated," Roger whispered to me. "He must be human."

Marsh seemed to be too much into remorse to focus on us.

"He collapsed but came out of it."

"So, why did it affect him at all?" Roger asked.

"Call Doctor Connor. Maybe he can figure this out."

Marsh was sitting with his head in his hands, crying when Connor peeked in the door.

"What's going on?"

"Two or more students in the class are androids. This guy had a change of personality after an EMP was used."

He went over to Marsh. "Hi. Would you mind if I ran some tests on you?"

"Maybe he can figure out why you hated your mother," I said.

"I hated this girl I saw the other day too. She reminded me of my mother."

"Golden hair, green eyes?" Roger asked.

"That was her. I wanted to kill her, and I didn't know her."

I thought of asking him about Denton and the project, but I didn't want to distract from his breakdown before we were able to check him over.

"The hospital? Are you taking me to the hospital?"

"There is a clinic where I can do the exam," Connor said. "I'm not privileged in either Valley or University Hospital currently."

We waited in an outer office while a CT scan was run on Marsh. Marsh came out and sat with us and then was called back into an inner office. "Will you go with me?" he asked, taking my hand.

"Of course," I said.

There was something really helpless about him.

Marsh showed him the images. He pointed to objects on both sides of Marsh's brain. "These should not be there."

"What are they?" I asked.

"It looks like some old microchips of the kind they had around twenty years ago. They could inject them with a needle."

"Twenty years ago was before the poisoning," I commented.

"In medical school, they were speaking of experiments that were being done on younger people, making them less dependent on families. Sometimes the insertion of chips facilitated the agendas, such as turning children against their families and stopping them from wanting children of their own. It was believed to be an environmental thing, lowering the carbon footprint. Humans are carbon."

"Unitee spoke of the importance of lowering the carbon and how we needed to stop caring about hurting others. We needed to go for ourselves," Marsh recalled.

A thought occurred to me. "Was it just teens or did they do it with little kids?"

"I heard they did it with babies as young as one month old. Their parents would take them in for an exam and vaccines or chips were implanted."

"Can they reactivate his chips?"

"I don't know. From the images, it looks as if they are damaged. The device may have permanently deactivated them."

"Can that harm him? Would it be better to remove them?"

"If they are inactive, it might be better to leave them in place. There are procedures for removing them."

"They made me hate my mother," Marsh lamented. He started crying, again.

"What are we going to do with him? Can he teach class like this?" Roger asked as he and Kal joined us.

"Brenden, you have to get yourself together. There are kids who depend on you," I told him.

"I've been mean to girls."

"The androids will notice if he starts being nice," Kal pointed out.

"What is the purpose of the class?" Roger asked.

"The government wanted to explore possibilities for stopping robots," Connor related.

"So, the government knows about the underworld?"

"A couple have made it up here."

"The countdown timer?"

"I told them I was concerned. Nobody in government seems to be worried."

"Denton's head?"

"He was a robot. We need to know how to stop them."

"You want to succeed in stopping the robots?"

"Yes."

"Then you have to go back to class and pretend to be the you from before you realized what had happened to you. You need to pretend to be cold and uncaring. Your class is making robots."

"The students were referred by WEFPD. They are protégés in this specialty."

"Is that an above-ground group? WEFDP is what the leaders who took the super-rich down below called their group. Could they have sent some of the kids? At least two androids were in it today. They won't be coming back, but there could be more."

"It's possible there are infiltrators."

"Or students were replaced. How were you selected?"

"The university put together the class on a recommendation from WEFPD and the government asked me to oversee it. Some of the best and brightest student minds often come up with solutions that seasoned geniuses overlook." Marsh started crying, again, and put his head in his hands. "My mother!"

Doctor Connor looked at me. "We have a room here where he can rest overnight. I'll give him a sedative and in the morning, I'll make sure the chips aren't working. What time does the class start?"

"Nine A.M," Roger said.

"Oh, Steve saw KaKool last night. I guess it was someone else who fell out of his closet," I informed him.

"I haven't heard anything about him or anyone else being found in an office. But then I'm not working there anymore and don't have all the sources."

As we were leaving, I asked Kal where Brad and Jennifer were.

"They've got a janitor's cart to carry away the waste and are busy sweeping the grounds, waiting for us."

After picking them up and putting the unconscious cargo in the trunk. I asked Brad, "Where are we taking them?"

"Same place we took your stalker. It's abandoned."

"Do you think they have tracking devices on them?"

"We ran the EMPs down the full length of their bodies. If they were there, they're not functional now."

"Let's just keep them away from the watch and necklace."

"They are heavy for their size."

"Probably human-looking security androids, then," Kal said.

Selini met us at the warehouse. "Nice," she said. She had a portable X-ray machine with her. "I'll need to use a stronger setting than the ones for humans. You should wait outside as a precaution."

"Do you have protection?"

"It's backed with a lead shield. I just don't want to take any chances with you, teens."

After checking them over, Selini called us in. "They are not humanoid inside."

"These were just two of the students. I wonder if the rest were robots."

"That's a possibility," she said.

"I did see one girl looking at me. I don't know if she suspected me or if she was real and looking for a comrade."

"One girl and one boy down. I wonder if we could take their places and join you," Brad said.

"You don't look anything like them," I rebutted.

"Did the other girls look like Barbie dolls?" Jennifer asked.

"Barbie dolls?"

"Those are missing from your education? Long ago, they were the in thing. Back at the time of the poisoning, junkie ones were sold in the stores. They even talked. My mom saved a couple that she showed me. I wasn't into dolls."

"If we had been born before the Elites went under, you would have been forced to have a sex change operation," Brad told Jennifer.

"Because I don't like dolls? I like being a girl."

"Before the Reset, if a girl liked blue or climbing trees, they cut off her breasts and if a boy liked dolls, his—thing was cut off," Selini said. "Back then, guys who were three hundred pounds but declaring themselves to be girls won girls' beauty contests and women were pretty much erased. But some of us survived."

"The Elites who went below were sexist in a different way, thinking girls didn't have the right to exist—except as obedient robots," Kal said.

"Maybe we should push in poison gas, blow up the entrances to the underground and let them enjoy the last of their psycho lives," Roger suggested.

"My mom's down there, I want her to be safe."

"I'm sure there are other good people down there too," Brad said.

"Like Robert Horton."

"The robot guy?" Brad asked.

"The real one was nice."

"Competition," Brad remarked.

"I'm fifteen. Nobody is winning my hand at this point."

"Below, you would have been given a mate at sixteen," Kal said.

"Not a surprise," Roger noted. "Before the Reset, the loonies running society went too far the other way, sending youth to fight in wars at the age of sixteen, removing organs or forcing jabs over parents' objections, and legalizing forced adult sex with kids."

"Part of the depopulation agenda," Brad said. "I'm glad my parents didn't get the jab."

"The Elites didn't either. Those who pretended to do so got saline," Kal said.

Selini looked over the girl. "How about you go home for a late lunch? I'm going to make an incision to see for myself what's under this covering and how it works."

"You're not going to skin her?" I freaked.

"It isn't skin, Natalia. It's a covering. It's not even the stuff my sister had. Hers felt like real flesh. This has a different feel."

"You're saying we can tell these from the regular androids by feel?" Jennifer asked.

"But not by looks," Selini said, "Except that they are as flawless as a mannequin."

———

Katerina was delighted when we all showed up for what Brad called "Dunch," late lunch/early dinner, to give Selini time to work. Eterra jumped into my arms, almost knocking me down.

"She missed you."

"I wish I could take you with me but believe me, you're better off here."

———

When we returned to the lab, I screamed as I saw two skinless, metal-faced beings sitting in chairs.

"They're deactivated." Selini handed Jennifer and Brad some boxes. "Their coverings have a stretch to them. I added a seam that self-seals when you put it on."

"You want us to wear someone else's skin?" Jennifer asked, grimacing.

"It's not skin," Selini said. "I hope you don't think I'm a monster."

"I don't know if I can do that?" Jennifer fretted.

"I've seen you at Halloween. You have no qualms about putting on full head coverings," Brad said.

"But they don't belong to—to—they were like people—real people when they had them on."

"I'll work on her," Roger assured Selini.

"It's easy for you. You don't have to wear someone else's skin and hair."

"It's not real skin or real hair," he countered. "Pretend it's like that Helen of Troy mask you wore last year. It looks a lot like that."

"You're beautiful. Why did you wear a face mask?" I asked her.

"I wanted to look like someone else."

"Tomorrow, you will." Roger patted his sister on the shoulder.

That night, we decided to get a good night's sleep. We met Selini at the warehouse in the morning.

"The EMP wiped out their programming. I managed to remove the chips and am trying to restore them on this computer, but it's a very slow process with so much of the program erased."

"Better erased than them coming after us and killing us," Brad acknowledged.

"And I'm expected to wear the skin and hair of a killer." Jennifer crunched her nose.

"I sanitized it and so it has none of their residue. It's as fresh as if it just came off a factory floor." Selini threw a cloth over the robots. "Now think of someone doing your Halloween face and hair to make you look like a princess."

"I like my princess red."

"I'm with Jennifer on that. I like red better than the blonde I'm stuck with. Well, now I'm not blonde," I said, putting on the short black wig. "

"I like your blonde," Kal remarked. "Chanelle's red wasn't real. When she was little, it was dark brown, almost black."

"And I still didn't realize they'd replaced her," I chided myself. I looked at the glasses. "The robotic students have got to know that robots don't wear glasses."

"Now that Marsh is on your side, maybe you won't have to wear them," Brad said.

"Let's do your eye makeup to make your eyes look different," Selini suggested.

A few minutes later, I didn't recognize myself.

"You look hot," Brad said.

"Not as hot as Jennifer."

"It's the robot who looks hot. I'm just wearing her yuck."

"I wonder if you are stronger than the robot," I said. "I mean, you are pretty capable."

"They are metal inside. It would be like fighting someone who's using iron knuckles."

"Maybe you can give my sister some of the robot's internal iron parts," Roger said.

Jennifer punched his shoulder. "I can still take you down."

We went to pick up Marsh at the clinic. "I think he'll be alright," Doctor Connor said as we squeezed him into the car.

Marsh looked at Jennifer and Brad. "How did you two—"

"These are friends who now look like your students. Those students turned out to be robots. They are sitting in a warehouse and their programs are hopefully being deciphered."

"Max said my chips are completely deactivated. I feel so much better and more alive than I've felt in years. And you two girls are beautiful, particularly you," Marsh said, looking at me. "You remind me of my mother—except she was a blonde."

"Do you know where your mother lives?"

"She has tried to call me a lot, but I never answer. I've been so awful to her. This year, I want to do good things for her: make her a Thanksgiving dinner, decorate her Christmas tree, celebrate New Year's with her."

"You might start by calling her."

"We're getting to school early. I'll call, but she's probably mad at me for the way I've treated her."

"Mothers love their children. My mom was willing to do whatever it took to protect me and I wasn't the most understanding girl in the world."

At school, Marsh went into the classroom. We gave Marsh some privacy. "Remember, we have to avoid being caught looking around, and we have to look like we have no emotions," I advised Brad and Jennifer.

"You two have lived around robots your whole lives. You were used to that," Jennifer noted.

"Pretend it's like in the movies," Brad told her. "Remember *The Invasion,* where Nichole Kidman had to pretend to be possessed by the alien stuff and she had to look very stoic."

"That was a great movie. People were lining up for a vaccine that took away their minds, and that was before that Fraudcy guy had people doing that same thing in real life," Jennifer recalled.

"I read about that in the history museum. It was sick. I hope Fraudcy wound up in prison," I said.

"He just kind of disappeared from public view, before the Reset. That's what my mom said," Jennifer related.

"I guess he served his purpose," I said.

"Let's go back in. We need to make sure that Marsh stays in character so nobody gets suspicious," Brad advised.

Inside, Marsh seemed elated, hosting a broad smile. "I called my mother. She loves me! She was so happy to speak with me that nothing else mattered. I was so awful, but she still loves me."

"That's great." I enthused.

"I told her I love her and I am so sorry about how I treated her. She cried and I cried. It was wonderful."

I went over and gave a hug to the guy that I previously despised. Now, he was like a lovable teddy bear, but thinner than one would expect a teddy bear to be.

My friends and brother gathered around and joined in giving him a group hug.

The bell rang. "Let's go out and watch the other students as they come in," I suggested.

Outside in the hallway, I told Brad, "There is nothing like talking to a mom to make a person feel better. Even though real communication was dangerous below, just talking to my mom always made me feel better because I knew she loved me."

"I wish I had had my mom growing up," Kal lamented. "She died when I was young. I'm sure my father was responsible."

"That's a good reason to hope he wasn't my father. Maybe you had a different father, too."

"My mom is really great. I feel for you, Kal," Brad said.

"Me, too," Roger added.

"She's my best supporter," Jennifer said. "It's sad when children are separated from their moms, especially when their moms are like Selini, having given so much only to have their kids close their hearts."

"I wonder if Tarinda is autistic. She has no empathy or any semblance of humanity," Brad pondered.

"Here they come," I said, nudging my head towards one of the students. "That girl was staring at me yesterday when I was looking around."

Seeing who followed them down the hall, I exclaimed, "What? What is Steve doing here?"

"He might recognize us," Kal warned.

"I'll check it out," Brad said. He was in a full disguise and I hoped Steve wouldn't recognize him. He walked over to Steve while Kal and I stayed out of sight.

The girl I had recognized walked past the room and into the electronics lab we had hidden in.

We tried to stay out of sight. Steve went into a classroom down the hall. I felt like checking out the classroom. I hoped it didn't have robots.

Brad came back. "He said he had been assigned to give a lesson on modern surgical techniques. Apparently, Dr. KaKool was supposed to give the lesson but won't be able to make it."

"Dead people don't give lessons," Roger said.

"Except it may not have been Dr. KaKool we saw," I replied. "Steve said he was still alive."

A dozen students walked into Marsh's room.

"Look how controlled they are. They all look like androids," Kal observed.

"Do you think?" Roger asked.

"We still have the EMPs," I said. "Have any of you tried the defib?"

"Not yet," Brad replied.

"The dark-haired girl isn't in the class yet. Maybe she was switching classes."

Steve walked out of the other classroom.

He spoke with a woman and turned and walked in the direction from which he had come and down another hallway.

We started to follow, passing the woman. She spoke as we passed. "If you are looking for the medical lecture, it's in the main auditorium."

"Thank you," Brad replied.

"The guest speaker was mixed up about the location, too," the woman said.

We went back towards Marsh's classroom, entering robotically, single file. The other students were calmly looking at computer chips on their tables. I looked down at the floor and had to hold back a scream.

Marsh was lying on the floor, his neck turned to the side with his eyes open, staring at nothing.

CHAPTER 55

Kal and Brad leaned down and checked his pulse.

"Don't move his head in case his neck is broken," Brad said quietly, looking from the man to the calmly working students who seemed oblivious to what was going on.

Kal shook his own head as I dialed 9-1-1 on my phone.

Nobody at the tables seemed to notice.

"Do you think one of them?" I whispered.

"I don't even think they know he's here," Jennifer murmured back. "It's like they are deaf and blind to anything they aren't supposed to notice."

The dark-haired girl came in the door. She saw Brad and Kal kneeling on the floor by the body and screamed.

The other students started moving towards her. Roger rushed over to her, put his hands around her mouth and pushed her out of the classroom. I moved out with him. I heard what I thought was the door locking. I suspected Kal or Brad had surreptitiously done that.

But a minute later, a fist went through the door, and the knob area was pushed through.

Roger picked up the girl and ran down the hall into the men's bathroom as I followed. We went into a stall and I stood on a toilet seat while Roger held the girl over his head with her mouth covered. I heard the bathroom door open. Shadows poured in through the opening at the bottom of the door. From the shadows, it looked as if someone was bent over, maybe checking the feet in the stalls.

Nobody spoke but some of the stalls were being opened. Afraid they'd open our stall, I flushed the toilet as if someone was using the stall for legitimate purposes. The shadows and sound of footsteps moved away.

We waited. Roger opened the stall door and looked out. "They seem to be gone."

"What caught their attention?" I asked.

"The scream. I don't think they could even see us when we were in the classroom."

"Do you think it's safe to go back, now?" I asked Roger.

"Go back? Marsh is dead on the floor," the girl said as Roger removed his hand.

"We saw. Somebody broke his neck. Those metallic things are strong enough to do that," Roger said.

"I'm supposed to be assisting March. They'll kill me. I'm not going back."

"Assist him how?" I asked.

"We can't help unless we know what is going on," Roger said. "We need to see what they are up to."

She started crying. "I can't be here. They killed him."

"We have a defense if they get violent."

"They broke through the metal door."

"They've got stronger insides," I said. "They're robots."

"Marsh was part of the investigation."

"And you were investigating?" Roger asked.

"It's confidential. Marsh only knew part of my purpose."

"Which was?" I inquired.

"I'm an intern, a trainee, for SU, a government agency."

"SU?"

"Save Us is what we call it, but it really means something else. We believe the people from below will be coming up."

"This could be an advanced security force. The real androids have human organs," I said. "The security robots have metal insides."

"How do you know?"

"We know," I said. "We're trying to stop the invasion too. I'm Natalia and this is Roger, but our names are different on the rolls."

"I'm Brenda, but I'm Carly on the rolls. My work with Marsh is secret and I can't tell you any more than Marsh could."

"He's dead. He'd want you to help us catch his killer." I told her.

"This isn't the first person they've killed like that. They killed someone in the hospital the other night. Are you prepared to go back?" Roger asked.

"They'll recognize me."

"It was your scream that attracted their attention. But we can change your appearance. If they go after you, we'll protect you."

Her hair was nice and long. I pulled it into a knotted ponytail on top of her head. I took my old glasses out of my pocket. "They're not magnified. So they won't mess up your vision."

"Let's go. Hopefully, Brad, Kal and Jennifer are still invisible," Roger said.

"Whatever happens, androids don't have feelings. No screaming. No reaction to anything."

She wiped tears from her face. "I'll try. For Marsh, I'll try."

We went back to the classroom. The students, including our friends, were working at tables. Marsh's body was gone. I moved in between Jennifer and Brad, who was next to Kal on a side facing away from the door.

"Did 9-1-1 come?"

"Not yet?" Brad whispered

"Where—"

Jennifer shook her head as if to silence our conversation.

"Removed," Brad whispered to me. "You wouldn't believe." He stopped as one of the students seemed to turn his head in our direction. Brad looked down as if he hadn't said anything. I did likewise.

The door opened and I pretended not to look. "We got a call saying there was a body here."

Nobody moved or responded. I figured it was the paramedics, but I wasn't going to break the silence.

"It must have been a prank," a voice said from behind us. "Or maybe a different classroom."

I heard footsteps moving away, other footsteps walking in and the door closing.

"Students," a voice said and everyone turned to face the instructor: Dr. KaKool, the dead body from the closet.

CHAPTER 56

All kinds of thoughts clashed together in my mind. The body we had seen in the closet was clearly human and very dead. Yet here he stood before us, very much alive.

Kal looked at me, quickly, as if to let me know he was perplexed too.

I didn't dare look at Brenda or the others. Brenda probably didn't know KaKool. Brad and Kal had probably already experienced shock. I suspected it was this KaKool who had disposed of Marsh's body.

The likely scenario raced through my mind. *If the real KaKool is dead, then this must be a look-alike imposter, which likely means they could be preparing to impersonate all of us. Maybe that was their plan. Infiltrate and massively replace all above-ground humans with robots. Steve, I worried. He is working at the hospital with KaKool. Is he slated to be replaced? I have to find a way to warn him.*

Everyone was paying attention. KaKool looked at me, Kal and Roger. "Are you on the rolls?"

"Yes. If you look at the rolls, you will see our names: Abigail Wilson, John Cleveland, and Thomas McKinley. We were sent here to fill in for students who did not make the destination."

I wondered if the class was overfilled.

"There were to be twelve students. You make fifteen."

"There was a change. The new directive called for fifteen. We follow our instructions," I said in a monotone.

"Very well. What is the keyword?"

It had to be something I could grasp. Mom's office had something written above it: *Eternal Life. Eminence.*

"Eminence," I guessed.

"And what does that mean?"

I knew the dictionary definition didn't match what my mom had on the wall, but a fake would have given the dictionary definition. "Eternal life," I said.

"And you?" he asked Roger. "Eternal life, eminence," he repeated me.

I worried about Brenda. She undoubtedly didn't have answers.

He looked at Brenda. "Your number?"

"10291."

"You were here the first day. There is a note from Marsh. You are suspected of being a robot." She didn't answer. "You must try to act more human."

He put a check on a written roster. In this electronic age, I was surprised that schools were still using written rosters in the classroom, but then there was an anti-AI hysteria up here and with good reason.

"Student number 10285 is not here. According to the attendance, he has not been here since last week. Does anyone have any information?"

Robert! The carnival!

"I want all students here when we start on the next phase."

I wondered what that was. Would we be going out and mass slaughtering people? Or was there something else in mind?

"Hold up one of those robots you put together yesterday," KaKool instructed.

A student went into a closet and pulled out one of the tiny robots.

"This is what humans think robots are like."

He touched a plate on the robot's neck and it said, "Mama." That was my robot.

"Humor. I would have expected you all to show the stupidity of this assignment. Does this look like a robot?"

"No," Jennifer said. "It looks nothing like a real robot." That was gutsy, taking the lead in answering.

"Correct."

"What's off?"

"The covering. There is no covering over the formed plastic. Even simple security robots have a translucent sheath over them," Kal said.

"Does anyone disagree?"

No reaction.

"What else?"

"It's not AI. It lacks self-reasoning abilities," I said. "It just says what it is programmed to say and cannot adjust its observations."

"Very good. You've been programmed well."

"Do all concur?"

I heard an echo of emotionless "'yes"es.

Two days until D Day. I hoped KaKool would tell us what was going on. Brad and Jennifer weren't monitoring today, but Selini was from her apartment. I hoped the robots couldn't pick up on the signal. No such luck.

"I sense a remote signal. Someone is monitoring this classroom."

He pulled out a device and waved it around the room. "It's gone."

Selini must have remotely shut it down. I hoped it would be safe for her to monitor later.

Jennifer had a cell with her, but she had planned to take the battery out. Brad had informed me that removable batteries were back in use ever since the Elites went under. I'd left mine in the bathroom.

"Alright. We are not going to wait further". He opened a case and asked us to assemble a robot to look human. Inside the case was synthetic skin and hair. We took parts out of various drawers and started to work. The robot would not pass a metal detector undetected. It was basically a security robot but not quite. KaKool put a small disc onto a table. We attached it by wire to the uncovered head, which we had wired to the body.

"Now, we need to reshape the head." I figured he'd use some cosmetic dermal filler, as I had seen my mom do on some of the housekeeping robots. Instead, he pulled out some metal pieces and added them to the chin, lengthening the face and widening the jaw. He placed more metal over the cheeks.

Next, he had us add the skin covering. As we did, I held back my shock. It looked like Brad. No. It looked like Robert Horton.

KaKool finished the activation and removed the wire.

"We now have our final student, the missing one," KaKool said.

Robert looked at me and touched my chin.

Is he going to out me? Can he see through my disguise? Is the real Robert Horton only a robot?

He continued to stare at me and I almost went numb. I was surrounded by metallic creatures who could break my neck at any moment.

KaKool followed Robert's stare to me and back. I was about to be outed. "Defective program. The model must have an obsession with girls."

"Maybe she looks like his mother," Roger ventured in a monotone, but I feared he had spoken too much. KaKool looked at him and I wondered if both Roger and I had been caught.

"That is a possibility. Not his mother, but the source's mother. I will need to rebuild the program and we'll replace him tomorrow," he said, looking at the time. Put everything away for now. He chopped off Robert's head and slashed the skin off his body. I felt queasy. I guessed it was something you never got used to. I understood how Jennifer felt now about wearing the girl robot's skin.

As we walked out, I tapped Brenda's arm. Without looking at me, she managed to follow. Brad found an empty classroom and we moved inside. "They are creating human-looking security robots," Kal worried.

"Doctor KaKool is dead. The teacher is a replacement," I said.

"Replacement? How can you tell?" Brenda asked.

"We saw the original dead on the floor of his office," I replied.

She shook her head. "We need to notify someone."

"If there is someone who cares, notify them but keep us out of it as best you can. We have told you more than we should," Roger advised her.

"We'll keep your secret if you'll keep ours," Brad added, throwing in a little incentive.

She nodded. "How do I tell them I know?"

"Tell them it's from an anonymous source. You saw the instructor killed and the students made a human-looking robot."

"Why did he stare at you?"

"The last Horton robot tried to turn me into a zombie. They have necklaces and watches that mess with the natural electronic pulses in our brain and that communicate with the robots. Horton put the necklace on me. I went dizzy and felt I had to go somewhere. I wound up unconscious and only recovered some time after it was removed."

"There was a dead body in the hospital morgue. 3988. It was a robot named Aaron who had expired, but when we touched the watch to him, he sat up until we removed it," Brad said.

"Watch out that jewelry doesn't touch you," I further advised.

"Right," Brad said.

"And you can't tell us who you are working for?" she asked.

"No. But we are very concerned about everyone at the hospital and at the university. We don't know who will be replaced, next." I was especially worried about Steve.

"University Hospital?"

"No. The big one in Sutter Springs."

"KaKool was a department head," Kal said, almost reading my mind, "And now acting assistant chief of staff. I don't think they're going after underlings or they'd have already gotten Aaron's doctor."

I hoped they hadn't gotten Connor, and he hadn't been playing us.

We said goodbye and told Brenda we'd see her the next day in class. As we left, we made sure none of the students, including Brenda, followed us.

In the car on the way from the university, I said. "Steve was at the university and he knows KaKool. Do you think they'll try to replace him?"

"Thank goodness I have this thing off," Jennifer said, returning to her normal look. The rest of us removed our disguises as we continued the conversation.

"I think they're going to try to replace us all. And KaKool will probably start with the hospital and university staff. But that flaw in the one we built today could delay things," Brad conjectured.

"He's got two days," I said.

"He'll probably be working overnight," Kal guessed.

"Did someone put KaKool together or did he put himself together?" Roger pondered.

"Someone must be overseeing the project and have the names of people to replace first. If we were the first to come up here, how do they know who to replace?" I asked.

"There was Aaron," Brad said.

"But he was damaged."

"Someone had KaKool replaced. The original was killed and replaced."

"That was just yesterday or the day before. He was replaced very fast."

"We replaced Robert in a short time today."

"But he was defective," Brad remarked.

"He looked at me. I knew Robert, and he was always nice to me down below. The Robert in the House of Horrors and Mirrors put his arm around me before he put the necklace on me."

"And did you like that?" Kal asked.

"He turned me into a zombie. I didn't consider it endearing," I reacted.

We went to the warehouse. "They're still inactive. I've been looking at the programming. They are a part of an advanced force. They are security robots, as you said."

"Did you see what happened in the room?"

"I was on an audio monitor."

"I got video," Jennifer said.

"You left your battery in?" I asked.

"Airplane mode. It should have been undetectable. I continued it after he said the device was turned off."

Jennifer downloaded the video onto Selini's computer.

"The metal is stronger than steel or titanium," Selini said. "I've been examining them. Don't ever get into a fight with one."

"How did the fake Robert Horton's head get smashed in?' Brad asked.

"Whoever rescued you must have known what he was dealing with, knew his weak points, and had something stronger to smash him with."

"So, whoever rescued me knows about the robots and how to fight them physically?"

"Apparently," Selini said. "I don't expect you to be carrying around pipes to kill them. The EMPs have worked so far."

"So far. They may come up with a defense against the EMPs if they discover we are using them," Brad noted.

"Did you tell Brenda?" Selini asked. "That's who you said the girl was, didn't you?"

"We pretended we were working for a different government agency. We gave her minimal information. We did tell her about the bracelet and the watch," Roger informed her.

"Did you find anything new about the countdown timer?" I asked Selini.

"I'm not sure if they set it up or if it was set up by someone who was warning us. But I did find a program called Replace."

"Replace?"

"There are numbers, rather than names, associated with the replacements?"

"In the class, we all have numbers, including Brenda. Maybe the numbers will tell you something. For instance, who is to be replaced?"

"I made up numbers for you, Kal and Roger," Brad said. "But they were logical additional numbers for those already on the list. They looked as if they would be the next set of numbers."

"I didn't know my number," Jennifer said. "It's a good thing KaKool didn't ask me."

As we left the warehouse and went to see Doctor Connor, we had more questions than before.

"You are saying the same KaKool you saw dead was replaced with a duplicate?"

"Ten to one, it's an android," I said. "He had us build a duplicate of a friend of mine from below. It looked at me. So, he destroyed it."

"Does he suspect you?"

"He thought it was defective."

"When they uploaded his consciousness, he must have been thinking about you."

"Clearly," Kal said, seeming rather upset. "I guess a guy with an empty head has very little to think about."

"You told me they are destructible," Dr. Connor continued.

"But they're strong. Today, they were punching through a metal door."

"Is there a way to destroy their heads?"

"When KaKool smashed today's Horton, he had a wrench that looked very heavy."

"He's teaching your class at the university?"

"Someone killed our professor, Brenden Marsh. It was the same way KaKool was killed. Twisted neck." I recounted, thinking of the horrible loss.

"What happened to the body?"

"KaKool removed it," Brad said.

"There is a removal list. We don't know who is on it," Kal added.

"You think I might be?" Connor asked.

"You brought Aaron to KaKool's attention. It's a possibility," Kal pointed out.

"But I brought him to the real Dr. KaKool's attention."

"Your name is on the robot's body," Brad noted.

"Also, we think they uploaded KaKool's brain. I saw marks on the side of his head," I said.

Connor turned to Roger and Jennifer. "What do you think?"

"We didn't see KaKool's body, but we saw Brenden Marsh's," Jennifer said.

"I'd take a vacation," Roger suggested.

"Marsh had seriously changed. He loved his mom, and he was eager to make up to her for all he had done to her," Connor lamented. "It's terrible timing."

"He called her and made up with her before he was killed," I told him. "They were making plans. It's awful." I felt like crying thinking of his mother waiting to see him and now it would never happen.

"At least she'll remember that he loved her," Kal pointed out.

"Tarinda!" An inspiration that had been digging at my brain exploded. "They were doing it to little kids. I know she's older than me. Do you think?"

"That she's chipped and not a bitch?" Jennifer asked.

"Maybe, she's both," Roger said.

"We have to be home soon, but maybe we could swing by her place," Kal suggested.

"What if she has a human side that is worse?" Brad asked. "Like she eats babies for lunch?"

"Oooo," Jennifer reacted.

"Or maybe she'd been replaced," Kal suggested.

"Then they'd know how to reach Selini and they'd want Tarinda to get in touch with her mother, wouldn't they?" I asked. "Wouldn't Selini be on their hit list?"

We knew we had limited time. We rushed to Tarinda's apartment building. Brad knew how to get us into the building and her apartment. This time, there was a male security person and Jennifer and I distracted him while the others went up to the apartment. Jennifer asked for water as she was totally dehydrated. Of course, when he returned, we were gone.

Inside the apartment, Jennifer looked in Tarinda's refrigerator. "This thing has the most unhealthy food I've ever seen. Where did she get this garbage? A poison factory?"

"Do we wait? We don't want Steve and Katerina getting suspicious." I worried.

Jennifer pulled out her phone. "I know...Hi. Mrs. Drake...The students are going out for slushies and to discuss the class. I hope you don't mind if it takes an extra hour or two to get Kal and Natalia home. Everyone is so impressed by how amazing they are in math. In fact, Kal is showing some calculations to this nice boy from the class. His name is Jim. Thank you. We'll have them home as soon as possible."

"If there are negative points for lying, we'd be on probation or worse," I said.

"You know about probation?" Brad asked.

"Students in the leadership group sometimes get put on probation if they are out of line. Some leave permanently," Kal related.

"Probably turned into robots," I remarked.

"That's on your mom."

"I cannot believe my mom would kill live kids."

The door opened. "You, again." Tarinda whipped out her cell phone and started punching in numbers as Jennifer and I swept back her hair with the EMPs in our hands, each of us tapping twice and giving her a double dose.

She dropped the phone. "That was weird. What are you doing?"

"Hoping you'll be a better person," I said.

Jennifer picked up the phone and said, "Wrong number." She turned it off.

"Give me back my new phone."

"I think you were insulting parasites when you said you are a louse," I derided her.

"And are fine with it," Brad added.

"Yeah," she said, unsteadily. We sat her down on the couch.

"Think about what a terrible daughter you are and how much you've hurt your mom," Jennifer remarked as we started to leave.

"Did she send you?"

"She doesn't know we're here. But we are fans of hers," I replied.

"You don't deserve a mother that good," Brad added.

"You belong with a mom who uses whips and chains," Jennifer said.

As we arrived downstairs, the security guard asked Jennifer, "What were you doing up there?"

"My friend arrived and invited me up. Sorry, I couldn't wait for you."

He held out the water.

"She gave me a glass. Thank you."

When we got home, Katerina had already prepared dinner. It was mushroom ravioli again. Steve was sitting at the table, not saying anything.

"Hi," I said.

"I'm glad Jennifer called," Katerina replied. "I was worried about you. I know, it's stupid. But I'm a worrier."

"Thank you for letting us stay out later, and thank you for watching Eterra while we've been at the university."

"It's good you're home," Steve said. There was no inflection in his voice and his face was expressionless. I didn't know if my concerns were because of KaKool or Marsh but I started to worry. I looked at Kal. He looked worried too.

CHAPTER 57

"What happened at work today?" I asked.

"I was only there for part of the day. I started at the university."

"And?"

"I saw Dr. KaKool. I tried to speak to him, and it was as if he didn't hear me."

I was starting to feel relieved, but robots don't always know they are robots and he still hadn't shown any emotion.

"Maybe he was in a hurry," Katerina guessed. "He may have had something on his mind."

"There is something odd about him," Steve shook his head, grimacing.

I relaxed. I could see Kal had relaxed too.

I went over and gave Steve a hug. He hugged me back. Then he smiled. "It's so refreshing to come home to a wonderful family after such a strange day."

"You aren't worried about your job?" Kal asked.

"I don't work for him."

"How is the head of your department behaving?"

"Fine, I guess. I didn't see him today. I shouldn't bring my concerns home."

"Talking is two-way. We're supposed to tell you what's happening with us, and it makes us feel better when you tell us about your day," Kal said.

Katerina hugged me. "How was your day?"

"Weirder than yours," I said to Steve. "We had a change of professors and a girl came into the room and freaked out."

"Is she alright?" Katerina asked.

"Oh yes. And we've bonded with a couple of the other kids."

"When I went to work, I heard that KaKool had ordered up Connor's files."

"Aren't they computerized?" I was more than a little nervous. If he looked at the files, he might figure out about us.

"They were erased and the physical files are missing."

"Including ours?"

"Including yours."

I wondered if the robotic force already had them, but if they did, KaKool wouldn't have been looking for them. I wondered who had erased them, though.

"Who is the acting Chief of Staff?"

"My department head, which is why it was strange he wasn't at work."

In my room, Kal and I spoke. "Weirder and weirder," I said. "For a moment, I thought Steve—"

"Me too."

"The files. Mine was just altered. We didn't get around to erasing anything after we found the body."

"Somebody erased them. We searched for Connor's physical files Saturday night. They weren't under the disciplinary section or anywhere else we looked."

"Either KaKool removed them before he was killed or Connor did it before he left."

"If an android had killed KaKool, the android could have taken the files at that time."

"Unless the killer wanted to get out of there fast, figuring the replacement would get the files later."

"Kakool could have taken them yesterday or today, but he told the staff they weren't there."

"Or he lied."

"Maybe he was searching and finally asked someone."

Kal called Brad with the information on the developments.

"I'm going back to Connor's place tonight," he said.

An hour later, Brad called us. "I'm at his apartment. Security remembered I was a regular guest and let me up. I used my card to get in."

"And?"

"He's gone. I don't know if he's alive."

"We told him to leave."

"I searched his place for the files. I didn't find anything, but I found some ashes in the fireplace. I swept them into a bag. I know ashes can be reconstructed by certain people. I'm bringing the bag with me."

"Shit," His next line was whispered. "Somebody's at the door."

I heard a loud noise and the phone went quiet.

CHAPTER 58

"We've got to help Brad," I said. "I don't have Roger's or Jennifer's number on my phone."

"I just have Brad's. Let's go," Kal urged. We left our usual way, leaving Eterra on the bed in case of danger, and rushed to Jennifer's house. I threw a pebble at her window. She looked out. A couple of minutes later, she and Roger were downstairs.

"What's up?" Roger asked.

"Brad was at Connor's. His phone went silent," Kal informed them.

"That was after someone arrived and we heard a loud noise," I added.

"Let's go," Roger encouraged. We jumped into Roger's car and sped away.

As we arrived, we saw a familiar corpse walking out of the building. I warned, "Don't let him see us."

Roger turned left, just before the building. Through the back window, we could see Kakool getting into a car.

Kal's phone rang. "Thank goodness. We were worried about you." He put it on speaker.

"When he started breaking in, I rushed into the hallway and went out the living room to the kitchen area, which had its own door."

"People should always have two doors to their apartments," Roger commented. "KaKook drove off."

"That answers the who. If he were there, before—"

"He wouldn't have needed to break in," Kal finished Brad's sentence.

"I didn't see any signs of a struggle, and the closet looked partially empty."

"So, either you have the files in that bag or Connor took them with him," I surmised.

"Or they're still in the hospital," Kal noted.

The next morning at the university, we walked into the classroom to find Robert standing next to KaKool. I held back my reaction and tried not to be seen looking around. There was a curtain around a section of the classroom as if a new project was hidden there.

"Our final student has returned and will be taking over the instruction here," KaKool rattled off Robert's number. He was not looking at me. In fact, he seemed very much under control.

I was sure Kal recognized him, too.

"I have to complete the hospital project," KaKool said.

I had to make sure my eyes did not show my concern.

KaKool left the classroom. I wondered if we should run after him and deactivate him. We were supposed to be androids. We couldn't fake a need for bathroom breaks. Though humanoid androids did take breaks, security robots didn't. No quick excuse to leave came to mind.

I stood there as Robert started speaking. "We will start by creating another android. I have a new mental upload for the robot, an unflawed one," Robert said.

"The administration insisted I go to the office. There seems to be a problem with the class. I was told that my enrollment didn't have the correct authorizations," I informed him.

"They should have contacted me or the former instructor."

They couldn't contact Marsh as he was dead. "We'll need to recreate Marsh. They'll need to interact with him," Kal said.

"We don't have his upload," Robert noted.

Why is a supervisor telling us underlings his problem?

"Suggestions?" He turned to the class.

"Create a second android to look like Marsh but imprint on it with your upload. You two will complement each other," I said.

"Smart girl," he responded. There was no reaction to me so far.

"The administrators will be here soon if I don't go to the office. May I be excused?"

"Go."

"I was told the same thing," Brad related. "I will make sure all goes appropriately."

Kal started to speak but may have felt it would be too suspicious if all three of us left.

In the car, I freaked. "Hurry."

Brad removed his mask. I pulled off my hair and we headed for the hospital.

"Do you think KaKool will recognize you?"

"I don't recall him from down below," I said. "They've got to be doing security robot replacements up here for people in positions of authority. That's the only thing that makes sense, as fast as they replaced KaKool. Only my mom can properly replace the humanoid ones. The security robots are a different matter. Maybe they plan to bring her up here after it's safe. The countdown is set for tomorrow."

"Why the hospital?" he asked.

"I don't know. Maybe they have a doctor fetish."

We walked in through the entrance. Something was very off. The Acting Chief of Staff, Steve's department head, according to his nametag, came out and looked right past us as if we weren't even there. We kept going.

"He's not programmed to see us," I noted.

Steve was a general practitioner who was currently working in emergency. We rushed into the emergency room. "I don't see him here," I worried.

As we rushed down the hall, a nurse asked, "What are you doing?"

"I'm here to see my dad, Steve Drake. It's an emergency."

"We can page him."

"Just tell me where he is."

"I think Dr. KaKool just paged him to his office."

My eyes widened.

"Wait. Aren't you the girl—" But the end was lost as we rushed towards KaKool's office.

"Remember, act like a robot when you see KaKool," I told Brad.

Steve was just entering the office.

"There's a major emergency. You are needed," Brad advised Steve calmly in a monotone voice.

"I'm sure someone can handle it," KaKool said.

"The person asked for Steve. As Chief of Internal Medicine, I'm sure you realize the importance of following protocol," Brad responded.

Steve didn't let on who we were.

"Sometimes protocol does not serve its purpose," KaKool countered.

"We were told a life is at stake. And I know you have a busy schedule right now. An hour's delay won't hurt," I said, rather officiously.

"Make it quick," KaKool replied.

In the hall, Steve asked, "Why would emergency send you?"

"Say as little as possible, sir. The life we are saving is yours," Brad warned.

Steve stopped. "What is this? This is a serious hospital."

"I promise you will get all the answers you need if you simply come with us. You know I'm on your side." At least, I hoped he did.

"KaKool won't wait all day. He's meeting with all the staff."

"But he is not your supervisor."

"Not directly, but he is one of the top administrators here and taking my department head's place as Assistant Chief of Staff while Montrose is Acting Chief of Staff. It will reflect badly on my record if I don't meet with him."

"But you work under Montrose in his department, not under KaKool," I said.

"KaKool is doing the staffing evaluations while Montrose handles the other tasks."

"Are you sure? Have you had an extensive discussion with Monstrose?" I asked.

Steve looked angry. "You are both teens. This is my job. It's how I cover the costs of our family."

"And there are things about this hospital you don't know," Brad advised.

"This is absurd."

"You asked me to trust you and Katerina. You need to trust us for just this once. We'll explain everything outside."

As we walked out past emergency, there really was an emergency. A multiple-car accident had resulted in a dozen critical patients. There was lots of blood in spite of the bandages the EMTs had placed on the injured. A couple of people were unconscious. Others were crying in pain.

"Whatever you need will have to wait," he told us.

"Promise me that you will come with us before you see KaKool."

"I don't—"

"My life and yours depend on it."

"This could take quite a few hours. I'll find an excuse to delay the meeting until tomorrow," he said, less irritated with us. "But you'd better have a good reason for this."

"We do."

———

Resigned, we returned to the university with our disguises back on. In the classroom, there were two Robert androids and one that looked like Marsh. "This one should be able to deal with Administration," the Robert in front of the class pointed to Marsh's double. "Did you have any problems?"

"No. I think the matter is handled," Brad said.

"Tomorrow is the day," Kal whispered to us. "Is everything coordinated?"

Robert almost looked like he had caught Kal whispering. "Everything is underway. After tomorrow, there will be no problems."

I looked at Marsh. I again thought about his mother. They had just made up and she would not know why everything had changed again. He wouldn't even know who she was. I loved Chanelle, but I somehow sensed her feelings were on the surface. Marsh had lost his human side as well as his memories. Part of me wanted to cry. I kept wishing I had my mother back, but I couldn't even speak with her or know how she was doing.

I looked at the primary Robert to see if any part of the real Robert, the guy who had been so nice to me, the one I had had a crush on, was still in there. I didn't see any indication of that.

"Now you all have your assignments for tomorrow. We meet here."

As the class ended for the day and students exited the classroom. I backed up towards the curtain. Jennifer was the last one leaving and she was slowly exiting the classroom. Horton was looking at the students leaving as I picked up one end of the curtain. I could see androids that had not yet been activated. One of them I recognized as Sam, the records clerk for the University.

CHAPTER 59

I wondered if there was a plan to replace all of the university staff.

I turned. Horton was not looking at me. He hadn't seen me lift the curtain. What this meant was that the university staff would likely be killed that night. *What about the hospital people? Will they survive that long?*

I suspected Brad and the others were already speaking with Brenda.

As I left, I heard, "Nat." I didn't respond. "It's okay," Robert stated.

I continued on. He knew me. He had seen through my disguise. But there was something about his voice. It wasn't robotic. I looked back. He had gone back to his electronic pad that wrote on the large whiteboard on the wall. He seemed to be ignoring me.

Maybe I had misheard. Maybe it was a memory from long ago. I thought about how the carnival Robert had put his arm around me and how the second Robert robot had stared into my eyes. Was Horton's real mission finding me and eliminating the human version of me?

As my companions and I went into an empty classroom to speak, I asked Brad, "Did you speak with Brenda?"

"She is in major fear. She wants to back out. She asked if our agency could handle everything if she's out of here."

"We could use a real agency backup," I stated.

"She agreed to show up in the morning, but she isn't eager to do anything."

"They're planning to kill at least part of the staff here, and they could do it this afternoon or tonight."

"I'm pretty sure they are replacing hospital staff as we speak," Brad noted.

"What do we do?" Jennifer asked.

"I remember from the history books. They used to close facilities for bomb threats," I said.

"They can trace our phones," Roger pointed out.

"So we don't use our phones," Brad said. "I lifted this from the hospital. I don't know who it belongs to."

"Oh, good. We're going to trash another career and maybe frame a good person into prison."

"Except if they run voice prints, they won't come close to the owner."

"No. They'll nail us," Jennifer said.

"Hmm. We mess up the receiver such that they can't get an accurate reading. The location will show we're not at the hospital."

Brad recorded two recordings onto Jennifer's phone recorder and used her phone's editing to alter the voice.

"It doesn't sound anything like you," Jennifer acknowledged.

"But Jennifer's phone—" I worried.

"We'll erase the message after we send this and the second message and toss the other phone."

First, Brad called, not one but two numbers for the hospitals. One was for emergency and another was for the city oversight of the hospital. He played the recording.

"They'll be tracing," Roger warned.

Next, he called several offices in the school, including the Administration office and played the bomb threat recording. After that, he smashed the stolen phone, used a tissue to pick up the pieces and disposed of it in a trash compactor.

We started to rush from the school. "I can't," I said. I turned and went to the records office.

Susan was at the desk as I entered. She came over to us. "Your purpose?"

"To see Sam about my records."

"Sam is busy. Come back tomorrow," she said.

"Certainly, see you tomorrow, Sam," I said more loudly and then turned towards the door. As I did, Sam came out of his office and she turned towards him. I crossed my fingers and closed the door, hoping the sound would make her think I was gone as she focused on him.

"What is going on?" he asked. She moved very methodically towards him.

Something inside him must have told him to be afraid. "Susan, what are you doing?"

She reached up towards his neck with her hands. I picked up a computer monitor and threw it at her, but it just bounced off. I jumped over the counter as he backed up and she moved faster. I prepared to wave my EMP at her skull but at that point, something came flying from behind on my side, smashing into her head. Brad had opened the door and thrown a heavy wrench at her. It dented her head somewhat and sparks started flying but it didn't stop her. I continued on with my EMP. She turned towards me and then stopped.

"What the—" Sam started to ask.

Brad came in, picked up the wrench and started smashing at her throat until her head came off, sparking. "I think that's how we kill them."

"Susan?"

"It's not Susan. The real one has probably been killed." I knew it sounded cold. "I'm sorry. Maybe she's alive."

"I don't—what's going on?"

"Do you know about the Reset and the countdown? They are planning to replace you and the lead staff at the university."

"Replace?"

At that moment, sirens burst out and I could hear footsteps in the hall. Over the loudspeaker, a voice said, "There has been a bomb threat. Everyone is to go home for the rest of the day."

Kal, Jennifer and Roger entered the office.

"A bomb?" Sam asked.

"That's the least of the university's problems. They are planning to kill the staff. They have replacement robots. I know it's insane, but look?" I pointed at Susan.

"She's correct. And if you tell anyone directly, they won't believe you. We're trying to handle things, but we can't if we're outed," Brad said.

"And Brenden Marsh is dead," Kal added. "If his robot double comes near you, hide. Let them think robot Susan succeeded in replacing you."

"Robots are really calm, neutral. They don't get excited," I said. "Convince them you're a robot if you come in tomorrow. If you see others who have no emotion, they could be robots who would kill you if they figure out you aren't one."

"And they are very strong. Physically, you can't outfight them," Brad noted, pointing at Susan. He held out the wrench. "They do have vulnerable spots, though."

I thought back to what had happened to Chanelle, how it had devastated me. She was my friend and had organs immolating those of humans, at least. But these killer robots were different, I told myself. I still felt bloody, though there was no blood in these robots.

"If you are afraid, go on vacation. If you are willing to protect your colleagues, then stand up. Good luck," Brad said.

We left, joined our friends and started down the hall towards the exit.

"We can delay them further," I said. "Let's destroy the faculty robots. They were behind that curtain. They'll have to be replaced like Robert."

"Smash them?" Roger asked.

"How about blowing them up?"

"You mean like arson?" Jennifer followed up.

"The school is made of fireproof materials that will contain what happens in the classroom, I think. I hope," Roger said.

"Anyone know where the chem lab is?" Brad asked.

Roger handed us some gas masks he'd picked up in the chem lab. We drenched the robots with ammonium nitrate, silver nitrate, bleach, picric acid, ethyl alcohol, kerosene and a few other chemicals. "I got this from a book, called *Kitchen C4 Revisited*, I found in an old attic," Brad related.

Brad ran back out and returned with more chemicals he added to the mess.

We pulled some of the wiring in the walls free and figured that an electrical trigger would be best to create a combination chemical explosion and electrical fire. We set the planned explosion on a timer and took off, hoping the robots would be blown to smithereens.

"If they were human, the smell would have killed them," I noted.

"I'm surprised the mixture didn't blow us all up before we got out of there," Jennifer said.

On the way to Brad's vehicle, we took a couple of detours and removed our disguises before we got to the parking lot.

"We need to get back to the hospital and hope that Steve isn't finished with the emergencies," I said.

"Have they already gone through the department heads and administrative staff?" Jennifer asked.

"The Acting Chief of Staff, who is Steve's direct boss, looks programmed," Brad responded.

"Each replacement can turn more people, cutting the replacement time way down. They could go through the hospital in an hour," Jennifer warned.

"We shouldn't have left Steve alone!" I panicked. "Hurry!"

As we arrived and entered through the main lobby, it looked as if we were walking through a factory of animated mannequins. "Are there any humans here?" I asked. Patients could be heard crying and were suddenly silenced. "They're killing the patients."

"The bomb threat didn't work," Brad lamented.

"The robots must have answered it or the humans at the phones didn't care. Tomorrow is the day," I replied.

"On the flip side, they seem to be ignoring us," Roger said. "I guess they aren't programmed to see us."

"We have to find Steve. Let's pray we're not too late," I said.

"There's Emergency." Kal pointed to the sign above the wing. The officer who had taken the Social Worker away from the hospital was present with a gun, aimed at us as we entered the ER.

"Don't shoot," I shouted.

"We're friends," Brad called to him.

"How do I know? I'm not taking any chances." He cocked the hammer as he prepared to fire.

CHAPTER 60

Kal knocked me down as the gun went off. I looked up and Steve had knocked the gun out of the officer's hand. "They're with me."

"We have to get out of here," I said. "They've taken over the hospital."

The outer door to Emergency opened. Robert Horton walked in, followed by four other Robert Hortons. I turned towards the inner door through which we had entered. KaKool and the Chief of Staff briskly walked through. Behind them were several other doctors, all looking very unemotional. The five Robert Hortons moved into position around my group of friends and Steve. Brad had a wench. But he could only take out one.

"We've got to protect the patients," Steve told the officer. "You kids need to get out of here."

"We're sort of locked in," I observed.

More robotic doctors and two more Robert Hortons moved in.

My friends and I each grabbed a wheeled hospital bed. We pushed them towards the ambulance entrance. The Roberts moved to the side out of our way.

As they did, Brenda walked in. "Help us," I told her.

She went over to the bed I was pushing and twisted the neck of the patient lying there. "But you were Marsh's assistant."

"So, I told you."

"You screamed."

"I was programmed to scream."

"You weren't that heavy?" Roger recalled.

"They deactivated a humanoid robot and gave me some of its parts."

"Why the hospital? I mean, since you're planning to kill us, you might as well tell us."

"Is that what they do in the movies you watch?"

"We'd like to know what's ahead before we die," Brad said.

"The hospital was always the key to the plan," she said. "And it will be ready."

"Key?"

"National leaders are planning a tour of our hospital tomorrow," Steve explained. I recalled he had said the new national capital was in California.

The androids were all closing in. My friends and I had EMP devices in our pockets. At least, I assumed my friends also had theirs. But who to take out first? I picked one of the Roberts and he froze.

"Remind me to avoid that," Brenda said as she approached me from one side and KaKool approached from the other.

Brad turned quickly and struck out at KaKool with his wrench but missed. KaKool moved forward to grab Brad's throat as Kal picked up a metal bedrail and smacked KaKool back. It didn't seem to damage him.

KaKool turned towards Kal. Brenda came after me.

The officer started firing bullets at KaKool. The bullets seemed to bounce off his chest. Brenda strode past me towards the officer and slammed him against the wall with her hand.

I looked around. We were surrounded.

CHAPTER 61

The Roberts started closing in around me, but were facing away. Maybe they planned to spin around and catch me by surprise.

KaKool was about to grab Kal when, from under a sheet, a patient jumped up with a sledgehammer and smashed his head.

"Lancaster?"

"Later," he said.

He turned his hammer on one of the other doctors, who quickly collapsed in a pile of sparking electrical junk.

Three of the remaining six Horton's started swiping at the necks of the robotic doctors with their fists. *Is this a rebellion of robot factions?*

It was hard to see who was going to win the fight. Brenda had picked up the guard's gun and was aiming it at me.

One of the Roberts pulled the ends off the chest attachments of a defibrillator machine and fried her. I used my EMP to make sure she was out.

The doctors fought against the Hortons, destroying several of our protectors. My friends aimed EMP devices at the doctors' heads as they turned. Two of the Hortons, including the one who took out Brenda, were still intact. The others were a mess, along with the robotic medical staff.

"Let's get the patients into an ambulance and out of here," Steve said as more android doctors started to enter the room through the inside doors. One Robert threw an oxygen canister at them, which cracked, and then threw a lighter into the mess. The escaping oxygen caught fire, holding the androids back.

We got the patients who appeared to be alive into multiple ambulances, pulling them away as quickly as possible as the fire spread. Jennifer and Brad were driving two ambulances, following one driven by Steve. In all three, the patients had been packed in tightly to fit.

Using the keys Brad had thrown to him, Roger jumped into the driver's seat of Brad's car and Kal and I joined him. To our surprise, the two remaining Roberts jumped into the back seat.

"Wait. We can't go without Lancaster," I insisted.

The ER was on fire and multiple explosions could be heard from inside it as flashes of light were visible from the door. Lancaster had eliminated a number of androids but something inside told me that he needed help.

I started to run back.

"You can't! You'll get burned!" Kal shouted.

"I don't care. I've got to save him."

Another explosion blew the doors out and all we could see were flames. "If he's in there, he didn't make it," Roger said.

"But I don't know who he is, and he saved us."

"I'd be dead for sure if he hadn't nailed KaKool," Kal acknowledged. "There's nothing we can do. If he made it out in an ambulance, he's alive. We can hope for that."

Brad called to say they were taking the patients to University Hospital. "I'll meet you at our special place." He didn't know if Lancaster was among the ones in his ambulance.

Roger drove us to the park. "This is where you two Roberts get out." They agreed to wait for our return.

Roger drove us over to the warehouse, where I informed Selini of what had happened.

"So they were planning to replace the President and top Congressional leaders tomorrow, along with anyone else who might get in their way," she commented.

"President?" I asked.

"We have honest elections these days," Brad said. "We copied the Venezuelan model to ensure election integrity."

"Smart. I read about that in the history museum. The President is going to be at the hospital tomorrow?"

"And then the university," Selini said. "Smart plan for the underworld. As with the poison jabs they gave back before the Reset, people will line up for whatever experiment the replacement leaders tell them is necessary."

"Haven't they learned to stop following leaders yet?" I asked.

"We can hope. But fear brings back mass formation psychosis. I would have expected them to refuse, and yet they walked off the cliff at the urging of braindead Presidents and psychotic governors during the plandemics."

"I don't think the leaders will go to Valley Hospital," Roger said. "We blew up the ER."

"They'll simply relocate their plan. They'll replace the leadership at their next stop," Kal guessed.

"I wonder if the university was a backup plan," I pondered. "They were prepared to replace the heads of the university, but we blew up the replacements."

"We've seen the speed with which they can replace the security androids," Roger reminded us. "They were putting them together every couple of minutes while you and Brad were gone."

"Did we get all the university replacements?" Kal asked.

"I didn't count when I pulled the curtain. I was trying to make sure Horton didn't notice me. Why did the Hortons protect us?"

"For the same reason the first Horton replacement robot looked at you," Roger said. "They uploaded his consciousness and he liked you. He turned on his own for you."

"Do you think we can trust him?"

"I don't know," Roger said.

"If they join our side and are found out, they'll deactivate them. Robots don't care if they're deactivated," Kal stated.

"Shall we go pick them up?" Roger asked.

Kal looked at me. "I know you like him. But he's a robot."

"This isn't about romance. We need to stop an invasion. They might be able to help us."

"Brenda turned out to be a fake."

"She didn't kill any robots for us."

"Why didn't she turn us in right away?"

"She may have wanted to find out more about us first and who we were working with. We were wearing disguises."

"Let's take a vote," Kal said.

I turned to Selini. "You join us."

"That would make it harder to get a majority."

"I respect your opinion. Please join in," I said.

Twice, it was Selini and me for bringing in the Hortons against Kal and Roger. Finally, Roger joined me and Selini.

I turned to Kal. "Remember, I deactivated one of the Roberts at the hospital. Romance isn't on my mind. But as my brother, you shouldn't care."

"Maybe I don't want to be your brother, anymore."

"It seems you're stuck with me, whether you like it or not," I said.

We went back to the park. No Hortons were in sight.

"You think they went to squeal on us? He had Robert's upload and undoubtedly recognized us," I pointed out.

"All I know is that people who know too many of our secrets are out there somewhere," Kal remarked.

"Maybe, they'll show up if I'm alone."

"I'm not leaving you alone with those things," Kal said.

"Then watch from elsewhere."

Kal and Roger went back to Brad's car. I sat on a bench and put my head in my hands. I didn't know what to do.

More than Horton, I was thinking about Lancaster. I wanted him to be alive. It was somehow really important to me. I thought back to when he chased me at the museum and in the park and later showed up in my neighborhood. He kept saying he wanted to help me. He had helped and it may have cost him his life.

"Who are you, Robert Lancaster? Did you really know my mother? Were you married to her before she went down below?" I asked the air.

If so, why was he trying to save a child she had had with maybe Kal's dad? He must have really cared for my mother if he was the real Robert Lancaster.

I thought about Kal. He was very confusing. He had been so attached to my being his sister and now that had changed—maybe. He didn't like me dating Brad. He didn't like me being around Robert Horton. Brad had said Kal was acting more like a jealous boyfriend than a brother. Yet, he was devastated when Jennifer suggested Lancaster was my dad.

I needed to take off. When they finished at the other hospital, Brad and Jennifer would be back at the warehouse. I hoped they would bring Steve. What was I to say to Steve? Was the truth stranger than anything he could be thinking after today's encounter with the robots? Would Steve turn in our little operation at the warehouse? He hadn't turned us in so far, but he might think saving the world from two invaders was worth more than two teens.

I started to get up.

"Nat," a voice I recognized said.

"We need to talk," another voice I recognized added.

CHAPTER 62

I was surrounded by Roberts.

"Which one is the security robot and who was created by KaKool today?"

"Neither," the one on my right said, laughing as he sat on the bench next to me. "I'm not an android. I'm the real thing."

"I don't get it."

"They sent a security android to participate in the class with my upload. He found you, and I was watching."

"Watching?"

"He had a camera that was sending video back home."

"Then they know?"

"I erased the video. They assumed he was damaged or destroyed before he saw anything relevant."

"Are we being watched?"

"I am not an android. Somehow, my camera has been malfunctioning." He smiled.

"How about him?" I tilted my head towards the other Robert."

"Humanoid."

"I'm confused."

"Your mom created a duplicate to attend to my studies below—in addition to him and the security robot they sent up for the class, the one who found you at the carnival. They think they sent another android up here to replace him and that I'm still down there, hanging out with you and Kal."

"My mom! She's alive?"

"Yes!"

I jumped in the air with excitement, dropped back on the bench, and thrust my fists up high.

He smiled, seeing a side of me I wasn't allowed to show down below. "Very much so. I don't know what will happen after today. KaKool was a duplicate of someone up here and was created up here. I don't know if he had a camera. I don't think the others they've put together up here had properly functioning cameras. The ones I put together didn't."

"My mom would be in real danger if they discovered I got out."

"I know."

"Why did you do it?"

"Do what?"

"Come up here? Rescue me? Hide the truth from the leadership?"

"You're my friend. My good friend. I've always liked you best."

"Best?"

"Of all the girls, you were the most real."

"I guess so. I want to rescue my mom."

"First, we need to save the free world so she'll have something to escape to."

"Hanging out with androids again?" I hadn't seen Kal and Roger approaching.

"This is the real Robert."

"Hi, Kalandro."

"Kal will do."

"What are you doing up here?"

"I like it up here. If we can stop the invasion, I think I'll stay."

"My mom's alive. Robert's going to help me rescue her. That is, after we save the world."

Kal crossed his arms. "Certainly. Would you sit a little further away from my sister?"

"Sister?"

"Apparently, my dad isn't my dad and Kal believes his dad is my dad."

"Interesting."

"I hear that word a lot. Both our dads are jerks. His dad chopped off Chanelle's head and my not-dad was eager to do the same to me."

Robert grimaced and shook his head. "Some of those leaders are really sick. Was Chanelle real?"

"Not for a long time. Mom pretended I was a robot too. She gave me a drug that lowered my heartbeat and blood pressure."

"Reversesave?"

"You know about that?" I asked.

"My dad was one of the leaders in the pharmaceutical industry. I've had to face it. He was evil too. Even so, he was good to me and he loved my mom."

"Thank you for the save," I said.

"Yeah. Thanks," Kal remarked flatly.

"How did you manage to bring so many backups to the hospital?"

"I had to work fast. I knew they'd have already turned a lot of doctors."

"What do we do about that?"

"The important thing is we have to save the above-ground leadership tomorrow."

"We will do that, how?" Kal asked.

"They were supposed to get checkups at Valley Hospital. That's out. They might go to a different facility or they might just cancel the check-ups. University Hospital is more of a small research facility and I don't think they'll go there. The backup plan was to tour the university."

"And nobody would believe us if we tried to warn them."

"That's a problem with humans. They follow narratives. don't want to look at unpleasant facts. Back during the first plandemic, the mass psychosis took out a huge chunk of the population. People and even kids threw their families into the trash and worshiped at the feet of Fraudcy, making the drug scammers, including my dad, rich and powerful. But an equal-sized group saw through the lies. Then, there was the bigger midsection. We don't have time to set up an opposition to educate a midsection. Replacements can be built too fast."

"So what do we do?"

"We show up at the university and save the leadership."

"We called in a bomb threat."

"You saw how well it worked at the hospital," Roger pointed out.

"If the Dean of Students is replaced, he'll call off all concerns about a bomb."

"We destroyed the robots."

"They can build more. But it might cause a slight delay in their plans."

I noticed Kal was continuing to stand there. arms folded, glaring at us. He looked anything but happy.

"Kal, we're going to save the world and then my mom. That's what we've been working toward."

"We also need to seal off the underground and make it impossible for them to return," Robert said.

"Did our leaving open up the top to them?"

"No. They had to dig through the collapse. But they had the robotics force to do that. And there are other exits that will have to be sealed."

"If my mom hadn't arranged a rescue, in another minute, I would have been in the incinerator and a robot would have replaced me."

"I have a message from your mom."

"Yes."

"She had to find a way to slip it to me that they wouldn't see. She gave me a note and I had to eat it."

"That's an old movie trick," Roger said.

"They can reconstruct trash in the underground."

"What did it say?"

She said, "Tell Natalia I love her very much and I want her to be safe. I don't want her to risk herself for me."

"That's exactly what I plan to do."

"I was sure you would."

"Shall we go see Selini?" I asked Roger and Kal.

"You sure we can trust him?" Kal responded.

"I'm sure."

"He saved us. I'm in, too," Roger said.

***

On the way to the car, Kal pulled me back. "You're not going to date a loser like that, are you?"

"He's not a loser. And I'm not dating him."

"He was the one in the Youth Leadership Program with the least innovative ideas."

"Maybe he didn't like it there and didn't want to give them a heads up on his ideas."

"He's totally dull."

"He just saved your life, and he is anything but dull. He was the one person, other than Chanelle, who was really nice to me down there."

"I'm sorry for the way I treated you."

"I get that. Now, we're friends, but we weren't then."

"I thought you were a messed-up robot."

"You've said that like a hundred times. I guess I followed my mother's instructions too well around you. That's all in the past. Now, we're friends and family. You and Robert have a lot in common. You were both part of the Youth Leadership Program, and neither of you liked what was going on. Now, you're both up here, trying to stop the takeover. Maybe you can be best buddies."

He shook his head. "I'll get along with him as long as he behaves."

***

We went back to the warehouse. I noticed Selini taking equipment out of boxes.

"What is this?" I asked.

In the door, walked Doctor Connor.

Relief rushed through me. "I'm so glad you're safe. Dr. KaKool visited your apartment last night."

"I was expecting that. I burned my written files. I scrubbed them from the computer before I left for the suspension."

"Dr. KaKool was really interested in those files, yesterday."

"I figured."

"3988 had your name on him."

"I haven't been able to get back into the morgue."

"I wonder if KaKool found Aaron and that's why he was looking for your records."

"It could be."

Doctor Connor looked at the two Roberts.

"They saved our lives," I said.

"Lost a lot of my duplicates, including the one that was hacked at the Carnival. Do you remember who did that?" Robert asked.

"I was too out of it."

"He had my imprints and knew you were to be protected."

"Why? Why me?"

"Like I said, you were the only kid I wanted to get to know down there. The others were stuffy elitist jerks." He looked at Kal and then back at me. "But you were nice. That's how I knew you were real. We were supposed to be neutral in our attitude. I had trouble controlling it. You may have heard the expression. 'It takes one to know one.'"

"I thought Chanelle was real."

"She was programmed to look real and pretend to be human. I think you brought out the best in her," Kal said. "I thought you were both pretending when you were together."

"Now, we're all up here and we have more friends. That Brad guy looks a little like you. Any chance you are related?" I asked.

"Maybe distant cousins."

Kal almost scowled as he said, "Yeah, well, Brad also likes my sister and it's hands off to both of you."

"I can't imagine you two being brother and sister. It just doesn't fit."

"It fits just fine," I said, knowing it was important to Kal.

"So, this equipment—" I started to ask about.

"I was worried they would take over the clinic. We had double equipment and so I brought a lot of it here."

"How did you know Selini?"

"I contacted him at the clinic—" she said. "—after I reviewed the programming from those two androids and found that some kind of attack was imminent on the hospital."

"And you didn't notify us?"

"I was afraid you'd put yourselves in even more danger."

"I'd been hiding out at the clinic until Selini called," Connor explained.

"What about the clinic patients?"

"I told the rest of the staff to be careful and that I suspected someone was trying to harm doctors. Also, to pretend I hadn't been there. Still, my connection to the place could be uncovered."

"I've also set up a large EMP device to go off if someone I don't know comes to this warehouse," Selini said. She looked at the Roberts. "It hasn't been activated yet."

"We found this place abandoned," Roger said. "But we don't know who owns it."

"I do now," Selini stated. "But under an alias. I purchased it yesterday."

"Nice." Roger smiled.

"So who are you?" Real Robert asked.

"I was a close friend of Natalia's mother. We tried out new ideas together. She was, she is, a true genius."

"She's alive," I said. "Robert says she's alive." I smiled and whirled around again.

Robert looked at me with a big grin on his face. "Eterra sent me here with a humanoid version after my security duplicate was wiped out at the carnival. I had gotten a glimpse of Natalia and erased the images. Eterra asked me to go up, pretending to be an android and save her daughter, you." He smiled at me.

"I think she knew we were friends," I told him.

Kal was looking down, fidgeting. Something was really bothering him.

"Kal, I really believe we can trust Robert," I tried to reassure him. "Remember, you were wrong about me, too."

"Yeah," he said, almost grimly.

We heard a vehicle. Selini turned her monitor to an external camera she had set up.

"An ambulance."

"It could be our friends," I said.

First out, I saw Jennifer, then Brad. They went around to the back and assisted Steve in pulling someone out on a gurney, along with an IV to which the patient was attached. There was a sheet covering most of the person's body and much of his face.

"The burn center at University Hospital is down and they are overloaded with patients," Steve said. "I was going to take him to a different hospital, but your friends insisted that a top expert was here."

Selini and Roger opened wide the doors to the warehouse and helped Steve roll him in.

"You didn't think you could trust me with the truth?" Steve asked me and Kal.

"Would you have believed us?" Kal responded.

"Probably not."

"Do you think Katerina is in any danger?" I asked the group.

"She's not a doctor. They might go to the house to look for Steve," Roger replied.

"Jennifer and I will get her. That way, nobody will recognize you two or Steve," Brad said.

Steve's eyebrows creased. "I shouldn't be sending you, kids."

"It's the least dangerous thing we've done lately," Brad assured him.

Steve shook his head and wrote a note. "Give this to her."

Robert tossed a wrench to Brad. "Take this."

"Make sure you still have your EMP devices on you," Selini advised.

"And bring Eterra, too," I said.

"Eterra?" Robert asked.

"My dog," I clarified.

"You named your dog after your—"

"I did. I miss her."

Steve looked confused but turned back to his patient, seeming more concerned about him.

As they left, I turned to Selini, "Do you think they'll be safe?"

"I just hope they get there before the confusion dies down at the hospital and they start looking up home addresses."

"Home addresses? Does that mean we should be doing likewise?" Kal asked.

"Maybe for the university personnel."

"They got Susan and almost got Sam in records," I said.

"Max, I need your help," Steve said. "This man has lost a lot of blood and will need extensive skin grafts."

"What about artificial skin?" Robert One, the real Robert, asked.

"We've used it from time to time. It's not the perfect solution."

"We destroyed the lab at school," I said.

"That was just the supplies for the workshop. There's another location we've set up in the basement of the history museum."

"The history museum?" Kal asked.

"That's where Kal's not-dad was blown up," I told Robert.

"Kal's not-dad?" Steve asked.

"Long story," Kal said.

"It was closed after the attack and the underworld took advantage of the closure to turn the basement into a warehouse in preparation for the invasion," Robert related.

"They'll need my mom for the humanoid robots."

"They've been working with AI on duplicating her work. It's failed so far but they're getting closer."

"Then we have to rescue her soon."

"The history museum is by Roy's farm," Kal reminded me.

"I hope Roy's safe," I said.

Steve moved the sheet a little and I could see his patient's face. It was Lancaster.

CHAPTER 63

Selini gasped but didn't say anything.

"You've got to save him!" I pleaded.

"That's the guy who killed my robot at the carnival," Robert One said. "I got a glimpse of him before he chopped off my android's head."

"He needs a transfusion but here's the problem," Steve advised us. "We need the correct blood type. Since the poisoning, RH-negative blood has been in shorter supply. It is believed that those who left had an over-representation of RH-negative. My hospital had some, but there was none at the hospital we just left."

"What's his blood type?" I asked.

"A negative."

"I can donate," I said. "I'm A negative."

"A negative, also," Robert Two said.

"You can't donate. Your blood just emulates A Negative," Robert One countered. "I can donate."

"A positive," Roger let out.

"If my sister is A negative, I should be too," Kal said.

"We can check. Sometimes there are family anomalies. Two kids could take after two different parents."

"O negative," Selini said. "I'm compatible."

"Seems like we've got an over-representation of negative blood in this room," Steve noted.

Steve took a pint of blood from me, Robert and Selini and then tested Kal's blood and analyzed it. "I mentioned anomalies. But we won't need your blood."

"I'm positive?" Kal asked.

"No. We can discuss it later. It's no big deal. This happens occasionally within families."

Doctor Connor helped Steve transfuse the blood into Lancaster.

I was feeling a little dizzy. Selini noticed and had me lie down. Steve gave me something to drink that he said would make me feel better.

"He's holding his own, but he's going to need either skin grafts or artificial skin. Complicating things, there is the possibility of rejection."

"They use artificial skin all the time down below," Kal said.

"We've used it some up here with mixed results."

"Ours may be more effective," Robert told him. "Some of the top scientists came down with our parents. Our leaders and future leaders have been counting on eternal life."

"Psycho-scientists, you mean," Kal said.

"If that's a crack about my mom," I started to say.

"I'm sure a lot of them were. But not all," Robert mediated.

"It would be nice if a medical team from down below came up here to show us some of the advances," Steve remarked.

"Isn't that what got us into this problem in the first place?" Selini pointed out.

"Kal, would you like to come with me to get the skin?" Robert asked.

"What you have up here works for androids but not for humans," Selini said, pointing at the covered android bodies. "It's just a costume covering."

"The humans will be coming up after the androids. I take it those two were security robots. The more developed androids have the good stuff. I know where they are stockpiling it for when the humans and humanoids arrive," Robert expounded.

"I injured my leg in a basketball game and they patched it up with artificial," Kal related.

"What about blood type? Does it have to match?" Roger asked.

"It doesn't depend on that," Robert said.

"It's not from vaccinated organisms, is it?" Roger inquired.

"You kidding?" Robert said. "Those who went below weren't dumb enough to get vaccinated for real."

"I'm going," I declared. "Lancaster saved me. It's the least I could do."

"You need to rest," Steve advised.

"I need to do this," I said firmly.

"I seem to be picking things up slowly these days," Steve reacted. "Boys, make sure she's safe."

"I'll guard her with my life," Robert One said.

"I will too, but I don't need to brag about it," Kal threw in.

"I could use some help setting up the rest of the equipment," Connor said. "Roger, can I count on you?"

Selini threw a long baton to me. "Hang onto this?"

"It doesn't look strong enough to smash a robot," Kal observed.

"That's not what it's for."

"I think I know how to use it," Robert One said. He turned to Robert Two. "You're coming, but stay away from the baton."

"You couldn't keep me away from this mission," Two said.

"It's in the history museum basement but we don't want to park too close," Robert advised as we took off for the location.

"Roy's," I suggested.

Robert looked at me.

"He has a nearby farm, a little to the southeast of the museum."

Kal and I instructed him on how to get to Roy's place.

"What brings you back here?" Roy asked.

"You are still you, aren't you?"

"Who else would I be?"

"I mean, you wouldn't mind giving your favorite sheep to me, would you?" I asked, trying to look serious.

"Maybe in my will," he snapped and then lightened up. "You were joking, right?" He laughed.

"Of course."

"We're going to leave the ambulance here for a little while," Kal said. "And if anyone asks, you don't know anything about the ambulance or us."

"It's not stolen, is it?"

"No. We're on a medical mission."

"You kids come up with the darndest things."

Roy looked at the two Roberts. "Are you two twins?"

"I'm the human one," Robert One said.

"Good one." Roy chuckled.

We hiked through the fields towards the museum. "This will be a long way to walk back with the skins. They'll have to be kept cool," Robert One said.

"I can run," Robert Two replied.

"And the rest of us?" I asked. "I can run, but not as fast as an android."

"I'll pick you up," Robert Two replied.

"I'm sure he's faster than me but not by that much," Robert One said. "Especially if he has to carry all those skins, inside coolers."

"The ones in the classroom weren't refrigerated," Kal pointed out.

"The androids made in the classroom were security robots with lower-quality skin."

"Robert Two?"

"He was the only one of the seven that was fully humanoid. He's pretty close to an exact double of me."

"I can tell the difference," I said.

Robert One smiled. "That's good. I guess I've made an impression on you."

"It's the way you look when you speak. You and Chanelle were my only real friends."

He looked at Kal. "You should have been nicer to the girls."

"I thought they were robots."

"You cared about the robot you saw killed," I said. "That's what made you want to get out."

"She was like a sister."

"Robot or not, you loved her—even if you won't admit it."

"Are you a robotphobe? Bigotry doesn't serve you," Robert teased.

Kal held up his fist.

As we approached the museum, we hid down in the hills. I could see the grave I had dug for the caretaker. I wondered if he knew what was coming. If we lost, he had managed to live a long life without the upcoming insanity.

"There's a grave up there. He must have been loved," Robert One commented.

"He was," I said.

"Did you know him?"

"Only his works," I replied. "He was a really good person."

"Were you there when he was buried?"

"Kal dug the grave," I said.

"She conducted the first memorial. His friends conducted a later one."

"Somehow, I'm not surprised about you, Nat, but I am about you, Kal. I guess her decency is rubbing off on you."

"Ha, ha, ha, ha," Kal said, flatly. "How do you get to call her Nat?"

"It's okay," I responded. "You can too. So how do we get into the basement?"

"There is the museum entrance, but there are guards up there who will see us if we go by the museum."

"What do we do? Dig a tunnel?" I asked.

"Don't need to. There's another entrance."

We moved through the hills, a ways past the museum downriver from where we had originally come. We slid down the cliff. "Careful," Robert One said, pushing me back against the cliff.

We could see movement on the riverbank close to the area below the museum. Several robots were walking back and forth.

"This isn't going to be easy," Robert One said. "We could have used some explosives."

"Sorry. We didn't stop by an armory on the way," Kal remarked, facetiously.

"Does the above-ground society even have an armory?" Robert One asked.

"I don't think they even have real guns up above," I replied to Robert.

"The officers, here, and at the hospital, each had one," Kal recalled.

"True, but have you seen any gun stores or anyone else with guns?"

"Let's see that baton Selini threw at you," Robert One said.

Robert One looked it over, examining a switch on it. "I think I know how to work this. You need to move way back," he told Robert Two as he pointed down the river.

After Robert Two moved quietly into position, Robert One moved closer to the museum, flicked the switch and threw the wand at the androids. They froze.

"Nice EMP," he said, as Kal and I approached him.

We rushed over to the wand. Robert One turned it off and signaled for Robert Two to join us. We were by an entrance I hadn't noticed before.

"They added this to make it easier to get things into and out of the basement." Robert pushed something on the chest of one of the robots and it separated into pieces. "This feature allows them to take parts from one and use them to rebuild another."

Robert One picked up an arm. Kal picked up one too. Robert One peered into the Iris Scan Reader, which opened the door. "Apparently, they haven't adjusted for my actions this afternoon."

We moved inside, where we were met by a security robot.

"I've been sent to gather skins."

"Your authorization key."

"It's an emergency."

"Your authorization key."

"Here," he said, bringing up the arm and smashing it against the security robot's neck. The head flew off and started sparking. "We'd better hurry before we wind up with an electrical fire," Robert advised. Robert, next, smashed what looked like a camera.

We moved through the basement past several rooms with Robert Two trailing. The basement walls looked like something the advance force would have rebuilt, as they were out of place for the original design of the museum. Robert One repeatedly used the wand to knock out more cameras while having Two stand back each time. It also knocked out the lights. Robert pulled a lighter out of his jacket.

"You don't smoke," I said.

"But these are useful tools, wouldn't you agree?"

"Better than going through the dark."

"My double can see better in the dark. An improved robotic feature."

"Still glad I'm not one of them," I said.

Inside some of the rooms, I could see various humanoid parts and glass-covered freezers with fake organs.

"They're planning to build an android force, here, aren't they?"

"Both security robots and humanoid androids." He stopped before a door. "Here. This is the room."

The room we entered had stacks of coolers. "We'll need dry ice. This stuff needs to be kept cool."

"Is it wrecked if it gets warm?" Kal asked.

"It can start to decay. We might have time to get back to the others, but it's chancy."

"The eye scanner. Will it know you were here?"

"I'm authorized, but I may have outed myself. That could catch up with us, later," he said.

He loaded up a portable cooler with humanoid skin as well as dry ice. We started to leave. That's when a security force of more than half a dozen security robots entered the room.

Kal smashed one with the hand he had carried as another robot started firing bullets. The smashed robot started to spark. Robert threw the lighter at the shooting robot but it landed short on the sparking robot.

I jumped on Kal, knocking him to the floor as bullets started firing in our direction. The sparking robot caught on fire and then exploded, causing a chain reaction of explosions threatening to wipe us all out as Kal and I got up. Another explosion threw Kal and me against the wall.

"Kal!" I cried, trying to wake him up in the dim light. I saw next to us, Robert, unconscious on the floor. The entire room was catching fire and explosions were continuing.

Somehow, through the fire, smoke and fumes, I saw an exit. I tried to pull both Kal and Robert up, but I couldn't, and I knew I only had seconds.

Jennifer had taught me a trick for carrying someone weighing more than me but I couldn't handle both of them. I knew that I was leaving one to die. I really cared about Robert. I had had a crush on him most of my life.

I could only save one.

CHAPTER 64

I chose Kal. I picked him up and rushed out the exit with him.

There were no lights in the hallway but the walls from the room we'd left were on fire and provided some illumination.

I didn't know which way to go. I started to move. "This way." It was Robert's voice. The fire seemed to move after us as I rushed off.

In the smoke-filled lighting, I could see Robert was carrying the other Robert. Had the android survived? He would have been the sturdier of the two and could easily carry the human Robert. I let him guide me out.

When we got to the basement exit, we used parts from the security robot to knock it open and rushed out.

Once outside, we ran down along the river. There was a tree in the river. The remaining Robert put the other Robert's body down in the shallow water next to the shore. The tree kept the body from going downstream.

There was no doubt he was lifeless, dead. It was my fault.

I looked at Kal. If I had made the other choice, that would have been Kal.

The surviving Robert spoke. "I didn't get the skins. But he's got the higher quality skin left on him. It should work," I looked at him, hoping he meant what I thought he meant. "You didn't think I—"

"No," I lied. "But he looks so human."

"Your mother does good work. He was the backup she gave me."

I had never felt so relieved. I had saved Kal, and Robert was still alive. I had deserted my friend to die, but he didn't. It was a miracle he had lived.

"You need to keep him cool until I can get closer with the ambulance. It's got four-wheel drive and a refrigerator unit. When I honk, run up that path and I'll handle the rest," he said, pointing to a path a short way down the river. Robert ran up the hill. At least, the water was cold, very cold. Did Robert know I thought it was him when I left Robert Two to die, instead of Kal? *Will he hate me when he finds out?*

Or was this Robert Two who died? The android would probably believe he was the real one without the other Robert telling him otherwise. I was sure Chanelle didn't know she was an android. It was hard to tell the two Roberts apart, and even dead, the Robert in the river looked as if he could be my Robert. His skin wouldn't turn blue yet, I didn't think. But it would soon if he was the real one. Of course, maybe there were chemicals, such as Reversesave, that would delay the bluing, and in the end, I'd see the horrible reality.

If it were the real Robert who had died, his skin wouldn't work for Lancaster and both would likely die. That would be my fault.

As I waited, Kal started to come to. "What happened?" He looked at Robert. "I'm sorry."

"The other Robert went to get the ambulance. If this is Robert Two, then his skin can be used to save Lancaster. The other skins were destroyed, along with the skin room in the museum."

He looked up and I followed his gaze. The fire had apparently spread through the entire building. The top of the cliff, where the museum had stood, was ablaze. I doubted that the exhibits had survived.

I thought about the legacy Mr. Malone had left, going up in flames. He had done so much work, and now it would be a miracle if any of it were intact.

It has to be the real Robert who survived, I tried to convince myself.

Otherwise, the loss would be too much. I didn't want to think about the alternative.

"I wish we had gotten pictures of everything in the museum for Mr. Malone's sake. So, people could remember him." Thinking of Malone took my mind off Robert.

"If this is the real Robert," Kal said, taking my hand, "I'm really sorry. I know you wish he were the one who made it out instead of me."

I opened my mouth to tell him I had chosen him over Robert. But I didn't want to look vulnerable to my brother. So, I didn't say anything.

It wasn't long before I heard a horn honking and bullets being fired. "We need to get up there before we lose both Roberts," I said.

"I think I'm strong enough to carry this one." He lifted Robert. "He feels about the weight I'd expect the real one to be," he said sadly. "He is definitely not a security robot."

Panic was still going through me.

"But it was a special android my mom made. It could be a good match, weight-wise."

I thought about the androids back home. Chanelle had weighed about what I expected her to weigh. There was hope, but Robert had indicated the android was stronger and faster. It was more likely that the android made it out than my Robert.

I reached the top before Kal with Robert over his shoulder. The ambulance was right by the cliff with the engine running as Robert got out and pushed me into the driver's seat. "Keep it moving," he said, as shots were fired and he rushed towards Kal and the river.

"They've got a cannon or bazooka," I said to myself as I took off driving the vehicle, side to side, turning several 180's, which I was glad the vehicle was able to make as blasts kept hitting all around.

Androids were rushing in our direction as I swung over to my companions and paused for Robert and Kal to jump in the back with the other Robert. I took off as fast as I could.

I'd never manually operated a vehicle before. My driving skills were possibly the worst for someone my age, but I kept swerving side to side, avoiding being hit by whatever they were shooting at us, while almost overturning the ambulance on my turns as it bounded down the hills.

When we got to the street, I stepped on the gas and drove as fast as I could back to the warehouse, making a number of sharp turns in case someone had spotted our ambulance. Robert had seemed a better driver on the way over there, but I didn't want to take the time to switch. Besides, I thought I had gotten the hang of it, or at least I hoped so. I had avoided being hit by bullets, cannons, missiles or whatever and the ambulance had stayed upright.

At the warehouse, I rushed in. Jennifer and Brad were there. Eterra jumped into my arms.

"We couldn't get the skins but we may have an alternative," I said, hoping this was true. "If—"

Robert and Kal carried in the body.

"What?" Steve said. "It might not be a match."

"It's top-grade synthetic," Robert said. "It's compatible. "

"I've used it on my leg if—" Kal started to say.

"If what?" Robert asked him.

"If this is the android. I can't tell," Kal continued.

"I'm me."

"You might not know," Kal said.

"I can tell," Jennifer declared. She went over to Robert and started tickling under his arms. He started laughing and almost went into a spasm.

"He's the real one," I said, relieved. "But the android would have been stronger, faster."

"There were explosions and an electrical fire in the room. It took out his programming."

"Where are Brad, Roger and Katerina?" I asked.

"Katerina wasn't at home. Brad dropped me off here with Eterra and took Roger with him while he went back to look for her."

I hoped she was alright. They had killed KaKool the night before the fake showed up. I didn't want to ask her in front of Steve if they had checked the closets. I thought back to the church service and started praying she was alive and well.

"Get him onto the other bed," Selina said. "I think I can do this. I need you to help, Max. Kids, go outside—except Robert."

"My mom—"

"Wouldn't want you to see this," Selini said.

Kal ushered me and Jennifer out. Eterra ran after us.

"Steve?" I asked, thinking he might be squeamish.

"I need to keep attending to my patient. I'm a doctor. I've seen some pretty gruesome things."

Outside, I said, "I bet this really freaks Robert out, seeing his double being skinned."

Jennifer's eyes widened. "I wish you hadn't said that. I think I'm going to be sick."

"It's a pretty disgusting image," Kal said.

I started to cry. "I was afraid it was the real Robert," I whimpered. "That I had left him to die. I'm sorry. I shouldn't cry."

"My sister has a crush on Robert. If she had had to choose between me and Robert, well, it's a good thing I got out. How did I get out?"

"I carried you. I picked you up the way Jennifer taught me and carried you."

"I guess you didn't see Robert."

"Aren't sisters supposed to protect their brothers?" I asked. "Family."

"Not over someone they're in love with," Jennifer said. "It's good, you didn't have to choose."

What she had said kind of got to me. Robert was the closest thing I had had to a boyfriend—even though he was just a boy and a friend. There had been times below when I had wondered if the two of us might one day become a real couple. *I must be a lousy girlfriend.*

"It all worked out," Jennifer said, giving me a hug.

"We don't know about Katerina," I fretted. "Did you look in the closets and any place an android might have put her?"

"Like with KaKool, before the replacement arrived, they probably got rid of—I'm sure she's okay," Kal said.

"She has to be. I don't want to lose another mother. My real mother is alive, but Katerina is like my mother away from mother."

"Let's assume she's fine and think about how excited she will be to see us all safe and sound," Jennifer tried to reassure me.

"We destroyed the museum. But the leaders are supposed to come tomorrow for an event at the university, and if the underground has its way, the university will be up and ready to replace them," I ranted.

"The whole basement with the android parts went up. And we destroyed the faculty androids today. That may have set back their plan a little," Kal said.

"A little? It better be a lot," Jennifer responded.

"And Lancaster. Who is he and why did he risk so much for me?"

Jennifer looked at me. "What if he was telling the truth? What if he cared about your mom and also you?"

"I remembered seeing him when I was smaller. He was really nice."

"He got out of there, and he's clearly not with them."

"I wonder why he left and didn't come back. Why didn't he stay?"

"Everyone was pretty well monitored down there, weren't they?" Jennifer asked.

"Totally," Kal said.

"Maybe he thought you and your mom might be in danger if he stayed."

"Why? It wasn't as if he was having anything to do with my mom when he was down there."

"Was your father or not-dad the jealous type? Maybe he knew about their past."

"Your dad didn't like my dad but if he suspected you were my sister, he might have found a way to eliminate my dad," Kal remarked. "I know my dad would have liked to eliminate him to move up."

"Except Not-Dad would only accept me as a robot. Maybe he knew I wasn't his and that was his way of erasing my connection to my real dad. Should we go and help find Katerina?" I asked. "We're just wandering around outside here and I'm feeling useless."

"She's going to be alright," Kal said. "I know she is. I mean, your real mom survived and maybe anyone related to you has a special blessing on them."

"They don't talk that way below," I said.

"I got that in church on Sunday," he responded.

"I'd like to go for a walk. Maybe you two and Eterra could hang out here."

"She wants to be with you," Kal said as Eterra jumped into my arms, again.

I handed her to Kal. "I need to think—alone."

I did need to think, but I also knew I was close to my neighborhood. I needed to find Katerina.

As I walked, I thought about what Jennifer had said about how, given a choice, a person would save the one they loved. I had saved Kal, but he was my brother. I started thinking back to the kiss. It didn't feel like kissing a brother. I needed not to feel about him any way other than as a sister. Before he decided I was his sister, he hated me. He only liked me now because I was his sister.

I didn't want to expose myself, just walking down the street. I went between trees and bushes, checking to see if anyone was watching the house. Nobody seemed to be looking at it. I finally snuck up to the front door and opened it.

Katerina came out of the kitchen. "I'm so glad you're home. I was wondering where everyone is. I'm making dinner."

I ran over and hugged her. There was something off. Her hug wasn't as warm as it normally was and her voice was flat.

"I suppose you are making my favorite," I said. "Chile peppers and asparagus."

"I didn't have any in the kitchen and so I had to improvise," she replied, once again using a flat, unemotional tone.

I hated chili peppers and asparagus. "Do you remember what I said the last time you couldn't locate them?"

"Oh, yes. A very sound response."

She'd been replaced.

CHAPTER 65

I went into the kitchen, followed by Katerina. I looked for something, anything that would work. "Is that Kal at the front door?"

"I didn't hear him."

"I know he was eager to see you."

She walked out into the living room. I opened some drawers and then the utility cupboard to find anything useful. There was an old-fashioned vacuum cleaner. I picked it up and went into the living room. She now realized he wasn't at the door and was facing me.

"How nice. I thought it needed vacuumed."

"Kal!" I shouted at the door. She turned. I lifted the vacuum and smashed it against her neck. Her head went flying. At that moment, the real Katerina opened the door and screamed.

I ran over to her and put my hand over her mouth. She was looking at the head and sparking body.

"That was to be your replacement," I said, happily, in spite of her obvious fright. "We have to get out of here."

"Steve? Kal?"

"They're waiting for you." As we ran out of the house, I saw Brad's car. It stopped and the back door was pushed open from inside. We jumped in.

"You were supposed to stay away so they wouldn't recognize you?" Roger said as we closed the door.

"It's a good thing I was there. The replacement arrived before the real one got home. Where were you?"

"At my place," Roger said. "My mom said Katerina had just left."

"Thank your mom for keeping her safe until I dispatched the fake one."

Katerina wasn't speaking.

"Are you okay?" I asked her.

"None of this is real. It has to be a dream."

"It's real, and what we told you before was real too."

As we returned to the warehouse, we entered quietly so as not to disturb any procedures. I saw something covered with a cloth in a long box. I hoped that wasn't Lancaster.

"That synthetic skin could have saved millions of lives if we had had access to it before," Steve said. "It's better than anything we've ever used up here."

I looked around the room. I could see Lancaster lying on a bed off to the side, partially covered with a sheet.

"He looks like himself," I said. "Actually, younger."

"No rejection so far, and I don't think there will be any," Dr. Cannon informed me. "And it mends to the body, instantly."

"Why is he still asleep?"

"He's been through a lot of trauma. He needs his rest."

"But he'll be alright?"

"I think he'll be fine," Selini joined in. She put her arm around me. I turned back to Katerina, who was just standing there, somewhat dazed. Kal and Robert were both watching me. Roger and Brad were looking over the situation. Jennifer was shivering.

Robert picked up a blanket and put it over Jennifer. "Are you alright?" he asked her.

"Yes. This just takes a minute or a year to get used to."

Steve rushed to Katerina. "It seems things aren't always as they look, honey." He took her in his arms.

"I've noticed that." She still looked and sounded stunned.

"They almost got her," I reported. "Fortunately, Jennifer's mom saved her."

"My mom?"

"Your mom invited me over to get to know me better." Katerina related.

"Thank you, Mom!" Jennifer whooped, as if her mom could hear.

"Do you think they'll go for the families of all the other doctors?" I asked.

"That wasn't the plan," Robert said. "I think they went after Katerina because Steve put up a fight. The plan could have changed."

"Plan?" Katerina asked.

"The plan to eliminate the President, several members of the current Congress and part of the Cabinet tomorrow when they attend the university."

"I bet our leaders will never go for another medical exam again after they find out what almost happened," Brad mused.

"I'm surprised they trust doctors after the various plandemic scams leading into the war that apparently wasn't," Robert responded.

"We were surprised, too," I told my first crush.

"My dad was one of those responsible for the scamdemics," he explained.

"My digestive system will never be the same," Jennifer commented, looking at the sheet. "I don't plan to become a doctor anymore."

I went over to Robert. "It had to have been horrible for you. I mean, you were here when they—"

"He wasn't me. Besides, five of my other doubles bought it at the hospital."

I gave him a hug. "Thank you for everything. You've saved me again and again. I owe you."

"I'll do whatever it takes to protect you."

"I will, too," Kal declared.

I went over to Kal and gave him a sisterly hug.

"Aside from helping the leaders, we need to figure out how to stop an invasion," Brad pointed out.

"It's too bad we aren't fighting this in the dark ages before the robots," Jennifer lamented.

I looked at Jennifer, as did Robert and Kal. "That's it. You may have saved the world."

"What? Time travel?"

"Can you do it?" I asked Selini.

She looked at Robert. "It won't be easy."

"I don't," Katerina reacted.

"I think we're dealing with some scientific geniuses," Steve said.

"We've had good mentors while we've been here," I pointed to Steve and Katerina. "Without you, we wouldn't have gotten this far."

I turned to Brad, who was looking at me. "We saw what our smaller EMP devices could do. What if we had one that wiped out the power for the whole city? And if we could do it for one city, we could do it for any city in danger."

"For tomorrow, we only need to start here," Selini said.

"What about patients who need electricity?" Jennifer asked.

"It can be restored. Doctors may have to go back to alternative methods of helping patients," Doctor Connor said.

"We've already stopped using ventilators," Steve advised us. "That's one of the ways they killed so many during the plandemics. However, the monitors could go out and—"

"Do you really think it helps patients to be constantly monitored? Maybe, some of the electronic devices are inhibiting more than helping," Kal contended.

"Brad, your dad is part of the public records system. Maybe we can use the public records network to drive through the EMP," Roger suggested.

"Which will blow out the system," he said. "It will probably wipe out all the birth and death records."

"Then we just treat everyone like equals," Katerina said.

"Bank records," Roger reacted with a smile.

"A nuclear bomb packs a powerful EMP," Jennifer said. "My parents said during the Reset or fake war, they thought we had been hit with one when the electronics went out, but it turned out the elites just cut the power lines."

"You want to nuke us?" Roger asked. "Not very sisterly."

"Radiation will kill us all," Robert advised. "A major aerial blast, without the radiation, coupled with an EMP, might knock out the computers, including the robotic force. One or more giant compression generator bombs could do it."

"But the real bad guys who did the Reset are still below, waiting to come up," Jennifer pointed out.

"They're cowards," Kal asserted. He turned to Robert. "Remember what they said in the leadership meetings? The governing council and those running the world must be protected at all costs."

"I remember. They'll stay underground until the invasion is complete," Robert postulated.

"And if it fails, they'll try again," Roger pointed out.

"Unless we seal them in," Brad said.

"Not without getting my mom out first. How about—" I didn't want to call him Dad.

Kal picked up on my drift. "Chanelle," he scowled. "Seal him in. I know she was an android, but—" He paused. A tear fell from one of his eyes. "You're right. I did love her."

I went over to him and gave him another hug. "I know you did. I loved her, too."

There were no major power lines. A lot of alternative energy was in use. This included solar power, wind power, water power, natural gas, and new forms of energy derived from water, air and regular soil. Houses and buildings were individually equipped. Some of the outlying areas would still be powered if the EMP took out the local power. A warning about bomb threats was sent to hospitals in the area advising them to prepare to transport their patients if necessary.

After previous fake bomb alerts, we figured the invaders would assume it was another fake warning---especially since no bomb had gone off at the university or hospital. The plans for the event appeared to be unchanged.

We needed to know if there were survivors at the hospital. Kal, Brad, Robert, Dr. Connor and I snuck into the hospital where Doctor Connor and Steve had worked while Steve attended to Lancaster and Roger,

Jennifer and Selini continued to strategize. Katerina kept watch over Eterra.

We used the wand Robert had with him to deactivate the cameras and the security robots at the main entrance. Part of the hospital was burned or blown apart, but fire extinguishers built into the hallways helped save large sections. In patient rooms, we saw what appeared to be a mass slaughter.

"Apparently, they don't care about replacing these people. They just wanted to depopulate them," Robert said.

"Isn't that how your father felt?" Kal asked Robert, "When he was killing all those elderly people during the fake plandemics with the jabs?"

"As a top pharmaceutical scientist, he put together the poisons that killed them. I think, I hope, he felt remorse over that. There were times I caught him looking very sad. But then he would see me and cheer up."

"I never met your mother," I told Robert.

"She died shortly after I was born. She was very depressed. They said that affected her health."

"But she had you. I would assume that would have cheered her up."

"I heard she tried to reject me. I guess it was post-partum depression. She didn't even want to look at me. I was told that she never tried to nurse me. The baby formulas had been made toxic before the Reset and my birth was before they came up with the synthetic milk they now use on leadership kids."

"How did you survive?" I asked.

"With donated milk. I was told someone who gave birth the same day provided bottles of pumped milk for me."

"I'm sorry about your mother. That must have been awful."

"I know my dad had remorse over her death. When we get your mom out, I'd like to give him a chance to leave there, too. I think he regrets what he did during the plandemics."

"It must have been awful for you kids," Max said.

"It was," Robert sadly agreed.

We opened another door. More bodies.

"They'll use the replacement leadership to claim any oddities about tomorrow either never happened or were handled," Robert contended.

"As before the poisoning, they'll create a news media that will call anyone telling the truth a conspiracy theorist," Doctor Connor asserted.

"I'm glad Jennifer stayed behind," Brad said. "She thinks she's stronger than she is."

"I know you like her," I told him. "I could see that when you were dancing. Why don't you tell her?"

"I like her, but I've known her all my life. Dating her would be like dating a sister."

"Real yucky," I said, looking at Kal.

"Yeah, real yucky," he responded, flatly.

"Most of my life, you weren't my brother," I told him. "You were just the guy I hated."

"A lot of sisters and brothers fight," Doctor Connor said. "How is it that you aren't reacting more strongly to this carnage?"

"My other sister. This isn't personal."

"I felt I had lost my only real friend." I turned to Robert. "I knew you were on the Youth Leadership Council. You were nice, but your friends were all snobs and—"

"You thought I might become one."

"Something like that. I was going to say, 'Like Kal.' I thought he was a total snob." I turned to my brother. "You know, I really hated you down there."

"I think you've said that enough for me to get it. I was living between two worlds. The one I wanted and the role I was supposed to assume. It's no excuse for the way I treated you and Chanelle. My last words to her before the transition, or, rather, execution, were awful."

"I believe in redemption," Doctor Connor said. "Extreme circumstances can activate a conscience, a higher self, in naturally good people."

"You've been wonderful since we escaped—for the most part."

"For the most part?"

"Not at first, but after we got to the museum and found Mr. Malone."

"You knew Ottis Malone?" Connor asked.

"Not alive. We buried him," Kal related.

"That was nice of you," Doctor Connor commented.

I reflected on Kal's transition or my impression of it. Down below, his jerkishness always overshadowed any positive qualities and had made him ugly to me. Now, I was noticing how good-looking he was, handsome in fact.

When I was in the museum, I read a book about abuse and the difficulty women had figuring out which men to trust. Abusers would often pretend to be nice to woo a girl and then turn into abusers once they had the girls where they wanted them. Would Kal, again, wind up insulting me in ten years? *What a weird thought. He's my brother. It isn't like I'm a girlfriend.*

We opened another door. "It doesn't look like there are any survivors," Kal said.

"If only I had been stronger, done more?" Doctor Connor lamented.

"Kal and I knew KaKool was replaced. We didn't stop this."

"You wouldn't have had the power as kids," Doctor Connor reasoned.

"I am fifteen and Kal is sixteen."

"We could have come up with something," Kal lamented.

"I could have stopped KaKool before he rushed from the classroom to the hospital for the final rampage," Robert said, shaking his head. "It's on me."

"You kids have nothing to feel guilty about. I was a doctor and I knew about Aaron some time back. I procrastinated and analyzed and didn't take sufficient action."

"That's another thing. Up here, we're kids. Below, we were treated as objects who had to learn, perform and behave. Even toddlers were expected to act a certain way, more like grown-ups and were punished if they didn't," Kal related.

"I remember goofing off with Chanelle when we were small. I remember other kids seeming more human before changing, too."

"Then at some point—" Kal started to say.

"They replaced her," I finished.

"The coldness they created in families during the plandemics is something they took with them," Dr. Connor postulated. "Those people were as evil as they come."

"I don't think they always killed little kids. I remembered my dad saying he saw it coming, but from our conversations, I don't think they fully implemented it until about eleven years ago. At first, they just drugged kids to make them behave," Robert said.

"When I was four," I said. "I think that's when Chanelle changed."

Kal closed his eyes. "I remember Chanelle, too. We were friends long ago. I think you and I were friends, but you may not remember. Then she changed some and it wasn't just a growth spurt. One of the boys at the youth council told me that girls were being replaced with androids. I blamed your mom for her role in my real sister's death."

"Dad raised her for four years and then had her killed? That's sick," I reacted with disgust.

"I wish he weren't my father."

I didn't want him to be my father either.

"Now, we have Steve," Kal said.

We opened another door. On the floor lay a nurse with her neck apparently broken.

We were about to leave the room when I heard a noise. Something was crying from inside a closet. I opened the door. Wrapped up in some little blankets, inside a box, was a baby.

CHAPTER 66

I picked up the baby and one of the blankets and tried to comfort her.

"She's probably hungry," Doctor Connor said. "We have some almond milk back at the warehouse."

"An almond milk fan," I commented.

Brad picked up the chart. "She's an orphan, being checked out for physical problems."

"Orphan?" I asked.

"The hospital checks out children who are about to be adopted," Doctor Connor said.

"She's only a month old," Brad read.

"I thought babies and parents were valued here," I responded.

"Her mother could have been young, or maybe something happened to both parents. Adoptions are rare, but they do sometimes happen."

After being held, the baby calmed down a little and started chewing on her toes. "I'm told I used to do that," I said.

"You're pretty flexible," Kal remarked. "I bet you still can."

I put her back in the box and covered her as best I could while making sure she could breathe. "Let's get out of here before we run into any more robots," I advised.

Back at the warehouse, everyone turned as we entered with a crying baby. "I think she's hungry," I said.

Steve went to the refrigerator and pulled out some almond milk. He put it into the coffee maker to warm it. Doctor Connor cut the end of a vinyl glove liner and tied the other fingers off as he put it over the cup of warmed-up milk.

The baby kept crying as the doctors tried to feed her.

"Let me try," Katerina said. They handed her the cup and she got the baby to drink.

"We need real baby bottles," Steve said.

"I'll pick some up," Roger offered as he went out.

"Do we get to keep her?" Jennifer asked.

"She was up for adoption," I said.

"What about the patients and the other doctors?" Steve asked.

Robert shook his head.

"It was horrible," I said.

"We shouldn't have sent you kids there," Katerina replied. "I'm sorry you had to see that."

"I'm sorry we didn't stop it," I responded, finding myself crying.

"You saved this little girl. That's important," Katerina comforted me.

"She's beautiful. She reminds me of Tarinda when she was a baby, so sweet and innocent. I never thought she would—"

"It wasn't your fault," Brad said. "I think she was chipped or just had too much of your ex's evilness in her."

"Chipped?"

"I ran the EMP by her head and she started reacting as if she was having some internal changes, almost like Brenden did," I informed her.

"Is she alright?"

"She was fine, but a bit confused when we left."

"When was this?"

"The other night," I said. "Has she contacted you?"

"My cell is back at my place. But I doubt she would even try. She feels nothing for me."

I recalled Selini's number wasn't on Tarinda's phone. She might not even know it. "Brenden hated his mother until the chips were deactivated." I looked around at an electronic whiteboard that had arrows and circles around words. "What did we miss?"

"We've created a multi-prong approach to stop the replacements." Selini went into more detail. "The team, your friends, are going to create several nearby chemically activated electrical explosions while using an amplified EPM locally."

"Is there a military base around here? "Robert asked.

"We don't do war anymore," Steve responded.

"But there is a closed and deserted base not far away," Brad said.

"Does it have airplanes?" Robert asked.

"Do you know how to fly?" Steve inquired.

"No," Robert said.

"I do." It was Lancaster. He was starting to come to and had apparently heard our conversation.

I went over to him. "I'm sorry I told you to stay away from me. I thought you were one of them. I'm sorry."

"It's okay. I didn't tell you the whole truth," he said.

"You apologize a lot," Robert told me.

"I've made so many mistakes since I've been here," I said.

"No, Natalia," Steve said. "You've done a lot of right things. You saved me and Katerina. Look." His eyes rested on his wife and the baby. "Katerina's fallen in love with your latest save. You said she's up for adoption?"

"That's what the paperwork said," I replied.

Doctor Connor pulled the baby's chart out of the box and showed it to Steve. "The baby needs a mother."

"It looks like she's got one," Jennifer said.

Roger returned with baby bottles, more almond milk, some coconut milk and formula.

"Good. Formula was a good idea," Jennifer commented.

"My dad said they poisoned the formula during the Reset," Robert informed us.

"That was long ago," Doctor Connor replied. "Things are different today."

"This will do for now," Steve said. "Where did you get the formula?"

"From Margery's Market."

"It's got clean food," Steve responded. "I wouldn't trust anything from the hospital after today."

"That's why we didn't pick it up when we picked up the baby girl," Kal related.

"She isn't even named on the chart, just 'Baby Girl,'" Doctor Connor said.

I turned back to Lancaster. "I'm so glad you're going to be okay." I looked at Steve. "He will be, won't he?"

"He should be fine. But he needs to rest."

Lancaster reached out from under the sheet. His arm looked normal. He put his hand on my hand, which was resting on the edge of his bed.

I turned to Selini. "Is he related to the Lancaster you said had died?"

"He didn't die. You're looking at him."

"You knew my mom?"

"I knew your mom. She was, she is the finest woman I've ever known."

"I remembered you. You were down there. You were kind to me when I was a little girl. But then I didn't see you again."

"I was afraid that my presence would endanger you. I had had to go undercover, pretend to be a robot, until I got out."

"You rescued me. At the carnival, you rescued me."

"I knew it was an android who had picked you up and that you were in an induced trance. After I got to the park, I watched you until Selini arrived."

"You knew?" I asked Selini.

"Not until he called that night. He asked me not to say anything."

"And you used my phone to text Brad. Thank you. The necklace. You figured it out."

I turned to Robert. "Why did your robot do that to me?"

"That android had double programming. In addition to having my information, the security team assigned him to the invasion group. I was still able to monitor him, but that necklace was a test product they were using to make it easier to replace humans if he saw any. They only had a couple of them, the necklace and a watch, both of which disappeared."

"He was going to replace me?"

"Not after he saw you. From what I could see remotely, he was trying to get you somewhere safe, but he believed the necklace would get you to come with him. With my upload, there is no way he would have hurt you. I am concerned about where the devices went."

"They're in my hands now," Selini related. "They are encased and contained."

"Good."

"I didn't know his intentions," Lancaster said.

"You were protecting me. But why? Because of my mom?"

"Because of you," Lancaster responded.

"Let him rest," Steve said. "You can speak more tomorrow."

"I've been waiting to talk to this little girl for a long time."

"After you build up your strength," Steve instructed him.

As I watched Katerina with the baby, I remembered what I had heard at the hospital—that she had lost a baby she had really wanted. She had been a wonderful second mother to me and she would be a great mother to the little girl.

"You are going to give her a name, aren't you?" I asked.

"How about Ever? I want her to live forever. She is so beautiful."

"I'll second that," Steve said.

Katerina looked at me and Kal. "This doesn't change us. We still love you, too."

"I know. It's possible to love more than one person." I loved my mother, Katerina, and Steve. I looked at Kal. I loved him, too.

Sleeping was not easy that night. I was very agitated and worried about the next morning. Steve gave me something. I don't know what it was. In my dreams, my mind went through the events of the day, the death of Marsh, the battle at the hospital, Lancaster saving me, the two Roberts, learning that my mom was alive, picking up Kal and leaving Robert while hating myself for not rescuing both, and finding the baby.

When I woke up, it was still dark. Kal, Robert, and Roger had gone off to the military base to locate old stored explosives. Brad was out putting the finishing touches on a plan he and Selini had created to turn internet and telephone transmissions into EMP boosters. Giant EMPs were already set up around the university, ready to be activated at the right time.

Lancaster was pacing. It was good to see him up and awake. How had he recovered that fast? *Of course! Selini is a genius.*

"You need to relax," Steve told him.

"Not until I know the boys are alright."

"I feel useless," I said. "I need to be out there."

"You and I will be at the university with the new EMP attachments Selini created," Jennifer said.

"If anything happens to any of you kids, I'll—I should be out there, not Natalia, Kal and Jennifer," Katerina contended.

"You've got a baby to take care of," I countered. "We're ready for this. Jennifer knows self-defense and she's taught me some. I was schooled below by the people we are fighting."

"I have a pass I can use to get into the airport," Lancaster said. "From there, it's a point of absconding with an airplane."

"That could get you locked up in prison, especially when you steal the plane," Steve warned.

"Not if he puts on a disguise," Selini said. She was holding the face that had been peeled off the male robot from the classroom.

"You're going to be near the center of activity, Natalia. Promise me you won't take any chances," Lancaster told me.

"I will do my best to stay safe,"

"You are very important to me."

"Because of my mother?"

Lancaster paused as if he were thinking about his answer. "Steve said you donated blood to me. I've got your blood running through my veins."

"Robert's and Selini's too."

"I'll be activating a number of things from here," Selini said. "Brad, Roger and Kal will be assisting me, mostly from the outside."

"What about Robert?" I turned to my childhood friend.

"He's planning to be at the university," Selini responded.

I wondered if, after the incident at the museum and the hospital, the invaders were on to him. "Have Roy and Holiday been warned about the likely power outage?" I asked.

"We can drop by the farm on the way to the university," Jennifer said.

"I was hoping to see Mr. Lancaster off."

"My first name is Robert, but everyone can call me Bob to avoid confusion with your friend Robert."

"I'd like to take you to the airport."

"You won't be able to get onto the airfield. You and Jennifer can drop me off outside and then take off to warn your friends."

"We'll need to come back to pick you up after you fly back."

He looked at Selini and then back at me. "Don't worry about that," he said. The look the two of them gave each other concerned me. They were keeping something from me.

It wasn't long before the boys came back. "Some of these explosives are needed for the airplane," Brad said.

"Won't they check you going into the airport?" I asked.

"This is after the poisoning. We don't have an active military or TSA anymore. In other words, violence is not a concern here. No metal detectors or X-ray machines."

"We have two large military trucks. You can take one to the airfield," Brad suggested.

"I think I should go with you to the airfield," Roger said. "Pretend I'm a trainee. I can help load the plane."

I looked down. I had really been hoping to take Lancaster to the airfield. But Roger was right. The plan was more important than my desire to ask Lancaster the questions that kept occurring to me.

"I guess I'll see you after we finish."

"The most important thing to me is your safety," he said. "As long as you don't take any unnecessary chances, everything will be alright. And defeating the underworld isn't as important as your life. Remember that."

"You remember that, too," I responded.

"He acts like more than a friend of the family," Jennifer whispered.

"I guess he really cared about my mother."

Something occurred to me that I hadn't thought about all night. "What did you tell your parents?" I asked Brad and Jennifer.

"I told my parents I was staying at your house and Roger and Jennifer did the same."

I watched as Roger and Bob walked out to the military truck Roger was driving.

I don't know why, but, I suddenly rushed to Lancaster and gave him a hug. "Thank you. Just be safe."

He smiled at me. "You've grown up into a wonderful girl, and I know your parents are proud of you."

He obviously didn't know of recent developments with my dad, or rather, my not-dad.

After Lancaster and Roger left, Kal, Robert and Brad took off to arrange some explosive excitement. "Everything will be set on timers, but it will all have to happen simultaneously so the EMP doesn't mess things up," Brad said as the guys, minus the doctors, left.

"They said they're not talking nuclear EMPs." I thought back to my training about the end of the world and how they claimed people had gone mad and how the nuclear war had destroyed everything. EMPs from a nuclear explosion would wipe out much of California, but I gathered we had a saner plan.

"No. Never. We know the dangers of nuclear anything. We're using an advanced version of EPFCGs—explosively pumped flux compression generators in successive events," Selini related.

"Steve, I've been wondering why Kal and I have different blood types."

"You had different mothers, right?"

"Definitely."

"The parent you had together must have been O, most likely O negative. Your mother must have been A negative and Kal's mother must have been B negative."

"But my mother was O negative. My Not-Dad was O negative too. Mom said that she changed her blood type to be A negative on the official records and didn't tell me why, but I was to know it was recorded incorrectly and only tell the truth if they tried to give her a transfusion. So, my father—"

"Would have to be A," Jennifer said. "If you both had an O mother, your father would have had to carry the A and Kal would have to be O or A. To be incompatible, he'd have to be positive."

"Is my brother's blood type positive?"

Steve looked away. "It's medical."

"I'm not a physician or bound by an oath," Selini said. "He's B negative."

"So, our dad gave birth to both an A baby and a B Baby?"

"That's extremely unlikely," Steve acknowledged.

"I don't understand. This doesn't make sense."

"Kal's not your brother," Jennifer said.

CHAPTER 67

"Is that what it means?" I asked Steve.

"In all probability."

Somehow, I didn't feel shocked or even stunned. Disappointed, yes. I had gotten so used to Kal being my brother that I felt as if I had lost something important. But part of me felt happy, and I didn't know why, when this was really awful. Kal would be so upset if he found out. Why was I almost smiling?

"Please don't tell Kal," I said. "It means so much to him that I'm his sister—especially after what happened to Chanelle."

"If he doesn't press me, we'll let it drop," Steve said.

Selini looked at me. "That means you do have a father and your mother's double told you it was not the man who raised you."

"My mom. Did she love my not-dad at all? If so, why did she marry him?"

"Maybe to protect you," she said.

I thought about what I knew. "The toy robot Steve brought home had the inventor's name as Eterra Lancaster. Is Bob her brother or cousin?"

"He's not." She seemed very closed-mouthed.

I looked at Jennifer. I remembered her wild hypothesis. "Bob has A negative blood. Selini, the truth."

"Robert and your mom were married before the Reset and then she thought, we all thought, he had been killed. Cambridge had always wanted her. I know he promised her safety and many other things. She was carrying you when she went below sixteen years ago."

"Bob's my father? You are saying Bob's my father."

She nodded.

"And I didn't get to see him off. He's got to be okay."

"You've all got to be okay," Selini said.

I looked at Steve and Katerina. Katerina put the baby into a small cradle she had created from a little tub and blankets. She hugged me. "It doesn't matter who your father is. We still love you."

"Don't tell Kal," I cautioned everyone. "I don't want him hurt."

"Just because he's not your real brother doesn't mean you don't love him," Katerina said. "I know he loves you."

"Will my animals be in danger?" Roy asked. Claire was there. We had picked her up on the way.

Roy had been skeptical at first, but he'd lived through the Reset and the destruction my Not-Dad had created before going below.

"It may be very loud. But your farms will be outside the blast area. The main problem is your electricity."

"We have our own generators."

"I'd turn them off," Jennifer said.

"Won't the robots just reboot themselves after the explosions?" Roy asked. "Bet you didn't think of that."

"There's a fail-safe my mom added at the request of the council. If a robot goes down, it might have been compromised or captured by enemies. Its programming is automatically erased. New files would have to be uploaded and it would need to be returned for reprogramming or replacement."

"That would create a delay," Jennifer noted. "And that might be enough. We have a plan to deal with that."

Claire and Roy discussed how they could help each other protect the animals.

"What about crop contamination?" Claire asked.

"They are focusing on large localized blasts, not widespread blasts. Anything higher up won't be over your farms. We figure their whole above-ground team will be around the university for the changeover."

<hr>

After I pulled my hair up under a cap and Jennifer used makeup to give me a different look, we arrived at the university.

Jennifer pointed to a man in a suit. "He's Charles Brent, the University President. His picture was in the records office."

He wouldn't have recognized us. I hoped Robert was correct about the security androids created above not having cameras. But what if they'd added some since yesterday and they could see through my makeup?

Jennifer went over to Brent. "It's great to see you again, Charlie." That might have caught him off guard.

During the distraction, I popped some headphones, carrying an EMP current, on him. Shortly after, he collapsed. I pulled off the headphones.

"Hi," Robert said, catching the collapsing university president and helping him walk into the building.

"He collapsed."

"He's drained. We have to refill him." Robert attached one of several tiny cards he was carrying in a packet in his pocket to a micro-computer he was also carrying. He copied the card, made some alterations to a file, and attached the microcomputer with similar headpieces to Brent's head. As he removed the headphones, Brent got up and walked out.

"Is he—"

"Don't worry. He now has different instructions. We need to identify three more. Brent can help."

"What did you fill him with?"

"His new role is to defeat the invasion. There are other androids in the group. Look for classmates and anyone who looks like a robot. But be careful. You've changed your look a little but if any have come up from the underworld, you might still be recognizable. Jennifer and I should take the lead. I suspect the Secret Service has been infiltrated by robots."

We spotted a likely robot. It was a security guard.

"Excuse me," Robert said to the robot as I watched. "I think the university has created a counter plan. I need you to come over here."

He guided the guard into the building. Jennifer came behind and did the same thing as the guard collapsed.

Robert proceeded to upload something onto the android, which got up and walked out.

He and Jennifer repeated this several times.

"Before they replace the leaders, they'll have to kill the originals," I said.

Robert looked at the screen in front of the university with a live showing of a motorcade. "Oww. We need to make sure the leaders are safe. The President and other leaders will be coming down Sacramento Street. The road is mined. It's part of their plan."

"We need to stop them before they get there," I said. "Suggestion?"

"A temporary roadblock."

I called Roy and he agreed to help with our plan. We rushed, at first in a car we'd borrowed from Selini, and then on foot towards the route the leaders would be taking to Sacramento Street.

As we got to Sacramento Street, I saw several tractors blocking the intersection.

"My fellow farmers and I are glad to be of service," Roy said.

"Won't the mines create an EMP?" I asked Robert. "Why would they do this to themselves?"

"They are minor blasts, set under the surface, just enough to damage and roll the limousines. Any survivors will be killed by a crew of robots coming down from Sacramento."

A string of limos stopped. Someone got out. "What is this? A welcoming party?"

"Come here and I'll show you," Robert said.

As he introduced the Secret Service man to Roy, Jennifer performed the emptying and refilling process. The Secret Service driver started to fold and then straightened up. Then the reprogrammed driver got the other Secret Service men and the limo drivers, one by one, to be fixed by Jennifer and Robert.

"Do you think they infiltrated in San Diego?" I asked Robert

"There was a special Secret Service unit that was supposed to greet them at the airport. The invasion team likely replaced them last night or earlier this morning. Additional Secret Service Androids are floating in the crowd at the university."

All seemed to be going well. Then one of the leaders got out. "What's going on?"

"He's the Speaker of the House," Jennifer whispered.

I looked at Jennifer. Had they gotten him, too?

As he approached, I turned and said, "Rumpelstiltskin!" on a whim.

He laughed. "What?"

"You're clean, I hope." I remembered Brenda. Jennifer brushed her hand with the EMP over his head.

"You're pretty, but don't touch," he said.

"There's an assassination plot. These tractors will safely escort you to the university," Robert said.

"How do I know you aren't the assassins?"

"I'm Roy. The other local farmers and I would be in a heap of trouble if anything happens to you or the others in your convoy."

"The route is mined and the invaders will be arriving soon. The timer counted down to today. Do you want to risk your life and everyone else's to worry about conspiracy theories?" Robert asked.

"I know about the countdown timer."

"The invaders are androids, look-alike replacements for you and the other leaders. After the mines go off, they plan to take your place. We want to bring the androids out in the open. We're trying to save the world," I said.

The Speaker shook his head. "You're a kid. Common sense tells me this is ridiculous, but I've never ridden on a tractor before."

The Speaker went back to speak with the others, including the President, in the motorcade. He returned and got on Roy's tractor. Others left their limos and climbed onto other tractors. A security force could be seen approaching.

"Get out of here," I told Roy as Jennifer, Robert and I prepared for battle.

CHAPTER 68

The androids marched towards us. Robert pointed to the limos. They got inside. The limo drivers and Secret Service men got in as well.

"I guess you weren't outed to the Security Force Robots. Don't they notice the leaders aren't in the limos?"

"Limited programming. Fortunately, I still have authority. With the limos stopped early, their current job is to escort the limos down the mined road. All the drivers and agents have been reprogrammed. And after the crash, they'll notice there are no living occupants to execute."

As we proceeded back towards the university, we heard what sounded like crashes and small explosions. We could see flames rising from the roadway.

"Pollution," Robert commented. "I trust your society knows how to handle it," he said to Jennifer.

"After the Reset, we found ways to remove pollution and poisons without resorting to eliminating carbon or rather humans and it was discovered there was no need to remove the food supply, either—or to eat bugs."

I was pretty sure the sound of the crashes and mini-explosions helped convince the replacement leaders, who were probably ready to step into their roles, that all was on schedule.

The real Speaker was at the front of the tractor procession and the President was a ways back, probably for safety reasons. The tractors were moving slowly and it would take a while for the real procession to reach the University. But just because they were human didn't mean they were the best. I'd read in the history museum about past Presidents and members of Congress who had dementia that the public had ignored.

The necklace. They didn't need to be replaced to do as programmed. They could already be under control. I hoped that wasn't the case.

"Hey, they went on the tractors—instead of the programmed route," Robert said, as if he read my mind. "That's a good sign that they're human and can think."

"When they show up alive, the androids we haven't reprogrammed will kill them. Let's hurry."

We ran and managed to arrive before the real leaders. The grounds were filled with students and people eager to see their elected officials and members of the Cabinet.

"I see some people are still waiting like good little groupies for political leaders to save them," I commented.

"In the leadership program, we were told about that human quirk," Robert said.

"I read about it in a history book."

Cheers went up as fake leaders approached. The real ones were still back a ways. I could hear people gushing, which almost made me sick. *Wasn't the failure of people to think for themselves the reason the Elites were able to pull off the Great Reset?*

I looked at the crowd oohing and ahhing over the fake leaders.

As the leaders greeted the crowd, loud explosions could be heard everywhere. I suspected the real leadership team would have to continue on foot after the tractors conked out from all the EMPs going off around the university.

"Look," Jennifer said.

She pointed up to the sky where a plane was flying with a string of mid-air explosions going off behind it. I assumed it was Bob with the compression bombs.

"No!" I freaked as it started dropping, looking out of control.

A second later, it exploded in midair. The pieces fell upon the Administration Building, causing further explosions.

My dad! It was a suicide mission, I realized.

CHAPTER 69

I rushed through the crowd, as students gathered around fallen individuals in suits and university security uniforms. One of the fallen looked like the Speaker. I assumed other fake leaders were among those who had fallen, along with fake Secret Service agents, robotic university personnel and other androids.

I had to get to whatever, if anything, remained of the plane. As I raced toward the Administration Building and the burning remains, a hand caught me. It was Kal.

"I've got to get to Bob." He picked me up and carried me away from the blast area that was spreading out as students and others outside the university rushed back.

I pounded on Kal's back. "Let me down. I've got to get to Bob. I can't lose him. Please."

"I'm not letting you die. The pieces are still exploding."

"I don't care. I need to speak with my—" I didn't finish. I would have said my father. I was certain in my heart that Bob was my father, and I had just watched him die. All he cared about was protecting me.

Kal put me down and I collapsed on the ground, crying. Robert came over to me. He and Kal tried to console me, but I didn't want to be consoled.

"That plane just proved our parents right about 9/11," Roger said, joining us. "Except for where the explosions directly hit it, the building is still intact. A plane fire can't bring down a steel-framed building."

"Roger!" Jennifer called as she caught up to us. She hugged him. "I'm glad you weren't with him on that plane."

"Bob wouldn't let me. He said the EMPs would wipe out the plane and it could turn into a suicide mission. He martyred himself."

"Shhh," Jennifer whispered, looking at me, crying.

Roger touched my arm. "Sorry."

"Over there!" Jennifer exclaimed. I ignored her. I was too upset to think of anything but losing my father.

"Nat," Robert said. "Look." I glanced at Robert. He and Kal were looking in the distance past me.

Robert helped me up and turned me in the direction my friends were looking. I put my hands to my mouth, not believing what I was seeing.

It was Bob, walking towards us, awkwardly holding a mostly rolled-up parachute. I ran over to him. "Don't you dare die, again," I said, hugging him. "Father."

"I've wanted to hear you call me that for so long," He said, hugging me back.

"Your rescuer survived." It was Kal, rushing up behind me.

I turned to him. I looked between Kal and Bob. I wanted to acknowledge my dad, but Kal's feelings were too important to me. For some reason, they mattered more than anything, and I didn't know why.

"Yes, my rescuer survived. We all survived. I think. Where is Robert?"

"He's coming." He pointed to Robert walking across the lawn towards us.

The real leaders had arrived and were moving through the crowd, talking to people and making sure everyone was alright. Makeshift tents were put up to assist those who had been traumatized.

I pulled Bob aside. "It means so much to Kal that I'm his sister. His dad cut off his sister's head, and he's alone. His mother is gone. He hates his dad, and I'm all he has."

"It's okay. I don't need any announcements. I just want you and your mother to be safe."

"My mother!"

"That's next?"

"You're going to go back down there with me?"

"I'd prefer you stay up here."

"Not a chance. Not with my mom down there."

"She's the most important person in my life other than you." He paused. "When I managed to find her, I discovered she had believed reports of my death. She had married Cambridge to protect her unborn child, you. They were already depopulating—except for the leaders and their families."

"Were you there when I was born?"

"I didn't find a way down there until after that. I could see that she was safe and you were safe and I wanted to make sure she stayed that way. Everything above had been poisoned. If I had contacted her, Cambridge would have forced her into a life-and-death choice. I wasn't going to put her through that. So, I never contacted her. I—"

"He wanted me replaced. She saved me."

"He must have resented that you weren't his. I would have rescued you if I knew you were in danger."

"That wasn't necessary. Mom kept me safe until she arranged for my escape."

"I knew she would. Did Cambridge hurt you?"

"He was actually pretty good to me. That is, until he was ready to kill me for my transition and Mom's double got me out of there. Her double told me he wasn't my father. Kal said there had been rumors about his dad and my mom."

"Your mom and Fenton? There is no way on that. He was a womanizer, and your mom never liked him. Did Kal tell you how his mother died?"

"How?"

"Denton claimed it was suicide and nobody questioned it. I'm pretty sure he killed her."

"Did Kal know the details?"

"He may not remember. He was maybe four years old when he

found her body. His tutor had just accompanied him home. His mother was lying in a pool of blood with contusions all over her body. Not realizing or not believing she was dead, he kept trying to wake her. It was before there were cameras in all the directors' homes."

"Poor Kal. Were you there?"

"I was on the cleanup crew. The directors didn't like questions."

"Hey, Sis, these leaders are great!" Kal said, excitedly coming over to us.

As we watched the warm reaction of people towards each other, we found we had more company. People were rushing from all directions to the university on foot. I saw Jennifer's, Roger's, and Brad's parents. They all seemed very excited. To my delight, Brad, Selini and my second parents arrived with Ever.

"Your generation is underestimated," Steve said.

"My generation let everyone down and ushered in the Reset," Selini remarked. "It's good a more positive generation followed us."

"Not all Millennials and Gen Zs sold out," Brad said. He glanced around. "Look at all the older generations celebrating. We wouldn't have succeeded without you and Bob."

"And my mom," I added.

I went over to Robert. "We also wouldn't have succeeded without you."

"We make a good team, don't we?"

"We do," I said.

"Where is Eterra?" I asked Steve.

"Max is watching her."

After people settled in, the President, the real Speaker of the House and members of the Cabinet who had accompanied them gave speeches. The topic was unity and resilience.

"Visions of our passing have been wildly fabricated," the President started. "I hope someone will disassemble our robotic doubles before they reanimate."

Someone yelled, "Incinerate them."

"The idea of my image going up in smoke is unsettling, but there is a reason humanoid robots or artificial intelligence are banned. I know that today was disturbing, but it proved something. When the community comes together in peace for the benefit of all, there is nothing we can't accomplish. Everyone get to know others in your communities. We need to reach out to each other, to our neighbors and our family members, so that if anything happens to them, we'll be the first to know. By protecting each other, we protect ourselves.

"Long ago, they claimed suppressing speech and poisoning the masses was protection. Former leaders broke up families and taught neighbors to hate neighbors. That's not protection. Free speech and kindness are protection. Let us never forget what happened today, and let us never forget to listen to those who speak out against dangers and injustices. Those who caused all the suffering long ago abandoned us and this world. We will welcome all who come in peace, but we must see to it that no organizations or small groups of people, no matter how rich they are, ever take the reins again. Vigilance is necessary for a harmonious future for all." He continued on with his plan for the future.

"I wish we had leaders like these down below," Robert remarked.

"If the former leaders had been like these, the Reset never would have happened," I pointed out.

"Next, we have to stop the underworld leaders from infiltrating and destroying this world." Kal declared.

"Right now, after the failed takeover, may be the best time to for part two of our plan. Prepared?" Robert asked.

My friends and I all responded affirmatively.

"You've taken too many chances," Katerina advised.

"And we are the best equipped to stop an invasion and survive. You'll have to trust us on this," I replied.

"We entered upriver. I guess they reopened that," Kal surmised.

"I didn't," Bob said. "But a landslide closed the opening I took. With some explosives, we can blast the debris out of the way of the one I took and close all other entrances.

"If it's where that quake was, I don't think they're monitoring it," Robert told us. "Remember, Kal, they claimed that some radioactive zombies tried to come down near Plathorya Central and the earth swallowed them up. They didn't tell us about any exits, including the one up the river, until the Invasion was approaching. Even then, they didn't mention this one."

"I missed the final meetings," Kal pointed out.

"Your double didn't."

"I was replaced?"

Robert nodded. "You, too. Nat. It was a good match, but I could tell the difference."

"I bet mine looked a little older, more sophisticated."

"A little older—but not prettier. Kal's android is much closer in appearance."

"If we blast through the landslide, they'll hear us," Kal pointed out.

"Unless they think it's another landslide," Robert suggested.

"What about tractors and steam shovels. I wonder if Roy and his friends can get us equipment to do it more quietly."

"A lot of their equipment will have been knocked out—at least temporarily. It will go back up at some point."

"Maybe we can utilize equipment located further away from the blasts." I went over to Roy to ask if he had any old-fashioned resources. I was pretty sure our cars were no longer working for the time being.

His resources included horses to get us out of the area and towards our destination. "My brother has a farm over near where you want to go and I know a farm equipment distributor in that area," he said.

Bob drew us a quick map of the passage system from the tunnel to the Operations Center as best as he could remember. The region-wide power systems could only be wiped out from the Operations Center and my mother's Bio-Enhancement Lab was also located there.

"Mom's double was able to work remotely from closer to the exit we took," I said.

"She surreptitiously told me about that. She created a temporary backdoor to hide your exit and then erased the tracks before it was discovered. She's a genius, but if her double had waited another five minutes to blow the link, the AI would have found it."

"She *is* a genius."

"You realize we may be working against the clock," Robert said. "They were probably monitoring the event from below and are already working on a backup plan."

"Which is why we're taking an alternate route. They'll be expecting us the other way," Bob noted.

"I think Bob is right," Selini told us.

"You don't have to come. You are safer up here," I told her.

"And let you kids go down there unsupervised."

"What do you call me?" Bob asked Selini. "I guess I'm young again. I'll take that as a compliment."

"We don't know how prepared they are. We may need to adjust plans repeatedly. Your mother was more skilled, but I was with her when she had some of her insights," Selini pointed out.

"You're not going to change Selini's determination. Even when she was younger, she always knew what needed to be done," Bob advised us.

"But I didn't stop the Reset," she lamented.

"None of us did. They had the money and media. We didn't have a shot."

Robert gave copies of a map of the various entrances he had learned about to the President. "If explosions start down there, seal the tunnels quickly. It's best if everyone stays above ground for their own safety. Plathorya runs the show and if we get to the controls, I'll use the central controls to seal off escape routes from other areas of the region. But they have scientists and engineers, people up here have always underestimated."

As the President pulled Robert aside for further discussion, Brad told Steve and Katerina, "Don't mention to my parents what we're up to. They'll worry."

"Ours too," Roger added.

"We shouldn't be a party to these kids risking themselves," Katerina said.

"They just saved the day. I'm going to keep trusting them," Steve responded. He turned to Brad. "Your parents don't know about your part in today's events, do they?"

"They'd worry. Let us save the world and then they can chastise us.

Maybe they'll even thank us for saving them."

"I don't like it," Katerina said.

"Be safe or my wife will hate me forever," Steve advised.

I knew she wouldn't, but she would feel regret if we didn't survive.

"We've got this," I assured her.

Steve, Katerina and Ever returned to the warehouse to wait for us after Katerina repeated her objections to the idea of letting us go below. Steve told her that we were experts on the Underworld.

Knowing the tractors might go out, Roy and others had stationed a number of horses within walking distance. We rode to his brother's farm and arranged for other local farmers and equipment operators in that area to join with the major equipment I hoped would do the trick. The farmers worked fast to clear the tunnel.

"I wonder if they could have built tunnels faster in the old days if they had used farmers instead of miners," I commented.

"I don't think they had these conveniences back then," Roy replied.

"Remember, the power, cameras and all, will be on when we go down there," Selini warned.

"How monitored is this entrance?" I asked Robert.

"I didn't even know this existed. Maybe it's forgotten, but when we get past it, everything is monitored."

"Will that wand work?" Kal asked.

"Yes, but it may signal a malfunction. If there's a pattern, they could figure it out," Robert noted.

"My mom's double used a similar wand," I recalled.

"Then it's a good thing I made a second one," Selini said, pulling another one out of her pocket.

"You really come prepared," I acknowledged.

"You got in and out of Plathorya," I said to Bob. "How?"

"Stolen uniforms and knowing where the cameras are."

"You can point them out to me," Robert said.

"I left over a decade ago," Bob explained.

"A decade ago makes you better informed than any of the rest of us on this route," Robert responded.

I knew their plan involved stopping a robot invasion but found myself worrying about the people below---though I knew they would kill us if they had the chance. I had no idea whether many or any people still existed outside of Plathorya. If the rest of the region involved robotic slaves doing the harvesting and other work, Plathorya might be the only human sector—a sector of leaders believing in their natural superiority and right to kill.

Once the mouth of the tunnel was cleared, we still had to move some debris out of the path. We used an infrared light to limit detection. As we walked through the opening, we came to a panel. "This used to be openable," Bob said.

"It's locked from the other side," Robert noted, trying to open it.

For a minute, I thought we'd have to turn back. Brad pulled out some explosives.

"They'll hear those?" I said.

"They'll come to check," Kal guessed.

"And we better be gone before they get here," I advised. Brad taped them to the panel where he assumed the lock was and we moved back. The explosion set off a cave-in as rocks fell, trapping me under debris.

CHAPTER 70

The rocks were heavy. I was choking on the debris.

The guys worked to get me out. It was Kal who finally pulled me free. "Can't lose another sister."

"If I weren't your sister, would you have left me?"

"We've got to rush," Robert advised. We moved quickly into the passage as he used the wand to cut the cameras.

We came to two giant vertical tubes that looked like they were bottomless.

"We'll have to take these," Bob advised us.

"And live?" Jennifer asked.

Bob took a hammer from his backpack and dropped it. It moved quickly down as we watched.

"That's not freefall," Kal said.

"The descent tube has strong wind resistance and an anti-gravity device that gets stronger as you approach the bottom and it's large enough to take continuous large groups. The ascending one over there is like a vacuum tube. We'll need to be up through the upbound one before the power is cut."

"We'll blow it on a timer," Brad said.

We held hands as we jumped in.

We followed Bob down a corridor to a fork. "You studied my map?" he asked Robert and Kal.

"I can handle it from here," Kal said as Robert nodded.

"We'll see you at the pass," Selini remarked as Brad, Jennifer, Robert, Kal and I went one way and Bob, Selini and Roger moved the other.

We moved from corridor to corridor. Robert had us wait while he went down other corridors and back. "The more cameras that are out, the more confusion there will be."

"You said they created our doubles?" I asked Robert.

"True."

"They didn't take an upload from me," Kal said. "I wasn't supposed to be replaced."

"Everyone was uploaded, but yours won't be recent," Robert replied.

"And mine doesn't look quite like me. It should be easy to tell yours and mine apart," I said. I had grown some since I had been above ground. They could have properly predicted my changes in the time I'd been gone but the face I'd seen before I left was definitely older than my current look.

As we approached the Operations Center, we saw security robots surrounding the door to the Headquarters. "Do you think the robots above sent back my image? Maybe Mom's a prisoner."

"If so, we'll rescue her," Robert reacted. "We need to take them out." He flipped a switch on the wand and tossed it. The robots froze.

Out of the Operations Center's Headquarters came someone I recognized. He picked it up. "Surrender. You can't get out of here."

"Dad," Kal breathed.

Brad tossed something else he had put in his pocket. "Oh well, I guess it only works on androids."

Kal's dad looked at it and laughed. He picked the thing up. Something steamy came out of it. He coughed and fell to the ground.

"What is it?"

"Delayed release Mustard Gas."

"Our government stockpiled it?" Jennifer asked.

"It wasn't our government," Brad said. "It was theirs before the Reset. The base was abandoned."

"Can we breathe?" I asked.

"You might want to wait for the air to clear." A tech I had seen before walked out of the Headquarters, choked and collapsed on the floor.

"Are they dead?" Kal asked.

"Probably not, but they should get their lungs treated," Robert replied.

"How do we get past that?" I asked.

Brad pulled out some gas masks from his backpack.

"Masks. You've got to be kidding," I said.

"Never will I ever," Jennifer reacted.

"You want to wind up like them?" Brad asked her. "These are real gas masks, not the joke anti-virus ones."

"I'll wait here," she said.

"Brad and I can handle this," Robert responded. The two of them put on the gas masks, picked up the wand and went inside.

"Oh!" a voice behind me exclaimed. I turned. It was me, a little older looking.

CHAPTER 71

"Hi," I said.

"Who are you?"

"Natalia," I replied. "You're an android."

"That's ridiculous," she responded.

"Ridiculous?" I remembered that I had had several small uploads taken from me and logged by my mother. Those would have been for the record and for the androids she destroyed instead of me.

"Ridiculous."

"You used to look like me. Chanelle was your best friend until she changed."

"The change is for the better."

Somehow Mom had programmed her to fit in, maybe convince them she was me. "Look, we both love Mom," I said.

"Of course."

"Her life depends on us succeeding with what we are doing here."

"Why?"

"Because she's better than the rest," I said. "You can't say you don't believe me. You have enough of me in you to have seen that."

"Why should I believe you are on her side?"

"Look at me. One of us is an android and regardless of which, Mom did the work. She would not have created an evil me."

She seemed to be reflective, as if processing something.

That's when the power went down. "What happened?" I asked.

"Electrical problems," Robert said, rejoining us.

"I recognize that voice," my double noted.

"Robert, meet the other Natalia," I introduced them.

"We've met," he responded.

"My mother liked you," she told him.

"She does," he said. "And she better be safe. Please take us to her."

"In the dark?"

"You can do it." It was Kal's voice. "I'm sure you have improved vision."

"You're that mean kid who hates me."

Apparently, she had been given that memory of mine.

"He likes us now," I said. "We have to move fast if we're to save Mom."

"I think it's this way," she said.

As we entered the lab, the power went back on. My not-father was surprised to see both of us.

"Natalia?" he asked. Anger flared across his face. He turned towards my mom. "Why are there two Natalias and why is one younger than the other?"

She didn't say anything.

"You've been lying to me all along?" He walked towards my mom, his face red with anger and bearing an iron expression.

I knew he was going to do something violent to her. He never had before, but still, I knew what he was about to do. She had been disobedient, gone against him. The EMP wouldn't work on him. I had to stop him—even if it meant my life. But how?

He started to move towards the side of the room to reach for it but before he did, the ax was in my hand, not his.

"You will not kill my mom," I said, raising it.

"Natalia, I love your mom and you. Why would I?"

"You were going to incinerate me and replace me with this." I pointed to my double. He lunged for my arm. It happened so fast that before I knew what was happening, my not-dad fell to the floor, his headless neck spurting out blood.

CHAPTER 72

I looked at my double, who was holding the ax she had grabbed from my arm.

"He was going to kill Mom," my double said. "Mom has always been there for me."

"Yes, she has," I agreed, feeling relieved when I knew I shouldn't.

Brad took the ax away from her as Mom hugged me.

Selini, Bob and Roger entered the lab.

"Bob!" my mom gasped. She rushed into his arms. "You're alive!"

"I'm alive. And I'm here to rescue you."

Brad grabbed Bob's arm, pulling him away. "We have to go."

"Selini—"

"There's no time," Brad interrupted.

I took my mom's hand and told Bob, "Get her out of here."

"You, too," she told me.

"I've got to save my dad," Robert said.

Selini had a mixed expression on her face as she looked at Robert. "He was part of the depopulation."

"He regrets it. I know he does."

"I'll go with Robert. Bob, Kal, Roger, Selini, get my mom and Jennifer out of here."

"Natalia."

"Mom, you trusted Robert to rescue me. I'll be safe with him."

"You might need this," Brad said, raising the ax.

"Not with my dad," Robert reacted.

"Go with Mom," I told the others.

"I'm not leaving you," Mom insisted.

"I'll be safe."

Mom hugged me.

"Trust me. I'll be fine," I whispered.

"You better," she said as Brad pulled her towards the door.

Jennifer quickly gave me a hug.

"Bob, you and Eterra need to get out of here," Brad said as we left the office. "This place will soon be a tomb and we all need to be up the vacuum tube before the power on it goes out."

"Come on, Sis," Roger said, tugging at his sister's arm. "You're going too."

I looked at the other me. She was standing there, confused, disoriented by the events. I didn't want her to die—even if she was my replacement. "Go with Mom and help keep her safe. We'll be fast. Go."

Mom looked back at me, "There's so much I haven't told you. Be careful, Nat and Robert."

"I know. About Dad."

"There's more. A lot more."

"Tell me when I get out," I urged.

"Roger, Kal and I have a job to finish," Brad said. "We'll meet you at the exit."

Bob and Selini pulled my mom away. The other me followed.

"Go, Sis," Roger said. Jennfier looked between her brother and me and then reluctantly joined Bob, Selini, my mom and my double.

I turned to go towards Robert's residence with him and that's when we saw them. People, normal people, hundreds, maybe thousands, of them, flooding into the underground streets.

"What's going on?" I asked.

"I guess they breached some of the other entrances. I shouldn't have left a map," Robert lamented.

Brad, Kal and Roger looked at each other as if something had affected their plans. "We need to get them out, too," Brad said.

He and Roger spoke to some of the people rushing through the streets, who gathered with some of the others. It was somewhat chaotic. We had to push our way to Robert's place. I lost sight of Kal, Brad and Roger as we did. The others in our party had already left and I hoped I really would see them all again.

Robert's father was inside his living room with his head in his hands. "Dad, we've got to go. I think this place is about to blow."

He shook his head. "I belong down here."

"Nobody belongs in an underground prison," I said.

"Do you know what I've done? How many deaths I caused?"

"We know."

"We don't want you to die," Robert pleaded.

"I lost my wife. She killed herself because she couldn't live with what I had done," He looked up at Robert. "She couldn't even acknowledge you because she hated everything we had become."

"She was traumatized," he replied

"She said you weren't her baby, that her baby was dead and it was our curse for what I had done."

"Robert is very much alive."

"You're nothing like me. You have the goodness and the conscience I wish I had had. Save yourself."

"We're going to save you, too," he said. "I'm not going to let my father die. I'm not leaving without you."

"Could you get me a glass of water?"

"Sure." Robert went into the kitchen to get the water. I followed him.

"We can always knock him out and carry him," I suggested.

"That's plan B."

We went back into the living room. Roger's dad was on the floor, blood pouring out from a knife wound in his chest.

"No!" Robert yelled, rushing to him.

"It has to be this way. I love you, son." Those were his last words before he went still, lifeless.

Robert was crying and I found I was crying too.

I heard feet running past the door. I opened it. Robert was still on the floor by his dad. "We've got to go," Kal said. He grabbed my hand.

"No. I have to wait for Robert. You were supposed to be with Roger and Brad."

"I have to save you. You're coming with me." He started pulling me with him.

"That's the wrong way," I said.

"We're going a different direction," he advised.

"Stop," another Kal said from behind him. "Don't trust him. He's taking you to Dad."

"The other way doesn't work," the Kal who was holding my hand said. "They're waiting to catch you there."

"He's lying," the second Kal countered.

I looked between them, not certain who to believe.

CHAPTER 73

"Okay," I said, addressing the Kal who had greeted me at the door. "If you want me to go with you, kiss me."

"What?"

"Kiss me or I'm not going anywhere with you."

"No."

"Bye."

He leaned and kissed me, and I kneed him, pushing him away, as the other Kal pulled the ax out from behind his back and decapitated him.

"Oh my God," I said, leaning down to the floor, feeling panicky as the blood poured from his head.

"It's what Dad did to my sister."

"But he's you or not-you?" I straightened up and looked at him.

"Which is the real me?" the second Kal asked as he swept me to him and his lips met mine.

I couldn't speak. That kiss was even more amazing than our first. As he released me, I reached up and pulled his head towards me and kissed him again.

"Hey, Sis," he said as he released me. "If you weren't my sister, you'd be—never mind."

I laughed. "Have I got something to tell you. Or maybe not."

Robert came out of his home, wiping the tears off his face. "How soon will the place blow?" he asked Kal.

"Fifteen minutes. The oxygen and water will blow first and flood the place." We've got to get up through the tubes to the exit by then.

"This way," Robert said, urging the people rushing through the underground street past the headless corpse to follow him.

One of them had a megaphone and shouted, "This way," and they did.

I thought about who else might have heard. "The Elites are cowards. They're probably hiding in their homes," Kal said.

The Elites may have stayed home, but we saw numerous groups of security robots, which Robert and Kal took down with EMPs as we and the remaining stragglers headed to safety.

"Selini handed me her second one," Robert said. "I guess she didn't want to accidentally deactivate your double."

We rushed through passages to the tubes. They continuously sucked up each group entering the upper passages, which we took at top speed to the exit into the tunnel.

As we made it through to the mouth of the tunnel, we were shaken by a long string of underground explosions. I hoped the others in our group had already made it out.

Bringing up the back, we continued to help the crowd out of the tunnel. I hoped they were all real people.

"I've been using my EMP on the crowd. Any robots would have collapsed by now," Kal said.

"Is this the last of them?"

"It should be."

That's when the ground beneath us started splitting and we rushed forward as everything collapsed behind us, blocking anyone who was still below from following. We heard more explosions.

"I hope all the good guys got out," I said.

When the dust in my eyes cleared, I could see my friends watching as we made our way over to them.

"I think we were the last of the crowd," Kal said. Another explosion closer to the surface caused the rest of the tunnel entrance to collapse.

That's when I felt a hug. It was my mom and dad.

"Where's my double?"

"She's over there in the field," Brad said. "Away from the now-defunct entrance. A precaution—even though the explosions were underground."

"She looks sad for a robot."

"I programmed some of your feelings into her. I had always told Stan they were part of your special programming and I had to be consistent."

"She might need you, too, then," I acknowledged.

"You sure?"

I nodded.

"The Elites are still down there—unless they joined the crowd."

"We'll know one of them made it if he or she tries to create a new plandemic or war," Kal said. "I didn't recognize any of the Elites in the crowd we came out with."

"I didn't either," Robert said. "The maps I handed out to people before we left the university included directions on how to seal each of the other entrances. We may be safe." Robert looked at my expression. "There were multiple tunnels. Hopefully, those who didn't accompany us got out elsewhere."

"Do you think the Elites will devise another plan?" I asked.

"They'll be pretty waterlogged and oxygen-deprived," Roger said. "They'll have to use their elite brains to figure out their own survival."

"With top scientists down there, count on it," Robert replied.

"I wonder if this means we're like them," I pondered, guilt hitting me.

"It was the only way. They want us and everyone above ground dead," Kal pointed out.

"That won't stop the security robots," Roger pointed out.

"The EMPs I set to go off will." Robert smiled. "And the President is having EMPs placed and activated nationwide, wherever they might come up—except in the areas radiated by those power plants they set off to help convince people a real nuclear war had taken place."

"With the EMPs, we could wind up in the Stone Age, I noted.

"Is that so bad?" Roger asked.

"One android made it out," I told Brad, looking at the other me having a conversation with Jennifer.

"I've never dated an android," Brad stated. "It could be interesting."

"What about Jennifer?"

"I think she actually prefers Robert," Brad said. "She kept going on and on about how courageous he was all night while you were sleeping."

"Oh," I commented. *Good taste.*

Roy waved at me from where he and a couple of his friends were attending the horses. Kal, Brad and Roger went over to them. I looked for Robert and saw him, sitting on the grass with his back turned to us. I could tell he was sobbing. I went over to him.

"I'm really sorry about your dad. I know you loved him."

"He was my only parent. I didn't know my mom committed suicide. She rejected me. She must have hated me to claim I wasn't even her kid."

"Your mother loves you very much." I turned to the voice I recognized.

"Mom?"

CHAPTER 74

"I knew that Stan was agitated I was carrying Bob's baby. When I had twins, I knew both of you could be in trouble. And then I learned that another baby born that night, the son of another of the more renowned leaders, had been stillborn. I convinced the doctor to switch the stillborn boy for my son. Robert, I knew you would be treated well. At least, I thought you would. I wasn't expecting Horton to give you the same first name as your real father."

Robert was looking at Mom and I was looking between her and Robert. I stood up to address my mom. "My brother? Robert's my twin brother?"

"You two were always friends. I think inside you knew."

I dropped back onto my knees and hugged Robert. "I'm so sorry about everything that happened to your family, but I'm glad you're my brother. Mom's right. I've always cared about you."'

He hugged me back. "You were my best friend," Robert said. "I always knew there was a connection. I never knew what it was. And you were the only girl who really showed any feelings."

"I blew that directive," I said to Mom.

"That's why I asked him to help. I knew you were up there and the two of you had a connection. They wanted him to assist with the invasion."

"And you knew he and his double would save me. Dad saved me, too."

Bob walked over.

"They know," she said.

"You knew I had a twin?" I asked him.

"I told him just before you came up," Mom explained.

I helped Robert up and Bob and Mom gave us a joint hug.

"I never knew I had a son, but I'm proud it's you."

Robert was crying again. I was, too.

"Oh, Mom, Kal thinks he's my brother. We'll have to break it gently to him."

"Brother?"

"He thinks you and his father."

"I couldn't stand that guy."

I laughed. "Neither could Kal nor I."

I looked at my double. She had killed the guy I thought was my dad in order to protect my mom and me. She had my upload. Or did she do it so I wouldn't have to? I was ready to do whatever it took to protect Mom—including taking out my not-dad. I guessed I was capable of killing.

"I think she will make a nice addition to the family," I said. "Are you okay with what happened to—I mean, you were married to Cambridge."

"No mother could ever love someone who wanted to off her daughter and replace her with a robot. I only married him and stayed with him because it seemed the safest thing for you. Your brother was safe and so I had to focus on keeping you safe."

"Thank you, Mom. I loved you before, but now I love you even more." I hugged her again.

I looked at Robert. He seemed a little stunned. "You'll get used to the idea. I'm not such a bad sister. Ask Kal."

"She's a great sister," Kal said, coming over to us. There was something off about the way he said it. He was staring at Robert. "Thank you for helping keep her safe," he added. He turned, looking sad about something and went over to the horses.

"He's probably thinking about Chanelle," I said. I was hoping he hadn't heard the rest of the conversation.

"Mom, were they confused after they tracked Kal above and his double was down there?"

"When I saw he'd taken the escape route, I deactivated his tracker, erased his route, and put together his double, updating an old upload."

"Then Denton's double didn't track us."

"His timing was a coincidence."

The crowd that had come up with us was dispersing, some of them walking off. Some went over to the farmers and conversed with them. Kal, Brad, Jennifer, and Roger quickly got onto horses. Mom and Bob mounted one. I had a feeling that some of the others were going to have to double up as well.

"Hey, bro, how about a lift?" I asked Kal.

I noticed Robert getting onto Jennifer's horse and the other me getting onto Brad's. I wondered if this pairing was indicative of things to come.

EPILOGUE

The electricity was still out, but all was well as we arrived at the warehouse. Eterra rushed to me and jumped into my arms. "Mom, this is my dog, Eterra."

"That could be a little confusing, but I think it's sweet," she said, hugging me again.

Katerina and Steve came out and rushed over to me and Kal. They each gave us a hug. I turned to my mom. "Mom, Kal and I never would have survived up here if it weren't for Steve and Katerina. And your song brought me to Selini."

"My best friend," my mom said, reaching her arms around Selini. The two hugged and I could almost swear I saw tears of joy in their eyes.

"I can see why you're best friends. Selini is amazing and we wouldn't have succeeded without her and Bob, and of course, our other friends."

We all walked back to our neighborhood. Brad's parents invited us to their house for a barbecue and swim in their pool.

"Isn't it cold without the heater?" I asked.

"We boiled some water on the barbecue grill."

"How do we protect my double from future EMP blasts?" I asked Mom.

"I remembered your reaction when you saw what happened to Chanelle, and I didn't want you to experience that if it happened to someone who looked like you. So, she'll go down for an EMP, but, like my double, her memory has a protected backup. If she comes back up, she'll still be her. But don't think she could ever replace you. Nobody can."

"I know. I'm glad you made her that way. Of course, when I'm eighty, I'll be jealous of how young she looks. But don't change that. Promise?"

"Promise."

I looked at Robert. "Robert's double was wiped out at the museum. Could he have come back up? Did we declare him dead too soon?"

"He had the same physiology as the other humanoid androids below. The leaders wanted them vulnerable as they didn't fully trust the technology, even though they touted and used that same technology. I went against the rules with your double as well as mine. She had to survive long enough to get you out."

Selini joined the conversation. "If you are worried about your double, I can construct a pendant that will provide additional protection from EMPs. I have the material for that at my place. But if she ever tries to replace you, it's curtains for her."

"She's got too much of me in her. I'm not worried about that."

"The second verse of the lullaby. The part about sounds and zombs."

"That was the second part of their plan. It was to program the subconscious of anyone still alive with sound waves. They didn't get to that."

"The necklace."

"It operated on a similar principle. If they could get someone to turn into a zombie and come below with the sound waves it was emitting, they'd know they could do it on a larger scale."

"Robert's first android put the necklace on me."

"Robert's androids had different instructions—to protect you if they saw you."

"What about the other regions of the underworld?" Selini asked my mom.

"I think ours was the most technologically advanced, but we'll be prepared for them if they try to invade elsewhere."

"Natalia, would you like to accompany me to my place?" Selini asked. "I'll show you what I can do to protect your double."

"Sure," I said. I turned to Kal. He was sitting, looking depressed. His father was below, maybe gone. His mother was gone. He had nobody but a sister, whom he didn't yet know wasn't his sister. Could I ever acknowledge Bob as my father? "I'm going to Selini's place for a bit. Would you like to join us?"

As we were leaving, Katerina came over and told Kal, "I don't know what your plans are, but you're the best son I could have hoped for. If you don't have another mother, little Ever could use an older brother and I've always wanted a son."

"Every girl needs a brother," I said.

He hugged her. "I'd be glad to be her brother. Thank you," he paused. "Mom."

She looked at me. "And I need you to refresh my calculus skills."

"You're my second mom," I told her. "Thank you for everything."

"Our home is your home, too."

I hugged her. "I think Bob and my mom might want some alone time. So that would be great."

"You feel that way?" Kal asked.

"I guess you're stuck with me."

As we arrived at Selini's place, the door was slightly open and it was clear that someone was in her apartment. Kal grabbed a fire extinguisher hanging on the hallway wall. It was mostly for decoration as the ceilings all had fire-retardant dispatchers in them.

"Let me open the door," I whispered.

"I can do it." Kal kicked the door inward.

Selini breathed a sigh of relief as she saw Tarinda inside, sitting on a couch and drinking a glass of what I assumed was lemonade.

Selini moved quickly over to her daughter. "I'm so glad to see you. I always worry about you."

"I know. I've been thinking. I've been really mean to you, and there is no real reason for it. You weren't responsible for what Dad did to you."

"The guy I thought was my father tried to kill me and almost killed my mother," I said. "You were lucky your mother protected you, just like my mom protected me."

"As my sister said, you are lucky Selini is your mom and that she's still speaking to you," Kal remarked. "I wish my mom were alive. I'd be proud to have Selini for a mom."

"I realize I haven't treated you well. In fact, I've been awful."

"Haven't treated her well?" Kal reacted. "Robots make better children than what you've been."

"It's okay," Selini told him. She turned to her daughter. "I'm glad you're here now. The past is the past. I love you. That's what mothers do. No matter what, they love their children."

Tarinda got up and hugged her mother, who hugged her back. I turned to Kal. "Everything seems to be working out perfectly."

"Yeah, you've got a mom and a boyfriend. I have no real family except a sister I wish weren't my sister."

"I can go back below and if your father's still standing, he can chop off my head—if that would make you happy."

"No. I just. I mean, your mom has Bob and Steve and Katerina have each other and Ever. Jennifer is crazy about Brad. And…" He paused. "I wish you and Robert well."

"You wish me and Robert well. That's really good, because I expect you two to get along like brothers."

"Yeah. I guess that's inevitable. You've always been crazy about Robert."

"Yeah, but that's to be expected. Turns out that Robert is my twin brother."

"Brother? Robert is our brother? I have a brother?"

"Not exactly."

"Half-brother."

"Why don't you want me to be your sister?"

"I mean, forget it. It's just that, oh forget it."

"But you said you wished I weren't your sister. Why?"

"It's not important."

"Maybe this will make it simpler. Bob's my and Robert's father, and your dad isn't."

"Then I'm nothing to you?"

I shook my head and put my hands to my head as if in shock, "Oh no! I think I made a terrible mistake."

"What?" Selini asked.

"There were two Kals below. I think the real one is the one that didn't make it." I turned to Kal. "You're an android. Nothing to me."

"You're crazy."

"No. That other Kal was really cute, hot really, maybe the love of my life and this is terrible."

"Terrible! I'm the real—" Kal stopped mid-sentence and smiled. He pulled me into his arms and kissed me so passionately, explosions erupted in me and the universe and world seemed to collapse around us.

"Hey. Not in front of the children," Selini said, interrupting us.

"I'm older than they are," Tarinda said.

"If you ever decide you want another mother in addition to Katerina, Tarinda could also use a brother, and I could use a genius son."

"And now you have two new sisters and two new mothers."

"Brothers, yuck," Tarinda said.

"Yep, she sounds like a sister," he remarked.

RESET, RESET BECOMING REALITY

When *Reset, Reset* was written during NaNoWriMo in 2022, elements of the novel were already happening. Each day, the world comes closer and closer to the world presented in this book.

The UK has mandated digital ID to control the masses and has made telling the truth on unapproved matters a crime. The US has been going in that direction, attempting to institute mass surveillance, mass censorship, forced medical procedures, digital ID, digital currency, prosecution of speech as a hate crime, and the virtual obliteration by the government of the *Constitution of the United States.ci*

Our food, water and air have already been poisoned with chemicals being sprayed on or injected into plants or animals or dropped from the sky. States working to ban chemtrails, GMOs and toxic chemicals placed into the water or food have met opposition from the U.S. Government. Poisons banned in other countries are pushed by the U.S. Government in spite of objections from the American people.

Artificial Intelligence logarithms in the US, UK and Western Europe have resulted in censorship of the world's greatest journalists, scientists, attorneys, doctors, and other truthtellers, too many of whom have been imprisoned, placed on official kill lists or actually executed with the implicit support of the US and other Western Governments. With the installation of digital ID and digital currency, anyone not supporting the government narratives can be deprived of food, shelter and even the right to live.

Elitists who believe they can survive a nuclear war in their underground bunkers are intimidating and threatening nuclear powers for illegitimate reasons, not caring that that they are risking the lives of everyone on the planet. Elite corporatists controlling the US Government, who want Venezuela's oil, gold, lithium and emeralds have created lies about drugs and are threatening war with a country that has the most verified and legitimate elections in the world, a country that has never done anything to harm the USA. The U.S. Government regularly topples democratic governments whose people refuse to bend to an elite agenda. Our country continues to sell arms for use in genocides on innocent populations and refuses to listen to the American populace calling on our government to spend its resources for the betterment of the people of this country, instead.

Whole work forces are being replaced with AI and androids. AI has also contributed to injustice in the courts, with attorneys filing briefs containing non-existent cases that AI says are real as judges and other authorities use AI-generated logarithms to remove rights and property from domestic violence survivors and other law-abiding citizens. The NaNoWriMo organization no longer exists because, after it authorized the use of AI in 2024, human writers revolted.

Artificial Intelligence lacks the heart, compassion and humanity of real writers, journalists and workers. We can make a difference by saying "no" to AI-created literature and by patronizing business that refuse to replace *human* workers with cold, uncaring machines. The best hope for the people of the USA to stop the destruction of our country and the planet is for all of us to stand up for *human* rights and freedom of thought and speech while we still can. Instead of electing purchased politicians, we can choose leaders with integrity, like Dennis Kucinich, Cynthia McKinney, Cindy Sheehan, Ron Paul, Thomas Massie and Jose Vega.

ACKNOWLEDGMENTS

This was written during 2022 NaNoWriMo (National Novel Writing Month), and though the NaNoWriMo organization no longer exists, I met many great writers through it. I encourage everyone who wants to write to join a write-in group.

There are so many people in my life who have been very supportive or who have been mentors to me that it is impossible to name them all. Just to name a few: Susan Estrella, Nancy Howell, Tammy Rief, and Cindy Sheehan have been very supportive and inspiring through the years. My children have inspired some of the characters I've written about in various books and my God-daughter Shannon Ream has also been a positive and encouraging influence in my life.

I would like to thank Rose de Guzman for her work in editing my books and Jessica Verrill for her vision and work in publishing my books. Both have been a delight to work with.

I also have to acknowledge my papillons, who have been very patient and cooperative while watching me write my books. They are a very important part of my life.

ALSO BY NATALIE TRIUMPHS

Best Sellers Now Available

Silent Deathfall

#1 Best Seller in Animal Law (Australia)

#1 Best Seller in Environmental & Natural Resources Law (US)

#1 Best Seller in Animal Law (US)

#1 Best Seller in Human Rights Law (US)

#1 Best Seller in Teen & Young Adult Environmental Science & Ecosystems eBooks (US)

Abandoned by her family in Yosemite National Park, Treasure Dover discovers America's national parks, popular vacation spots and cities have been poisoned by toxic clouds. As Yosemite is turned into a FEMA prison camp, Treasure, the Yosemite Rangers, and their friends take action to save the Park they love so much, as well as other places hit by silent deathfalls.

Summer Heat: Education: American Gulag Style

#1 Amazon Best Selling Book in Young Adult Schools & Education

#1 Amazon New Release in Teen & Young Adult Politics & Government Fiction

#1 Amazon New Release in Teen & Young Adult Fiction about Parents

After a break-up with her boyfriend, fifteen-year-old Summer Tanner, a survivor of the Family Court Injustice System, finds herself kidnapped and imprisoned in one of America's Gulag Camps, part of a behavior modification system where thousands of teens are taken against their will annually to be "fixed," often returning home in body bags or psychologically damaged for life. There, Summer meets allies, including a new love interest, who, like her, wants to escape and bring an end to America's teen torture programs. But how high up does the corruption of the multi-billion-dollar industry run and how far will the forces in power go to silence Summer and her new friends to keep the truth from coming out?

Taking Down the Deep State: Summer Heat II

#1 Amazon Best Seller Teen & Young Adult Media Studies eBook

#1 Amazon Best Seller Teen & Young Adult Sociology eBook

#1 Amazon New Release in Young Adult Politics & Government

Having escaped their American Gulag Camp, Summer and her friends, now known as the Wilderness Five, return to the States to expose the torture and deaths in the behavior modification programs and close them down. To silence the truth, Deep State retaliates in full force, threatening the lives of the teens, university students and anyone else taking a stand for human rights and against the mistreatment of America's youth. When Americans stand together for rights and justice, even the most powerful forces on Earth cannot defeat them. This book, written in 2017, has predicted numerous real-life events which have taken place in more recent times.

Kakistocracy of the Technocrats

#1 Amazon Best Seller in Young Adult Politics & Government

#1 Amazon Best Seller in Young Adult Fiction Alternative History

As White House researcher for a non-existent department that oversees a demented robotic President, Karissa James finds herself in the middle of a string of murders, fires, earthquakes, embassy bombings, assassination attempts, bribes, wars and an Administration that can best be described as a Kakistocracy.

Everything

#1 Amazon Best Seller in Human Rights Law,

#1 Amazon Best Seller in Young Adult Adventures and Adventurers

#1 Amazon Best Seller in Young Adults Politics and Government

After the deaths of her parents, Meadow Clarkson finds herself woven into the world of child trafficking, false flags, mass disappearances, rogue government agents and secret government operations. Her primary companions are a two-hundred-and-fifty year old talking dog named Everything and Cal, a mysterious guy who keeps appearing in her life, as Meadow fights to save children from capture and slaughter, to protect her canine companion and other dogs from a dog-killing frenzy that has swept the nation and to discover what has happened to curious people who have suddenly disappeared.

Coming Soon:

Everything II: Meadow, her talking Papillion, Everything, Cal and their friends continue their adventure as they work to save the lives of dogs and other animals in a world that will forever be changed by judicial corruption, murders, dognappings and trans-species experimentation. Also coming, the final book in the series is

Everything III: Once again, Meadow, Everything, Cal and their friends fight to expose government corruption so extreme that it threatens the future of humanity.

ABOUT THE AUTHOR

Natalie Triumphs is a criminal defense and civil rights attorney, private investigator, investigative journalist and best-selling author. She is a strong advocate for youth rights, for human rights, for Constitutional Rights and for eliminating the NDAA, the Espionage Act and other unconstitutional laws used to target whistleblowers, journalists and truth-tellers. She has fought for protections for domestic violence survivors, for victims of child trafficking and for vulnerable individuals falsely targeted by the criminal justice system.